What the critics are saying...

&

"The storyline surrounding this glimpse into our possible future is extremely unique with enough action that I was obsessed with it for hours on end." ~ *JERR gives it the GOLD STAR AWARD!*

5 stars and a RECOMMENDED READ "Lorie O'Clare once again employs her fabulous world-building skills in Dead World." ~ *Fallen Angel Reviews*

4 1/2 blue ribbons! "DEADWORLD is a fantastic story that draws the reader into a fantasy world of passion and mystery." ~ *Romance Junkies*

5 coffee cups! "This book is a masterpiece of gargantuan proportions. I absolutely adored it!" ~ *Coffeetime Romance*

5 stars! "As always, Lorie O'Clare never fails to please her readers by bringing us a fantastic new novel featuring three genres, paranormal/futuristic and adventure." ~ *Ecataromance*

"A fast paced love story with twists, turns, lies, secrets and fantasies, Dead World has all that and more!" ~ *Erotic-Escapades*

4 roses! "Clever, energetic, and very hot, this erotic adventure promises an entertaining read to all who open its pages." ~ *A Romance Review*

DEAD
WORLD

LORIE O'CLARE

ELLORA'S CAVE
ROMANTICA PUBLISHING

An Ellora's Cave Romantica Publication

www.ellorascave.com

Dead World

ISBN 9781419956188
ALL RIGHTS RESERVED.
Dead World Copyright © 2006 Lorie O'Clare
Edited by Sue-Ellen Gower.
Cover art by Syneca.

Electronic book Publication January 2006
Trade paperback Publication January 2007

Content Advisory:

S – ENSUOUS
E – ROTIC
X - TREME

Ellora's Cave Publishing offers three levels of Romantica™ reading entertainment: S (S-ensuous), E (E-rotic), and X (X-treme).

The following material contains graphic sexual content meant for mature readers. This story has been rated E–rotic.

S-*ensuous* love scenes are explicit and leave nothing to the imagination.

E-*rotic* love scenes are explicit, leave nothing to the imagination, and are high in volume per the overall word count. E-rated titles might contain material that some readers find objectionable — in other words, almost anything goes, sexually. E-rated titles are the most graphic titles we carry in terms of both sexual language and descriptiveness in these works of literature.

X-*treme* titles differ from E-rated titles only in plot premise and storyline execution. Stories designated with the letter X tend to contain difficult or controversial subject matter not for the faint of heart.

Also by Lorie O' Clare

ଚୈ

About the Author

ଋ

All my life, I've wondered at how people fall into the routines of life. The paths we travel seemed to be well-trodden by society. We go to school, fall in love, find a line of work (and hope and pray it is one we like), have children and do our best to mold them into good people who will travel the same path. This is the path so commonly referred to as the "real world".

The characters in my books are destined to stray down a different path other than the one society suggests. Each story leads the reader into a world altered slightly from the one they know. For me, this is what good fiction is about, an opportunity to escape from the daily grind and wander down someone else's path.

Lorie O'Clare lives in Kansas with her three sons.

Lorie welcomes comments from readers. You can find her website and email address on her author bio page at www.elloracave.com.

DEAD WORLD

Dedication

❧

In a world that judges a book by its cover,
I would like to dedicate this book to Syneca Featherstone,
who continually makes the covers of my books shine!
Syndi Stone was created because of you! Love you, Syn!

Chapter One

෨

Syndi Stone didn't know hot, sudsy, long baths. She'd never enjoyed the pounding of a shower until the hot water was all gone. In her world, such luxuries were for the very wealthy. And the Stone family was far from wealthy.

Walking into the warm pond, Syndi closed her eyes as the water soaked through her parched skin. This was better than sex—almost. Refusing to focus on the parched dead lands surrounding her, the worn-out earth faded from her vision until all she saw was the glistening water brushing against her naked body.

The sun baked her skin, burning her flesh, but she ignored it. The brightness made the ground wavy, droplets of sweat clinging to her shoulders, under her hair at the base of her neck. The warm pond sank into her pores. Deeper, closing in around her, enveloping her.

No dream compared to this. So much water. Covering her, surrounding her, enough to walk into. It covered her ankles, her knees then her thighs. She wouldn't lose her mind over this. Paying attention to all sounds around her, terrified she'd be discovered, she walked deeper into the pool. Water closed around her waist. She swallowed a feeling of terror. Being discovered would mean death. It just felt too damned good. Never had she seen so much water.

Spreading her arms out, they floated, the water supporting them while her long hair lifted off her back, drifted around her. A few more steps and it would consume her, take her away, enclose her in its depths. Desperately she ached for that moment when the water would cover every inch of her, carry her, control her with its power.

Breaking the law never felt so damned good. Nerves gripped her, making her legs wobble with every step she took. Mud and pebbles slowly covered her feet, squishing between her toes.

One more step.

Water soaked her shoulders, closed in around her neck, and then brushed against her cheeks. Slowly, she submerged under the water. Just a few more minutes and all the frustrations and agonies of her life would be gone — if just for a short time.

Submerging completely, the muffled silence underwater surrounded her, her hair floating around her face. This was too perfect to be wrong. She wouldn't think about the repercussions, about being arrested for enjoying the water. No one would find her here.

The police didn't cover the dead lands. Overused and worn-out, all natural resources depleted so that not even grass grew. Nothing grew in the dead lands. There was no explanation why this water was here.

Syndi wouldn't question the godsend. She needed the water — needed it to survive. More so than she would ever let anyone know.

The sensation to laugh, to kick her feet and splash her arms, made her giddy. No one had ever taught her to swim, playing in water wasn't something anyone in her world did. The thought that she wanted to do exactly that made her feel like a little girl again. But not even children played in water. And this was a hell of a lot more fun than kicking dust clouds in the dirt.

Not once in her life did she remember her entire body being surrounded by water.

Fear and excitement twisted her stomach. Getting caught would disgrace her, humiliate her family, more than likely mean her death. Her tummy twisted with painful nervousness. Quickly she dived underwater. If just for another minute, she would enjoy this needed pleasure.

Her private getaway, she'd learned every corner of the pond over the months she'd been coming here. Kicking harder, feeling her lungs begin to hurt, she moved deeper into its depths.

Her eyes were wide open, her mouth shut, holding her breath. The pressure built in her lungs, the pain from holding her breath increasing. But still she kicked harder, swimming into the darker depths.

It wouldn't be much longer now.

Her lungs burned. Her brain hurt. God. She wanted to gulp in air so badly.

She kicked harder, moving deeper and deeper. The water grew colder. Sunlight couldn't travel down this far. Darkness surrounded her, closing in around her, but she wouldn't panic—wouldn't let the sensation to frantically kick to the surface take over.

All that mattered was that she remembered the right way. She shoved her floating hair out of the way. It was hard to concentrate from the pain in her lungs. Her body ached for air.

She'd almost reached where she needed to be. And there was no turning back now. Endure the pain just a bit more. Concentrate. Focus.

Pop!

The release of the pain was like a sweet chocolate, melting through her, a forbidden treat. The small gills behind her ears opened, sending a rush of oxygen from the water through her brain. For a moment she was lightheaded, almost giddy.

Cold water pressed against every inch of her naked body, her nipples hardening, energy tingling through her like she'd never experienced before. Brushing her hands down her front, cupping her breasts, tracing paths through the water over her ribs, her belly, her heart pounded in her chest. Her hair floated around her. She twisted underwater, spreading her legs, cupping her pussy and feeling the throb there.

She closed her eyes, letting her mind enjoy the experience. Kicking her legs, in her mind she was graceful, beautiful, the weight of her body, the heat that usually tortured her skin gone — replaced with blissful paradise.

Parting the folds of skin between her legs, heat captured her, contrasted by the cold water engulfing her. A sensation she never experienced, feeling cold, it was the most incredible feeling in the world. Well almost.

She stroked her pussy, penetrated herself with her fingers, blowing bubbles as her muscles clamped down. Her small muscles hardened and she straightened in the dark water, no longer knowing or caring which direction led to the surface.

Almost laughing, the sensations so wonderful she never wanted to leave her private paradise. If only a perfect man would join her. Not any of the men from her village, but someone who didn't exist, someone strong, powerful, capable of moving beyond the suppressed existence she endured.

Her hair floated in front of her face, her body light and agile. Spreading her legs wide it was almost as if she flew. She stroked her cunt, fire building. Her breasts swelled, her nipples hard and perky. In her dark underwater paradise, she was beautiful. Pressure built, her fingers working to hit that spot that would take care of her needs, keep her from surrendering to the sorry saps who shared her village.

She would never do that. Taking care of herself, stroking her pussy, brushing her hands over her body, she would rather get off with her imagination than allow any of the lame excuses for men who were in her world touch her. Spinning in the water, rolling over, she plunged her fingers deeper inside her.

Images of her perfect man, muscles all over him like the pictures of men she'd seen on magazine covers in the city, had her rubbing harder. Someone like that, someone with eyes only for her, who would know her needs, know where to hit her deep inside, know just how to make her scream his name.

Twisting as she masturbated, loving how her body could move, the positions she could master, she thrust deep inside her, feeling the pressure so close to breaking. Cold water touched her everywhere, stroked her like thousands of tiny fingers, barely touching her. Sensations pulsed inside her, growing, building. She stroked harder—faster.

The small flaps behind her ears fluttered, gills she never knew she had. Gasping for breath after climaxing was such a normal reaction and she gulped in water unnecessarily. Coughing, she then laughed, too much oxygen hitting her brain and making her feel giddy, like she was drunk. The freedom that surged through her—her deepest secret—made her want to dance.

Waiting until her heart quit pounding, she kicked with a new energy, determined to travel a bit further today, explore the underwater caverns that she'd discovered months ago.

Syndi had been terrified the first time she'd learned the truth about herself—that she had gills. Always she'd craved water. But who didn't?

A rare commodity, expensive and used in small rations, it had never seemed odd to her that she enjoyed the sweet treat every time she was around it. Even a cup of water, fresh and confined, appealed to her as much as a good orgasm.

What a turn-on to pour a cup of water over a man and then lick the clinging beads from his body.

"You're supposed to drink it, not play in it," they had teased her in the past.

No one had ever treated her differently. Not once had a guy complained if she asked to include a bit of water in their foreplay. But none of the men satisfied her. She wanted more, a man with strength, with power, someone as strong as she was.

Her pussy throbbed from her self-induced orgasm. She kicked deeper. If this much water meant death, then what a way to go. The day she'd swam too far, her lungs threatening to explode, small slits had opened in the soft flesh behind her ears. The explosion in her head had been deafening. But then she'd been able to breathe—underwater. Like a damned freak!

Several times since that day she'd managed to escape the village. Using water like this broke more laws than she dared to count. Having gills though, the ability to breathe underwater when she lived in a world with no water, was too damned insane to dwell on. A secret she'd take to her grave, just like this water. Each time she came out here, she'd dive quickly underwater, hurrying to be hidden in the depths, the only way to enjoy this pleasure without being caught. And to dream about a man who didn't exist, get herself off in her silent, wet sanctuary.

That's how she'd learned about the underwater tunnels. And today, she would figure out where they went.

Excitement urged her on. Her mundane life left behind, anticipation pulsed through her. The water was almost black now, her eyes no longer any good to her. But this time she'd come prepared. Fumbling in the darkness, her heart pounding in her chest, she felt her waist, found the flashlight she'd secured to her belt.

She grinned and water filled her mouth. The beam of light glowed through the dark underwater abyss. Not too far below her, she spotted the boulders. Nibbling her lip, ignoring the twisting of nerves that put a painful rock in her gut, she kicked to make herself go deeper. The water grew delightfully cold. Her naked body tingled, her nipples puckering. Before her, captured in the path of her light, she saw the entrance to the long tunnel.

Dark and forbidding, it traveled further than her beam of light. Return home to help plan small groups that would panhandle the streets in the city, or kick her way into the darkness, discover what lay on the other end. She didn't hesitate.

Earlier the men had teased her. "You're scared to hold out your hand and ask for a few dollars. We have the right to survive."

The words burned through her. She'd grown up with most of these idiots. "Detroit won't even let us sleep on their streets. What rights do we have again?"

"You have the right to spread your legs for whoever you want." The lot of them had burst into laughter.

Syndi had turned her back on them. She was no fucking whore. She didn't put out for a pitcher or two of water. To hell with all of them. Perry, the only one of them she had actually been with, at least had the decency not to laugh.

For that she was grateful. But the rest of them. They had no clue how much guts she had. And she had nothing to prove to any of them.

The first few times she'd traveled through the tunnel, she'd turned back around, unsure of herself. Today no one would miss her. New laws were being passed. The village was in an uproar. Water would be even harder to get. Detroit controlled their actions and disowned them at the same time. Most of the villagers would be heading to the city, screaming of the injustice in the streets. Like that would do them any good.

"You aren't heading into the city?" Perry had come up behind her at the public tent.

No matter that she'd had sex with him once and turned him down every time since, he still always put his hands on her whenever he could. He'd done that earlier, stroking her long brown hair behind her shoulder. She ignored the gesture, and had dipped her hands into the large barrel of community water, then brushed it over her arms to cool off.

"Seems like everyone is going." It was none of his damned business that she wasn't heading out with the rest of them.

"They can't ignore us and leave us out here to die."

"Seems like they're doing a pretty good job of it to me."

Fortunately, several others joined them at the public water barrel, and Perry had been distracted with their comments. Syndi slowly moved around the other villagers, waiting for the right moment. Heading into the dead lands was dangerous—and something she had to do.

Goose bumps traveled over her skin as Syndi swam through cold water, moving through the darkness of the tunnel. She held her flashlight in her hand, using it as a guide so she wouldn't run into hard-packed earth surrounding her. This was her third trip into the tunnel and once again she studied the strange carvings on the walls around her as she swam past them. It made no sense that they were there.

Plenty of graffiti covered the sides of the buildings in Detroit. She remembered thinking some of them pretty as a child. That was when they'd still been allowed to live in the city. Before Detroit, and all the other cities, had grown sick of the amount of homeless on their streets and sent them packing. Villagers. It wasn't politically correct to call them homeless anymore.

These carvings, people swimming, intertwined underwater. And there were other images, pictures she didn't understand. The paint had faded, the water wearing the images down. The circular beam of light strayed over the strange paintings, distorted by dark muddy water.

Once there had been a lot more water on Earth. Rivers and lakes had dried up as the sun slowly baked the planet. Wars and industry were credited with thinning the atmosphere. Less land was habitable than even just a hundred years ago. But that wouldn't explain what she saw now. She imagined once this tunnel hadn't been underwater, but how the water got here was the mystery. Especially when there was so little water to be had.

The fact that it flowed freely, and for no apparent reason, boggled her brain.

She swam further than she had before when the pictures on the walls surrounding her grew more colorful. Images of people, symbols she didn't recognize, appeared to float as she stared wide-eyed through the water. A nervous rush tightened her tummy. No one knew she was here. God only knew what lay ahead. Her heart pounded in her ears but she ignored it, ignored her fear. Kicking harder, pushing herself forward, she had to know where the tunnel led.

What struck her as odd was that the flashlight seemed to be gaining strength. It was easier to see around her. Pain ripped through her muscles, shooting up her legs and down her arms from swimming for so long, but she couldn't make herself stop, wouldn't turn around yet. The tunnel had widened. Looking around, she realized she'd swam into another pool, and there was light above her.

Her heart skipped a beat. If she surfaced, where would she be? She held her hair away from her face and looked up.

Curiosity bested her. Securing her flashlight to her belt, she used both hands to push herself closer to the surface. She hadn't come this far to turn around and go back without learning anything. There was barely enough oxygen in the water for her to catch her breath. Her heart beat so ruthlessly she swore her ribs would break. In spite of her nervousness, her fear, she had to know what lay ahead. But if she reached the surface, floated to the top, and was somewhere she wasn't permitted to be, it would be a certain prison sentence. Syndi kicked underwater, holding her position, while her belt slid against her hips. Indecision rushed through her.

It would be prison or worse if she'd somehow swum into a public bath in the city. Nervous jitters crawled over her skin as the horror stories of the gang rapes, being starved, tortured, crept through her thoughts. Not that growing up homeless, on the streets, had been that much better.

Public baths were always crowded. There wasn't anyone else in the pond with her. She frowned, looking through the growing light in the water at a sky that seemed too dark, a sky that wasn't blue, more like green and brown. A pond wouldn't exist underground. Her breathing came harder. From what she could tell, it either opened into another cave, or it was dark for some reason. And she hadn't been gone long enough for the sun to set.

Indecision could cost you your life.

Acting quickly, making a show that she was in control and knew what she was doing, had saved her ass more times than not. She kicked at the water. This wasn't a public bath or there would be tons of people in it. Wherever she was, she was alone. That was almost more terrifying. Her teeth chattered, and she clamped her jaw, wishing her heart would quit pounding so damned loud.

Being scared pissed her off. The unknown wouldn't stop her. Floating closer to the surface, the water warmed, grew brighter and easier to see through. The surface was just above her.

Someone stood there, looking down at her.

The water had to be distorting her vision. A man stood on the bank, tall and thin, his head shaven bald, and with the darkest eyes she'd ever seen in her life. They weren't grotesque, but larger than they should be. They were the most intense eyes she'd ever seen.

Without thinking, she fluttered her hands, forcing herself deeper into the pool. It wasn't like she could run underwater, and it was a long journey back through the tunnel, but a little distance made her feel safer.

She hadn't expected to see someone who looked so, so — different.

The pain in her chest grew, making it hard to breathe. The gills behind her ears fluttered open and shut, feeding her, the skin stretching as she fought for air.

Damn it. Panicking was a sign of weakness.

But what in the hell was this place?

Moving under the water was awkward. Every movement she made was in slow motion. There was no way to escape quickly. Swimming wasn't a skill anyone she knew had.

In fact, if she'd been a better swimmer she never would have discovered the gills behind her ears. She wouldn't have been foolish enough to go so deep that she couldn't recover from a cramp.

Those black eyes continued staring at her. They were damned unnerving. Her heart raced and she opened her mouth, forgetting she was underwater for a moment, and gulped in too much water.

She coughed and bubbles blurred her vision. She might as well have sent out an announcement that she was here. The bubbles floated toward the surface. Her arm muscles ached but she forced herself lower, moving backward deeper toward the tunnel entrance.

The man knelt down on the edge of the pool, still watching her. Or maybe he was searching the water to see where she'd gone. Either way something told her to retrace her steps, pray he wouldn't jump in and try dragging her out. Something was wrong with the way he looked. Syndi had seen mutilation before—and this wasn't it. There were plenty of villagers deformed for one reason or another. Even city people, with all their money and their homes, sometimes weren't born right. But that man, staring down at her...those eyes were damned unnerving. His eyes were more than mutated—they were way too large.

Forgetting she couldn't breathe with her mouth, she inhaled deeply, once again setting off a world of bubbles in front of her face.

Damn it.

If he couldn't find her, she was sure sending out enough indication as to where she was. All her life she'd practiced doing nothing to stand out, keeping a low profile. The police would use any excuse to arrest a villager.

The easiest way to do that was to look like everyone else—act like everyone else—live like everyone else. Syndi's eyes were dark green, almost brown, while most in the village had pale eyes. That wasn't questioned. She was an orphan, had no solid memories of her parents—like many villagers. Even taller than most everyone she knew, she'd managed a low profile.

She could fight with the best of them, hold her own when needed. That was enough to keep trouble away.

But right now, trouble seemed to surround her. She was alone in a pond with no clue what lay beyond the surface. Damned hard to keep a low profile under these circumstances.

Her feet slid against the slippery stones at the bottom of the pool, and she ran her hand over the rocky entrance of the tunnel. Moving so the tunnel hid her, she peered back up toward the top of the water. She couldn't see the man anymore.

Who was he?

City people didn't look like that. Shaving one's head would cause the sun to burn you. Most people, in the city or the villages, kept their hair longer, possibly wrapped up off their neck, but always long. But it wasn't the hair—it was the eyes. They were way too large.

Her tummy twisted into a knot thinking about it. Not to mention her ribs hurt from her heart pounding so damned bad. Talk about a nerve-racking experience. Usually she didn't freak out so easily. She should go back, return to the village before anyone missed her—return to a mundane life with no surprises.

Once she got home, she would go nuts thinking about this place until she found time to return, explore further. Fighting for something none of them would ever get was a waste of time. For twenty years she'd managed to find what she needed on the streets. City laws would never change in their favor. Syndi was homeless, born that way, would die that way. No one in politics gave a rat's ass about her.

Whoever was up there, they weren't part of her village, and she doubted they were from the city.

Damn. Damn. Damn.

Floating toward the top of the pool once again, moving slowly, just far enough to let the surface come into focus again, she held her breath until it hurt. This time she didn't see the man.

But there were images, some darker than others. They blurred and wavered while she stared wide-eyed under the water until her eyes burned. Floating until she surfaced, her lungs stung when she inhaled air through her mouth.

Then she coughed, and looked around in shock. The dark images had been trees. She'd seen pictures of them. Tall with limbs spreading over the width of the pool, they blocked the sky above her. If that was a sky. Thick grass grew in clumps along the bank of the pool.

Where in the hell was she?

Places like this didn't exist anymore. Fear gripped her, twisting in her gut. She'd seen the history books, learned what everyone else learned. There were special gardens in the city that could be walked through for a steep price. Other than that, vegetation like this was a thing of the past.

And Syndi wasn't going to buy into the fact that she'd just swum into her past.

"What passage are you from?" The man she'd seen before appeared from behind one of the trees.

Syndi's heart exploded in her chest. He'd hidden from her to make her surface. Fear gripped her until her heart about exploded. Unsure what to say, or how to run away, she stared at the mutated man. At the rate she kicked her legs and moved her arms just to stay above surface, she'd cramp again and never be able to escape. Panicking, she worked her way backward in the water, scared escape was impossible.

"It's okay. You're safe." He held his hands out in front of him, stepping away from the tree that had concealed him. "I won't tell them that you're here. Just tell me your name." The man cocked his head, frowning for a moment.

Tell who that she was here?

Escape was impossible. There was no way she could move that quickly in the water. All he had to do was jump in and he'd be on top of her.

His gaze strolled down her naked body, obviously quite visible through the water. "I'm Roln Storn, guard of the passages. And you are?"

Hiding her nudity wasn't an option. If she tried covering her breasts with her arms, she'd sink. Heat burned her cheeks. Embarrassment and frustration rushed through her. She hated being stuck in a bad situation.

If he was aware of her predicament, or her fear, he gave no indication. His calm expression, bordering on curiosity, annoyed her. He seemed content to wait for an answer.

Perfect white teeth contrasted his deep black eyes. His skin was a creamy white. Dressed in tan pants that looked like they were made from animal skin, smoothed and stretched and hugging long slender legs and a snug long-sleeved shirt, he didn't look like anyone she'd ever seen before. His bald head didn't look shaved but more like he just didn't have hair growing there. And his face was smooth, not a blemish on his skin. The man, this Roln Storn, was the most bizarre-looking human she'd ever seen.

But there was something about his eyes. Usually she could tell a man's business through his eyes, if he were up to no good or not. Those incredibly dark large eyes made her shudder. No matter that she was in water up to her chin, her mouth suddenly was too dry to speak.

"You're from Dead World, aren't you? They told us there were no survivors, but I never believed it. This isn't a passageway. How did you get here?"

There was no way to respond to complete nonsense.

He squatted down by the water, appearing just as he had when she'd first seen him. Syndi floated further away from him, although she doubted she'd be able to escape if he jumped in after her.

"Maybe you don't understand my language. Can you speak?"

"I can speak," she said. He just wasn't making any damned sense.

"What's your name?" he asked, again letting his gaze travel over her.

She hated feeling vulnerable. It was a sign of weakness. There wasn't a damned thing she could do about not having any clothes on.

"Syndi Stone."

"Well, Syndi Stone, you stay above water much longer and your gills will close." He extended his hand to her. "I'll take you to Tor. He'll protect you."

All she could do was stare at his hand. He knew about her gills. And he spoke about them as if he understood how they worked. She searched his face, but he looked at her straight on. Even though he had no hair, she couldn't see behind his ears. For the most part, he appeared as normal as she did. Except for eyes that were way too large, clothes like nothing she'd ever seen before, and a shaved head.

Still staring at his hand, she shook her head. "I don't think so."

"Well, at least let me offer you my shirt and see you to the right passage. Do you know which passage you're from?" He straightened and began unbuttoning his shirt.

She found herself staring at smooth, hairless skin as the material parted to show off his chest. Never in her life had she seen a man like him. It was as if he had no hair at all. The few men she'd fucked in her life had all been fairly hairy. And admittedly, a bit of hair on a man was a definite turn-on. His fingers moved down his shirt, until he had it open.

"No," she said finally, feeling suddenly foolish that she'd allowed him to almost disrobe before stopping him.

Her muscles burned from treading water so long. Now her stomach was in knots too. A few more minutes of this and she wouldn't be able to make it home.

Roln called out to her, something about her going the wrong way, but she was already underwater, hurrying back to the tunnel that would take her home. Trembling made it damned hard to kick, but she did it anyway, refusing to look back.

* * * * *

Syndi worked her way down the rocky hill, ignoring the postcard view of the small village of Camden below. Instead she focused on the faded blue sky, her attention riveted to the rolling lavender clouds that consumed the horizon. The pending storm made the air hotter than normal.

High winds and lightning would make the dead lands very dangerous, the sand blinding if someone got stuck in it. And the winds could get hot enough to burn your skin from your body.

"Syn. Syn. Look what we found!" Two of the village boys, all legs and a mess of unbrushed hair, grinned and laughed as they ran along the hill, fighting to keep balance so they wouldn't topple down the side of it.

Syndi stopped, holding her long auburn hair from her face. It was almost dry under the scorching sun. Walking over the uneven sandy ground was almost impossible to do with cramping leg muscles. She craved the water, needed it. But she'd hurried away from it as quickly as she could, almost running over the burning sand. Thankfully the children hadn't spotted her until the small pond was out of view. It didn't appear that she'd been followed, although she wouldn't feel safe until she was back at her tent.

The breeze that picked up would bring the storm quicker. The village would need to prepare. If they weren't ready for the storm before nightfall, lives would be lost. The intense thunder and lightning brought fires. Her tent would barely protect her, but nonetheless she couldn't wait to get there.

"You know you shouldn't leave the village," she scolded.

They ignored her, their faces showing their excitement.

She stared down at their thin tanned bodies, dirt stuck to every inch of them. Preoccupied with whatever they'd found, they didn't notice her slightly damp hair, or the exhaustion on her face.

"We found this buried in the sand." Joey, who was small for being ten, proudly held up a small wooden box.

"Maybe it's buried treasure," Nicholas said, grinning from ear to ear. "We can't open it."

"Open it for us." Joey held the box out to her.

"Let's get to the tents. I'll open it there." She took the box, tucking it under her arm while the boys took off running in front of her.

They didn't notice her shaking and she did her best to keep up with them. It seemed like they would never get to the village. The winds picked up, searing her skin. At least she wouldn't have to worry about explaining her wet hair. By the time they reached the dirt road lined with tents that made up the village Camden, the first bolt of lightning screamed across the sky.

"Get under cover, we'll open it tomorrow." Syndi watched the two boys hurry to the main tent.

Like most children, they had no parents. Raised by the rest of them, left to survive by their wits or die, she watched the two boys until she knew they had reached the large tent in the middle of the village.

Ignoring the rest of the people who hurried around her, seeking cover from the impending storm, she ducked her head and entered her dark home. Scraps of wood, bound and nailed together, made her small home secure. Securing the patched blanket that made up her door, she almost collapsed on to her hard dirt floor.

"You want to tell me where you were today?" Perry shoved the blanket that was her door to the side, and hovered over her.

There was barely time to shove her belt and the box she'd had in her hands under blankets before Perry made himself at home on the dirt next to her.

"Something wrong with your own tent?" she asked, ignoring his question.

"I figured the storm might scare you." He grinned, stretching his long legs out in front of him.

His lanky body took up most of the space on her floor.

"Yeah right. Go home, Perry. I'm not in the mood for company."

Her mind lingered on her adventure. She couldn't get Roln out of her head. Somehow she'd stumbled onto some forgotten place. There was no way she would accept that the city officials didn't know it existed. The government kept everything from them. Today she'd found land so rich it reeked of water, yet her people died from lack of it. More than anything she wanted to share her adventure, but confessing what she'd found would mean she'd have to tell him about her gills.

That wasn't an option. No one would ever know that she was a freak. Knowledge like that would be too hard to believe. She'd have to prove it. And she knew telling anyone about the pond could put them all in danger. Water was an incredibly expensive commodity, one that villagers didn't have at their disposal. Sharing what she knew would bring trouble.

"What's this?" Perry noticed the hidden box and pulled it out from under the covers.

Syndi shrugged. "I don't know. Some of the boys dug it up and gave it to me."

Perry turned the box around and studied it. She studied his unruly blond hair. It curled at his neck, which was just as hairy as his face. Unshaven, he wasn't all that bad-looking. His skin was dark, like hers. His pale blue eyes always reminded her of a dried-out summer sky. He had larger muscles than many of the men in the village, although quite thin, just like the rest of them. Perry found work when he could, and probably got a few decent meals a week. The T-shirt and jeans he wore did nothing to show off the fairly decent body he had.

Having known Perry most of her life, his presence didn't usually bother her. The casual sex they'd had once didn't impact their relationship today. But trust him. Did she? With normal stuff, probably. But what she'd just experienced, just witnessed, just done, was anything but normal. Syndi couldn't guess how he'd react.

He ran his hand over the box, wiping dirt off it. "Where'd they find it?"

Blurred painted images appeared on the box, initially concealed by sand and dirt. Faded, unclear, with one thing being obvious. Her stomach twisted in knots. They were identical to the pictures she'd seen in the tunnel while swimming to the lost world she'd found today.

Chapter Two

ജ

Thunder shook the ground. Lightning charged the air, momentarily stealing the darkness from Syndi's small tent.

"I told you. A couple of the boys found it. I figured I'd open it for them after the storm." She wouldn't mention the dead lands, then she'd have to explain what she'd been doing out there.

Mischievous boys wandering where they shouldn't go was one thing. She'd have a harder time explaining what she was doing out there.

Perry messed with the clasp that kept the box closed.

"Let it be." Her fingers scraped over the wood as she tried snatching the box from him. "You've got your own tent. Why don't you go to it?"

"You'd throw me out into the storm?" He reached for her breast, trying to tweak her nipple.

Syndi slapped at his hand. She wanted to be alone. The box had something to do with the underwater world. Too many mysteries, secrets, had just been revealed. It would take time to sort them out, and Perry was an annoying distraction.

"Why's your hair damp?" He gave her an appraising look.

"I'm sweaty." She pulled her knees to her chest, wishing he would leave.

Fortunately, he didn't mess with her. Returning his attention to the box, it took him a minute to force it open.

A small book fell out between them. Syndi snatched it up, staring at the plain cover. It was worn, the pages brittle and smelling like dirt, but the entry on the first page, handwritten in simple script, grabbed her attention.

May 10, 2145

We brought our precious bundle home today. She is so adorable. Don managed the paperwork. I don't even dare to write the details here. But she is ours. We just returned from city hall in Detroit and she is legal now, on the books. No one questioned a thing. I am the happiest mother in the world.

I wish I could share the adventure we had. But we've agreed to put it behind us, forget any of it happened. What matters is we're truly a family now. We have our daughter. I'm scared though. The man stressed that she had to be bathed every day. She'll need more water than we do. Somehow I'll make sure that she gets it.

Syndi didn't realize she was holding her breath.

Exhaling, she scowled at Perry. "Don't you have somewhere to go?"

"I'm there," he suggested, scooting closer to her, his large hand running over her leg, heading for her inner thigh.

Her muscles screamed, but she jumped to her feet anyway. His touch made her cringe, and she had no problem letting him know that.

"You're not getting a piece of ass from me tonight," she hissed. "Give me the box, and get out of here."

Another streak of lightning exploded outside the tent, and then rumbled through the air, shaking the walls around them. Wind nearly blew her blanket that served as her door to the side, opening her door for him. The elements agreed with Syndi. She wasn't in the mood for company.

"Like there's anyone else around here decent enough to take the edge off for you. You'll come begging for some." Perry ignored the weather outside, and grabbing her blanket-door, he scowled at her. "I thought you'd like to know that they're passing new legislation. You now need a medical examination, and proof that you've had one with some new card, before you can get in the public baths."

He let the blanket fall behind him as he stormed out of her tent. Pompous ass. Like she had time to focus on his bruised ego right now.

"Shit." None of them had money to get official medical examinations. Without water they would all die.

No one in Detroit, or any of the cities, gave a damn about villagers. Cast-outs. Street people who embarrassed them. Out of sight, out of mind obviously wasn't good enough anymore. Now they'd pass laws to ensure the villagers wouldn't survive. If she weren't so distracted by the box in front of her, the small notebook, and the underwater world, she'd be damned pissed off.

Running her fingers over the faded scroll on the small book in her hands, she ignored the clap of lightning outside. Her legs were like jelly and she almost fell onto her blankets. Once again she read the entry on the page.

"Oh my God," she whispered, nervous excitement tightening inside her.

She was born on May 10, 2145. And her parents' names had been Don and Samantha. She remembered being told that by the other villagers as a child. She delicately turned the page.

Suddenly there wasn't enough air to breathe in her small tent. Her lungs ached just as if she were underwater.

She flipped back to the first page, looking again at the entry. The tall flowing handwriting looked so elegant, classy. There weren't any pictures of her parents. None of the villagers talked about them. All she'd been told was that her Mom and Dad had been arrested. She'd grown up on the streets of Detroit until they'd all been banished to the village. Legislation had been passed, outlawing street people. Now they all had the polite name of villagers. Many of them had no clue who their parents were. Flipping through the pages, she stopped at the next page that was legible.

September 3, 2147

It had to be a dream. We both woke up last night. We both saw it. There is no way we can talk about it. No one can ever know. But there she was. Our little Syndi, completely submerged in the tub of water we'd bought earlier that day. Don had the barrel of water at the entrance to our tent so we could use it for cooking and cleaning.

She just sat there, staring up at us under the water. I screamed but Don silenced me. He held his hand over my mouth while we both stared down at Syndi. When she smiled up at us, her hair floating around her face in the water, I knew it had to be a dream. I was so scared. There was no way she could breathe. But when we pulled her out she was fine, giggling and happier than I'd seen her in days. We've both agreed not to talk about it.

Her fingers shook so hard she could hardly turn the page. Glancing quickly through the rest of the book she realized there was only one more legible entry. She devoured the words on the page, excitement tearing in her eyes.

October 15, 2147

I'm not sure what we're going to do. They just raised the price of water – again. At four dollars a gallon, I can't let Syndi play in it at night like I have in the past. We just can't afford it. We tried bathing her just twice a week. No other child has more than a couple baths a month. I didn't think it would hurt her. But now I feel so terrible. I'm not good at describing things, but I swear, her skin is falling off, shedding from her body the way a snake sheds its skin. She won't play. She just sits there, looking so lethargic. I give her cups of water and she sticks her fingers in it, tracing paths over her skin with the water. If only we could visit her people, just for a little while, for Syndi. I've promised Don that I won't write about it. He's outraged if I even mention where she came from. Somehow, no matter the price, I will make sure my daughter gets to bathe every day. We promised that when we got her, and I'm scared if we don't give her water, she'll die.

Tears burned her eyes and she rubbed at them angrily. She hadn't been the one to die, her mother had. Her throat swelled shut, and she let out a whimper, unable to stop her tears. Pain, confusion, bitterness over a life she barely remembered raged inside her, like a narrow sharp sword, piercing her from head to toe. She'd been told her mother had been arrested for not paying for the public baths. Syndi had never questioned the information. Most who were arrested were never seen again.

"I didn't die, Mom."

Anger soared through her, making her already sore muscles tighten. Fighting for rights to water had become part of her life. Yet earlier today she'd swam through free, flowing water, and had discovered a place none of them knew about. Something wasn't right here, and she had to figure out the mystery.

She could no longer see the pages on the book. She shut it carefully, not wanting to damage it more from her tears. Clasping the notebook in her lap, the same book that almost twenty years ago her mother had held, she let her tears fall. So many questions flooded through her. The entries didn't say where she'd come from. Her mother had stressed that she wouldn't reveal that information. Wherever that place was, water had been a major part of her life. And now she lived in a world where it was almost the hardest thing to get a hold of.

* * * * *

Syndi was lost in another world the next day—literally. She couldn't get images of the tall trees, the lush environment, out of her head. A harsh cruel sun scalded her skin as she fought to tighten the walls on one of the wood and plastic homes that had collapsed in the storm the night before.

Sand piled against the makeshift screens used as walls. The roof had been patched and repatched over the years. There was no money to buy supplies. She'd done her share of roaming the city streets, gathering anything thrown away in the dumpsters that the villagers could use. No funds would be coming in. If something needed fixing, they got out there and fixed it.

The sand made her ankles itch, while the sun burned her skin. Intense heat always made her miserable, grouchy if she were under direct sunlight for too long. But that was how it was for everyone. She'd never questioned it. Her dreams of water, craving it, needing it so desperately she couldn't think straight. Everyone was like that, weren't they?

If there were any way, she would make it to that pool again today. Her body screamed for the water.

"That should hold for a while." Syndi stepped back, surveying her work.

Warped wood, hemmed together with old nails, steadied the wall that had collapsed. Blankets wove through two-by-fours creating the roof.

"My hands just don't work like they used to." Randy Porter was a heavyset older man. He rubbed his arthritic hands together, and gave her a toothless grin.

"There are a few more tents that need repairs." Perry walked up to them, balancing a bundle of blankets over his shoulder. Sand stuck to his sunburnt cheeks, and he had the ripe odor about him of a man who'd gone a week without taking a wet towel to his body.

"You found food for me more times than I can remember when I was a child," Syndi told the older man, ignoring Perry. "You know I'm always here if you need help."

Perry scrutinized the work she'd done on the old man's shack. His gaze then moved to her, traveling down her with a hungry look. Syndi shook her head, looking away. Some men didn't understand the word no.

"I'll talk to you later." Waving at Randy, she turned toward the large tent in the middle of the village.

"Watch where you're going." Marla Hannaway jumped to the side to avoid Syndi walking into her."

"Sorry, Marla." Syndi nodded to the small bundle in Marla's hands. "I haven't seen your new baby."

Marla and Syndi were the same age, had gone to school together. The tiny infant lay naked in her friend's arms. Being a mother right now would absolutely ruin her life. There was so much still to learn. Marla beamed though, grinning as she turned the infant to show her off.

"She's beautiful," Syndi murmured, while the infant wrapped her tiny fingers around one of her fingers.

"When are you going to find yourself a man?" Marla asked.

Syndi blinked. None of the guys in the village evenly remotely impressed her.

"You might be tall, but you're pretty. Don't tell me the guys don't come around."

It didn't matter that they came around. None of them were getting between her legs. Guys in the village were puny, no muscles. Most of them were lucky to get a few meals a week. She'd known almost all of them most of her life. Getting herself off appealed to her more than any man she laid eyes on around here.

"I guess there just isn't time to find anyone," she said, letting go of the baby's hand to head toward the middle of the village.

"Did you all hear the news?" Joanie Wagner held her hand over her eyes, squinting against the hot sun as she walked up to them, her boyfriend Alex Froth in tow.

"No. What?" Marla adjusted her baby, her eyes wide with excitement over the possibility of new gossip.

"They've closed down the public baths in Detroit," Alex piped up, and Joanie scowled at him that he'd gotten the latest gossip out before she could announce it.

"Why did they do that?" Syndi couldn't believe it. Without the public baths, no one but the extremely wealthy would be able to bathe.

"They say the water is infected." Joanie rolled her eyes. "They're just coming up with new ways to make water more expensive."

"Now you have to buy a health inspection card so that you can get water." Alex's words silenced them all.

Everyone fell into a discontented silence. Not once in her life had she been to a doctor.

"If the water is infected, why don't they just clean it?" Randy grunted. "Makes more sense to me."

"They say they found skin in the water," Perry spoke up, adjusting the boards still resting on his shoulder. "Like it had flaked right off someone."

Syndi's heart quit beating. Heat from the sun burned her skin. She couldn't look down at herself, couldn't move her gaze from where she stared past Joanie and Alex. God. If the sun sizzled through her for a second longer, she swore her skin would peel off in front of everyone.

"I've got to go," she mumbled.

"I agree. It's disgusting." Joanie misunderstood Syndi's sudden urge to run.

"It's a bunch of bullshit is what it is. Like anyone's skin is going to flake off their body." Perry grabbed her arm. "Come on. Give me a hand."

Syndi jumped from his touch, his sweaty grip simply adding to the heat that threatened to boil her alive. Hurrying past him, the large tent that housed the small market booths, the place where the villagers did their bartering, wasn't too far away. Maybe the shade would help her get a grip. Water. Just a bit of water. It wasn't any cooler when she stepped under the shade of the large tent. Her skin felt like it would sizzle right off her bones. Standing under the glaring midday sun always did this to her, and she hated it. Hated having to be exposed to its cruel glare. There was always the fear that she'd start peeling, and now with the news of the public baths closing, and why, panic made it even harder to breathe in the crushing heat.

Politely she waited her turn then dipped her hands into the barrel, which was only half full of water. Their supplies were running low. Guilt stabbed at her when she brought her damp hands to her face, enjoying the sensation as the moisture seeped through her pores. They had such little water, and she knew where a pond was just outside of town. What the villagers wouldn't do to prance and play in that water as she had. If she told them, and somehow the city found out, it would be taken away, guarded. None of them would be allowed access, not without paying an exorbitant price none of them could afford.

The others had followed her to the tent. More villagers surrounded her, but the conversation didn't change. She blinked through moist lashes, staring at the others around her.

She did stand taller than all of them. And while they were all fair complexioned, her hair was brown. She'd never given thought to how different she looked from the other villagers.

"How do we get these cards?" Syndi couldn't remember when she'd ever had any kind of health inspection.

"They're bringing a clinic here next week. We have to wait that long unless you want to go in to one of Detroit's clinics." Joanie showed her disgust, frowning as she spoke. "Now we have to have a checkup just to get water."

"Even to buy water?" That didn't make sense.

"Well, we just had a checkup at the clinic. It was expensive but you get more pan-handling when you're pregnant." Marla cuddled her baby to her. "Maybe they will count that."

Syndi stumbled over her feet several times, lost in thought, while hurrying down the dirt road, wishing she could go home and out of the sun. Dust clouds burned her eyes, her skin was about to peel right off her, and her muscles hurt more today than they had yesterday.

But it was her thoughts that really plagued her. She'd found a large pool of water. Up until now it had been her private sanctuary, a place to go when her skin hurt too much to handle it any longer. But her village would die if they had to pay for health cards just to get water. None of them had that kind of money. And she knew no one in the cities cared about villagers. They were the poorest of the poor, those unable to survive in the cities who'd migrated into small communities throughout the United States. The cities had banished them, deciding their homeless existence would be better off elsewhere instead of marring their streets.

Camden had been around for over ten years, the people here working together to make sure everyone had some form of shelter. The thunderstorms were cruel and the sun harsh, but they all managed.

With another forced expense on all of them, many would die before being able to meet the city's requirements simply to get water. And no one would give a rat's ass.

She walked around a large tent that had no sides. The center of the village, it was a huge structure with many tarps sewn together and stretched over poles that held it high enough to stand under. Some lived here and all bartered here.

Her Uncle Paul stood with several other men alongside one of the water barrels.

Remembering the journal entry from her mother, she wondered to what expense her parents had gone to get one of those barrels in their kitchen. They must have loved her very much. Her heart swelled painfully. She wished she had memories of her mother and father. There were no images, no sensations, nothing anywhere in her deepest thoughts that she could pin as a vague recollection of either of them. What kind of person didn't remember their parents?

"We were there earlier this morning," Shef Winfrey was saying to the other men when Syndi stopped just far enough away for her uncle to notice but for her not to be part of the group. "And it's all true. They passed legislation the other day. Something about skin being found in the water being reason for everyone now having to have a physical before getting in the baths."

"But they've made it so that you have to have that damned physical card just to buy water," old Ralph said a bit too loudly. His hearing never had been that good. "Next time the water vendor comes around they say he's going to have security with him to make sure everyone's got a card before they can buy."

The large meeting area was where most of the villagers spent their days, catching up on gossip and bartering whatever service they could offer. A fair amount of people had joined the group of men where her uncle lingered.

"You know anything about physical cards?" someone yelled to Bertha, their village doctor.

"No one tells me anything," Bertha yelled back from the pile of metal slabs that she sat on under the patchwork roof.

"We're all going to die," someone wailed, and the others said nothing to console him.

"Whoever heard of skin falling off a person anyway?" another argued. "The city is just trying to kill us all off."

Standing there while everyone groaned would accomplish nothing. Syndi left the group, catching her uncle's appraising glance as she left them. Her aunt and uncle had kept watch over her off and on while she grew up. No specific memory came forth of either of them commenting on it, but she knew her skin had shed repeatedly when she didn't get enough water. The worried look in his eyes made her stomach turn.

Worrying wouldn't help the matter any. Something needed to be done.

If the sun didn't kill her, then her sore muscles would. Staying busy was better than standing around griping about something.

"Did you get our box opened?" Little Joey hurried up to her with Nicholas right behind him.

Both of them were just as dirty as they'd been the day before.

"Was there treasure in it?" Nicholas grinned, tugging at her shirt.

Appraising the mangled tent that Perry and some of the others were working to reassemble, she looked down at the two boys, smiling at their enthusiasm. Their life would be filled with poverty, hardship, and no place to call home. Yet the two children embraced life, knowing no other way.

"It was empty. But you come to my tent after I'm through here, and I'll give you the box."

Perry wrinkled his brow, overhearing her but fortunately not commenting.

Ignoring his look, she helped get the tents fixed from the storm.

Every inch of her ached when finally homes were repaired, and life after the storm had returned to normal. Every step she took hurt as she headed toward her tent, wanting no more than to collapse and escape the wrath of the sun. If it were possible to bake alive, she swore that was what she was doing.

"I bet you'd love a sponge bath right about now." Perry fell into stride next to her.

"You're the one who needs a bath." She wrinkled her nose at him.

"Sounds good. You bathe me and I'll bathe you."

"Dream on." The ground was hard under her shoes. Even the muscles in her feet hurt.

"I'm not a dreamer." Perry pressed on. "I've got five gallons of water at my tent, and I'm willing to share."

"I'm not interested."

Perry ran his rough palm down her hair. His hot hand rested in the middle of her back, making her itch more than she already did. If that were possible. Twisting against his touch, she wrinkled her brow and pointed a finger at him.

"Just because you fucked me once," she hissed under her breath, "don't think you have rights to it again."

Turning from him, irritation coursing through her, she tossed her heavy hair over her shoulder. Damn it. Water. She needed water.

"Well, if you don't look like you're in a foul mood," her Aunt Mary said, cocking her head at her the way she always did when she was trying to figure what Syndi was up to.

Forcing her facial muscles to relax took more effort than she realized. Syndi pursed her lips, doing her best to match a smile.

"It's been a long day." She twisted her hair off her back, fearing one more minute in this roasting heat and her skin would start peeling.

Aunt Mary knitted her brows, giving her that look when she was deciding something. A bit on the stocky side, she carried her weight well, and was rather pretty considering her age. Her mother might have looked like her. There had never been reason to ask. Thinking of the journal entries, having been given a glimpse at her mother's thoughts, suddenly made her want to know more about her. Dwelling on her before hadn't mattered. Staying alive had mattered.

But now...

"Come here," her aunt said, disappearing into her tent.

Syndi ducked her head, holding her hair up as she left the direct sunlight. Tight heat inside the tent made her skin stretch, pulling against her muscles and bones. Squinting, she fought the burning in her head, the need for water. It consumed her so desperately she could hardly think.

"What's up?" she managed to say.

Her aunt dipped a towel into a pot of water and brought it to Syndi, then stroked her arms and face with the cloth. Syndi almost melted against the touch.

"I look that bad, huh."

"You look worse."

Her aunt hummed to herself while rubbing Syndi's arms, neck, back of her neck, then her forehead and cheeks with the damp cloth. The soft melodic tune soothed her as much as the cloth did. Water soaked through her pores, relieving the tightness in her skin.

Something triggered in her memory. "You used to do this for me when I was a child."

"Sometimes," her aunt said indifferently.

Thoughts of the journal, of the small box found buried in the dead lands, distracted her. Her stomach tightened.

"Aunt Mary," Syndi said and then hesitated.

"Yes dear?" Her aunt met her gaze and then frowned, sensing something was wrong. "What is it?"

"Where did I come from?"

Chapter Three

ဢ

Tor Geinz didn't like the hard rocks in the narrow cavern. Too many memories of persecution, of humiliation, rushed through him as he climbed out of the water, situating himself. Cries from battles, screams as good warriors died, still echoed through the cavern.

Roln Storn swam up alongside him, dutifully allowing Tor to climb out of the water first before mounting a nearby rock.

"What is it that's so mysterious we had to come here?" He scowled at the dark damp walls, wiping the bitter water from his mouth.

"Agreed it's a morbid place, Sir." Roln was one of his most loyal guards, or Tor never would have agreed to such a meeting.

Morbid hardly described the place. Bloodshed permanently stained the water. Even the rocks were darker, permanently marked from a time when they'd fought for the right to rule their own passage. It was an eerie place. None of them came here anymore. When Roln suggested they meet here, Tor knew something was wrong.

Roln looked around him, those dark eyes of his taking in the place. Tor didn't doubt it was secure but also knew Roln would keep guard even while talking.

"So out with it," he prompted.

Pulling the thin sleeveless shirt away from his chest momentarily, water dripped down his shorts. Staring down at the four triangles that connected at the corners, the emblem of his rank, he knew any knowledge Roln was about to give him would go no further. Tor had reached top rank. Controlling the entire West Passage would not be something he'd give up easily. Just being here was reminder enough of how many had given their life fighting for his right to rule.

"Yesterday, at the meeting of the passages," Roln started, and then sucked in a breath.

Tor studied the bald man. "Yes?"

"One of the ponds," he began again, rubbing his head with his thick hand. "It doesn't make sense. There's no passage there. But you need to know. I'm not sure who she was. But there was someone there."

"You're not making any sense." Tor studied the calm dark water that surrounded the rock he sat on. The slightest ripple would indicate someone approaching. Not that anyone in their right mind would come here.

"I know I'm not making any sense." Roln shook his head. "A young lady, with hair that was so long it drifted around her naked body, surfaced in one of the ponds surrounding the passages. It's not a place we keep well guarded. We've no reason to."

"A naked lady? You brought me here to this place to tell me about a naked woman?" Only Roln, his loyalty to the West Passage so strong, would leave a naked woman alone while on duty.

Roln didn't blink an eye at Tor's sudden aggravation. Letting out a sigh, he watched his guard look up and down the narrow dark cavern as Tor's voice echoed from the walls.

"No. I didn't bring you to tell you about a naked woman." Roln had the good sense not to sound exasperated. "I brought you here to talk to you about a woman found where she shouldn't have been. No one should have been there, naked or otherwise. The pond is just an uprising of water. It doesn't go anywhere."

"Then what was she doing there?"

"I don't know."

"Where is she now?"

"Well, that's just it. She dove back down into the pond and never surfaced again."

"Then obviously the pond is a passage."

Roln shook his head. "That would mean there are more than four passages."

Running his hand through his thick dark hair, drops of water streamed down his back, keeping his skin wet. Roln had a point. There were only four passages. The North Passage, ruled by Tren Fal, the West Passage, which he'd recently taken over, the South Passage, which Shara Dar had control over at the moment, although Tor would wager she wouldn't be able to keep it, and Ran Mose, who'd ruled the East Passage since Tor had been a boy.

"There are only four passages," Tor said, frowning at Roln. "Where would another passage lead to?"

Roln shook his head. "Exactly. But the fact that she disappeared into the pond isn't why I called you here. There's more."

Tor allowed the brief silence, waiting for Roln to share his thoughts.

"Tor," Roln said slowly. "She looked different. Her eyes were too small. I know this sounds crazy, but she almost looked like the pictures in our history books of what humans looked like on Dead World."

Anyone else and Tor would have broken out laughing. Roln didn't joke though. He'd known the man since they were boys. More so, he'd never looked more serious than he did right now.

Sliding off the rock into the cold dark water that led toward the passage, Tor focused on Roln. "Pull some of the trainees out tonight to guard the passages. Make it appear that it's a trial run for them to start into rotation. That way you'll have extra men out, and you can focus on this pond. Take a look and see if you find a passage. And keep me updated."

Roln nodded, sliding into the water next to Tor. "And if there is another passage?"

"Then we find out where it leads."

Leaving the dark cavern lifted Tor's mood. Battle was a necessary evil. But harboring where so many of his friends had died, entering once again into the dark tunnels where they'd fought so savagely to gain their independence as a passage of their own, had surfaced so many unpleasant memories.

It had been necessary at the time. Only his youth had allowed him to survive the terrible civil wars. Today boys weren't initiated into manhood by annihilating and mutilating just to survive. The memories would be with him for life. And he didn't regret them. But there was no reason to dwell on them. Peace existed in the West Passage now. His armies were strong. And life would stay this way. Many had died for the rest of them to have such a peaceful existence today.

Reaching the warm aqua sea, he glided through the silky water, his thoughts slowing his actions. Roln obviously worried the naked lady, and the pond, might bring them trouble. Not many men had his trust the way Roln did. He'd be anxious to hear what Roln learned after diving into the pond.

And what if there was another passage?

People appeared through the aqua green mist, bowing politely as he passed. Appreciation of his rank. Their respect would come with time. Acknowledging each bow, he picked up speed, swimming through the calm sea toward the swift currents that surrounded the caves.

The green hue changed to blue, dark seaweed floating without direction while lazy and well-fed fish drifted around him. Reaching New Dallas, the water darkened, grew colder, and the underground mountains slowly took form in front of him.

Currents pushed hard against his body as tran-buses sped through the water, carrying citizens from one end of the mountains to the other. Silver and shaped like long tubes, the tiny windows glowing with light, he barely focused on them. Tourists on vacation, people getting off work, the city's main form of transportation housed them all. Just another busy day for most of them. Life as usual.

Tor would see to it that they were able to continue their peaceful existence.

"It's about time you got back." Fern Rosh paced the rocky cliff, her tan dress clinging to her, damp, showing off her tight ass and plump breasts.

His communication's officer, Fern always seemed upset with him. It was just her nature, and he respected the young woman for trying so hard to impress him.

Lifting himself out of the water, he walked to where Fern stood. Her dark eyes lowered, moist lashes fluttering as she quickly let her gaze travel over him. A look most women gave him. He was accustomed to it. Most shied away when he came on to them. His status and size intimidated them. Fern was no different. She turned before he reached her, carrying her portable computer in her hands while her feet made small slapping sounds against the rocks.

"Glad to know you missed me." He looked down at her short blonde hair, cropped close around her head in the contemporary style.

"I hope this all-important meeting you had to hurry off to was good for you." She thought he'd gone off to get laid.

Hiding a smile at her protective jealous nature, he ignored her comment. Walking along the narrow path that bordered the pool of water, which was the entrance into his office, they passed through the oval-shaped carved doorway into the large cave. Humming computers and the brightness of large screens on the wall, transmitting different parts of New Dallas, his office was the usual busy atmosphere of his staff running the city.

"There you are." Ben Osk, his senior computer specialist, turned in his chair.

Fern stood next to him, glancing at the panels in front of him.

"What's up?" Tor asked.

Fern's gills fluttered behind her ears. That and her attentive look was enough to tell Tor something bothered her.

Ben, having run the city from his computers for years, was a little harder to read. Nonetheless, he straightened in his seat, pressing several buttons on the panel housed in the desk secured to the stone wall behind it. He pointed a finger at his screen when an image appeared.

Fern looked up at him quickly, her expression wide-eyed before she returned her attention to the screen in front of Ben.

"Give me a second for audio," Ben said.

Every muscle inside Tor hardened as he stared at the image of Ran Mose, leader of the Eastern Passage. During their civil war, Ran Mose had sat quietly, word whispered among the soldiers that he watched, waiting to see who would be victorious without interfering.

Other than pictures, Tor had never laid eyes on the man. More than likely somewhere in his fifties, permanent creases in his forehead didn't hide the distinguished look. Here was a ruler who'd passed the test of time. And for whatever reasons, he sent a message to Tor.

Speakers crackled on either side of the computer before a soft hum sounded and then the image began moving, his voice muffled but audible.

"Tor Geinz. I will have a personal unmonitored conference with you at your earliest convenience. Reply immediately." The transmission ended.

"That's it?" He'd never met the man and with no preamble the leader demanded a conference.

"I've prepared a channel for the conference in your office." Apparently Fern had guessed he'd honor the East Passage leader's request.

He'd chosen those who worked closest to him because they could act on their feet, make decisions without running to him with a thousand questions. They'd all grown up studying the leadership qualities of Ran Mose. Tor stifled the wish that the leader would have respected him enough to ask for a meeting, instead of demanding one. He wouldn't let his irritation show over that minor detail. Not bothering to respond, Tor headed toward the tunnel that led to his office.

Diving into the small opening at the corner of the large cave, Fern was right behind him. He swam through the tunnel, illuminated with underwater lights since often they carried office equipment as they swam. Fern did that now, holding her waterproof portable computer in her hand as she moved easily alongside him toward his office.

Water puddled at his feet as he lifted himself out of the small opening in the floor to his office. The round hole in the ground, no more than five feet in diameter, was similar to all openings leading to rooms in houses, or offices in buildings. Fern lifted herself out after him.

Wiping water from his eyes, he left a path of water behind him as he moved across the stone floor, barefoot, and sat down at his conference table. Fern was right there, setting up the computer in front of him. A task he could manage easily enough, but apparently she was just as curious to know what the reputable leader wanted.

Disappointing her didn't bother him. "He's requested an unmonitored conference."

Fern took a moment to get his meaning. A protest was on her lips before she got the better of herself.

"Fine," she said with a noticeable pout and then turned sharply, marching over to the hole in the ground and jumped, not dived, into the water, splashing it in her anger.

Her tantrum would pass. Right now, learning what Ran Mose was about mattered more.

Alone in his office, a decent-sized cave, his home away from home, allowed him space to think. Just a few matters to take care of, and he'd be ready for this unmonitored conference. Reaching for his portable computer, he brought up the program to record. No one would monitor what was said between him and the East Passage leader, but he would have their conversation recorded so that he could play it again later. There was no doubt in his mind the East Passage leader would do the same.

Reclining in his seat, he pulled his belt from his waist, which holstered his gun and his phone. Glancing up at the small camera housed in the corner of the cave, he decided there was no harm in leaving it on. No doubt existed that Fern and Ben hovered over the monitor in the main computer cave watching his every move. They were dying to know what the East Passage leader wanted.

And so was he.

More than honored that Ran Mose wished his time, he stared at the blank screen momentarily, gathering his thoughts. There was no reason to impress the leader, although he wouldn't deny his urge to do so. Tor had fought hard for his rank. He'd earned every bit of it. There was nothing to be nervous about, nothing to fear. Ran Mose was a man, just like he was. Nonetheless, a twitch of anxiousness hit his gut.

Pressing the necessary buttons, he pulled up the transmission, still open, to the East Passage. For a moment he stared at the mountainous symbol that represented that side of the world. A place he'd never been. The symbol displayed two rugged mountains, rocky and desolate-looking. A cold, hard image.

The image faded, Tor's muscles hardening, in spite of the fact that he was alone and safe in his own office. Immediately he was on the defensive, ready for anything this known warrior might have to say to him.

"Tor Geinz." Ran Mose's deep voice rang with authority, a man who'd lived most of his life ruling his passage, a man who'd earned respect of all on Earth.

"Ran Mose." He wouldn't bow to him. They were equals. No matter that Tor had just recently fought to reach his rank, they were damned equals.

"We have a situation. Another passage has been discovered, a people we didn't know existed. You will assist me in taking over this passage."

Tor wouldn't change his position, and sure as hell wouldn't let his expression show how Ran's words had just hit him. Adjusting his legs under the table, water streaming down his skin, he gave the image staring back at him total concentration.

"We're aware of this passage already. Tell me what you've learned." Best to show he had the upper edge. "The people there seem quite different."

"People?" Ran leaned back, his image blurring for a brief moment. "This doesn't surprise me a bit that you'd be wise to this already. You remind me a lot of myself, Tor, in my earlier years. You're definitely the only leader I would give merit too."

Tor wouldn't argue that point. At the same time, his demand to know what Ran knew had been ignored.

"This isn't an issue to discuss over a transmission," he said, needing to buy himself some time.

"Agreed. In two days we'll meet at the four passages. First thing in the morning." Ran reached out, and his transmission went dead.

Tor stared at the blank screen. But only for a moment. There was a lot of work to do. And information to gather. No longer could he wait until this evening to explore that pond by the four passages, the same location where Ran wished to meet.

That in itself seemed a bit odd. A strange naked woman appears in a pond that shouldn't be a passage and then Ran contacts him. Excitement hit him, and he almost grinned. Almost. He wouldn't be stupid enough to think Ran contacted him simply to share this knowledge, or because he needed Tor's help. There was another reason.

Securing his belt to his waist, he yanked his phone free from its clasp.

It rang once.

"Roln," he barked.

"Yes, Sir."

"Meet me at the four passages immediately." He'd be damned if Ran Mose gained the upper hand on him.

"Yes, Sir."

Tor hung up his phone, clipping it to his belt and then dived into the tunnel of water that led to his computer cave. Fern and Ben waited with anxious looks on their faces.

Two other computer assistants worked along the wall, their backs to Tor. Loyalty wasn't an issue. Every one of his people would die for him. There were no doubts. This was a puzzle though, and he hated not having all the facts.

He lowered his voice. "We have a situation."

Both of them followed him to the oval-shaped doorway. He walked a short way over the stone path that bordered the water leading out of the cave. Both waited for him to speak again.

"There is another passage," he told them quietly.

"You mean a fifth passage?" Fern's jaw dropped, her small mouth forming a perfect circle while she looked from Tor to Ben.

"Keep communication open. I've got my guards already handling the matter. I'll be in touch shortly."

"Why are we just finding out?" Fern cried out, but he'd already dived into the canal that led out of the cave.

None of this made any sense. The world was mapped. There were no uncharted areas. The passages had developed over the course of time, after war and devastation had altered the planet drastically. Every soldier studied this in extensive detail in the academy. Where could a fifth passage possibly lead?

Tor wouldn't enjoy swimming through the ocean this time. Reaching the outer side of the mountain, he hailed one of his guards who immediately brought over his personal tran-bus.

His personal vehicle, a cream-colored, cylindrical tran-bus moved silently toward him until stopping in shallow water inside the cave. Tor pressed buttons on the outer hull and a door on the side of the tran-bus slid open silently. Water washed into the small compartment as he stepped inside. The outer doors slid shut, enclosing him in the airtight area. Water drained out of the compartment and then inner doors slid open. He entered the small cabin, which housed a driver's seat and passenger seat, and then several bench seats behind them. His personal driver Peg looked over her shoulder expectantly at him.

"Head to the four passages," he told her, taking the seat next to her.

She nodded, not asking any questions, and gripped the large steering wheel, her muscular arms still damp with water. Slim and shapely, Peg was probably one of the best damned warriors he had. Having fought next to each other in their early days, he knew she'd have his back before any of them would. She was shrewd and sexy, her wet brown hair sleeked back and tapering at her neck, while her soft brown eyes focused ahead of her, giving him the impression she didn't have a thought in her head.

Which he knew damned good and well wasn't the case.

More than once he'd come real close to fucking her. They'd worked closely over the years, and her quick wit and hot muscular body had almost pulled him over the edge on a handful of times. Fucking her would quite possibly ruin the tight bond they had. And that wasn't something Tor was willing to risk.

Running his hands through his wet hair, he did know her input and methodical way of thinking might help him sort out this matter. Not to mention, he didn't know what he was walking into here, and wanted her on the alert for anything that might happen.

He reached over to the panel next to her steering wheel, and flipped off the transmission switch. All conversations were recorded. Although not always reviewed, if needed, Tor always had access to everything going on around him.

Peg glanced over at him, raising her eyebrow. "Don't want them to hear us fucking?"

He didn't smile, although her crude comment was just like her. It was that relaxed bond the two of them had that made her the perfect candidate to discuss this with.

"We'll fuck later," he told her. "I just talked to Ran Mose."

"No shit?" She looked at him wide-eyed. "Have you ever talked to him before?"

"No." He looked out ahead of them, as they sped through a large school of fish. "He's told me that he's discovered a fifth passage."

For some reason, telling her how Roln had spotted the naked woman seemed like too much information. He wouldn't let loose a school of minnows by mentioning the possibility of this fifth passage being populated. Not yet. Too many questions would quickly be raised that he didn't have answers for. And nothing was worse than not having answers.

"A fifth passage?" she whispered. "No way."

"I think it might be at the four passages. But if there is one there, then there is another entrance to it in the East Passage. Head to the four passages. And I want you to hang around. Until I have some clue as to whether this passage is for real or not, I want a low profile on why I'm at the passages."

"Okay…" The way she drew out the word matched her expression.

Peg was taking it all in, digesting what he'd told her. And in her own good time he would hear what she thought. Of that he had no doubts.

She slowed at the next mountain, navigating the tran-bus through the underground tunnel that lead to the four passages. A natural anomaly inside the hollow mountain, the tunnel was short. No longer were they underwater, but suddenly floating, until the tran-bus hit land, and came to a stop.

Tor didn't have to use the airtight chamber that kept water out of the cabin this time. Overriding it, inner and outer doors opened quietly and he walked out onto the thick grassy terrain.

Roln walked over to him, his calm manner the same as always.

"Show me this pond you told me about."

"It's not too far from the south passage." Roln didn't question him, as it should be.

Tall thick trees reminded Tor of growing up, except then the trees had been barriers, providing both protection and means for an enemy to spy unnoticed. The wars before the separation of the passages were best put behind him. Nonetheless, something as simple as a thick growth of trees could trigger memories he'd like to forget. Pushing the edginess that the trees brought on out of his head, he searched for this pond Roln had told him about.

The trees barely parted when Roln slowed and then pointed. "There it is."

Tor stared down at the calm water, no bank or anything, the trees bordering it as if protecting whatever lay beneath.

"It's obviously deep."

Tor jumped in and Roln splashed right in next to him. Surfacing, he shouldn't have been surprised to see Peg at the edge of the water.

"Let me explore the water, Sir." Roln wasn't insulting him, but simply pointing out that Tor wasn't expendable.

Too much weighed on understanding this passage—if there indeed was one.

"Keep anyone away from this water until we return. Message me if needed," Tor said to Peg, patting his phone that was secured to his belt in the water.

The look she gave him made it clear she wanted to explore as well, but she simply nodded.

"I'm going with you," Roln said, daring to put some authority in his tone.

"Let's go then." Tor dove down into the water, anxious to learn what was down there.

There was no way this water could have been here before. It made absolutely no sense that it was here now. Especially so close to the four passages. The area was guarded so heavily, word would have gotten back to him that it existed. Hell, he would have noticed it himself.

Yet it was here, and too deep just to be a pond. There had been no reports of shifting ground in almost fifty years. After World War Three, the Earth changed substantially, most maps being rewritten. But since then little had changed. And nothing so drastic as a new passage.

Roln pulled a light from his belt, which flooded through the darkness. And still they swam deeper. Anxious to see something, anything, that might explain what this pond was, Tor took the light from his guard, leading the way into the murky depths.

Roln tapped Tor's shoulder and pointed. The action wasn't necessary though. Ahead of them was a tunnel, lost and forgotten, and ornately painted with symbols he'd never seen before.

Excitement surged through him. This was fucking unbelievable. A lost passage. He kicked with all his might, more anxious than a teenager getting laid for the first time.

History was being made here. Passing the light to Roln, Tor took his phone from his belt and then gestured for Roln to hold the light just right so that he could snap pictures of the paintings on the wall. Saving them on his phone, later he would transfer the images to his computer and match them with what they had stored on history files.

Most tunnels weren't this long, or narrow. Before they reached the end of it, they swam single file. Roln probably didn't like the idea of following Tor, but Tor didn't give a rat's ass. Curiosity urged him forward. The tunnel finally ended, another pond appeared, the water way too warm.

Breathing almost became a chore, the water temperature making his gills swell. Roln gave him a wary look when they neared the surface of the pond. Anything could be out there, and there were only two of them. There was no turning back at this point. Pulling his gun, he gestured with his head for them to swim to the surface. Roln's mouth formed a thin line and he looked above them, squinting. It was also too bright in the water.

Light surrounded them with so much intensity that Tor could hardly see. Masking his eyes with his hand, he broke through the water, hit with a heat he'd never experienced before.

"What is it?" Roln spit water as he surfaced next to Tor.

"I'm not sure, but I think it might be the sun."

Chapter Four

∞

"There's going to be a meeting later tonight." Perry's words disturbed Syndi.

If the villagers were in the main tent, it would be easier to be seen when she headed toward the dead lands. Waiting until dark to go could be more dangerous than risking being seen while it was still light. Wild dogs coursed over the dead lands at night, scavengers anxious to tear into anything they could find to eat.

Finding her can opener, she ripped into the tin can, the thick aroma of canned meat filling the tight air in her tent. Perry walked up behind her, his thick hands dampening her waist with sweat when he gripped her and pulled her back against him. His hard shaft pressed into her ass.

"The smell of meat turn you on?" she asked, pulling away from him in search of her fork.

"You can only say no for so long," he grumbled. "I know you're not getting it anywhere else. You've got needs just like me. Fuck me and make both of us happy."

She curled her lip. "You are such a romantic."

"It's one hundred thirty degrees out. We've both worked all day. And I've got an ache." Now he sounded like he was whining. "At least take your clothes off and let me look at you while I jack off."

"Get out of here." She pointed to the tent flap with her fork.

"You know, there are those who plan to smuggle water, an act that would surely get the entire village in a lot of trouble." He pulled the tent flap back, but then wagged his index finger at her. "If you aren't at that meeting tonight, some might think you could be one of those smugglers."

"I don't do threats," she hissed.

He grunted, leaving her in peace finally. Not that being alone in her tent offered any solace. Water cried out to her. Deep and plentiful. Her skin was so tight it burned. But Perry had a point. His words bothered her with their truth. Not being at that meeting might look bad for her. Maybe just going to the pond for a while, long enough to ease the pain, ensure that her skin wouldn't start peeling.

Granted, her aunt had done some good when she'd soaked her down with the damp towel. Something inside Syndi's gut twisted, an uncomfortable sensation. The words from her mother's journal ran through her head. Her parents had known she could breathe underwater, and that her skin peeled. What if her aunt and uncle knew also?

There were others out there like her. No way would she believe it was a mere coincidence that the city had shut the public baths down due to peeling skin. They could have made up any lie. But to say that—to indicate others lost their skin without water—other people out there had gills too.

She looked down at the can of pressed meat that she'd managed one bite of. Suddenly she'd lost her appetite. Too many questions floated in her head. Questions that she needed answers to. Her head hurt trying to figure out how she'd possibly get those answers.

What she did know was that she needed water—needed that pond. Like an addict needed his fix, she had to go there. None of her thoughts would fall into place until she did.

Covering the can with foil, she slipped it back into the box with the rest of her rations. If she was going to enjoy a swim, best to do it now before it got dark, and before the meeting.

Light blinded her at the same moment that heat scalded her skin. Late afternoon brought the cruel sting of the sun. Everyone would be resting, staying out of direct sunlight, and waiting to finish chores and socialize once the sun began setting. Pain ripped through her, as if someone had set her on fire. Hurrying to the edge of the village, she took off into the dead lands, praying she wouldn't get caught.

Intense sunlight made it hard to tell where she was going. She couldn't see a damned thing. Worrying she might have traipsed past the pond, it suddenly appeared before her.

Brightness reflected from the water and she lowered her eyes, quickly undressing and then finding the rock she'd buried her clothes under before. The first step into the pond was like an electrical shock. Her nerve endings shot to life, while every inch of her pulsed with newfound energy.

Instantly her body pulsed, her pussy throbbing, already accustomed and anticipating her private masturbation sessions deep in the privacy of the water. The pond was like the Earth's womb, soaked and dripping with pleasure while she entered it, bringing it pleasure while she gained her own. The water splashed around her, greeting her, eager for their intimate session to begin.

It took a minute to recover from the initial reaction her body had to the water, but then she took a few more steps, her body like a sponge.

Needing every inch of her covered, she bent down, crawling until water covered her cheeks, soaked her hair, filled her with new life. If only she could bring the villagers here and make it so none of them would get caught. The pond was so deep all of them could enjoy it without it drying up. This was simply too good to keep to herself. Maybe at the meeting tonight. Maybe…

Something moved ahead of her, closer to the middle of the pond. Unable to focus in the bright sunlight, she ducked her head underwater, squinting while her heart skipped a beat.

It had never crossed her mind that others might already know about the pond. Damn it. She didn't have any clothes on.

She focused slowly, her heart skipping a beat, her lungs instantly filling with water as she gasped underwater.

Roln Storn, the bald man she'd met at the other end of the tunnel, floated in the middle of the pond. His bald head shone brightly against the intensity of the sun. And there was another man with him, slightly bigger in stature, more muscular, with black hair pressed against his head and tapering to the end of his neck.

Underwater, their entire bodies were visible, both of them kicking almost in unison, a slow, steady movement. Roln wore the same tan pants she'd seen on him before, making her wonder if it weren't some kind of uniform. Whoever tredded water alongside him wore shorts that floated around an ass that almost had her drooling underwater. With each kick of his legs, strong large muscles moved rhythmically under smooth white skin.

Damn. He was a work of perfection. Roped muscles twisted under his flesh. His back was broad, shoulder blades gliding back and forth while he controlled the water, moving his hands through it. His arms bulged and flexed, every inch of him better than anything her imagination had ever conjured up. Her pussy throbbed, her heart swelling to her throat. Her nipples puckered in the water, taking him in, imagining what it would be like to fuck such a large man, such a powerful strong-looking man.

And she was out of her fucking mind.

Her heart picked up pace as reality sunk inside her suddenly fogged thoughts. What the hell was she doing lusting over this stranger? No matter that they weren't villagers who'd discovered her secret hideaway, or officials from the city come to set up guards around her coveted water. This was worse — it had to be. No more than ten feet in front of her, two men floated from a world underneath her own.

It took two glances down the magnificent body of the dark-haired man to catch sight of the belt wrapped around his waist. On one side hung a dangerous-looking gun.

They were armed.

She was naked.

This was bad.

Backing up on her hands and knees, her face surfaced from the water, and she coughed. The two men spun around.

"God. No." She cried out in spite of herself.

"That's the girl." The bald man had his hand almost covering his eyes.

Her breath caught in her throat when she stared into the face of the larger man with his black hair stuck to his head, falling in small curls that clung to his neck. He, too, covered his eyes, but not so much that she couldn't see their milk chocolate color, long lashes that clung together from the water, and that they were definitely larger than they should be.

But dear God! He was fucking gorgeous. Dark chest hair clung to well defined muscles. Every inch of him rippled, corded muscle begging to be touched, to be stroked. What she wouldn't do to rub her breasts over a chest like that, experience what it would be like to have a body so powerful-looking, so strong, pull her to him, fill her with his hard cock.

"That's the one I saw the other day," Roln said excitedly.

"Grab her. We'll get answers later." The larger man barked the order like he was accustomed to giving them.

Syndi's hair clung to her, falling around her arms, almost causing her to trip. Sunlight coursed over her bare back, frying her skin, drying it instantly. Her heart raced way too hard, her breath coming in quick pants. This wasn't fair being robbed of her precious time in her pond. Every inch of her tingled with lust, but fear gripped her almost as hard as anger did.

Grabbing her simply wasn't an option. But they were armed. She was naked.

Damn. Damn. Damn.

"Get away from me." It was the first thing out of her mouth as she stumbled backward.

"Come here," Roln said, his tone way too calm, as if he spoke to a child. "No one's going to hurt you."

Water from his hand soaked through her skin when he grabbed her arm. His grip wasn't hard, but when she tried to pull away, he had more strength than she was prepared for with his gentle touch.

She slid over the sandy bottom of the pool too easily. Water soaked through her pores when suddenly she was in it up to her cheeks once again.

"Let's go." The other man took her other arm and before she could cry out they dived underwater, taking her down with them.

Syndi had never moved so quickly underwater. She gasped, sucking in too much water, and started choking. The two men slowed, looking at her curiously. Swallowing more water than she probably had all month, she was so damned scared she was sure she'd drown, her gills suddenly deciding not to work.

Glancing from one man to the other, they came to a full stop under the water, both of them still holding her arms. Her lungs burned, the need for air so great she was sure her brain would explode. Everything around her seemed to blacken. For the life of her she couldn't remember what she'd done before to make her gills open. Panic rushed through her and she fought their hold, suddenly struggling with all the strength she had to get back to the surface.

Bubbles floated around her, the water rippling and making it hard for her to focus on either one of them. She couldn't see, couldn't breathe. There was no way she'd live through this.

A strong arm wrapped around her, holding her firmly against a body so hard, so virile, that she forgot about struggling. Minutes before she'd imagined that hard corded muscle stroking her body. Now he sent every nerve ending in her body screaming as he held her against him. A hard long thick muscle throbbed against her hip. If that was his cock...

Bubbles slowed between them. Breathing wasn't an option. His hardened expression, eyes too large, too intense, watched her without blinking. There was no fear in his eyes, no hesitation. Broad cheekbones with a regal, straight nose, made him beautiful. No. More than that. Fucking gorgeous. Stilling his body, holding her so tightly she couldn't move, Syndi forgot all about breathing.

Her breasts swelled against his hairy chest. His body as hard as rock, their legs entwining in the water, breathing no longer seemed to matter.

With his free hand, he reached up to her, pinning her while she stared in awe as he touched her behind her ear.

He stroked her skin, his look intent while she stared at him, frozen with fear and amazement. Gently stroking her then moving his fingers to the other side of her head, his touch sent tingling sensations rushing through her. Charges of electricity rushed over her skin, giving her goose bumps, while a quickening in her womb added to her sudden sensations. The touch was so odd, yet damn arousing. The pulse in her chest moved between her legs, growing, throbbing. Even in the water her pussy moistened, ripened, heat rushing through her and lodging deep inside her.

His expression remained relaxed, dark hair floating slowly around his face, giving the entire moment a surreal feeling. The solid beat of his heart throbbed against her breasts. Her nipples so hard they ached. Sudden awareness of bristly chest hair, stroking her flesh, sent a carnal rush of desire spinning through her.

Syndi couldn't even manage to swallow. His fingers continued stroking her behind her ears while his watchful gaze devoured her. If the water didn't drown her, she would drown in those eyes. Powerful and confident, yet relaxed. He cocked his head, a small movement, barely noticeable, showing his curiosity.

The man who held her so close to his body, able to feel every bit of her nakedness, was intelligent, and on a mission. That reality fought to seep through her suddenly clogged thoughts. This wasn't some Neanderthal she was dealing with. She didn't detect raw seduction. No matter that his touch turned her on more than any man in the village, any creation of her imagination had ever been able to do, that wasn't his intention. Those large dark eyes revealed an agenda, one she couldn't figure out, but that he was heartfelt on accomplishing.

Her lungs were about to explode in her chest. At the same time heat rushed through her unlike anything she'd ever experienced before. Her pussy pulsed harder than her heart. God, he would make her come, holding her like this. A complete stranger, in a foreign world. She was out of her fucking mind.

When her gills popped open, oxygen rushing through her, it hit her so hard that for a second she thought she'd pass out. Her heart pounded, pumping blood through her veins at a pace she could barely handle. All she could do was stare.

Their legs entwined, floating underwater, not rising to the surface, but staying still. Those large brown eyes mesmerized her and she couldn't think, couldn't get her wits about her.

Realizing she had relaxed in the arms of a stranger, a stranger who was abducting her, reality rushed into her brain as quickly as the oxygen from the water had. She fought again, this time with more control. Her gills supplied her with strength, coherency. Drowning in that gaze, allowing his hard body to brush against hers, was a fool's mission. This stranger was stealing her away from her world.

Fight. Overtake the son of a bitch!

She kicked, as best she could underwater, clawed, twisted, her hair blinding her as it floated in front of her face.

Once again strong hands gripped her arms, and the two men sped through the water, pulling her down with them toward the tunnel.

They moved too quickly for her to fight them. All she could do was keep her legs straight, prevent her feet from scraping the walls of the tunnel as they flew through the water as if they were propelled by some motor.

At twice the speed that she'd reached the other pond before, the three of them swam out of the tunnel and toward the surface of the pond in the underground world. At least she was pretty sure she was underground.

"What the hell have you done?" a woman's voice said as soon as Syndi got her head out of the water.

"Roln, secure the area," the man behind her barked.

She managed to wipe the hair from her eyes, and clear her vision in time to see a woman standing at the edge of the pond, looking down at her in shock. Damp hair hung close to her round face. She stood with her fists pressed against her hips, her legs parted, looking down at them like an irate mother.

Roln let go of her arm and eased out of the water with more agility than looked right. He disappeared into the trees, not even bothering to dry off. Syndi turned quickly, the other man letting go of her. Escape was impossible, but she had to try. Even though she couldn't outswim him, allowing him to abduct her without a fight went against everything she'd been taught. Maybe at the least she could disable him long enough to get a head start.

Bringing her fist out of the water, she aimed for his face, not hesitating.

The man grabbed her hand, twisting her body so that her back pressed against his hard body.

"Don't fight me," he whispered into her ear. "I'm not going to hurt you."

The way he'd stroked her gills, made them open as if he knew her body better than she did, came to mind. That had done anything but hurt her. Hell, fucking him sounded a lot better than fighting him. What would it be like to have such a powerful aggressive man between her legs?

She shoved the arousing thought out of her mind quickly.

"Let me go," she whispered.

"I can't." His large hand moved down her body under the water, pressing against her belly and then stroking just a bit lower.

A sudden fire ignited between her legs, a reaction she wasn't ready for. This was kidnapping. Her assailant shouldn't be turning her on. He was more than just turning her on though—he was turning her into one oversized raw nerve ending. She pulsed from head to toe with a need so demanding, so raw and untamed, it was damned hard to focus on anything else other than running her hands over his body. She wanted to explore those rock-hard muscles, feel them twitch under her touch.

But then he was moving behind her, letting her go briefly, and she took advantage of the moment to swim away from him. Not having him touch her was all she could ask for at the moment. This stranger had some ability to turn her body into mush, ignite cravings in her that had never surfaced before, no matter how smooth the seducer.

The man quickly pulled his sleeveless muscle shirt from his body, and then moved toward her as if they were on ground. A complete klutz in the water, all she could do was splash water at him, doing anything to keep him from her. But his large strong hands were on her again, and suddenly she was blinded. It took a moment to realize he'd just slid his shirt over her.

And then climbing out of the pond, he pulled her out next to him. For a moment she wasn't sure she could stand.

"Let's get her out of here." He was walking through the trees, pulling her along with him.

"Tor. I swear to God you've lost your fucking mind," the woman in front of her muttered, giving a quick glance to their surroundings.

Syndi barely had a chance to look around her. The sensation of the soft ground against her feet, the cool air around her, distracted her too much for her to pay attention to where they were taking her.

In spite of the magnificent foliage, the air that was so cool it didn't burn her skin, one thing registered. They were taking her away from the pond, away from the only door back home. Getting lost in this unknown place wasn't an option.

The virile man walked behind her. He didn't touch her, although she could still feel every inch of him pressing against her in her mind. Focusing on the woman who walked in front of her, Syndi noticed a similar belt around her waist. A large deadly looking gun hung from the woman's side, barely moving as the woman's ass swayed with her strut.

Syndi hadn't grown up on the streets of Detroit without learning how to fight.

Moving quickly, punching the woman low in the back, aiming for the kidneys, Syndi grabbed the gun from the woman's belt. The woman managed a half-turn, crying out as she buckled to her knees. Syndi freed the gun from the belt then bolted to the side.

The man behind her was more of a threat. Running faster than she'd ever run before, it was as if she bounced off the moist ground, covered with cool blades of grass that she never dreamed would feel so soft against her feet.

There was one problem. She wasn't running toward the pond.

No. Two problems.

The large man barreled after her, sounding like a bulldozer clearing a path as he closed in on her.

She turned, knowing outrunning him wasn't an option. She didn't know the land, and he did.

"I'll shoot. I swear to God, I'll kill you." She held the gun toward him, straightening her arms, staring past the silver metal into dark eyes that had turned cold and hard.

A shiver rushed through her, turning hot quickly. Oversized eyes penetrated deep inside her, focusing on the source of the fire that burned out of control. It took a moment to remember she pointed a gun at that magnificent body.

The man came to a quick halt, standing bare chested before her, wearing nothing more than tan shorts that hugged him a bit too well. She let out a breath, demanding her gaze remain pinned on his face, which was really fucking hard to do.

"No, you won't." He raised his hands toward her, palms out. "You're as fascinated by me as I am by you. And you want to know more."

He wasn't speaking sexually, was he?

But she did want to know more. And conceding to her fascination with him sexually would give him the upper hand. No matter that he looked a little different with those large eyes. He was still a man. Dear God! Was he ever a man!

Fuck him first—then escape!

God. She was certifiably insane!

She narrowed her gaze, locking her elbows as she straightened her arms. This man had just abducted her. There couldn't be any good in him.

"Fascinated? Maybe with this place." Her voice was steady. She wouldn't let him see the fear and raw lust that tormented her. "But hardly with you. An abductor? A criminal? You don't rate my fascination."

His expression hardened, his dark eyes almost glowing black. A man this fucking hot—the lady had called him Tor—would have women begging him to do them every time he turned around. The look he gave her pissed her off though. As if silently he challenged her, not believing a word she said.

For the first time, she let her gaze falter, lowering it a fraction of an inch to get a closer look at the gun. There didn't appear to be a trigger, not the conventional sort. Shaped like any gun, this one had one difference—where the trigger would be, there were two buttons. She pressed her fingers to both buttons, willing to find out what each one of them did if he took another step toward her.

74

Tor didn't take a step. He lunged. Leaping at her, barely giving her time to focus on him, he took her down. The two of them landed hard on the ground. Someone ripped the gun from her hand, but she couldn't see. Her hair tangled over her face, and her arms and legs were pinned under his large, heavy body.

"You're fascinating me more with every minute," he whispered in her face.

A strong hand pinned her hands together, while he brushed her hair from her face with his other hand. His oversized shirt twisted on her body, exposing one breast to him. He lifted his body off hers slightly, allowing her at least the courtesy of breathing.

"Tor," the woman behind them said, sounding somewhat exasperated.

Maybe she was his girlfriend. If so, Syndi pitied the woman. Her man was a brute.

She glared up at him while he stared down at her, his gaze lowering to her exposed breast. There was no way to slow her breathing, adrenaline pumped through her too hard. The rise and fall of her chest added to the fullness of her breast. Her nipple hardened as her own hair, still quite wet, brushed over it and fell to her side.

"Get off me," she growled, hating being exposed like this, hating how her body convulsed with need.

Long lashes hooded his gaze. A moment passed like an eternity before slowly his focus moved to her face. Roped muscle stretched underneath his moist warm flesh. Everywhere he touched her burned with passion so raw, it was as if he'd branded her, marked her so that her body would respond only to him.

Her breathing slowed, until she swore her heart stopped in her chest, making it impossible to breathe. All she could do was stare into those large dark eyes that had found the source of her lust. His look turned triumphant.

Tor stood quickly, pulling her up with him. Then, much to her surprise, he threw her over his shoulder. She bounced against the hardness of bone and muscle as he took off through the dense trees. The woman ran alongside them.

When Tor put her down, it took a minute to get her bearings. She slid down rippling muscle, corded and strong. There wasn't a man in the village who could compare with the virility, the strength, the sex appeal, of Tor. For a moment she was too dizzy to move.

Rough hands stroked her shoulders, brushed over her arms, and gripped her hips. Her mouth was dry from breathing too hard. Daring to look up at him, the corner of his mouth twitched. Not a smile—more like acknowledgment.

His look assured her he'd put that fire out that burned out of control inside her. She looked away. He pushed her inside something that looked like an incredibly oversized silver sex toy. Solid metal with no windows on the side, and smaller in the front than in the back, it reminded her of an oversized dildo.

Dear God. Maybe she'd just drowned in the pond and now was hallucinating in limbo between life and death—with sex on the brain.

She stumbled forward, shoving her long wet strands over her shoulder. A panel slid open in the side of the thing— a door.

"Let's go," Tor ordered.

Inside there were two chairs facing windows at the front of the thing, and then benches behind them, well cushioned with backs. Tor shoved her down on the bench closest to the two front seats.

The door slid closed behind them and at the same time the woman entered from a door on the other side. She adjusted herself behind a steering wheel and within moments the thing lunged backward.

Syndi gripped the seat, watching as the trees through the windows grew smaller and water closed in around them.

Dear God. So much water!

"Head to my house," Tor told the woman, and then pulled something else from his belt that he held up to his ear. Again he started talking and Syndi guessed it to be a phone of sorts. "Roln, I don't have to tell you to stay quiet about this."

Syndi swallowed, her heart pounding so hard she couldn't catch her breath. They were underwater. Really deep underwater. She jumped back in her seat, her fingers digging into the fabric, when a large creature swam past the windows in front of her.

Heat rushed through her when she let out a yelp and the woman glanced back at her, looking somewhat amused. More than anything she wanted to lean forward, get a better look out the windows. So many questions rushed through her, the primary one being where in the hell was she? Next she wanted to know where they were taking her.

Pride kicked in at the woman's look. Nothing pissed Syndi off more than not having the upper hand in a situation. All her life she'd taken care of herself, fought for her meals, for water, for her life. At the moment she wasn't in control. And as they zipped through the water, passing fish she thought had been extinct since the last war, her life was falling more and more out of her control.

Tor hung up his phone, clasping it at the belt at the top of his shorts. Syndi took a moment to let her gaze travel down his well-shaped body. Dark hair clung to his legs and arms. Muscles rippled under his skin when he moved. She looked away quickly, taking in the woman sitting next to him, when Tor looked at her also.

"After you drop us off, head to the computer center and have Fern meet me at my house." He turned to look at Syndi and she focused her attention out the front windows, refusing to acknowledge his stare.

"She needs clothes. You can't just keep her naked," the woman driving pointed out.

"It's a tempting thought," Tor mumbled.

Syndi was about to tell him just what she thought of him when the woman interrupted her thoughts.

"Good grief, Tor. She's barely a woman. You've yanked her out of her world and scared her to death. The least you can do is get her something decent to wear. We'll stop by my place first. I'm sure I've got something that will fit her."

"Peg, remember your place." Tor's manner changed. Focusing on this woman called Peg, his lips thinned to a narrow line. "You'll take us to my home."

"Nice of you two to take into consideration what I want." A mixture of anger and awe at her surroundings almost made Syndi dizzy.

Nothing from her wildest dreams came close to comparing with what she saw outside the window in front of them. They continued moving through water. Other silver objects passed them, along with fish, and once she thought she even saw some people. They moved past them too quickly for her to be sure though.

"I'm sure you want to go home," Peg said, glancing over her shoulder at Syndi. "But Tor won't hurt you. He's not a bad man."

"I can handle brutes like him," Syndi told her. "I'm not a child. Just because I'm not as old as you are doesn't mean I'm incapable of taking care of myself."

Peg raised an eyebrow and for a moment she thought she detected amusement flicker in Tor's eyes.

Something dark and huge appeared through the front window. They moved closer and Syndi started seeing more and more ships, or whatever this thing was that they were in. Peg returned her attention to her driving, and slowed, the engines humming around them as she navigated.

Then Syndi did see people. A lot of people. They swam around them, above them, below them. This was beyond incredible.

"What is this place?" she asked, forgetting her fear as amazement took over.

"Undrworld," Tor told her. "You're in the West Passage and we're entering the city of New Dallas."

"Dallas? You've got to be kidding." She realized her jaw had fallen open and closed her mouth.

"You've heard of it?" Tor asked.

"I've never been there, but sure. Who hasn't? It's a huge city." But it wasn't underwater.

Several mountains, dark and filled with hundreds of cave-like entrances came into view. Ships of different sizes zoomed in and out of the entrances while people swam around them. Whatever this place was, it appeared to be just as populated as Dallas, or Detroit for that matter.

She fought the urge to duck when they entered one of the caves, hardly slowing down. Darkness quickly surrounded them but Peg navigated the ship skillfully, turning when the cave-like tunnel turned, and moving past other vehicles approaching them.

Minutes passed before she slowed further. It took a second before Syndi realized they'd come to a stop.

"I'm bringing back clothes," Peg told Tor.

"That's fine." He stood and at the same time the door next to Syndi slid open.

Tor took her hand and almost lifted her off the seat. This time another door prevented them from actually leaving the ship. She turned when the door they'd just walked through slid closed, confining the two of them in a closet-sized space. Suddenly water started filling the small area, quickly soaking her feet and rising up her legs.

"What's happening?" She tugged her hand free from his, turning to stare around her as the water continued to flood the tight area.

"Are you going to need help getting your gills to work again?" he asked her.

His tone was almost gentle, which surprised her. She looked up at him and at the same time the water rose high enough to reach her shoulders, then her neck.

They were underwater when the outer door opened. Syndi began floating before she could control her actions. She didn't fight Tor when he took her hand, and the two of them left the ship. A sudden current almost knocked her sideways when the ship they'd been in began moving, leaving the two of them alone in a tunnel similar to the one she'd found in the pond.

Tor's hand held hers securely and she had no choice but to hold on tightly. Her hair floated around her face, and she brushed it out of the way. Looking up at him, her uncertainty must have been written on her face. His smile was almost pleasant as he pulled her toward him.

This wasn't like jumping into the pond and then swimming toward a tunnel. Before there had been time to prepare, fill her lungs with air, and hold her breath until her gills popped open. Instantly the urge to suck in air through her mouth overtook her.

And at the same time, Tor had tucked her against his body, wrapping his arm around her and kicking his legs so that they brushed against hers. When the burning started in her lungs, her brain feeling like it would explode if she didn't get air, he pulled her up a small hole.

She cried out when they surfaced. Gasping for breath, she couldn't focus on where they were. Tor lifted himself out of the barrel-like opening. She tried to brush water from her eyes when he reached down and pulled her out too.

They stood on slippery stone and she looked down at the hole where she'd just been. Water splashed up from the circular hole, soaking her bare feet.

"Come on." Tor took her hand and guided her along a narrow stone path.

They were inside the mountain and rock surrounded her, making up the walls and ceiling. It was dimly lit but she could see well enough to notice lamps secured in the walls and water dripping in random paths toward the floor.

Tor's world was nothing but water. Her world was dying from lack of it. What she had to figure out now was how in the hell to get back to her pond so that she could tell everyone about this.

What little she knew would change existence on her planet forever.

Chapter Five

∞

The way his shirt clung to her, nicely showing off every curve, and barely reaching the top of her thighs, Tor could hardly keep his thoughts straight. Her long hair draped over her body, ending at her ass. And damn, the shirt was so wet, hugging her like a second skin, offering him a tempting view of her tight rear end when she turned.

Taking his home in with a quick glance, she stepped further into his living room. Her breasts were large, and her nipples puckered to hard points against the material. Too much of his concentration focused on keeping his cock from going hard as a rock. Peg had been right about one thing. She was young. Granted she was a woman—but barely one at that. He shouldn't be thinking about fucking the shit out of her right now.

"My guard tells me you are Syndi Stone." Tor pressed several buttons on the maintenance panel that controlled the environment of his home. "I'm Tor Geinz, leader of the West Passage."

Adjusting the room temperature to give the air a level of humidity to keep their skin damp, and brightening the lights, he also figured it best to secure the door. Miss Syndi would bolt without more than a moment's thought. The last thing he needed was her running without direction through the city. Until he had a lot of answers, no one would know she was here.

"What is this place?" She had as many questions as he did.

She'd moved from the door and ran her fingers along the back of his seawood couch. Syndi wasn't short, but her body was thin with small muscles. She didn't have the athletic build most women in Undrworld had. Swimming from birth built muscles quickly.

Those large breasts of hers had his mouth watering. Her ribs were outlined through the clinging material of his shirt. Hipbones were visible too. If he hadn't seen her display so much energy fighting them earlier, he'd guess her half starved.

"This is my home." When he moved closer to her, she gripped the back of his couch, her look wary.

"No." Her brows narrowed over soft small dark green eyes. She waved her hand in front of her. "This place. All of it. I've never seen so much water in my life."

"West Passage is an entire ocean."

She made some kind of snorting sound. "There haven't been oceans since the Third World War. And they were filled with salt."

"It's all fresh water." He'd never seen such long hair on a woman. And those eyes, so small, and such a soft sensual green. She was physically different than women in Undrworld, yet he'd bet she wasn't that different. "So you know of the war?"

She looked at him like he'd lost his mind. "Everyone knows about the war. It destroyed Earth."

"And made the surface uninhabitable."

"I've lived there all my life." Her mind churned, he could see her thinking process in high gear just by the way she chewed her lower lip and studied him. "You didn't know there were people on the surface."

He shook his head. "Just like you didn't know all humans moved underground."

"Not all." She moved away from him when he stepped closer. "Obviously some of us weren't enlightened that you'd relocated and taken all the water with you."

She had no water yet she had gills. Scientists worked hard after the war mutating humans and ensuring they would be born with gills. There had been many failures and still occasionally an infant had to be altered at birth so they could breathe through gills.

Now this was interesting. Humans on the surface had gills but no water? How had they survived? How had they adapted? More important, Ran Mose knew about people on the surface. This news would alter all of their lives forever. Matters had to be handled delicately.

"Yet you knew we were here. When we found you, you were heading here…again." And this knowledge meant she would need protection.

Her world, and his, couldn't just collide without serious education first. Moving around the couch, he reached for her hair. Never had he felt such long hair, so silky and thick.

She slapped his hand away. "Apparently, you also know of my world. You were in the pond and abducted me."

Tor grabbed her wrist, holding it between them while he met her fiery gaze. "Today was the first time I've been to the surface. Honestly, I know nothing about it. But I'd like the education."

"It's obvious what you would like," she hissed, fighting to free her wrist from his hand. "You don't seem to need an education, just a lesson in manners."

"Manners?" He pulled her wrist toward him, and she almost stumbled into him. "Believe me. I have manners. You're lucky you weren't raped swimming naked in the pond. In our world, we wear clothes."

"My clothes are next to the pond where you abducted me." She spoke through clenched teeth.

She didn't have a lot of strength, but he'd give her this, she didn't seem to fear him. Her eyes widened, and he saw her anger — and her lust. But he also saw intelligence, the way she searched his face, as if taking everything about him to memory.

"I took them off so they wouldn't get wet," she added.

"You prefer to be dry?"

She looked confused for a moment. "Where I come from, it would draw suspicion if I were wet."

"Interesting." He wanted to know everything about her, about her world, and what it would feel like to be buried deep inside her.

The security of his passage was an issue, a major issue, but she intrigued him. Natural human curiosity, the explorer in him, came forth. That, and Syndi was the hottest woman he'd laid eyes on in a long time.

So small, so thin, yet feisty. She'd entered into his world, found them. Her craving for adventure turned him on as much as her tight little body did.

"Come here." He started around the couch.

Syndi yanked back on her wrist, so that he almost dragged her. "Why?" she demanded.

"I was going to find some clothes for you. Maybe you'd like something to eat or drink?" It didn't take that much strength to pull her around the couch and lead her out of the living room. "Allow me to show you some of those manners you claim I don't have."

Her laugh surprised him.

"If you had manners you wouldn't be dragging me through your home like some caveman."

If she had any idea what he really wanted to do with her, she'd be grateful all he was doing was leading her by her wrist.

"I'm offering to clothe you," he growled, stopping at the edge of his shallow pool in his kitchen. "Of course, if you'd rather stay as you are, I have no problem with that."

He intentionally let his gaze travel down her, his cock hardening, blood draining through him no matter that he ordered himself to stay relaxed.

She yanked her wrist out of his hand. The force she used had her stumbling backward. There was a look of surprise on her face when she fell backward into the shallow foot of water in the center of his kitchen, landing hard, splashing as her rear end hit the bottom with a thud. Her legs spread ungracefully while she struggled to a sitting position. Quickly she brushed hair from her face, distracted with her predicament and not bothering to cover her body.

Tor stared at the light brown hair covering her pussy, her exposed breasts, and his cock roared to life. Every inch of him demanded that he shed his shorts and mount her. With her defiant, almost wild nature, she would be an incredible lover. If he didn't fuck her soon he'd go mad.

Stepping into the water, he reached for her.

"Get away from me." She almost sounded like she was crying.

Syndi pulled her legs to her chest, yanking the shirt over her legs, and rested her chin on her knees, not looking at him.

"Have it your way." He should have predicted this.

Syndi Stone had shown him characteristics of being a strong woman, willing to approach the unknown. But she'd just humiliated herself, or that was how she saw it, by tripping into the water. Her pride ran deep. He respected that.

Sitting down in the corner of the water, he stretched his legs out in front of him, soaking in the warm water. Resting his elbows on the edge of the pool, he watched her as she stared at her toes.

"I want to go home," she finally said, still not looking at him.

"I'd like to see your world." He needed to explore it, become more familiar with it before his meeting with Ran in two days.

"You wouldn't last an hour," she grunted.

"Oh really? And why is that?"

She looked at him briefly, her expression sobering. "The average temperature is anywhere from a hundred degrees to a hundred and thirty degrees. Water is five dollars a gallon. Sitting like this," she cupped her hands on either side of her and then let the water run through her fingers, "isn't something anyone even dares dream about."

Well, that explained why she had a problem working her gills. But she had them. She had to be a product of the hybrid results after the war.

"You have gills," he prompted, hoping she would shed light on how she survived without water.

She nodded but didn't say anything.

"Does everyone on the surface have gills?" There had to be a way to get her to talk to him.

She seemed to be giving his question some thought. What he wouldn't do to know what was going on in that pretty head of hers.

"I think there might be others," she said carefully.

"You think? So you don't know anyone else with gills?"

Slowly she shook her head.

She wiggled her toes in the water and he imagined what it would be like to not have water. His people would die. Thanks to the results of the alterations after the war, they needed water more than they needed to breathe air.

But if gills weren't common knowledge in her world, more than likely those on the surface were the humans who wouldn't take to the scientific breeding. There wasn't mention of any failures in the history books, but he could see it happening. No project ever pulled off perfectly. Even now, generations after the success of mutating humans to have gills, there were still throwbacks, still babies born without them. It was rare, but it happened.

Syndi had gills though. And if she lived in a world where most didn't, she shouldn't be part of that world. For her, surviving on the surface must be pure hell.

Strands of her long hair had dried, taking on a slightly lighter shade. Her skin was so much darker than his, and her eyes, so small, probably a result of living under such a brutal sun. If the blinding light he'd experienced when surfacing from that pond was any indication, he imagined that humans had naturally evolved over the last hundred years so they could survive.

Her differences were appealing though—damned appealing. Dark and petite, with her small muscles, she was nothing like any woman in Undrworld. No matter how hard he tried, he couldn't get his cock to remain soft as he watched her.

"Syndi," he said quietly.

"What?" She was wiggling her fingers and toes in the water now, like a child would. Like someone enjoying a treat they didn't often have.

"Are you aware of the scientific studies conducted on humans after the war?"

She looked up at him, her gaze falling quickly to his cock and then darting back to his face. A beautiful rose blush spread over her cheeks but her mouth formed a thin line, as if she too were ordering herself not to be aroused by his presence.

"What are you talking about?"

"You don't know about the mutations done to humans after the war so they could survive in water?"

She frowned. "Why would they do that?"

"After the war, after the surface was rendered uninhabitable, humans migrated underground. With the destruction of Earth, the water sank underground as well. The only way we could survive was to evolve. But we weren't evolving fast enough, so a project was created to help us evolve. It was successful in almost all cases. As a result, humans now have gills." He gave her the edited version, but it was enough to see that she'd never before heard what he was telling her.

Frowning, she brought her fingers up to her legs and let the water droplets trail down her skin. "That doesn't make sense. I've never heard of it. And there are millions of people on the surface who I'm sure don't have gills."

Somehow he had to see this surface, witness these people who lived without water, who'd continued living there after the war. Major research needed to be done. He needed answers. And he had two days to get them. There was no telling what Ran Mose knew, but whatever his knowledge, Tor had to be able to match it. For the safety of the West Passage, for his people, he had to learn why only part of the planet was brought underground. And why, apparently, none of them knew about the other.

"You're right. It doesn't make sense. The only thing I see right now that does make sense, is that for whatever reason, you are part of our world, and somehow ended up on the surface."

Her eyes grew wide. Color washed from her face as she stared at him. He might as well have just stabbed her in the gut from the look of pain and panic that covered her expression. Just as quickly, her expression went blank. She wasn't telling him something. "You said you were the leader. Are you the President, or something?"

He searched his memory, the word not familiar to him. Then something registered, from his early grades in school.

"That's a pretty old fashioned word. We don't have presidents anymore. There are four passages, and four leaders. I'm one of them."

Slowly she stood up, the bottom of the shirt clinging to her more so than the top. He moved also, allowing her to step out before following her.

"Then you have the authority to do what you want," she said with her back to him.

"I have council members that I consult with." Who more than likely at the moment were cursing his name for turning off all of the phones and recording devices in his home.

She turned around, a glow in her eyes that matched what he'd seen when he'd first laid eyes on her.

"Are you going to let me go home?"

"Of course." He wouldn't add that he worried she'd be in danger there, severe danger.

If Ran Mose got his hands on her, she wouldn't be treated as well as he was treating her now. No matter where Syndi went, from this point forward, he would have to protect her.

"I'll take those clothes you offered me now." She licked her lips, a small movement yet so sensual every muscle inside him hardened.

Moving suddenly became a task. Not to mention, he didn't want her covered up.

She followed him through his kitchen, into his bedroom, and then paused inside his doorway. Pushing the button on his wall to open his closet, the same clothes that were always folded on the shelves inside greeted him. Nothing in here would fit her any better than what she wore.

"How long will it take that woman, Peg, to get back here with clothes?" she asked, seeming to read his mind.

"It's hard to say." More than likely she'd be here any minute. "How about a blanket?

Taking one of his softer blankets from the shelf he unfolded it as he took the few steps needed to stand in front of her. She didn't move when he reached around her, draping the blanket over her shoulder.

"I'm not stupid, you know." She focused on his chest, her long lashes hooding her gaze. "Now that we're aware of each other's worlds, things will change."

"No change ever happens quickly."

"If it did, our worlds would collide," she said quietly.

He gripped the blanket that wrapped around her shoulders, seeing her fear that life as she'd always known it was about to end.

No. She wasn't stupid.

"I won't let that happen." Nothing would happen to West Passage, not under his command.

Having captured her in the blanket, he pulled harder. She pressed her small hands against his bare chest, her palms almost dry, and warm. Slowly, her gaze lifted, lashes fluttering, until she stared at him with those alluring green eyes.

There was hesitation. But he saw the curiosity, the unbridled lust that plagued her as it did him. Tor had been through his share of women, most of them willing conquests in his early days. He knew desire when it filled a woman's gaze.

She moistened her lips, her small tongue parting her mouth, hesitating, and then disappearing again, leaving her lips full and wet. Her breath deepened, pressing her breasts against his shirt, the outline of her nipples barely visible through the fabric.

Something rose from deep inside him, more than a protector's instinct, something more carnal, more primitive. Syndi stood by her own agenda, fought to take care of herself. And he had a feeling it had always been that way with her. This battle would be hard, terrifying in fact. Everything as they knew it might soon come to an end. She wouldn't be able to take this on herself.

Her touch was gentle, unsure. She measured him up, worked to determine in her thoughts if he were trustworthy or not. As she'd already shown, Syndi would take on the unknown, explore it, accept a challenge.

And he had one to give her.

Fisting the blanket, binding her with it, he dipped his head and nipped at her lip. Soft and full against his teeth, the slightest of contact sent a fire burning through him.

"Tor," she whispered.

His name escaped her lips, but that was all he would allow. Taking her mouth, parting her, opening her so that he could have what he needed, Tor devoured her mouth.

She let out a cry, a gasp so soft, so enticing—definitely the sound of submission.

Letting go of the blanket, wrapping his arms around her, he growled fiercely as he slammed her body against his. Tor lifted her from the ground, opening her mouth wider with his tongue as he relished her taste.

"Oh God," she breathed when he released her mouth and ran his tongue over her cheek.

Carrying her to his bed, he collapsed on his blankets, tucking her under him as he feasted on her neck.

The shirt she wore twisted around her, and he ran his hand up her thigh, her small muscles hard and her tanned skin smooth and tight. As human as he was, yet so different, the urge to know every inch of her, explore every part of her, learn what made her cry out his name and what made her sigh in satisfaction became all that mattered.

Spreading his fingers over her, a fever surged through his brain when he parted the hot folds of skin between her legs.

"Oh shit," she said quickly, instantly arching against him, her leg muscles tightening while she clamped down on his hand.

It had been a while since Syndi had been with a man. He doubted she was a virgin, the passion coursed through her with too much energy, but she'd yet to learn how to control her orgasm. And she came hard when he barely touched her.

"You are too ripe to enjoy quickly," he told her, lifting himself on his elbow to enjoy the flush that had spread across her cheeks.

The cloud of lust lifted from her eyes and she stared up at him. Lazily, he ran a finger over her gill. It was small, closed tightly, but he felt the flesh pulse there when he touched her. She blinked several times, her mouth forming a tiny circle as she sucked in a breath. No one had ever shown her how erotic stroking gills could be.

Lowering his mouth to her hard nipple that poked through the shirt, he captured it between his teeth, breathing heavily over it while her body spasmed. Continuing to stroke her gill, her pulse pounded against his finger.

He cupped her large breast in his hand, while continuing to torture her nipple. Then slowly lifting the shirt, he sucked in a breath at how fucking sexy she looked spread out next to him. Quickly, he sucked in the nipple, no longer kept from him by fabric.

He looked up at her, her eyes closed tightly, her mouth open while she gasped for air. Long hair fell over her shoulders, clinging to her barely moist body.

"I wonder how many times I can make you come before I fuck you?" he whispered over her nipple.

She turned her head from him and then quickly rolled off the bed.

"No." She had her back to him.

Turning around quickly, her expression had hardened, defiance replacing her lust.

"I won't fuck you." She sliced her hand through the air. "For all I know you're the enemy. I won't let you do this."

She marched out of the room, and he pounced off his bed after her. No way could he race after her with his cock holding every ounce of blood in his body. Stripping out of his shorts, he took a moment to regain some oxygen in his brain before going after her.

Tor was no rapist. There was no need to be. She'd turned him down on the question of his loyalty, of whether he could be trusted. Well, he had no problem proving to her that he was definitely not her enemy.

Syndi sat in the middle of the shallow pool in the floor. Her legs were straight in front of her, locked at the knees and pressed together. Her hands pressed flat against the bottom of the pool and she looked up at him, determination etched on her face.

"Don't come any closer," she warned but then stopped speaking, her mouth still open as she stared at his hard cock.

He hid his smile. "This is my home."

"Fine. I'll leave."

"Go ahead and try."

She didn't move. Her gaze didn't leave his cock. He stepped into the water.

"Tell me no again and I'll stop." He went down on his knees, crawling over her.

Syndi leaned backward, then fell back on her elbows.

"I…" she began, and then met his gaze.

He captured her mouth, tasting her heat that matched the fire burning inside him.

Pushing his legs between hers, she opened for him, falling onto her back. Long brown hair fanned around her in the shallow water. His cock found her soft flesh. Thrusting forward, unable to slow the movement, he buried himself deep inside her.

She screamed, reaching for him. He grabbed her legs, lifting them out of the water, stroking her smooth flesh while her pussy muscles about squeezed all life out of him.

"Dear God, you're fucking tighter than a virgin." And about to pump him dry if he wasn't careful.

"Maybe you're just accustomed to fucking whores," she hissed, her teeth clamped together while her fingers dug into his arms.

He grinned, seeing no reason to enlighten her either way. All that mattered right now was that he was inside her, deep inside her. Taking all she had, stroking the source of the heat he'd seen in her eyes, he built the momentum.

"God. You're too big." Her small fingers scraped down his arms.

"It's a perfect fit." No woman had ever felt so damned good.

Her cheeks flushed, her mouth forming a perfect circle. Water splashed over her large breasts, over her hard tummy, while her soft brown hair floated around her. Almost like an angel, but with the fire of the devil, he watched her come, saw how her entire body hardened, while heat rushed around his cock.

Tiny muscles were like thousands of little fingers stroking his shaft as he repeatedly impaled her. No matter that she was from another world, that acknowledging each other's existence might destroy life as each of them knew it, Syndi wasn't going to get away from him. Hitting her harder, discovering that spot that almost brought her out of the water, he planned on putting his mark on her, branding her with the knowledge that she would be his.

Damn it!

Not once in his life, no matter how fucking good the sex was, had he ever had thoughts of keeping a woman around permanently. What was the point? Life was good. There were women everywhere.

The room swayed around him, every inch of him hardening while blood slammed through him. His cock thrust in her one last time, then exploded, leaving him so dizzy that for a moment he couldn't move. He stared at her through fogged vision, loving those small eyes, and the sated look that showed up like crimson against her tan skin.

A buzz through the speaker on the wall made her jump and shriek.

"We have company," he told her, managing to stand and then find his shorts before heading to the front door.

Peg immediately looked past him when he opened the door. Pressing clothing to her breast, she pushed past him into his living room.

"Where is she?" she asked quietly.

"In the kitchen."

Peg knew him well. They'd fought alongside each other and struggled to rise in rank while securing the West Passage. He wouldn't say he had a true best friend, but she came close. At the moment, her attention wasn't on him though.

Tor followed Peg into the kitchen where Syndi still sat in the pool. She looked up, her gaze shifting from him to Peg.

"I brought you some clothes. I'm pretty sure they'll fit." Peg sounded like she was talking to a child.

"My clothes at home fit me nicely too." Syndi stood slowly, adjusting the wet shirt that moments before had been pushed up to her armpits.

"Go in the other room and change." There were a few things he needed to address with Peg.

Taking the hint, Syndi stepped out of the water and took the clothes, leaving Peg and Tor alone.

"Isn't your computer in there?" Peg brushed her hair behind her ear as she stared after Syndi.

"If she starts trouble, I'll stop her." It would be a good excuse to get his hands back on her.

"So what have you found out?" Peg's eyes lit with excitement.

One of his personal guards, Peg often also sat in as counsel. She had good insight and often helped him brainstorm. Following her into his living room, he hit the switches on his maintenance panel so that his communication lines opened. It wouldn't be long now before Fern or Ben got in touch with them.

"According to Syndi, there are millions of people on the surface."

Peg spun around, her jaw dropping in astonishment. "No way," she exclaimed.

"There's more." He walked over to his computer, tapping at the buttons until he pulled up some simple history files. "Apparently their leader is a president. They don't have gills. And water is scarce. They have to pay for it."

Peg walked up to him, resting her hands on the panel while he searched for images of old Earth.

"We were taught that humans successfully mutated, moved underground after the war." He pulled up images of a city, the blue background of a sky giving it an odd look. "What if that weren't true, that only some of us moved underground, while the rest continued above ground just as they had before the war?"

"But that's impossible. The planet lost its atmosphere. The sun fried the surface."

"I got a glimpse of the surface earlier today." He remembered the burning heat. It had been impossible to see, to breathe. "It might not be inhabitable for us, but it's where Syndi's been born and raised."

"Her eyes are smaller, and her skin is darker."

"It's got a different texture than ours," he added.

Peg narrowed her gaze, her expression showing that she guessed how he knew how her skin felt. And it wasn't just because he'd hauled her to the tran-bus. There was no reason to acknowledge her patronizing stare. As soon as he could, he'd bury himself deep inside Syndi again.

Peg glanced behind his shoulder toward the other room. "What are you going to do with her?"

He didn't want to let her go. Nothing he'd heard so far sounded like her world was a better place to be. But it was all she knew, and he wouldn't force her to stay.

"I haven't decided yet. What I do know is that I need answers, and quickly. Ran Mose will be at the Four Passages the day after tomorrow, first thing in the morning. I want to know why so many humans are on the surface and we never knew about it." He stared at the pictures he'd found in the history files of old Earth. Landscapes and pictures of tall buildings, animals and people. "One thing I know, our life will not be changed, or suffer, because of these people on the surface."

"If you let her return, she'll tell her people about us." Peg was her usual blunt self. "If they have no water, they will try to come here, invade our cities. You can't let that happen."

"Maybe I'll keep her here for a while." He wouldn't force her to leave her life, but maybe a few days, and he could gain her trust so that this thing could be handled without either world bursting into a panic. "Her people aren't going to ransack our lives."

"Well, if they don't have gills, then they wouldn't survive here." Peg frowned, again looking over her shoulder. "But that woman has gills."

"A mystery. One I don't think she has an answer to either." Another thought hit him, one that left a foul taste in his mouth. "Her people don't have water. If they are desperate for it, they could dig and tap into our water."

"If you let her return, and she tells her people about us — they might be desperate for water. You can't let that happen." She looked up at him shocked. "You can't let her leave."

The slightest noise behind them grabbed his attention. Tor turned, more amused than concerned when Syndi stood in the doorway, pointing his stun gun at them.

Chapter Six

ജ

Syndi's heart beat so hard in her chest that the pain rushed through her entire body. The shaking came from anger though. It shouldn't have surprised her that Tor would seduce her, gain her trust, and then keep her prisoner here so that she couldn't tell her people about all this water.

No matter that he had his nation, or ocean, or whatever it was, to protect. She had a duty to her people. Her village struggled every day for water. The rest of the world could rot, but she wouldn't turn her back on her friends and family. Staying here wasn't an option.

"You are not keeping me here." Closing her eyes, gritting her teeth together so hard her jaw hurt, she pressed the button on the gun.

A large thump made her jump.

"Oh God," she cried out, as she stared at Tor's limp body.

She'd shot him. He crumpled to the ground. His large frame lay heaped at Peg's feet. Peg's jaw dropped, staring in disbelief at her leader, and then slowly meeting Syndi's gaze.

Syndi pinned the gun on her. "You're going to take me home."

"Okay." Peg lifted her arms, stepping away from Tor. "But if you shoot me, you're stranded."

"Let's go." Syndi's mouth was suddenly so dry that her tongue felt like sandpaper against her lips.

She took a deep breath as she moved past Tor's body. He wasn't moving. He wasn't breathing. Dear God. She'd never killed a man in her life. Her legs were like jelly, and for a moment she thought she might pass out right on top of him.

Ignoring the severe pang of regret that rushed through her, she followed Peg out of Tor's home.

Peg wouldn't help Syndi's gills open as they moved through the watery tunnel to the tran-bus. Adrenaline rushed through her so hard her lungs would explode before her gills opened. Closing her eyes and focusing on making them open might cost her life. Peg swam ahead of her, and Syndi kicked with all of her might, gripping the gun with one hand while she used her other hand to help push her through the water.

Peg was lifting herself out of the tunnel when Syndi's gills finally opened. For a moment, too much oxygen rushed through her brain. Stopping wasn't an option. If Peg got away, she would be trapped in this world, the only person who'd brought her here, dead.

Oh God. What had she done?

Again regret slapped her so hard that her eyes burned when she hoisted herself out of the tunnel. Peg had just reached the tran-bus and slid the door open. She couldn't focus on Tor. It had been his life or hers. She had to believe that.

"Take me back to the pond," she told Peg, grabbing her arm, and then climbing in the same door, over the driver's seat, and then pulling Peg in after her. "And I swear, I'll figure out how to drive this thing myself if you try anything."

"I believe you." Peg sounded resolutely calm.

She started the thing and Syndi watched, doing her best to learn in a split second how to maneuver the contraption when she'd never even driven a car. Too many thoughts spun through her to be able to focus.

No matter how she tried, she couldn't get Tor's limp body, sprawled on his living room floor, out of her head. Her heart swelled to her throat. Tears burned her eyes. She'd just killed the leader of a nation. Peg had witnessed it.

It had been her life or his. Tor's nation would retaliate. Her people wouldn't defend her.

Damn it.

But it was more than that. He'd touched her, more than just fucked her, reached a spot inside her no man had ever been to before.

And she still felt him inside her.

Maybe he wasn't dead. *God. Please. Let him not be dead.*

The tran-bus sped through the water, once again multitudes of people and other similar-looking ships moving around them. Then they were in open water, less populated, an incredible creamy blue color surrounding them. She should be taking all of this to memory, allowing herself to witness every bit of their world, a world full of all the water that her life was deprived of.

All of it was terribly wrong.

For a moment she thought she might cry. That would resolve nothing. Possibly Tor wasn't dead. Maybe somehow this gun thing she gripped in her hand didn't kill people.

He sure had looked dead.

God. What was going to happen to her?

She could get back to her village, possibly tell her people about the pond, but how long before this world came after her? Murder, or even shooting someone, had to be a crime here just as it was in her world. Nasty bile coated her throat. Breaking laws in her world meant almost certain death.

"Are we almost there?" She wouldn't ask what the punishment was in this world for shooting and possibly killing their leader.

"Yup." As Peg answered, she slowed the engines.

Within minutes the water lowered down the windshield, trees coming into view as they floated toward the dense growth that surrounded the pond.

Peg stopped, and then turned to face Syndi. "What are you going to do?"

"Go home." Syndi almost jumped when Peg pushed a button and the door next to Syndi slid open.

She let out a sigh, staring down at the gun in her hand. Probably would be wise to keep the thing with her.

"Syndi," Peg called after her when she was almost out of the tran-bus.

Syndi stood outside, her bare feet sinking into the thick grass — a feeling she may never experience again in her life.

"What?" she asked.

"Good luck." And the look on Peg's face showed she meant it.

A dull throb weighed heavy in Syndi's chest as she changed out of the clothes Peg had given her, and into her own sandy, hot clothes. They itched and burnt her skin but that was the least of her worries.

The sun hung low, almost touching the horizon. Sand burned her feet, the early evening rays slicing through her skin. Her world was a parched, waterless place. And tonight she would participate in a meeting where desperate measures would be discussed so that they could have enough water to continue to dampen their towels, wipe their bodies, and take frugal sips periodically throughout the day.

She'd almost made it out of the dead lands when heavy footsteps sounded alongside her. Gripping the clothes Peg had loaned to her, with the gun wrapped inside them, she knew her life was over. They had come after her. Everything she'd known all her life would disappear for her.

"What are you doing out here?" Perry fell in alongside her, matching her pace.

Relief flooded through her so hard she almost broke out laughing. Perry didn't stand as tall as Tor, his skin was so much darker, and wrinkled. The man she'd dodged for the past few years suddenly seemed anything but a threat. He didn't have that aura about him that Tor had. There was no self-confidence, at least not to the point of cockiness like she'd sensed in Tor. His sandy-blond hair was thick, not shiny and dark like Tor's. Her gaze fell to his arms and the pale sprinkling of thin hairs that almost appeared white against his tanned skin. There was no wiry dark thick hair like Tor had.

She looked away quickly, realizing what she was doing. God. She had to quit thinking about him, even more so she had to quit wondering if he were alive or dead.

"You aren't going to tell me?" Perry asked.

"What?"

They'd almost reached the village and she could see children squatting and playing in the dirt through the wavy heat that settled over the ground.

"Why are you out here?"

She grinned when the perfect answer popped into her head. "You know that box the kids found the other day. I wanted to see if I could find anything else. The contents of the box intrigued me."

"Oh?"

She'd managed to get his mind off her being in the dead lands. Now he'd want to know what was in that book. Like he always did, Perry stroked her hair. She moved away from his touch.

"Your hair is damp."

"I'm sweaty." She should turn around right now and tell him about the water, show him where the pond was.

If the people from Undrworld came after her, sought her out, at least her villagers would know about water. No one else needed to know. They would all willingly keep the secret to have their own stash of fresh water. Free water, easily accessed, would be something all of them would agree should be kept a secret.

"You're coming to the meeting, aren't you?" he asked when she turned toward her tent.

"I just want a little water," she told him, keeping the small bundle of practically dry clothes in her hand next to her body.

He didn't notice them. "Better hurry. We've got some important news to share."

It wasn't like Perry to hurry off, leaving her without attempting to maul her. He had something on his mind. She couldn't imagine any news he might have to share would hold a flame to what she could tell all of them.

The box the boys had found still sat among her things in her tent. Opening it, she placed the page-worn journal in the bottom, the gun on top of it, and then the clothes she'd worn earlier on the top. The lid barely managed to close.

"Syndi?"

She jumped, almost dropping the box, when she turned to see her aunt holding back her tent flap. Syndi almost fell to her rear from her squatting position before standing. Uncle Paul stood behind her Aunt Mary just outside her tent. Trying not to make a show of it, she bent down to slide the box under her bedroll and then stood again.

"I was just heading to the meeting," she told them.

"I've been looking for you for the past hour," her aunt said, frowning. "Where have you been?"

She had to tell them about the water. If not the underground world, at least the water. No one had to know about Tor. Every inch of her throbbed while his crumpled body appeared in her mind. Like he would ever fuck her like that again after she'd just shot him.

Her nerves were still way too frazzled, but having made the decision of how she would handle matters sent a rush of relief through her. There was no future for her and Tor anyway. They were from different worlds. Ignoring the regret, the sinking feeling that made her want to cry, she toughened up inside.

"I've found something—something wonderful," she whispered to them. "Let's go. I'll tell everyone at the meeting."

Aunt Mary glanced at her uncle. He looked straight ahead, frowning. That wasn't the reaction she'd expected after mentioning she had news.

They walked across the hard ground toward the large tent in the middle of the village. Heat dried her skin, the setting sun still brutal as it baked her flesh made her ache for water. Her private pond was no longer her perfect sanctuary. As badly as she craved going back there, the thought of returning twisted her gut into a painful knot. There was no telling who might be waiting for her there when she returned.

Shooting Tor meant that the pond could be more dangerous now than trying to sneak into public baths. At least two people from Undrworld knew that the pond connected their worlds. It would be a matter of time, maybe even hours, before they came after her. And she knew they wouldn't just let her escape. Not after what she'd done.

By her own actions, she'd ruined offering her people what they needed more than anything else. Somehow she had to figure a way out of this mess. Her world needed water too badly to just run from what she'd discovered.

"What's this?" she whispered, stopping in her tracks when she noticed the strangers standing under the tent.

Two cars were parked alongside the tent. No one in the village owned a vehicle.

"They're on the city council," her uncle explained.

"I tried to find you this afternoon to tell you they'd be here," her aunt added.

They entered under the hot tent, the rest of the villagers brushing against each other, trying to make room for each other but at the same time ensuring they had a good spot to see the visitors.

An anxious mood had settled among them. Something had happened here while she'd been gone. Whispered concerns caught her attention.

"We'll make this quick." One of the city council members began speaking, sending a hush over the crowd. "We've talked to a handful of you already throughout the day. And all of you have been very helpful."

The murmurs in the crowd worried Syndi. From what she gathered from the whispers around her, the council members were helping officials search for someone.

"We didn't feel a need to send law enforcement over here. Camden has always been a peaceful, pleasant village." The other city council member gave them all a toothy smile that looked anything but sincere.

Pleasant, my ass! Disgust at the two men smiling at them made Syndi's stomach turn. What he really meant to say was that these two council members were sent because the police didn't want to waste their manpower on Camden.

"As we mentioned to some of you," the first one continued, sweat dripping down his temples profusely. He tugged on the tight collar of his suit and glanced around. "Suspicious strangers have been spotted in Detroit. They are easily spotted due to mutations. These mutants are infecting our water, which is causing all of us to have to pay higher prices to keep our water from becoming contaminated."

Syndi's heart stopped in her chest. There were too many people pushing against her, making her skin crawl. And it was too hard to breathe.

"We will offer twenty gallons of water to anyone who can validate seeing them." The second councilman held his arms up in the air when the villagers immediately began commenting. "These mutants need water. If they don't have it their skin falls off."

"My skin peels from a sunburn," one of the villagers on the other side of the tent said a bit too loudly.

Roars of laughter followed. Pushing and shoving around Syndi increased. It burned her skin every time a hot and sweaty body pressed against her. Meanwhile, her mind raced over what she was hearing. Her world had already learned of Undrworld. People from there were on the surface. If the council members were discussing this with them now, they had spotted these "mutants" a while ago. One thing to be certain of, the city didn't move that quickly on anything. They'd learned of it, debated possibilities of handling it, and then made decisions. Speaking to all of them was probably just one method of approach they were taking.

That meant that Tor might have known about life on the surface before he met her.

"We have artist interpretations of these mutants," one of the councilmen was yelling. "They will be posted for you all to see. Remember, validated spottings means free water!"

This was all too much for her to handle.

Most of the villagers pressed forward after the pictures of the mutants were nailed to the posts holding up the tent.

Falling back to the side, she wanted more than anything to run, escape the suddenly uptight atmosphere as the villagers turned into a mob squad, determined to track down and capture these mutants.

But there was nowhere to run. The pond was no longer her safe sanctuary. Telling the villagers about the water would make matters worse. If someone from Undrworld surfaced, her people would attack them on sight. And if Tor's guards came after her, more than likely they would be armed.

"Are you okay?" Her aunt wrinkled her brow and Syndi realized her face was wrinkled with disgust over the situation.

Several around her overheard Aunt Mary's question and looked her way. The two cars the councilmen had arrived in pulled out, leaving a cloud of dust that surrounded them as they hurried back to their air-conditioned homes and comfortable lives. Their civic duty done, they had no concerns as to the chaos they'd planted in the village.

"You know there's more to the story than what they're telling us." Those around her nodded quickly in agreement. "I was just trying to figure out what it might be."

"You'd be at that all night," Uncle Paul said, putting his hand on her aunt's shoulder.

A few of them speculated and immediately the conversation drew away from her. Syndi met her aunt's gaze and realized she hadn't fooled the older woman. There was concern in Aunt Mary's eyes.

"Go take a look at the pictures posted before someone thinks you don't care about what they look like," her aunt whispered. "I'm headed over to share a bath with old Margaret. Why don't you come with me?"

Just like in the city, it was common practice to share bath water among the villagers. If there was a large family, then family members simply took turns with their own bath water. But in cases where someone lived alone, or it was just a couple, people grouped together and shared tubs of water to bathe.

The last thing Syndi felt like doing was bathing with old Margaret and her aunt. "Sounds good," she said numbly, and then turned to take a look at the posted pictures.

Everyone had begun to scatter. It would be dark soon and tents needed to be prepared for night while they could still see. Syndi stared at the artist interpretations of what these mutated people looked like.

Heat rushed through her with the fierceness of a knife, cutting deep into her. For a moment she didn't breathe, but simply stared at the cold expression in the drawing. Large dark eyes, and dark hair caught her attention. She then took in the look of hatred the artist had drawn on the face. One of the images was of a man, the other a woman. Both looked exactly like people from Undrworld.

This was no coincidence. Her government knew about the land underground. Which meant they also knew about all of the water. Anger twisted her gut. They were dying, barely hanging on. Children who ran around her would grow up with no hope to live any better life than she'd had.

"Are you ready?" Her aunt tapped her arm.

"Sure." Syndi turned, having no desire to study the drawings further.

Something had to be done about this. She was only one person, one human female on a planet that didn't care if she lived or died. Yet somehow she had to make a difference. She knew too much not to.

Old Margaret had a cluttered tent set up on the edge of the village. Aunt Mary and Syndi moved quickly to set up the bathing area, just outside the tent. A shallow tub, just large enough to sit in, was set behind the tent. Water covered the bottom of the tub. It was only a few inches deep. The trick to bathing was to not let any water splash out of the tub. That would guarantee that each person bathing would have enough water to lather and rinse. Of course the third person who bathed would rinse with pretty soapy water, but the soap was used modestly too.

After situating the tub, Syndi straightened and squinted out toward the dead land. Not more than a half an hour walk out there was her pond. Danger lurked around it now, and yet she still craved splashing in the water, diving underneath and feeling it soak through her pores. Her skin tightened just thinking about it. The pain as her lungs filled, the sweet sensation of her gills popping open, more than anything she wanted that experience again. She wanted Tor again.

You shot him.

Touching herself, stroking her neck the way Tor had, she closed her eyes for a moment. He'd stroked her gills, shown her sensations she had never known her body could experience. Fucked her like she'd never been fucked before.

She'd fucking shot him.

"Is he good-looking?" Old Margaret pulled her out of her thoughts.

"Huh?" Syndi turned as the old woman approached, several worn towels in her hands.

"The guy who has your thoughts hundreds of miles from here." Old Margaret chuckled. "I'm sure you'd much rather be with him than with a couple of old ladies taking a bath."

"Who are you calling old?" her aunt teased, but once again the worried look crossed her eyes when she stared at Syndi.

"There's no one." Syndi reached for the towels, which old Margaret gave her willingly, as if they were way too heavy a burden.

And there wasn't anyone, not anymore—not since she'd shot him. Regret hit her so hard, for a moment she struggled to catch her breath. Maybe he wasn't dead. Maybe that gun-thing didn't fry his brain, or whatever it was designed to do.

"You're both so kind to bathe with me," Old Margaret was saying.

Syndi helped her out of her clothes, the woman's old wrinkled body a reminder of where she would be. Old and worn-out and alone.

If she lived that long. Again she glanced out at the dead lands, worry engulfing her that at any minute she'd see strangers hurrying through the dusk. They would come after her—hunt her down.

"Syndi." Her aunt sounded exasperated.

She looked up quickly and then grabbed the cup that sat next to her, dipping it into the tepid water to rinse the soap from old Margaret's sparse hair. The woman sat contentedly in the tub, allowing the women to wash and rinse her, a luxury they shared with each other, making bathing the best experience it could be.

Small residues of soap lingered in the shallow water when they helped old Margaret stand, and then wrapped one of the towels around her. A small mat was placed on the ground, so that their feet wouldn't immediately get dirty when they stepped out of the tub.

"While you're helping your aunt, I'm going to get a treat for us. I have a bottle of wine." Old Margaret looked almost skeletal with her wet hair stuck to her small head.

She grinned at both of them, pleased with herself to be offering such a treat. With her thin towel clinging to her naked frame, she hurried toward her tent. Aunt Mary stripped out of her clothes and stepped into the water, sitting down and adjusting herself in the shallow water. Syndi knelt next to her, cup in hand, ready this time to perform her duties.

"Something is bothering you," her aunt prodded.

Lying had never been something she did well. But the truth of this matter was too damaging to share completely. Especially after what she'd heard at the village meeting. No matter that her aunt cared about her. Anything she said to her right now her aunt would share with Uncle Paul. If he decided the matter merited further discussion, she wouldn't be able to stop him.

"Tell me about my mother," she said.

A slow smile crossed her aunt's damp face. "I guess it wasn't fair of me to not talk about her when you were a child. Kind of like now, at the time, too much controversy wrapped around her death. It scared me."

Old Margaret reappeared, wearing the same dirty dress she'd worn before bathing. More than likely, it was the only dress she owned. She grinned, holding the bottle before her. The cork had been removed and she downed a good-sized gulp before handing the bottle to Aunt Mary.

"I remember Samantha," Old Margaret said, and then covered her mouth and burped quietly. She smiled apologetically. "She was a pretty thing. You look just like her."

Aunt Mary nodded. "And you act like her too," she added, her expression changing.

"How did she act?" Syndi thought of the journal she'd found, the tiny window that had been opened for her into her mother's thoughts.

Aunt Mary finished rinsing herself, and then reached over the edge of the tub for one of the towels. Her gaze met old Margaret's, as if silently the two women were trying to decide how to explain her mother to her.

"She wasn't afraid to take on a challenge," old Margaret finally said.

Aunt Mary pursed her lips, busying herself with the task of drying her body.

Syndi stripped out of her clothes and sat down in the milky-colored water. Accepting the bottle of wine, she put it to her lips, the bittersweet liquid instantly sending fumes to her brain. She'd only had alcohol a few times in her life, and she didn't remember it being quite as strong as this bottle of wine was. There was no label on the bottle, which probably meant old Margaret had obtained it illegally.

"What kind of challenges did she take on?" she asked, the water soaking through her pores while the wine seemed to slow the racing thoughts in her head down a bit.

Aunt Mary quickly dressed and then the two women worked to soak Syndi's hair, pouring cup after cup of the soapy water over her head. She was like a sponge, absorbing the water as fast as they poured it over her. There was no doubt in her mind that if she opened her eyes and looked down, there would be no water left in the tub. She was sure she'd soaked every drop of it through her pores.

"I remember her trying to get all of the villagers to help her make a stand against Detroit," her aunt said.

Syndi sputtered water out of her mouth, rubbing her eyes as she looked up at her aunt. "You're kidding. How did she do that?"

Old Margaret laughed. "Oh yes. She was still a young thing when she did that. Claimed the city actually had more water than they claimed they did. Samantha had half the villagers convinced if they started digging, they would have water spraying up around us in no time."

The two women laughed. Her mother had been thought a fool. Syndi's stomach twisted, and she straightened a bit while the women diligently tried to rinse soap from her hair. Samantha had known about Undrworld.

It made sense. Syndi didn't have a clue how her mother had learned about the place, but Tor's words came back to her.

He'd believed since she had gills, she wasn't part of the surface. Syndi had been born in the Undrworld.

"Don't get us wrong," Aunt Mary said, obviously thinking that the frown on Syndi's face was because she didn't like her mother being laughed at. "My sister was always ready to take on the world, make it a better place for everyone. Even as a kid she wanted to do that."

Her voice faded, the pain of Syndi's mother's death obviously still affecting her aunt.

"Is it true she died because she was bathing me in the public baths without paying?" Syndi asked.

Darkness shrouded them. Standing in the tub, she took the last dry towel and lightly wiped her body, wanting the moisture to remain on her skin as long as possible.

"That's what we were told," her aunt said, sipping again from the bottle.

"She was always in the city." Old Margaret grabbed the edge of tub.

Syndi quickly pulled her clothes on over her wet body then helped drag the tub to the side of the tent. Margaret would wash her clothes in it, and any other items she wished cleaned, the next day. The water would be used for cleaning until every last drop had been absorbed into clothes and towels.

"Why did she think there was underground water?" Syndi walked alongside her aunt through the quiet village.

They'd left old Margaret, who sat contentedly with what was left of her bottle of wine, and headed toward their own tents.

A few tents glowed with light although most were dark. Batteries and candles were expensive commodities. She stared at her cloth shoes, still dusty from the dead lands. Water droplets had dried into her skin, taking the tightness away. Her damp hair would make it easier to sleep. Although with all the thoughts in her head, she doubted she'd do anything but toss and turn.

"She had all kinds of stories," her aunt said, making a tsking sound with her mouth.

"So tell me the story about the underground water?"

"Why do you want to know?" Her aunt gave her a reprimanding look.

It didn't fool Syndi. Her aunt was hiding something, some old knowledge. She wanted to protect Syndi from something.

"I want to know more about my mother," she said, sighing, hoping her aunt wouldn't think she had any other motive.

They slowed their pace as they neared her aunt's tent. A dim light glowed inside. Her uncle waited up for her. No one would be waiting up for Syndi—she hoped. Icy tingles crept down her spine. Guards from Undrworld wouldn't be able to just strut into the village—would they?

"She told me she knew because that is where you came from." Her aunt crossed her arms over her chest and gave Syndi a hard look. "I loved my sister, very much. We took care of each other, until I found my Paul and she found Don.

But she had crazy ideas. And when she didn't want me to know the truth, she told me even crazier lies."

Syndi nodded, unable to say a word. Her mother had known about Undrworld. More than likely, more people on Earth knew of its existence. The city men showing up today were proof of that. What she didn't understand, and had to figure out, was why it was such a well-kept secret.

"Thanks for telling me a bit about her," she mumbled, and then bent so her aunt could peck her dry lips against Syndi's cheek.

Walking past the quiet tents toward her own, she glanced nervously through the dark. No one stirred. The stillness of the night didn't relax her though. Anyone could walk around out here and not be questioned. There was no security, no laws. People settled matters among themselves, and they took care of their own. Just like it had always been. Even on the streets with the nightlife around her, Syndi had no protection.

Hurrying toward her tent, she secured the flap behind her, and then crawled onto her mat. Guards from Undrworld would be able to take her, possibly just as her parents had disappeared, and no one would ever know the truth of her disappearance.

Stretching out on her mat, her thoughts jumping from image to image, she tried focusing on the cool dampness of her hair. Usually a soothing feeling, one that cooled her body and relaxed her skin, tonight it was barely a distraction.

She jumped when the tent flap rustled, and then a small slicing sound let her know someone had just cut the ties that secured it shut. Scrambling to her feet, she wasn't fast enough when a large figure pounced on her.

Strong hands wrapped around her and then covered her mouth when she tried to cry out.

"I don't take lightly to being shot at," Tor whispered in her ear.

Chapter Seven

§

For a moment, in spite of the suffocating heat, Tor simply held her to him. No matter that she'd wanted to get away from him so badly that she'd shot him, something about her had distracted him to annoyance. It was more than how her pussy had felt wrapped around his cock. Coming after her had been the only option.

It was a smart move too. As he'd told his council, his guards, all whom he trusted with the information, Syndi couldn't be allowed to leave after seeing his world. At least not until he had more information.

Her mouth moved against his hand, her lips and teeth scraping his flesh. She twisted against him. Dressed in loose-fitting shorts that fell almost to her knees, and a shirt that covered her modestly yet did nothing to show off her figure. Her body squirmed against his, her soft ass rubbing against his cock.

"You keep moving like that and we won't be leaving this tent for a while," he whispered into her damp hair.

She quit moving, straining her head to look up at him with wide, soft green eyes. The whites of her eyes glowed against her face in the dark. Never had he gazed on a more beautiful woman.

For all of his training, he must have relaxed just a bit too much. She managed to open her mouth, and then bit his finger.

"Shit," he hissed, moving his hand quickly to her neck, intending to give her a harsh squeeze to knock some sense into her.

"You're not safe here," she managed to whisper before he cut off some of her air.

Her words hit him though.

She cared about his safety?

From the moment he'd come to with a terrific headache after being knocked out with his own stun gun, he'd been on a grouchy rampage. Misjudging people wasn't something he did often. He hadn't made it to leader of the West Passage by being weak, or not thinking clearly. And when Peg had returned, first telling him she'd taken Syndi back to the pond, and then teasing him without mercy about letting a simple woman get the best of him, his mood hadn't improved at all.

At first he'd gone to his control room, paced his office while deciding his best move, and then finally conferenced with Fern and Ben.

"I've never in my life picked up any odd signals, but why don't you let me see if they have any kind of computer network," Ben had suggested.

That had been better than his first thoughts of simply taking on the surface, charging through the heat and confronting the unknown. The urge to do just that continued when they'd had no luck discovering if any media existed outside their world.

"Maybe if we find a place to surface and place a transmitter, then we can gather signals that way," Fern had offered a bit later.

Neither of them liked the idea at all of Tor being the one to place the transmitter on the surface. But their arguments fell on deaf ears. It was reason enough to look for Syndi, and get a better look at the Earth his ancestors had roamed.

There sure as hell wasn't much left of the place. Roln and one other guard, Ferris Bern, who he trusted enough to include on the mission, accompanied him. He'd ordered both of them to change out of the usual leather uniform they wore when guarding the passages, and to dress lightly.

Even in the loose-fitting shirt and shorts he wore, they were out of the water mere minutes when the heat had dried his skin. Thankfully the Earth had tilted enough that the sun no longer burned in the sky. Darkness had been welcomed, offering a natural shield against anyone who might notice them.

She struggled in his arms. His cock roared to life in spite of his efforts to remain unaffected with her in his arms. No matter how annoyed he'd been with her throughout the day—no, not annoyed, outraged—just touching her made him ache to be inside her again.

"I thought you were dead," she said when he finally let her go.

She stood, and he straightened as well, the darkness in the tent making it hard to see her face. Maybe he was fooling himself, but he swore she looked excited to see him.

"You can't kill someone with a stun gun," he told her. "Leaves one hell of a headache though."

"I'll remember that." Her gaze faltered, her head lowering as she looked away from him, focusing on the contents surrounding her.

With both of them standing, there wasn't a lot of room in the small area.

"I'm sorry I shot you," she said quietly.

He took her chin, forcing her to look back up at him. "Why did you do it?"

"I heard you talking to the woman, Peg. You seduced me, fucked me, to distract me. You didn't want me to be able to return here and tell my people about all of your water." She wouldn't meet his gaze.

No matter that he held her chin firmly, refusing to allow her to turn her head, her gaze darted to anywhere but his eyes.

"There's more." He didn't think she believed what she'd just said.

Remembering the conversation he'd had with Peg before she'd entered the room, he saw how she would think that. At the moment, it mattered that he gained her trust. Too much was at risk here. Although if the way she lived was any indication of how people on Earth existed, he didn't have a lot to worry about. They were a lot more primitive in their existence than he'd guessed. No wonder they hadn't picked up any computer signals. More than likely, they'd hauled the transmitter to the surface for nothing.

She moved around him, parting the flap that served as a door to her tent. For a moment he thought she would bolt away from him. Chasing her into her small community might prove a bit dangerous.

But she didn't run. Leaning her head out, looking around and then pulling her head back, she dropped the tent flaps.

"Yes, there's more." She crossed her arms, pressing cleavage together that he wished her shirt didn't hide. "You had your people's best interest in mind, as you should, you're their leader. But I have to have my people's interest foremost in my mind. We have no water, and prices are going higher."

She paused, nibbling her lower lip, and looked down. There was even more she wanted to say, yet she hesitated. Often the best way to get a person to speak, share what they knew, was to remain silent. He allowed the moment to pass, not commenting, but taking in the way her hair curved naturally around her face. So much darker than him, her skin tone fit her. There was a different smell about her since he'd seen her last. Maybe it was a kind of soap, faint yet clean. It would explain her damp hair.

She let out a sigh. "There's no way you would understand. Water is your entire world. But I had to return. And I'm glad I did. The villagers missed me, and there was a meeting tonight…"

Her voice trailed off.

"What was your meeting about?" He ached to leave the tent, walk with her through her community, get a glimpse, even if in the dark, of her world.

"You aren't the first from Undrworld to be here," she said.

That wasn't what he expected to hear. She met his gaze, her concern matching his.

"You aren't safe here," she added. "You have to return to your world."

The heat in her tent was about to make him melt. Not to mention, a discomfort he'd never experienced before slowly consumed him. It was as if his skin stretched too hard over the muscles and bones in his body, drying him out. The discomfort was easily ignored at the moment, but he'd never lived without being wet, having water around him. Finding out the hard way how long he could exist without water didn't appeal to him.

"Let's go." He took her arm. "You can tell me about your meeting once we've returned home."

"This is my home," she emphasized, tugging to be released. "I can't go back with you."

"Would you like to experience the effects of a stun gun?" he asked, almost enjoying her eyes widen.

But then her expression turned to disgust. "Don't threaten me."

He couldn't help but smile. She would go with him one way or another. There was knowledge that she had that he needed. And he needed her. Her spirit, her refusal to be intimidated, her willingness to take him on, turned him on as much as her sexy little body.

"Then behave," he told her, reaching over her and opening the flap of the tent.

She let out a very unladylike grunt, but followed him when he pulled her outside. It was just as hot once they left the tent, the air around them so stifling he could hardly breathe.

Keeping his grip on her arm, he retraced his steps to where he knew his guards were waiting. With every step his skin seemed to stretch more, burn, pull over his muscles in his arms and legs. The urge to take off in a quick sprint, reach the water as quickly as possible, made it hard to think straight.

Syndi had gills, yet she lived in this environment every day. Obviously she was accustomed to it, but he swore if he didn't have water soon, his skin would peel right off his body. It seemed he was drying out.

Ignoring the pain and discomfort, he forced himself to take in his surroundings. Syndi had the good sense not to make a sound, allow him to lead her as he walked through the group of tents. Sand burned his feet, and clung to his lower legs. The air was heavy, hard to breathe, and it burned his lungs as well as his flesh.

If he hadn't known there were people living in this environment, just a few minutes in it and he would have deemed it uninhabitable.

His two guards were right where he'd left them. Relief flooded their faces when they spotted him approaching. Syndi hesitated but he pulled her along, keeping her at his side.

"Let's go," he said quietly.

Although no one needed to be told twice. Maybe he imagined it, but it seemed to him that Syndi was pulled to the water just as he was. Their pace quickened, his small group trudging over the uneven sandy ground toward the pond. There was no sound around him, not a breeze, nothing. Their quiet footsteps were all that he heard.

Nonetheless, they were buried in the thick surroundings of darkness when Syndi balked, pulling against his hold on her.

"If you have one of those guns on you, we need it now."

Suddenly she'd turned into him, feeling his waist. Her small hands were damp with sweat as she hurriedly reached for his belt.

"Your gun. Where's your gun?" Her worried tone alerted him.

His guards faltered too, giving her their complete attention and then quickly looking around them.

"What is it?" he asked, not sure he wanted her to have his gun.

The one he brought wasn't a stun gun. He'd teased her in her tent, threatening to do to her what she'd done to him. But there was no way he'd enter this world without more severe means to protect himself.

"Dogs. Can you hear them?" Suddenly she sounded frantic. "They'll kill all of us. Give me your fucking gun."

His guards pulled their guns, suddenly alert. And then he heard it too. A pounding sound, a hard repetitive thud, as if a large group of something ran toward them. Heavy breathing that didn't sound quite right filled his ears. And then something else, large crisp screams, similar to the larger fish that swam in groups, but deeper, more sharp.

Tor pulled his gun, bracing himself and trying to shove Syndi behind him. She fought him though, and reached for his gun.

"Give it to me," she ordered, yanking at the weapon in his hand. "Give me your fucking gun now or we all die."

No sooner had she grabbed it from his hand than she'd managed to fire the thing, sending bullets screaming into the darkness. A hideous sound tore through the darkness.

And then he saw them.

"Fire," Syndi screamed. "They'll tear you up and eat you before they even kill you."

His guards followed her orders, firing at the beasts whose eyes glowed evilly in the dark. Tor didn't like being unarmed, and grabbed the gun back from Syndi, aiming quickly at the eyes and taking out as many of them as he could see.

One of them lunged at him, and he pulled Syndi down to the ground with him, managing to avoid the large beast, and firing as they fell. He swore the thing was close enough to feel its burning breath against his flesh.

Pounding feet, too many of them, made the ground underneath them vibrate as if it too were alive. The sand burned his flesh, sticking to him and making his skin stretch painfully and itch.

The creatures had varied colors of fur, and he didn't rely on them getting close enough to distinguish their means of attack. Syndi cried out underneath him. Her fear radiated through him. This was her home, her habitat, yet her scream, the tightening of her body, was enough to let him know that these creatures terrified her.

Her words of warning as the dogs had approached, and then the demonic glow of their eyes were all he needed to know that it was kill or be killed.

Holding her firmly underneath him, using his body to shield her, he aimed and fired repeatedly. His guards did the same.

Minutes seemed like hours before once again they were shrouded by the quiet blackness of the night. A metallic bitter stench filled the air though. Death and blood surrounded them. Even in the darkness he could see the beasts' blood stain the sand around them.

"We've got to get out of here before more come. They eat their dead." Syndi's warning was enough to have all of them leaping to their feet.

Ignoring the deadly heat, he hurried through the darkness, this time Syndi almost leading them as they returned to the pond.

None of them paused until they stood in the water, his guards turning slowly, surveying their surroundings. Syndi hesitated though, standing knee high in the water as she turned to stare at the black transmitter that they'd placed on the shore of the pond.

"What is that?" she asked.

"I'll explain when we get home." He'd had enough of this place for now.

There was information to digest, discuss, but he'd do it in the comfort of his control room.

Syndi shook her head, turning on him as if he had lost his mind. "You can't leave something from your world right there. My people know about you. Not just the villagers, but the city council. You don't understand. But leaving that there isn't a smart move."

"It stays." He had no idea what she meant by villagers, or city council. "Let's go."

When she would have protested further, he grabbed her arm, nodded to his guards, and then dived into the water.

Syndi didn't struggle too hard as they swam toward the tunnel returning to home.

He noticed that Syndi remained quiet as they traveled through New Dallas until they were home. There were matters to address at the control center. But until he determined that he had her complete trust, taking her there went against his better thinking. For now, she would stay in his home.

Besides, being alone with her sounded damned good.

Hoisting himself out of the tunnel at his home, he turned and pulled Syndi out of the water.

His phone rang before they were even in his door.

"You wouldn't believe what that transmitter is picking up." The excitement in Fern's voice grabbed his attention.

"What do you have?" he asked, waiting for his door to slide closed behind them and then walking to his maintenance panel and securing his locks.

"They are definitely as computerized as we are. We're picking up signals all over the place." Fern laughed, the whole thing an incredible adventure for her.

She hadn't just witnessed what he had on the surface.

"I'll be down there shortly." He hung up the phone, realizing he needed to go to the control center soon.

Syndi paced the length of his living room, stopping at the doorway leading to his kitchen then turning to glance at him before moving back to the front door. She moved like a trapped fish, her nervous energy contagious.

"Does everyone on the surface live as you do?" He'd seen no sign of computers where she lived, let alone any form of power, electricity.

Syndi snorted. "Why did you bring me back here, Tor?"

She continued to pace as if she hadn't heard his question, her own thoughts preoccupying her. Her brows almost met as she wrinkled her forehead, her expression a mixture of frustration and confusion.

Stepping into her path, he stopped her, running his hands down her arms and then up again to her shoulders. The way her wet hair wrapped around his fingers, clinging to him, and her shirt gathered as he brushed over it, it dawned on him that he'd craved having her with him again. Ever since he'd come to, she'd been all he'd thought about.

There was much to figure out, a lot to learn, and he'd master it much better with her at his side.

"Because you're supposed to be here," he told her, and then leaned into her, kissing her protest away.

She went stiff, her lips pursed together. Her defiance challenged him as he brushed his lips against hers, pulling her into his arms. Her head fell back, while thick locks of wet hair tumbled over his arms. With her neck arched, he left her reluctant mouth, allowing her to make a show of being stubborn. He sensed her arousal, knew it when she caught her breath, releasing a hesitant sigh. Tasting her flesh, running his tongue along her chin, he nibbled at her neck.

"God. Tor." She dug her fingers into his shoulders while her plump breasts pressed against his chest.

Her shirt wasn't made of thick material, but it was wet, cumbersome, and prevented him from feeling her. Running his tongue over her thin, exposed neck, he felt for the bottom of her shirt, and then found skin.

She breathed hard, her heartbeat pulsing through her body. Blood boiled through his veins as it drained through him. His cock pulsed with the eager beat that matched the throbbing of her heart. Pain stabbed through him, repressed sexual need surfacing with more intensity than he could handle.

Syndi was from another world. Although the same planet, they lived in extremely different environments and societies. Possibly they could be enemies. None of that prevented him from stroking her soft stomach, enjoying the warmth of her body, the different texture of her skin, tanned and firm.

Her breasts were soft, plump, more than a handful. Wrapping his fingers around one, he squeezed. Her cry raked over his senses, like tingles rushing over his flesh. She arched her back, letting her head fall to the side. It took more effort than he'd thought to focus his gaze on her. No matter that his entire body had hardened to stone, his brain a fogged haven of lust, he had to see the pure pleasure that tore across her expression.

She stared up at him, her sultry green eyes darkening like rare gems glowing. Her mouth formed a small circle and he leaned forward. There was no resistance this time when he kissed her. Syndi leaned against him, wrapping her hands around the back of his neck.

Her mouth was hot, sweet and so damned moist. Moving her small tongue around his, she kissed him like a seductress would her prey. Suddenly she was the aggressor, pressing against him, taking what he offered and demanding more.

Pulling her shirt up, he broke the kiss long enough to yank it from her body. Her arms raised, her body suddenly stretched out and on display before him when he pulled her shirt over her head.

"Everything. Take everything off." He could barely form the words to speak. "I want to see all of you."

She took a step backward, not speaking, but watching him as she slid her shorts down her slender legs.

Petite yet firm, young but experienced, hesitant yet demanding. Everything about Syndi was a contradiction, a mystery, and he couldn't wait to explore every detail until he had her figured out.

"If you think you're going to just drop your drawers and bang me, you better think again." She lazily moved her hand through her hair, stroking it over her shoulder to give him a better view. "All of your clothes...off...now."

All he could do was raise an eyebrow. Never had he seen such a powerful woman in a young lady's body. Slim and firm, her youth obvious in her perky breasts and hard, flat stomach, she belied all of that with the sultry way she stood before him.

"Suddenly I am yours to command?" Although he found himself pulling his clothes off like an eager and willing subject.

"Only if I decide that's how it's going to be."

He dropped his damp shirt and shorts to the floor, never taking his gaze from her. She walked to him, pushing against his chest. He took the step backward that she encouraged, enjoying her sudden wave of cockiness.

She pushed him onto his couch. Sitting, he pulled her onto him. Syndi straddled him, the heat from between her legs burning his flesh. His cock throbbed with anticipation, desperate to be inside her again, growing so hard he could hardly stand the pain. He gripped her hips, moving her so that he could thrust inside her.

"Not so fast," she whispered, fighting him.

Straightening her legs, she didn't have the strength to prevent him from entering her if he desired. But she had an agenda, one he was curious to discover. He allowed her control, holding on to firm hips. Her bones and muscles moved under his touch. She lifted herself over him, burying his face with her breasts and hair.

He couldn't think of anywhere he'd rather be.

Syndi gripped the back of the couch, holding herself over him. Offering him her breasts, he sucked first one nipple into his mouth, and then the other.

"Oh hell yeah," she cried out, her head falling back as she arched into him.

Her body pressed against him, his hands glided up her sides, feeling her ribs, how thin she was. But her breasts were full and ripe. Much more than a handful. Gripping them, squeezing and tugging, he made a feast of her, sucking and nibbling until he felt her body start to shake. Her leg muscles trembled against his, her breathing coming harder. He bit down on her nipple, scraping it over his teeth.

"God," she cried out, her legs clamping against his as she let go of the back of the couch and tangled her fingers through his hair.

Before her climax had ebbed, he released her breasts, capturing a glance at how the flesh there was now reddened, damp and marked from his touch.

She'd liked it a bit rough. He hadn't mauled her breasts enough to leave bruises, but his rough grip had left an imprint that would fade. At the moment though, the view drove him to madness.

He moved his hands, quickly grabbing her hips, and before she could regain her control, he forced her down on his cock.

"Dear God, you're soaked," he managed to say as he impaled her.

His cock glided through her hot pussy, soaked from her orgasm. So damned tight, and so damned perfect.

She screamed when he filled her, her body stiffening for a moment. Maybe he'd been a bit rough, but the little vixen had asked for it. Coming on strong, playing boss with him, he'd show her who was actually in charge here.

Lifting her off his cock just enough to feel her inner muscles glide over his shaft, he pushed her down on him again, filling her just as quickly as he had the first time.

Again she cried out, although this time she managed to straighten her head. Strands of hair fell over her face. Her cheeks were flushed and her mouth open, the cry barely escaping her lips.

Her fingers dug into his shoulders while her leg muscles seemed to return to life. Slowly she worked to take over the movement. He held her hips, but allowed her to lift herself slowly over him, creating a rhythm as she stroked him with her heat.

"That's it, baby. Ride me," he coaxed her.

She didn't answer, although watching him, her eyes glazed. Licking her lips, she continued fucking him, picking up momentum a bit. He sensed her next orgasm, felt her muscles quiver inside her.

"Now you're going to come," she told him, her voice raspy and winded.

Never had he seen a more seductive look. Her long hair fell over her breasts, parting to show her hardened nipples. Brown strands framed her face. Her lips moist and her eyes wide, she continued riding him. He loved the way her cheeks flushed, her breathing heavy. Those long lashes of hers fluttered shut and then lifted, her gaze hooded as her body tightened.

"Come. Now." She tried ordering him again.

But when she slowed the speed, her movements turning deliberate and meticulous, a fire burned through him that he couldn't control. He matched her breathing, running his hands up her body. Brushing her hardened nipples with his palms, she let out a small cry. He moved his hands up, caressing her neck.

She kept up the slowed pace, and leaned her head into his hand when he stroked her cheek. Again her eyes fluttered closed, and then opened partially, her lustful hue making her expression glow.

Reaching to the side of her neck, he stretched his fingers through her hair, caressing behind her ears, feeling the hollowed spots under her flesh where her gills were.

Suddenly her eyes opened fully. She didn't blink. Her breath caught in her throat.

"What—" she murmured.

Her movements faltered, her pussy clamping around his cock. Her muscles were so tight, so firm and small. She would suffocate the life right out of him, drain him before he could offer her a climax he knew she'd never experienced before.

Moving his index fingers over the softness behind her ears, he stroked her closed gills, knowing if she peaked just right they would open. The extra oxygen would flood through her as she climaxed. The high would be better than anything she'd ever experienced in her life.

Her body trembled, her legs quivering while her arms began shaking. She held on to his shoulders so hard he wondered if she might not draw blood. But the pain was sweet as her pussy throbbed around his cock, her heat growing with such intensity he could hold out no longer.

"Allow me to be your first," he told her, smiling slightly as he stroked her gills open, watched as her eyes rolled back in her head and her body convulsed with her orgasm.

His own release flooded through him, pumping out of his body with more aggression than he'd experienced in a long time. He'd fucked her better than she'd probably ever had it, but damn if she hadn't given him the ride of a lifetime.

There was no way he'd be able to let Syndi go.

Chapter Eight

 හ

The large cave, there was no other way to describe it, hummed with activity. It was damned hard not to stand there in awe, her jaw hanging open, as she stared at the computers along the rock walls.

A large table in the middle of the room housed even more equipment. A couple of men and one woman eyed her curiously, but looked away without staring too long, focusing on their work.

Tor moved through the room and joined two people working on the far side. He left a wet path on the rock floor and she walked through his footsteps, hating the insecure feelings that knotted her gut.

"Look what I've found." The woman sitting, looked over her shoulder, smiling.

"What is it?" Tor stood behind her, focusing on the images on her screen.

His expression was intent, serious, as it had been since they'd left his home. Having turned all business, his new mood put Syndi at a disadvantage. Handling him when he was the predator, the sexual aggressor, had been one thing. But now a leader stood before her, intent on the affairs of running his nation.

Coming over here in his small tran-bus, listening as he'd spoken on his phone, watching while he'd navigated the small two-seater ship through the water, he'd become a different person. He'd glanced at her only once or twice, and both times had appeared preoccupied.

She didn't know his mind, didn't understand his world, and it was making her unsure of how to behave. Sexually, she'd been confident. Now in the matters of business she didn't know how to act, where to stand, whether to comment or ask questions.

And there was nothing she hated more than feeling inadequate.

"Oh wow." The woman stared at Syndi, turning her chair more to get a better look at her. "This must be the woman from the surface."

Syndi straightened. No matter that she didn't have a clue what was going on around her, they would see her as intelligent and someone to reckon with.

She thrust out her hand. "I'm Syndi Stone. And you are?"

Surprise appeared on the woman's face only for a moment. She stood, glancing quickly at Tor before returning her attention to Syndi and accepting her hand. Her hand was damp and cool, but her grip firm.

"I'm Fern Leek," she said.

"And this is Ben Osk," Tor added, gesturing at the man who stood on the other side of him. "They are both my computer specialists. Now show us what you have here, Fern."

Syndi wasn't sure, but she thought Fern rolled her eyes at him. The young woman turned, thrusting a short strand of sandy blonde hair behind her ear, took her seat again, and moved her pointer on her screen.

Syndi frowned at the group of pictures on Fern's screen. "Those are the images in the tunnel," she said.

"Yes." Tor had his hands clasped behind his back.

Looking up at his profile, the hard definition of his chin, the muscles that flexed around his cheekbones, she could only guess at his thoughts. If she moved just a bit, their arms would brush against each other. But he held himself tall, alert, his attention completely on the screen in front of Fern. It was as if he didn't realize she stood so close.

"Well, look what I found." Fern drew her attention back to the screen.

"They look a lot alike." Syndi leaned forward, studying the pictures taken of the paintings that covered the walls in the tunnel that connected their worlds.

Fern had pulled up several other pictures, images drawn on what appeared to be a brick wall. The new images weren't taken underwater. They were from her world. Yet she didn't recognize them.

"The computer pulled them up as most possible match for being done by the same artist," Fern explained.

Syndi shook her head, not wanting them to know she knew nothing about computers. Like anyone in the village had exposure to anything electronic. The closest she'd been to anything like this was looking at it through store windows in the city as a child. They wouldn't see her ignorance though.

She nodded. "But they are taken from my world. Those pictures aren't in water."

"We aren't in water right now." Ben Osk glanced around Tor, his look placid. "It says right there these images are housed in the Polk Museum in the East Passage."

He pointed at the screen and Syndi read the caption she hadn't noticed at first. "The date is 2144. They are only twenty one years old."

She wasn't sure why she'd thought they would be older.

"The East Passage," Tor said, rubbing his chin.

He walked away from her, stopping at the large table in the center of the cave and picking up a piece of paper lying there. Barely giving it a glance, he set it back down and turned to face them. His expression suddenly appeared quite angry.

"You have one day to tell me what those pictures mean, and why they are in that tunnel." With several long strides, he crossed the room, muscles twitching against the sleeveless shirt that hung over his thick chest. "Syndi," he barked, and at the same time opened a door and disappeared into another room.

If that was a command for her to follow him, she wasn't sure she liked his attitude. Determined to tell him as much, she marched after him, almost jumping out of the way when the door brushed against her back as it slid closed behind her.

Tor had moved behind a large desk, and sat down, punching buttons on a panel in front of him while staring at a flat screen that stood on a small stand in the middle of his desk. He scowled as he stared at it, appearing unaware that she'd entered.

She'd yell at him in a minute. Since he obviously didn't yell for her to come in here to talk to her, she took a moment to glance around the room.

Not as large as the cave they'd just been in, although definitely what she'd think of as a cave, moist rock walls surrounded them. There were no windows, and long cylindrical beams attached to the ceiling provided enough light to see easily.

A table large enough to seat a good-sized group of people was at the other end of the cave. The floor was damp and cold under her feet. Even the air was moist against her skin. Whether they were in water, or not, this world had moisture everywhere. Her skin hadn't completely dried the entire time she'd been here, even while fucking Tor.

Her body still tingled everywhere from riding him. Never had she had better sex. When he'd rubbed her gills, she'd almost passed out. And the thickness of his cock had made her tender. A shiver rushed through her, heat growing between her legs as she thought how daring and demanding she'd been. Never in her life had she let her guard down, opened up to a man and let go during sex the way she had with Tor.

Not that she'd fucked that many men. And the experiences she had in the past faded in comparison.

But the way he'd acted since, cold and distant, made her cringe that she'd enjoyed it so much. His fingers made a hard tapping noise as he hit the keys in front of him. With her back to him, she wondered what he was doing, but didn't turn to ask.

Instead, she glanced at the items on the large table. It didn't surprise her that they had the same written language, that forms appeared similar to those she'd seen during her life. Originally, they had been the same people, divided by a World War, separated to evolve into who they were today.

Nothing she saw impressed her. She lifted a book, flipping through the heavy, glossy pages. Statutes and law written for a nation she knew nothing about. Reading through it would give her excellent insight into the life under the surface of her own world. But she glanced past the pages, pictures on the wall grabbing her attention.

Moving around the table, she studied pictures of Tor. There was a picture of him underwater, obviously a lot younger than he was now, grinning impishly at the photographer with his arms around an older couple. The man and woman on either side of him bore a resemblance to him, possibly his parents. Another shot showed him underwater, his body stretched with his arms over his head. It was an action shot. Remembering how quickly he'd moved underwater, she was amazed the photographer got such a good shot of him.

A certificate hung in a frame between the two pictures. Reading the fancy script, she noted the words, *Highest in Rank, Leader of the West Passage.* The frame enclosing the certificate was fancier than the other frames. He was proud of his rank. More than likely he'd worked hard to get to where he was now. She noted the date on the certificate. Tor hadn't been in charge of the West Passage that long. The date was less than two years ago.

Finally turning around, a large map behind Tor had her moving toward him. He barely glanced her way when she moved around his desk, studying the curvy lines that mapped out the different passages. The map would have anyone who didn't know better believe that was all there was to Earth.

Putting her finger on the words, West Passage, she struggled with the squiggly lines, trying to figure out where she was right now. None of the locations made any sense to her. She ached to ask questions, have Tor explain it to her, but his mood now made him almost unapproachable.

Growing restless, she turned to study his back. Muscles bulged against his shirt. Sleeveless with a wide collar, the material that went over his shoulders was narrow, similar to a muscle T-shirt that men in the city wore. None of them looked as good in them as Tor did.

Letting out a sigh, she looked past him at the screen he studied and her breath caught in her throat.

"What are you doing?" she asked, recognizing the skyline of the city of Detroit in the picture he studied.

Large bold words at the top of the screen read, "Public Baths Closed Until Further Notice." In the corner of the screen she recognized the name and logo of the newspaper delivered around the city. What he stared at was current.

"When were you going to tell me about this?" He didn't look at her.

"You haven't exactly sought me out for conversation." She didn't understand.

It wasn't that she didn't understand computers. They linked all of the cities together, and were used for most communication. Just because she didn't own one, didn't mean she didn't know about them. What she didn't understand was how he was viewing this website.

He scrolled down until the next pictures appeared on his screen. They were the same artist's interpretations of the "mutants" that had infected their water supply.

"And you knew about this?" he asked with an accusatory tone.

She'd had about enough of his sudden change in attitude.

"I found out at the meeting earlier tonight." She put her hands on her hips, willing him to look up at her. "When you showed up in my tent, I told you that you weren't safe there. Even then you didn't appear in the mood for conversation. Do people in your world think women are good only to fuck?"

That got his attention. Pulling his gaze from his screen, he appraised her body before lifting those powerful-looking dark eyes to hers.

"It would depend on the woman," he said with a low tone that sent shivers rushing through her body.

Damn it to hell, he wouldn't intimidate her.

"Just to set facts straight, I'm not one of those women." She nodded toward his computer screen. "Obviously, if you aren't aware of it, people from your world from one of the other passages must be on the surface. Unless your people explore without telling you."

"Have you ever seen one of us on the surface before me?" he asked.

"No."

"Then my guess is that they are from another passage." He leaned back in his chair, looking too damned good. "And since we're setting facts straight. All of the rooms here are monitored with cameras. My own doing. These are the offices that control the West Passage. If anything were to go wrong, it's all being recorded. Since I do respect you, I'm not going to treat you like my personal slut on camera — unless that's how you want to be treated."

Her cheeks flamed with heat, and she moved around his desk before she'd thought about it.

"Oh," she whispered, and then crossed her arms over her chest again, deciding she still had grounds to be upset. "That doesn't mean you have to ignore me."

"I've got a lot on my mind." Looking back at his screen, she watched his eyes move as he read further.

"How are you reading transmissions from my world?" Hadn't he told her that he knew nothing about the surface?

"The transmitter we put by the pond," he said, and then glanced up at her again. This time there was a glint in his dark eyes she hadn't noticed before. "It's sending us all of the transmissions from the surface."

"What are you going to do with that information?" A rush of defensiveness toward her people put her ill at ease.

"Be prepared." He didn't elaborate.

That bothered her. Hating that she could do nothing to defend her people, no matter what quick scenarios she came up with, she chewed her lip, watching him. Tor controlled everything around her. These people answered to him, and from the brief encounters she'd seen so far, respected him.

"Prepared for what?"

Something buzzed on his desk and, ignoring her question, he reached for his phone.

"Yes." He held the thing to his ear, corded forearm muscles twisting around each other when he flexed his arm. "I'll be right there."

When he stood, dark locks of his hair fell around his face as he leaned to turn off his computer. "Let's go," he said, without further explanation.

She focused on his thick, muscular legs, so perfectly covered with dark hair that she knew spread all over his stomach and chest. He hadn't answered her question. The best she could do was pay attention, do her best not to miss a thing. Although she was clueless how she'd pull it off, somehow she'd ensure her people remained safe. And if at all possible, get more water.

Tor pressed several buttons on a panel next to the door of his office, and turned to her. "We need to be prepared for when our worlds collide."

"You think that will happen?" She focused on where his shirt stopped, a tuft of black hair tempting her below his collarbone.

"Yes, I do." He lifted her chin with his finger and stared into her eyes with those oversized dark eyes of his. "So we learn everything we can about each other."

He traced a line down her neck, resting it between her breasts. "Every detail," he added, his voice suddenly huskier.

"What do we do with that information?" Her heart pounded, her skin overly sensitive to his one finger, barely pressing against her chest.

Tor ran his finger over her breast, and then across her to the other one. His touch was like fire, scorching her skin. His gaze never left hers, their eyes locked on each other while he created need in her so hard she could barely stand.

"That depends on our intentions."

"Oh."

She was sure the conversation had switched from their worlds, to the two of them. And at the moment, his intentions were very clear.

He pinched her nipple, tugging and pulling her closer. Tingles coursed from her nipple to her pussy.

"And what are your intentions?" she heard herself ask, speaking her thoughts.

One powerful arm pulled her against him, crushing his mouth to hers. His other hand remained between them, tugging and squeezing her breast.

Her entire body pulsed with energy, with a craving so strong she couldn't move. His tongue pressed past her lips, impaling her. Every inch of her throbbed, one huge steady beat stemming from between her legs.

He dragged his mouth down her neck, sucking and nipping at her tender flesh. "I intend to have you." His breath scorched her flesh.

Syndi's knees almost buckled, and she grabbed his shirt. Holding on while her world slowly spun around her, solid muscle pressed her against the wall. His hand moved down her, cupping the throbbing beat, the thudding reverberating in her ears. She was one huge fucking live wire, need beating through her.

She fought the thick fog that consumed her brain. "What about the cameras you mentioned?"

"I just turned them off."

"You did?" There were people on the other side of the door, official people controlling his city.

It wouldn't take too much for him to relieve the pain he'd created inside her, appease the growing pressure. Large roped muscle twitched against her hands. She stroked him, brushing over his hard body until she reached between them and wrapped her fingers around his thick hard cock.

"Take it out, Syndi." He'd pulled her shirt up and lowered his head to her breast. "I want to feel my cock in your hand."

None of the village men had ever spoken so boldly to her. Tor's demanding nature was better than anything she'd ever imagined. His confidence, his rock-hard body, the entire fucking package, made her boil inside. She needed him— now.

Freeing his cock, soft flesh moved with her fingers over hard muscle. Every inch of him hardened, a groan tearing through his body. It vibrated against her. For now, having him inside her mattered more than anything else. Their two worlds were about to change forever. People worked just outside the door behind her. Her village would die without water. All of them would still be there in a few minutes.

"Fuck me, Tor, please." She sighed, his fingers working magic as he stroked her pussy.

He almost ripped her clothes from her, his aggression one hell of a turn-on.

"Come here." He lifted her, pushing her against the wall next to the door.

The cold stone contrasted with heat burning inside her. Her hair fell over her face and she wrapped her legs around his waist, sinking onto his hard cock. His swollen soft head pressed against her vagina, parting her flesh. His fingers spread over her ass, stretching her as he slowly moved inside her.

The pressure between her legs thrust up her body. He was splitting her in two. She bit her lip hard enough to taste blood, scared if she cried out everyone on the other side of the door would know what they were doing.

She barely managed to open her eyes, and Tor had never looked more intent. He watched her, his creamy white skin flushed while his lips formed a thin line and dark eyes glowed almost black. Thick hair framed his face, falling to curls that bordered his thick neck. She stretched her fingers over his shoulders, dropping her gaze to the thick muscle that twitched as she touched it.

He lifted her, allowing room to move inside her, while his fingers dug into her soft ass. She held onto him, her legs wrapped around his waist. His cock stroked her pussy, reaching depths she didn't know a man could hit. Something about the way Tor looked at her, he knew he created sensations that rippled with every movement he made. He knew he brought her to a point she hadn't been to before.

He gritted his teeth, moving slowly, swelling and throbbing inside her. God, he had to have a cock larger than any other man.

A vein popped in his forehead, a dark thin line. He wouldn't last much longer. The movement was slow, but so damned intense she swore the room spun around them. Everything was a blur but his face.

"You're going to come with me," he growled, muscles in his arms bulging as he increased movement.

His cock stroked her harder—faster. Heat built between them, fire coursing through her while his face turned red.

Holding on for dear life, she no longer focused on the perfection of his body. Focusing on his hard packed muscle was impossible. He took her over the edge with him and all she could do was hold on, pray she didn't pass out. Never in her life had she experienced such a ride.

"Tor," she cried out, forgetting about the world around them.

Light flashed before her eyes, the wall stopping her head from falling back as the dam broke inside her. Tor gripped her, grinding hard and fast into her while a growl ripped through him ferocious enough that he sounded like a deadly animal.

She collapsed against roped muscle, desperately trying to catch her breath. She didn't realize he carried her away from the wall until he slowly slid out of her. Then she slid down him, her feet submerging into cool water.

"Somehow," he whispered, brushing his lips over hers. "Our worlds will accept each other."

"Hopefully," she agreed, although at the moment she'd probably agree with anything he said.

He ran water from a silver stem coming out of the wall and washed water over them before getting their clothes.

One thing she knew, she wanted this man around — for a long time. Never had she been more fulfilled, more satisfied, and at the same time craving more of him.

Two people sat with their backs to them when Tor led the way through the control room. The large cave, with its cool, damp rock floor, seemed like something she'd seen on old movies that she used to watch as a kid from the windows of video stores. But this wasn't fiction.

When they reached the tunnel of water, Tor jumped in, but then surfaced quickly, brushing hair from his face and looking up at her. She jumped in next to him, relishing how the water soaked through her pores, which had barely had a chance to dry out while in his office. What a life it would be to have water like this at her disposal all the time.

He pulled her down with him. More than aware of everywhere his hands touched her, she did her best to focus on swimming. He moved under the water so much easier than she did. Trying to match the way he kicked, the way he moved one arm while holding her to him with the other, she finally gave up. He kept her pressed against him, gliding through the dark tunnel with the ease of someone who'd obviously done this all his life.

It was as if he sensed when her lungs began burning. His hair floated around his strong face. His eyes wide open in the dark tunnel, he studied her, and then raised his hand to reach behind her ears.

The way he stroked her gills, a simple movement, was like bubbles rushing through her. He had a way of touching her, caressing the sensitive area, a small motion with one finger, yet it made her tingle to her toes.

Maybe she was giving him a funny facial expression, but he smiled, a sincere friendly grin, while little bubbles rose between them in the water.

He pulled his hand away the second her gills opened, tucked her against him again, and rushed through the underground water. He moved quickly, keeping them centered in the tunnel, which was wide enough that they could have swam side by side, if she could have kept up.

When the tunnel curved upward and they surfaced again in a circular hole with a small cave surrounding them, she almost regretted that their journey had ended.

For a moment, while they bobbed in the water with the damp air making her face feel cold, he held her close to him, his arousal tapping against her back. She didn't move, wasn't sure what to say or how to react. Instinct forced her to keep her guard up, but desire begged that she twist in his arms, rub herself against his strong body, tangle their legs together and tempt him further.

He spread his long fingers over her tummy, while his other hand moved up to her neck. Corded muscle tortured her back, and her long hair floated around them as they floated in the water.

"The room we're entering is very secure," he whispered into her ear. "It's got top security and is where all activity of all government offices is monitored. Control Center is where everyday business occurs. Here is where my military keeps an eye on things."

"Okay…" she said, trying to turn her head to look at him.

He tightened his grip, his fingers pressing against her chin so that she couldn't move.

"You'll stay by my side, and remain quiet. Is that understood?"

She could barely nod, but managed enough movement that he must have been satisfied. With a fluid movement, he shifted his hold on her and lifted her so that she could turn and sit on the edge of the small circular hole. Tor lifted himself out and then stood. She hurried to follow him through a narrow, very dim hallway. The cold, wet rock floor was as dark as the walls and ceilings. The place was almost eerie.

"Tor. This is most interesting." A young man, dressed in the clothing most of them seemed to wear, the simple tan shorts and a sleeveless shirt, turned to acknowledge them when they entered through a large oval doorway.

He stopped talking, his surprise visible over her presence.

"Go on. What do you have?" Tor obviously didn't see a need to make introductions.

The young man stared at her a moment longer before seeming to realize it was better not to ask questions. He turned toward the large panel on the wall he'd been facing, and pushed several buttons.

"First of all, you told me Ran Mose planned on meeting you the day after tomorrow. My monitoring shows he's already headed toward the West Passage."

"When do you anticipate him arriving?" Tor moved to stand next to the man.

Syndi stood behind the two of them, barely able to see over their shoulders. The two of them blocked the screens they looked at. She glanced around the small cave, wondering how someone could stand to be in here for very long and work. Knowing Tor didn't want her to make a scene, she took a careful step to the side, trying to get a better view of what they looked at.

"They are traveling through this passage here." The man pointed to something on one of the screens. "I'd say they will be at the four passages by the morning."

"What else do you have for me?"

The man shifted and Syndi wondered if Tor weren't quite as compassionate of a leader as she'd originally thought.

"There is one more thing," he hesitated, and looked down.

Her presence made the young man uncomfortable. Although he tried not to show it, he was trying to notice where she was, what she was doing. Syndi cocked her head at him then glanced up at Tor. Slowly, Tor crossed his muscular arms against his chest, watching the smaller man. It didn't take more than a second for the man to return his attention to his screens.

"I've intercepted a transmission between Ran Mose and one of his advisors. He's close enough to us that we picked up the signal." There was pride in his voice and he quickly punched more buttons. "Here it is."

Something crackled, and Syndi quickly studied the silver panel embedded in the stone wall until she noticed a speaker at the top of the panel. The voices she heard were tinny, distant, with static making it difficult to understand.

"No. You'd have to trace it back approximately twenty years." A man's voice echoed in the small cave.

"My point is that if there's no record of her today, possibly she's dead." The other voice, another man, was even more faint and hard to hear.

"Just determine where her last place of record was, we'll take it from there."

"Could there be any other names she went by?"

"Research the name I gave you. Samantha Stone."

Syndi stifled a gasp, able to remain quiet through a sheer act of will. A nauseating chill rushed through her while her stomach turned into a painful knot. Focusing on the spot of Tor's shirt in between his shoulder blades, she strained, trying to hear every word exchanged. If her heart would just quit thudding so loudly in her chest, she would be able to hear better. More than anything she wished they would turn up the volume.

Why would this person, Ran Mose, want her mother researched?

"We have been researching her." There was a sense of irritation in the voice. "She was one of the homeless—villagers they called them. The cities cast them out. What you're asking is almost impossible to do."

"How are the scouts on the surface doing?"

"One is dead. We got confirmation a few hours ago. The surface is miserable. The intense heat and no water makes it almost impossible to function."

There was a snorting sound, followed by a lot of static, and some of the words broke up.

The person reporting continued, "and yes, two of the surface people have agreed to the terms offered and are helping out. That's the best we can do."

"Then I'll replace you and find better. The threats are increasing. And as long as my bastard exists, they will continue. Kill that surface slut. I'll have no bastards threatening my son's right to rule after me."

"Yes, Sir," the other voice mumbled, and the transmission ended.

The man standing next to Tor shifted, daring this time to actually glance back at her before focusing his attention on his leader.

"I took the liberty of researching their most recently implemented laws in the East Passage," he offered.

"Make me a copy of that transmission." Tor pointed at the panel.

He turned and looked at her. Syndi straightened, hoping her expression appeared neutral, as if the message meant nothing to her. But she knew he wondered if the same last names meant that she might be related to the woman in question on the transmission.

"What new laws has Ran Mose passed?" Tor continued watching her.

"Well," the man hesitated, glancing at her again before clearing his throat. "Apparently he's recently passed a law making his firstborn next in command, without elections."

Tor looked at him as if he'd lost his mind. "Without elections? He has taken the vote away from his people? Damn."

Fumbling with a disc, the man turned his back briefly on them and worked the panel in front of him. The equipment hummed quietly and then stopped. The man slid the disc into a see-through bag, sealed it closed, and then handed it to Tor.

This time, they traveled through different tunnels after leaving the eerie small cave-room. The water around them was warmer, and the tunnels larger. More than once, they passed others in the tunnels. Although Tor swam with her tucked against him, he freed a hand each time, lifting it in greeting to whomever they passed.

Syndi's thoughts distracted her so badly, she took a minute to realize when they'd left the tunnel, entering a large underground body of water. When a large snakelike creature passed close enough that she could see its small circular eyes, she jumped, swallowing too much water when she let out a surprised cry.

Tor surfaced, still holding her, and she realized they were in a large lake with rock completely surrounding them. The water appeared almost black as it rippled around them.

"Are you okay?" he asked, slowing and adjusting his arm so that she could gulp in air.

"I'm fine." She was anything but fine. "Where are we?"

She didn't really care. They were underground in some pool of water. It all seemed to run together for her at this point. And any answer he gave her wouldn't be enough to distract her thoughts. Someone was trying to track down her mother. And they wanted a bastard killed. She had no idea what that meant.

He'd said his bastard. And a bastard was an illegitimate child. There was no way to prevent Tor from feeling her heart racing in her chest. She had gills, and knew she was different from others on the surface. Was she a bastard? Some deranged leader's cast-off child?

Tor brushed his fingers against her breast, yanking her out of her panicked thoughts.

"The water snakes are completely harmless," he told her, misunderstanding her reason for hyperventilating. "And we're in Norse Lake. It's our third largest lake in New Dallas. The majority of the city lives in that mountain." He pointed toward the large black stone that rose high above the water ahead of them. "And almost all of them work in the mountain behind us. During the day, this water is a lot more congested. I've always enjoyed the black water at night."

She took a minute to look around her. "Your world is really beautiful."

Dark water lapped around his shoulders when she gazed at him. Black hair clung to his head, strong hard cheekbones highlighted by the deep shadows surrounding them. Nothing she'd seen here was as beautiful as he was. Not that she'd say that to him.

His hand came out of the water, his movements so easily made, as if he stood in the water instead of floating in it. Stroking a strand of hair away from her cheek, his other hand pulled her closer to him.

"I want to give you another first," he muttered, nibbling on her ear while his fingers worked under her clothes and pierced her pussy.

"What's that?" Speaking suddenly was a chore.

She dug into his shoulders, wrapping her legs around his powerful thighs. Opening to him. He impaled her, stroking her inner pussy walls with his fingers.

"Fucking underwater."

She was looking at him wide-eyed when he pulled her down with him, the water wrapping around her face like a wet blanket. For a moment her vision failed her, the only sensations rushing inside her were his fingers, stroking the fire that quickly burst into flames.

His large black eyes were close, protective, and she focused on them while he stroked her gills. Holding on to his body with her legs, his cock pressed against her. His fingers slid out of her but then she was impaled again, stretched, consumed. He glided through her, the water making her muscles stretch, clamp down on him, as if she needed every inch of her holding on to him.

He filled her when her gills opened, and she swore she'd float right out of the water. Nothing came close to how he made her feel at that moment. Moving in and out of her, holding her protectively to him, his face was inches from hers, watching her. His expression remained relaxed, dark hair floating around his face while he filled her with his cock.

Blackness surrounded them. Nothing existed but Tor and her. His hands moved over her, stroking her breasts, caressing her skin. She held on to him with her legs, allowing him to control fucking her. His hips thrust forward, his cock gliding deep inside her pussy.

When he hit that spot, she cried out, bubbles exploding in front of her face while she swore they blew up inside her too. The water kept her tight, prevented her from being as soaked, and allowed her to feel every muscle that twitched in his shaft when he moved faster.

Crying out, she almost choked. His hands caressed her face, his black eyes so close she drowned in them. Her hair floated between them, around them, creating the extent of the world that was simply the two of them.

He caressed her, stroking every inch of her, and then rested his hands on her hips. Then he drove in harder, splitting her in two. She arched, clamping down on him with her legs. His expression contorted, and she fought to watch him when he exploded inside her. Slowly they drifted to the surface and she realized he relaxed on his back, while she lay sprawled over the top of him. Cold hair clung to her and she slowly managed to lift her head, the black water lapping at his body.

"There is nothing this amazing where I live." Something grabbed her attention, a shiny object twisting through the water near them. She jerked on top of him, forcing Tor to lift his head. Slowly they straightened in the water and she looked around nervously. "I saw something."

"I'm sure you did." He didn't appear the least bit concerned.

The shiny object twisted past them again and she clung to him. "What is it?"

"They're snakes."

"You must be fond of snakes," she muttered, pulling her feet up when she was sure something brushed against them.

"I think they are rather fond of you," he said.

"I'm not sure anyone in your world is fond of me."

"You're right. I don't see anything about you to be fond of."

She frowned at him and noticed the small curve in his lip. He teased her. After what they'd heard back in the cave, he seemed to find it fitting to pick on her. Maybe the words hadn't meant as much to him. Of course he wouldn't know anything about her background. With all the duties he must have, there couldn't possibly have been that much time to research her. Not to mention, he probably wouldn't have found anything.

One thing the voice in the transmission had pegged accurately, there wasn't much record kept on villagers. It wouldn't surprise her if her birth weren't even recorded. Having never been to a doctor, and never having reason to enter any city office, her people wouldn't even have her documented as existing.

Yet somehow these people knew of her mother.

Tor's powerful legs moved with slow, steady strokes, gliding them through the almost cold water, their heads remaining above water. "Do you know Samantha Stone?"

She pushed away from him, so she could see his face, and did her best to kick alongside him. Although splashing a fair bit more than he did when she kicked, feeling like a complete klutz while he moved gracefully, she managed to stay afloat.

It wasn't necessary to make a show of trying to swim. Never had she been in such deep water, so far from the shore. Doing her best to keep her head above water bought her time with her answer. He didn't comment that she remained silent for a moment, probably distracted by watching her. Possibly she would swim better if she weren't searching her mind for a reason not to tell him. Praying she wasn't making a big mistake, she allowed him the truth.

"She was my mother."

"Was?"

When she shoved hair from her face, she bobbed underwater. Splashing even more, she surfaced, spitting water, which almost hit his face. He grabbed her, once again pulling her body against his, and then picking up pace while swimming on his side.

"We'll never get home at this rate," he told her.

"Sorry. It's kind of hard to learn how to swim when there's no water."

"Then you're doing very well." Her backside stretched against the length of his body. His muscles swelled and stretched with his movements, caressing her. "You said she was your mother?" he asked.

"She died when I was very young."

"And you were her only child?"

"Yeah." All those corded muscles moving down the length of her body were beginning to distract her. "I was adopted."

"And you have gills, which I assume your mother didn't."

They'd already discussed this. Since she'd told him before that no one that she knew had gills, she didn't answer.

Tor was figuring out what she already worried might be the truth.

The leader, Ran Mose, quite possibly was looking for her.

Chapter Nine

ಣಿ

Tor didn't enjoy his usual morning ritual of relaxing in his pool in his kitchen while studying over the news uploaded every morning. The usual happenings in the cities of the West Passage, everything from editorial comments about good and bad laws, to any arrests that might have occurred the previous day, to births and deaths among his people, would have to wait.

By the time they'd reached his home the night before, Syndi had almost been asleep in his arms. They'd taken a long way home, swimming slowly through some of the quieter parts of the city. She wasn't used to the water, or swimming. That and the sex they'd had earlier had more than likely wiped her out. When they'd entered his home, he'd seen how stiff her movements were.

He'd tried to carry her through the water while returning to his house. But the damned woman was stubborn, determined to show him she could swim on her own. Well she'd paid the price with sore muscles. Her protests had been minimal when she'd tried telling him she should return to the surface. That wasn't an option. Once she'd collapsed on his bed, she was out.

Watching Syndi sleep in his bed, curled up under his sheet on her side, his cock stirred with desire. It was early, earlier than he usually got up. But he needed to be at the four passages. The sultry curve of her hip, the way the sheet creased and fell over her slender waist, and her breasts, pressed together and almost completely visible, had all the blood rushing from his brain straight to his groin.

"She'll be fine," Peg whispered from behind him.

Usually Peg's presence didn't annoy him. But for just another moment he wanted to watch Syndi, uninterrupted, without the reminder that he needed to get the hell out of there.

"She better be," he said, turning and walking past her without giving her a glance.

He grabbed his belt off his kitchen table and clasped it around his waist. Grabbing his phone, he punched the buttons to check in with Roln.

Heading out, he turned, Peg watching him from the kitchen doorway.

"I don't care if she pulls a gun on you or not, you take her to the surface, and I swear, I'll demote you to kitchen duty."

Peg had successfully detained life-threatening criminals on more than one occasion. She would never confess it to him, but he believed she'd taken Syndi back to the surface the other day out of sympathy for her. Nonetheless, Peg was the best candidate to watch her. He wouldn't leave Syndi sleeping in his bed with a male guard watching her.

She curled her lip at him. "Get out of here," she told him.

She better realize he was serious. But there was no time to threaten further. He was needed at the four passages.

Knowing he'd meet the great Ran Mose today, he'd ordered all of his guards in formal uniform. Tor adjusted the sash that crossed over his chest, the insignia of his rank, four triangles connected at the corners, covering his heart.

Up until yesterday, he would have been nervous about meeting Ran Mose. As a child he'd studied the leader, admired him for his achievements. The first to organize one of the passages, and the only leader the East Passage had known to date, Mose appeared in the public eye as one of the great figures of all time.

The three other passages had organized years after the East Passage, each of them going through a handful of leaders while Mose maintained control of his portion of the world. He'd offered advice to the other leaders, and his military tactics were mandatory lessons for all military.

But after yesterday, after breaking into Ran Mose' transmission, Tor's opinion of the great leader had faded considerably. All that mattered now was that he learn Mose's agenda, which he knew the leader wasn't here to share with him.

Brushing his hand down the sash, briefly touching the insignia on his chest, he walked through the thick trees, two of his guards already with him.

Roln appeared through the trees, positioned at the pond that led to the surface, as Tor had ordered. One of his computer specialists, Reece Goth, had arrived earlier, setting up a small camp with his equipment on a square table just outside a tran-bus parked nearby.

"We've verified that Ran Mose and his party are just inside the entrance to the East Passage," Roln told him, walking over to stand next to him as the two of them looked through the trees in the direction of that passage. "They haven't surfaced or made any announcement of their presence."

"Ran would know that I'd know he was there," Tor mused.

Second-guessing Ran Mose was a challenge he took on with enthusiasm.

"He wants us to send a greeting party, I bet." Obviously Roln struggled with why the East Passage leader hadn't surfaced as well. "I bet he wants us to go to him."

"Like hell I'm going in wading after him. He can come ashore for a formal greeting. He's the one showing up a damned day early."

Roln looked at him. "He would probably have a profile on you and know you'd stick to formalities."

Thoughts were churning in his guard's mind. Tor looked at him briefly, scowling. Roln was right. Ran Mose would have studied him—just like he'd studied Mose.

"Then what the hell is he doing down there," he said, voicing his thoughts.

"Tor?" Reece called out.

Tor turned toward the table where his computer specialist stood, frowning at the equipment in front of him.

"What's wrong?" He noted instantly that Reece didn't like what he saw.

"They're retreating."

"Retreating?" He moved around the table and studied the black screen that showed the four tunnels.

A white bleep moved slowly backward from the entrance of the East Passage.

"Why the hell would they be leaving?" Roln glanced at the screen too, and then squinted as he looked through the trees.

"I'm not sure," Reece said. "But they are definitely leaving. In fact, they've picked up their pace."

"Something isn't right." Warning bells went off in his head.

Tor didn't have a damned clue what Ran Mose was up to, but the transmission he'd heard the other day indicated he was determined to stop something, someone—some bastard. He'd told Tor to meet him here tomorrow morning, yet he was here today. Ran knew about the surface, had people above ground already searching the place. And now he showed up a day early, and then was leaving.

Something rumbled under his feet, the ground shaking slightly. Water splashed to the surface from the pond. Tor looked down at the water that had just soaked the grass.

"Everyone to the tran-bus now." He didn't give any thought to the order.

Following his instinct, he turned to his men, pointing to the tran-bus that waited at the shore to the ocean. They all looked at him, but only hesitated for a moment before carrying his order out. Reece reached for his equipment.

"Leave it. Vacate now." Tor felt the ground shake beneath him again.

He couldn't prove a thing. But damn it to hell, if his guess was right, this qualified as an act of war.

Damn.

His men ran to the tran-bus and he followed quickly. Jumping into the driver seat, he slammed the thing into reverse, quickly backing up until water began covering the windshield.

A sudden wave attacked the tran-bus.

"What the fuck was that?" one of his men yelled.

"The bastard is blowing up the Four Passages," Tor yelled back, fighting to maintain the tran-bus as he accelerated in reverse.

And along with the Four Passages, he would collapse the passage to the surface.

Another wave attacked them, knocking the tran-bus sideways. A muffled booming sounded, and water hit them hard enough to help accelerate them until they were in open water.

It took a minute to regain control. Tor glanced around him, noting that all of his men were all right.

"Get up here and tell me the standing of the Four Passages," Tor yelled at Reece.

Roln sat next to him and the two men quickly exchanged places while Tor navigated their path back to New Dallas.

"Holy shit. You were right." Reece's words created a moment of silence.

"Report," Tor said quietly. "What just happened?"

Although he already knew the answer.

"An explosion appears to have gone off in the East Passage. From what I'm seeing on my readings, that passage is completely sealed. But the shock of the explosion has done damage to the other passages as well. I can't tell you how bad at this point."

Tor slowed the tran-bus. "Can you pick up Ran Mose and his men?"

Reece pushed buttons. "There must be too much debris in that passage right now. Either they were killed, or the sediment just hasn't settled well enough for us to pick up their reading."

Tor's phone buzzed and he grabbed it from his belt. "What?"

"There's an incoming message from Ran Mose. Do you want me to patch it through?" Fern asked him. "And what the hell just happened at the Four Passages? We picked up something that looks like an explosion."

Well, that answered one question. Ran Mose was still alive.

"It was an explosion. No casualties at this end. And yes. Patch it through." He couldn't wait to hear what Ran Mose had to say.

Static sounded on the line before it faded to a dull popping noise. "Tor Geinz," Ran Mose said.

"This is Tor." He was more than aware of his men watching him, anxious to hear what the possible explanation could be for what happened.

"A pleasure to speak with you, young man." Ran Mose had chosen to play with formalities.

Well, Tor wasn't in the mood.

"I'm glad to hear you're alive," he told him, knowing he performed a lack of courtesy in not returning a polite greeting.

"There has been an unfortunate accident." Ran obviously realized it was time to get to the point. "We regret losing one of our tran-buses. Our equipment showed the engine blowing caused a bit of a shake to the passages. I assume no one was hurt?"

"No casualties at this end." Tor didn't believe a word the man was telling him. "We'll send assistance immediately to clear the passage and offer you aid."

"How kind of you." Ran Mose used the tone similar to the one Tor had heard in the transmission they'd picked up the day before.

Something Tor had just said to him upset him greatly. Either he'd wanted casualties, or he didn't want their aid. That made Tor want to assist him even more.

"Shut down your engines, and leave your communications open. We should have the East Passage opened again shortly. I have men working on it now." He had half a mind to leave them floating there all day.

Ran wouldn't argue about shutting down his engines. If they blew out the entrance of the passage, the tran-buses would float better in the rough water than if they were propelled, and their engines fought the sudden current that would hit them.

"Be sure they are careful about any aftershocks. I would hate to hear some of your people were injured in trying to rescue us." Again there was no friendliness in the man's tone.

"Noted." Tor severed communication, his anger mounting.

Something was up. He sensed it.

His phone buzzed again.

"I didn't like the comment about the aftershocks," Fern said when he'd acknowledged the call. Obviously his conversation with Ran had been monitored. "From what we see at the moment, the explosion was minor and the land is secure. I'm not sure why he would suggest aftershocks."

"Well, it doesn't make sense to me that an engine blowing would cause that kind of explosion in the first place." Ben Osk sounded in his ear.

He'd had the whole damn control room listening to his conversation. Since his people had obviously decided it was conference time, he switched the phone to speaker so his men in the tran-bus could hear as well. At least that way he had his hands free to drive.

"Ran Mose is up to something. He just informed me that the engine blew on one of his tran-buses. He doesn't report any casualties or injuries," Tor said, glancing over his shoulder so he could quickly inform his men what they hadn't overheard.

"Like hell that explosion came from an engine exploding," Roln said.

"I would have to read a survey of the land after damages are assessed," Reece added. "But from what my equipment shows right now, I would speculate a fleet of engines blew.

They weren't close enough to the entrance of the passage to have caused a collapse of the passage."

"The East Passage collapsed?" Tor asked.

"Agreed." Fern's voice came through the speaker, interrupting his question. "Our readings here confirm that the passage sealed shut, but I don't see any other damage."

"Why the hell would they want their passage sealed?" Roln wondered.

Anyone who entered the East Passage, or any of the passages at the Four Passages, had to have proper paperwork. Even if they somehow managed to get through without it, once they reached the other end, they would have to produce the paperwork again. All the passages were closely guarded. Tor agreed that it made no sense.

"What if that wasn't their motive?" He went over the transmission between Ran and his man that they'd overheard the day before. "What if they intentionally set off the explosion, but their goal wasn't to seal the passage?"

"What would their goal be then?" Reece asked.

Tor didn't answer. The passage to the surface wasn't too far from the East Passage. If any damage were done to it, they wouldn't have a way to get to the surface. Syndi wouldn't be able to return home. And no one else from the surface would be able to get to them.

"We're going back," he decided, and immediately changed course with the tran-bus.

"That might not be a safe idea." Fern immediately protested. "Let us run a more intensive survey first."

"Run your survey. Tell me if any of the other passages suffered any damages." He glanced over his shoulder at his guards. "We're going to run our own survey too."

Tor turned off the speaker, terminating the call. Immediately his phone buzzed again.

"What now?" he asked.

"We've received another call," Fern said, this time more quietly. "From your house," she added.

Well at least he knew Syndi was still there.

"And?" he asked.

"Apparently we weren't the only one's monitoring you," she told him. "I assured her you were okay."

He wanted to tell her to let Syndi know she better stay put. The last thing he needed to do was worry about her right now.

"Increase security over there," he told Fern.

"Understood," she said, and in her own best interest, didn't question him.

Within minutes they were back at the Four Passages. Tor placed one more call, ordering more guards sent to help with investigating the tunnels. He also arranged for more equipment to be sent for Reece.

"You'll work from here," he told Reece, after hanging up his phone once again, and then getting out of the tran-bus. "The rest of you take a passage, report back to Reece once you've confirmed that each passage is not damaged. Roln, you're with me."

Pulling the portable light from the tran-bus, he attached it to his belt. His guard didn't have to ask him where they were going. He knew. Tor waited until his men had split up, then led the way with Roln at his side toward the small pond.

"Do you think he somehow meant to close this passage?" Roln asked after they'd reached the small pond's edge.

"It crossed my mind." Tor made sure his phone and gun were secure on his belt. "There's only one way to find out."

He jumped into the pond, immediately kicking his way deep into the water. Roln was right behind him. Swimming down until the water chilled around him, he worked his way deeper, until he was sure no one would see the light from the surface when he turned it on. They'd damned near swam into complete darkness. But at the moment, protecting this passage seemed more important than reopening the East Passage. If he didn't believe Ran Mose had another way to get to the surface than through this tunnel, he'd leave the bastard trapped in his own passage.

Using the narrow ray of light to guide them, they kicked their way deeper searching for the narrow tunnel that would take them to the surface. There was more debris in the water than before. Clumps of dirt, rocks, sediment, floated around them. The other passages would be worse. They were furthest from the East Passage in this pond, but the South and North Passage ponds were very close to the East Passage.

Ran Mose would have been able to close the other two passages easily with that explosion. There was no reason that Tor could think of as to why Ran would want to seal him off from the other passages though. The only thing that merited any reason would be Ran wishing to seal this passage — the passage to the surface.

A tremor vibrated through the water. It took a minute to find Roln. Dirt cluttered the already dark water. He shone the light around him, concerned that the pond walls seemed to collapsing. Roln appeared in the beam of light, shielding his eyes when Tor shone it in his face. A large clump of earth, with grass attached, floated between them.

Roln's irritated expression matched Tor's feelings. They were in danger. That tremor meant only one thing — another explosion had gone off.

His phone buzzed, the vibration going through his belt. Grabbing it, he focused on the small screen and saw that

Reece was trying to reach him. Passing the light beam to Roln, he pushed the small buttons, letting Reece know his location.

A message returned immediately.

Another blast. Passages not safe.

The details would wait until he talked to Reece in person. Right now, they'd made it this far and weren't turning back until he checked out the tunnel.

He typed in a quick message. *Pull all guards out of passages.*

Putting the phone back on his belt, he gestured with his hand that they continue. The water around them shook, jostling them so that it became quite the task to swim deeper into the water. When his light hit the entrance to the tunnel, he grabbed the top of the rock, pulling himself down until he stood in the tunnel entrance, his hand flat against the wall.

The beam of light spread across the painted figures and symbols on the stone walls. Roln pulled himself down and then stabilized his stand by bracing his outstretched arms with his hands flat against the walls.

More sediment floated through the water behind them. Clumps of dirt hit his legs and back. The pond behind them was filling with dirt and rock. They would be swimming through mud if they tried to return.

All they could do was swim to the other side.

Praying the transmitter was still next to the pond on the surface, Tor gestured with his arm to Roln, and then pushed away from the wall.

Rocks brushed against his skin. Speed became imperative. The tunnel could collapse and they would be trapped. Already from the amount of dirt and rock floating around them, his guess was that the pond behind them was impassable. All that left was what was ahead.

The surface. The dry, waterless, burning with heat surface.

Being trapped up there didn't bother him as much as the puzzle as to why all of this was happening. Flying through the tunnel as quickly as they could swim, the water warmed instantly when they reached the pond on the other side. The temperature rose with each stroke until, by the time they hit the surface, the heat was already burning and stretching his skin.

"What the fuck is going on?" Roln was none too pleased to be on this side again.

Darkness still loomed around them, but the bright orb on the horizon, the deadly sun that would continue to cook them as it rose in the sky, made it almost too hot to think.

"Do you see the transmitter?" Tor asked.

They worked their way to the edge of the pond and then sat in the water, neither one of them having any desire to go to shore. Tor reached for the black box, thankfully right where they left it, and turned it so that it faced them.

"Our phones have no signals," Roln announced, holding his phone at one angle and then another until giving up and clipping it back to his belt.

"That doesn't surprise me." There was too much rock and dirt for the phone signal to get back to Undrworld. "There's got to be some way we can send a message through this transmitter. It would at least let them know where we are.

Tor never claimed to be an expert with computers and electronics. His specialty had always been in battle, organizing missions. His leadership qualities had gotten him where he was now.

Some leader—stranded on the surface of his planet when the nation he led was unable to reach him.

And all because he was hell-bent and determined to learn why Ran Mose was sabotaging the passages, and searching desperately for someone on the surface.

None of the signals or knobs on the black box made a hell of a lot of sense to him. The last report was that the transmitter was working properly and he didn't need to sabotage it as well. Flipping open a panel on the side, he grinned when he spotted a small phone inside.

"Maybe this works," he told Roln.

Roln had been squinting at their surroundings and turned his attention to Tor. "Does this pond seem larger to you?"

Tor looked around him for the first time. "I guess it's possible that the explosions forced more water up here. It's not like the surface couldn't use it."

"How far away would you say the East Passage is from this pond?" Roln asked.

"Not quite a mile." He frowned at Roln. His guard would know that.

"What if they were trying to create their own passage to the surface with those explosions?" Roln pointed across the pond. "They would create another pond maybe a mile in that direction."

"Let's see if we can check in first," he said, pulling the receiver that was attached to the box by a black cord. "Syndi's village is in the other direction. As long as we steer clear of these people, some exploring might be a good idea."

He'd been aching to learn more about the surface ever since he'd discovered it was populated. Roln nodded, his attention focused on the phone. But Tor didn't doubt his guard was up to some exploring as well.

When he put the phone to his ear, there was no sound. Nor was there a keypad anywhere that he could see where he could dial a number. Listening for a moment, it dawned on him the line didn't sound dead.

"This is Tor Geinz," he said, curious if the line was being monitored.

"Tor, Ben Osk here. Damn good to hear your voice, Sir." Ben said something to someone else in the control center. "We've been monitoring the passages. I take it you're on the surface."

"Yes. What's the status of the passages?" As relieved as he was that they had communication, he feared the worst with the status of things down there.

Roln gave him an anxious look. He quit surveying the area around them and gave Tor all his attention.

"Best as we can tell at the moment without sending down a survey crew is that the East Passage is sealed. Sediment is floating heavy in the North and South passage, as well as the pond that leads to the surface." Again Ben paused, more than likely gathering information as he spoke. "The explosions have stopped for now."

"Any more communication from Ran Mose?" he asked.

"None."

That didn't surprise him. The whole thing about him coming to see Tor had been a ruse. He had no idea at this point what the leader's real intention was, other than it had to do with the surface. Someone up here had him making some desperate moves.

"Hold for about thirty minutes. We're going to head east up here. We're curious if Ran Mose tried to create another passage to the surface through the East Passage." He squinted in that direction as he spoke, and ran the warm water over his quickly drying skin. "I'll check back with you in less than an hour."

"Be careful, Sir," Ben Osk said.

The ground was too hot to walk on. And the longer they waited, the higher the sun rose. Neither of them would survive too long under its extreme heat.

"I say we wrap our shirts around our feet, and just move quickly so we're back in the water before that sun gets much higher," Tor suggested.

It wouldn't be a pleasant expedition, but one both of them were game to take on. Tearing their shirts, and wrapping the wet material around their feet, didn't do much to deter the heat from the ground. They moved quickly though, leaving the pond and treading across the dead land.

Guns pulled and wary of any movement or sound around them, they'd walked about ten minutes when the ground started appearing more cracked than before.

"It could just be from the heat," Roln said. He sounded tired.

The extreme temperatures were affecting Tor too. Everything around them looked the same—desolate and abandoned. If he hadn't met Syndi, been to her village, from what he saw now he would have guessed the surface uninhabitable.

Another crack in the ground almost tripped him. Heat made everything in front of them seem wavy. It was hard to distinguish what they saw. He swore the temperatures seemed to climb by the second.

Glancing behind them, he could no longer see the pond. Everything looked the same no matter where he turned.

"We need to mark the ground somehow so we can find our way back." He aimed his gun at the ground behind them and fired briefly. The ground turned black, smoke rising, although the sand and rock didn't catch on fire.

They continued this method until Tor couldn't tell how far they'd walked. Nothing seemed any different though, just dried-out land with no life of any kind for as far as they could see.

"Think we should turn back?" Roln asked.

They risked the chance of passing out from the heat, if they didn't get lost first. Tor could risk neither. He studied the cracks in the ground.

"Just a bit further," he decided.

Maybe it was his imagination, but the cracks seemed bigger, deeper. And then something shiny caught his eye.

"Look." He pointed.

It was almost impossible to pick up their pace. But the two of them moved toward the sparkling object.

It was water, bubbling up out of the cracks, and trickling over land that hadn't been wet in probably a good hundred years.

Chapter Ten

🔊

Syndi had about enough of Peg telling her what to do.

"You can sit and stare at that damned computer all day if you want. I'm going after him." Ever since she'd woken up she'd known something wasn't right.

Peg glared at her over the monitor at Tor's desk. "You know that isn't an option."

"Watch me."

At first, waiting in Tor's home, knowing sooner or later he'd return to her, had its appeal. She'd explored, investigated how he lived. A whole new world had been at her fingertips.

Where her world had been sand and dirt, so little water, and extreme burning heat, Tor lived in a world of stone and water—water everywhere. In the corner of his bedroom a small fountain poured water electronically over rocks for no apparent reason.

There was the pool in the kitchen. Peg had told her most homes had water in the rooms where families could soak. It kept their skin from drying out. Syndi understood dried-out skin, the flaking, the pain as it stretched over her bones.

Tor's home wasn't large though, and after an hour or so of exploring, she'd grown restless. Peg might have felt a bit uneasy about Syndi standing behind her watching her on the computer, but that was just too damned bad. Syndi didn't have anything else to do.

When Peg got word that there were tremors, and then explosions at the Four Passages, Syndi had almost wrestled her to get out of the house. Living on the streets had its advantages. If needed, Syndi could and would take on anyone to save herself. And in this case, save a man who had more than intrigued her.

It had been more than a surprise when Peg actually slammed her to the floor.

"He said to keep you here. He didn't say a damned thing about not hurting you." Peg had proven she was indeed a good fighter.

It was always good to know what you were up against.

But now, the Control Center Peg kept communicating with had just informed her that Tor was on the surface, a couple of the passages had collapsed, and they didn't have confirmation yet as to whether he was trapped up there or not.

"How the hell do you think you're going to go after him?" Peg jumped up from behind the desk and hurried after Syndi.

"Just because I'm not from your world, doesn't mean I'm incompetent." And Syndi was starting to get the impression that's exactly what they thought. "I'm not some bimbo to keep locked up in this house."

Peg glared at her with her hands fisted against her hips, and her feet spread far enough that she looked like she might leap at her with a moment's notice.

"I've got my orders," she hissed.

"From a man who will die on the surface." She'd give Peg two minutes to see reason, or she'd take her down and figure out how to get to those passages. "What kind of loyalty are you displaying when you refuse to let the only person in your world who can help him, go to him?"

Peg's phone buzzed, and the two women stared at it. With a sigh, Peg turned from her and answered it.

"Well, it looks like you're getting your way," she said when she hung up.

Syndi's heart leaped in her chest. "It's about fucking time. Let's go."

"We aren't going to the surface," Peg told her when she led the way along the dark, damp stone hallway outside Tor's home. "They've requested that I bring you to Control Central."

"What for?" She watched her footing, the darkness around her slowing her pace as they reached the circular opening in the ground.

Water splashed over the edge, making the stone floor slippery. Placing her palm flat against the wet wall next to her, she met Peg's gaze in the dark.

"We're a society built on rank and structure," Peg said quietly. "When orders are given, we follow them. We'll find out what they want when we get there."

But even once they were in the large cave with more computers and equipment surrounding her than she'd ever seen in her own world, she wasn't sure why they wanted her brought there. Some kind of argument seemed to be going on. Peg had joined the two other people she'd met before, Fern and Ben. The three of them huddled around one of the computers, discussing something in whispers.

Quick glances from the other people working there made her uneasy. Left standing alone, she studied the incredibly large cave, with its black moist walls climbing a good twenty feet before curving into the smooth stone ceiling.

The large table in the middle of the cave and the desks built into the walls looked like they were made out of cement. Smooth and crystallized, they were like everything else in this world, hard as a rock with an intense beauty.

"Syndi?" Fern pulled her out of her thoughts.

Peg and Ben watched her carefully while Fern gestured she should join them in a private room. Ben closed the door behind her, and she looked around at what appeared to be a small cave with the long beams of light in the ceiling she'd grown accustomed to seeing. A long narrow table with several chairs on either side filled the small area.

The four of them each took a chair and she found herself staring at faces filled with curiosity, and something that looked like anxiety.

"What is it?" she asked, sensing they all wished to pounce on her with questions.

"Tor and one of his guards have gone to the surface," Fern began, speaking slowly as if weighing every word. "Our last contact with him was several hours ago."

Fern didn't trust her. For whatever reasons, the woman seemed reluctant to share any of this with her. The strained expression on her face showed her desperation. They were approaching Syndi as a last resort.

She fought the urge not to fidget against the rock-hard chair. Keeping her expression blank, she looked at each of them, sensing their worry and trepidation. No matter, sending her after Tor made damn good sense.

"I'll find him." It took everything she had not to jump up and order them to get moving.

Fern nodded. "We've been studying your world through transmissions we've picked up. Your current status in your society is not to our advantage."

"What do you mean by that?" They insulted her. And they didn't even know her.

Anger rushed through her, making it impossible to sit still. Shaking some sense into the large-eyed woman across from her sounded like a damned good idea. Everyone in the village respected her.

"What she means to say," Ben added quickly, "it would be better if we returned you to the surface with means to appear as if you are one of the city people. We've studied your currency and credit system. You will need more power to do what we need you to do."

There was more involved here than getting Tor. And they didn't want her to know the full plan. Wondering just how loyal these people were to their leader, she leaned back, knowing any questions might make her appear a risk. Best to remain quiet, allow them to send her on this mission, and figure things out as she went along.

"We've created an account for you at a financial institution in your city of Detroit. With a transmitter that we can put on your body, you'll be in continual contact with us." Fern relaxed her expression, but those large eyes yielded her mistrust. "That way you'll be safe."

Even when she smiled it didn't reach her eyes.

"What makes you think Tor is in Detroit," she couldn't help but ask.

Their offer of money meant little to her. It wouldn't give her any more power than she had right now. Explaining how her society worked, that she could gather just as much information on the streets as they could get from their computers, would be a waste of breath. She'd let them play it their way, get her to the surface, and she would take over from there.

The other two glanced at Fern and she guessed her to be the leader among the three. Fern looked down, pressing her fingers together, her damp skin leaving a small puddle on the table. When she met Syndi's gaze, she licked her lips and looked to be taking a leap of trust.

"There is a leader among us, Ran Mose. He leads the East Passage." Again she spoke slowly. "He successfully closed off his passage from us earlier today, and damaged the other two passages. The tunnel you entered our world from appears to be okay."

Relief swarmed through Syndi but she kept her expression blank, watching Fern as she struggled for some reason with what she would say next.

Her hesitation grew old. "Time is passing. Tor won't survive on the surface. None of you would. Let me go, and I'll find your leader for you."

"There is information you need to know first." Ben spoke up, and then put his hand over Fern's, patting it reassuringly when she gave him a sharp look. "There are others of us on the surface. Ran Mose has an agenda that we aren't fully aware of, but we know enough to know there is danger. We want you prepared before we send you back to your home."

"I gathered that," she said, nodding, but nonetheless scooted her chair back. The sound reverberated through the room. "What all of you are forgetting is the surface is my home. I can move easily in the city, or in my village. Tor cannot. If you're sending me up there, let's get moving."

She stood and moved to the door. The others hurried after her and Fern fell in line alongside her when they left the room, guiding her toward another door.

"We have a small transmitter that we can put on you. That way you can stay in touch with us, and we can stay in touch with you." Fern hurried over to a small desk in what appeared to be a supply room of sorts, with shelves lining the cave walls.

Syndi glanced at the variety of equipment setting on the shelves. "You don't trust me."

Fern quit moving with her hand in midair, holding the small transmitter that looked something like a wristband.

Her expression softened. "You're right. But my options are limited, aren't they?"

"Yes. They are." At least the woman was honest. Syndi looked down at the device in Fern's hand. "How does this work?"

Fern reached for Syndi's wrist, explaining while she put it on her. "This button allows you to contact us."

There was no way she would wear this thing and it not be detected. She didn't voice her thoughts though. Let the woman have her say so she could get out of there.

"Peg has agreed to go with you," Fern added.

"What?" Syndi shook her head. "She won't survive out there. The more time you spend talking to me here, the longer it will take for me to find Tor. I'll move a lot faster on my own."

"You're right. The more time we take down here, the longer it will take on the surface. And Peg is fully briefed. A plot to find and destroy one of your people on the surface is underway right now. Peg has all the details and will advise you while you two search for Tor." Fern wouldn't be swayed from her decision.

With a sigh, Syndi nodded, and then followed Fern back to the large cave where Peg waited.

Whatever information Peg had to share with her, she didn't enlighten her during their drive in the tran-bus. Peg would be nervous though. It didn't surprise Syndi at all. She'd been terrified the first time she'd discovered this world. And she could exist down here. Peg would have a hell of a time on the surface.

As would Tor. They'd told her he'd been up there for several hours. When he'd pulled her out of her tent the previous night, his skin had still been damp. He'd hurried from the pond, found her, and had hurried back. This time, he'd been up there a lot longer. Her stomach twisted in knots. She didn't want to guess what condition he'd be in.

There was little conversation when they parked the tran-bus, and then walked alongside each other toward the pond. Debris floated in the pond that hadn't been there before. Several guards stood alongside the water, which Syndi swore looked like it swelled over its banks. Maybe it had been a good idea that Peg accompanied her. The guards simply nodded, as if already briefed on their mission.

Syndi leapt into the water first, not waiting for instruction. From this point forward, she would be in charge. Kicking toward the bottom of the pool, Peg remained alongside her, making no effort to move ahead.

But when they surfaced on the other side, Peg reacted exactly how Syndi had expected.

"Holy shit," she cried out, her hand immediately shielding her eyes. "What's that?"

"The sun?" Syndi guessed what Peg meant.

Peg dipped her face into the water, fiddling with something attached to her belt. Her light brown hair fanned around her face in the water. When she lifted her head again, she adjusted dark sunglasses over her face and smiled as if very proud of herself.

"That helps a lot."

Syndi didn't mention that most in the city wore such sunglasses. They were a privilege those in the village went without. Accustomed to the glare, she shrugged it off and swam to the shore.

"The pond is larger," she noted, standing on the sand and staring at the pond that once had been her quiet sanctuary.

Water streamed over the baked ground, seeping through the cracks in the earth. She didn't have to look up to know the sun almost reached the middle of the sky. It was almost lunchtime, and the villagers would have realized she hadn't slept in her tent by now. They would be looking for her. Glancing that way, she remembered her instructions that she was supposed to head for the city.

There would be no way to explain to everyone why she'd simply disappeared. One wrong word said, and her friends would have her arrested, dragged from her tent on some trumped-up charge. Stories would fly. More than likely she would have to allow those stories to stick, just so they could be her cover.

"Where is everyone?" Peg sat in the water, pulling something else off her belt. "This heat is overwhelming."

Peg wore the shorts most everyone in Undrworld wore. Tan and ending at her thighs, those creamy white legs of hers would fry under the sun. Glancing down at the clothes she'd had on when Tor hauled her out of her tent, her simple villager's dress that would mark her as who she was the second they arrived in the city. Loose-fitting, although wet at the moment and hugging her breasts and hips, it fell to her thighs. Her dark tanned legs and exposed arms wouldn't suffer under the sun. And her long wet hair would help keep her cool for a while as they trekked over the dead lands.

Glancing back at Peg, she doubted the woman would make it that far.

"You get accustomed to it." Syndi looked around her, praying no one would be wandering the dead lands. "We're in an isolated area. If there is anyone out here, they wouldn't be someone we'd want to see."

Peg looked up at her quickly. Her lips formed a thin line. With the large black glasses on, it was impossible to see her eyes. Other than the fact that her skin was so much paler, she'd almost pass as normal-looking—as long as she didn't remove her glasses.

Peg touched base with Fern and Ben. Using the small wristband that matched the one Syndi had been given, they confirmed that the transmitter alongside the pond was in working order, and then, finally Peg got out of the water.

"He went this way." Pointing east, the two of them stared over the dead lands, nothing but sand and sky visible for as far as they could see.

It was going to be one hell of a long day.

Peg complained of the heat, asked how Syndi managed to walk in the shoes that both of them wore, and then grew quiet, the heat obviously getting to her. Syndi's skin already stretched uncomfortably over her bones. Living in Undrworld would spoil her quickly. She'd spent a lifetime without water, relishing every drop she'd ever had. Getting accustomed to it being otherwise was a dream she wouldn't allow herself to enjoy.

For the first time in her life, her future wasn't clear to her. Meeting Tor, discovering his world, had opened up hopes and dreams that were too dangerous to indulge in. She would find him, make sure he returned to his people, and let it go at that. Thinking for one minute that there might be a future for them wasn't something she could afford to do. The only thing she'd focus on at the moment was staying alive long enough to find him.

"What in the hell?" She stared down at the ground, at the black hole that tore through the sand and cracked earth surrounding it.

"Someone's shot a hole into the ground." Peg stopped next to her, squatting down and touching the black sand.

"With one of your guns." Syndi looked around her. "Tor must have done this. It means something."

"Let's keep walking."

After a few minutes, they found another burnt hole in the ground, and then soon after, another one.

"I bet he created a trail so that he could find his way back." Syndi squinted ahead of them. "We've got quite a few miles before we hit the city."

But just a few minutes later she stopped, staring at the water that bubbled through the cracks in the ground. She'd never ventured this far. But the way the water soaked through the ground around it, almost disappearing as soon as it bubbled to the surface, she guessed it hadn't been like this for very long. The ground wasn't accustomed to the water.

"Take advantage of it," she told Peg, squatting down to scoop the fresh water into her hands. "Water isn't easily found up here."

Peg didn't need to be encouraged twice. Cupping her hand, Syndi poured the water over her arms, and then her legs, all the while searching the area around them. Peg used her hands as a cup and drank at the water greedily.

"This water is bubbling up from your world. Maybe those explosions caused more water to surface." Syndi wondered what it would take to make more water break through.

Something her aunt had mentioned about her mother, her commenting that all everyone had to do was start digging and the water would be there, made her realize that possibly her mother had known of Undrworld. If she'd been down there, for whatever reasons, she hadn't shared the information with anyone else.

Or maybe she'd tried, and died doing it.

Chills rushed over Syndi's skin in spite of the incredible heat. If only she knew what her mother had done. That way she wouldn't make the same mistakes.

"Let's keep moving," Peg said.

Leaving the bubbling water, she guided them through the dead lands toward Detroit. The sun baked her back when the skyline of buildings, tall and silver, blinding as they reflected the sun, came into focus. Waves of heat made the ground move in front of them, and it took a minute for Syndi to realize something moved toward them.

She hadn't been to the city in almost a year, but she knew a car when she saw one.

"Oh shit," she said, grabbing Peg's sweat-covered arm. "We're in trouble."

"I don't think so." Peg sounded almost relieved. "There is supposed to be someone coming for us."

Syndi looked at her in disbelief. "And when were you going to tell me this?"

"Right now."

This wasn't good. All her life, a car approaching meant trouble. Living on the streets as a child, she'd instinctively run when any car came near her. Perverts looking for pretty girls, or the law, bored, wishing to start trouble, was all an approaching car meant.

The dark green vehicle with blackened windows crunched over the dried earth with large black tires. Whoever drove it wore dark sunglasses and was no more than a shadow behind the windshield. Thin solar panels on the roof blinded Syndi and she shielded her eyes, her heart thudding hard in her chest when the vehicle pulled to a stop next to them.

A slap of cold air briefly hit them when the dark window lowered and air conditioning filled the scorching air around them.

For a moment, the dark-haired man behind the wheel looked like Tor.

"Is this Syndi Stone?" the man asked, sounding nothing like Tor.

"Yes." Peg reached for the back door, opening it and allowing more cool air to rush around them. "Get in," she told Syndi.

Even though they'd spent the day together, Peg was a stranger. And it wasn't easy reading expressions of people Syndi didn't know. With a quick glance, something about the way Peg pursed her lips didn't sit right with Syndi.

"Where are we going?"

The heat would tear into Peg, but Syndi could stand out there for hours, and had most of her life. She watched a trickle of sweat brush down Peg's temple.

"To Detroit." Peg gestured with her hand for Syndi to get in the car.

Syndi lowered her voice. "Who is this person?"

"He's one of us. It's okay," Peg also whispered, and wiped her hand over her damp hair. Although it was no longer damp from water, but sweat.

"Like none of you are bad guys," Syndi muttered.

Something behind Peg caught her attention. A movement in the sand, like something burrowing underneath the ground.

"You have no idea how to follow orders, do you?" Peg grew truly exasperated.

"Is there a problem?" The driver stepped out of the car. "It's hotter than hell in this miserable place and there's plenty of water in the back. Get in."

He stood as tall as Tor, with dark hair that fell around his face, just past his ears. It looked like he might be trying to grow it a bit longer, to fit into the style of the people on the surface. He wore the dark glasses, hiding his eyes. The fact that she wouldn't have known he was from Undrworld if Peg hadn't told her, made her even more nervous.

"There's no problem," Peg said, and pushed Syndi toward the rear door of the vehicle.

"Yes. There is. I want to know where we're going." Syndi held her ground.

Something stirred behind Peg, except this time the driver had his back to the movement too. Both of them pushed Syndi into the back of the car without an explanation. Turning to protest, her words caught in her throat when a third person appeared behind them.

Too frightened to scream, she didn't know whether to scramble into the vehicle, or force her way back out. Whoever it was had caked sand and dirt clinging to his body and hair. It wasn't until she saw those dark eyes, large and outraged, that she knew who it was.

"The lady asked a question." Tor grabbed the driver, lifting him by his shoulders, and then slamming him down so that he screamed when his cheek touched the hot metal of the vehicle.

"Tor!" Peg looked at him wide-eyed.

And she was visibly shaking. Syndi jumped out of the car, wanting to run to him. His skin looked almost burnt, red patches visible through the dirt and sand that covered him from head to toe.

"Unless you've turned traitor," Tor hissed at Peg, his look venomous, "disarm him and then go get Roln. Drag him to the car."

Syndi then noticed the bump in the dirt next to the freshly turned earth. Tor had buried himself and Roln with dirt and sand, protecting them from the intense heat. From the looks of the burns on his legs and arms, they had suffered greatly before using the ground to protect themselves.

Heatstroke or not, Tor still had the strength to pull the driver back, hit him hard in the side of the head, and render him unconscious. Dragging him to the back door, he shoved his body into the backseat.

Syndi quickly brushed the sand and dirt off Roln. He'd passed out from the heat and it took her and Peg to drag him toward the car.

"Do you know how to drive this thing?" Tor asked her.

She looked at the open door to the driver seat. "I've never driven in my life."

"Peg, you're driving." He quickly disarmed the unconscious driver and then ran around to the passenger side.

Syndi climbed into the back, surprised at how much room was inside. A long cushioned seat faced the driver with another cushioned seat facing the back. The two unconscious men sat with their heads leaning against the windows and Syndi took the seat closest to the driver. Tor climbed into a single seat next to the driver, instantly looking around as he took in the surroundings.

As surprised as she was with the agility that Tor moved, considering he was obviously suffering, the interior of the car brought her serious pause. It looked very much like the inside of a tran-bus. Even though she'd never driven a car, she'd been inside them before. More than once as a child she'd played in the abandoned cars and sometimes even lived in them. None of them looked like this. The seats were the same material as those in a tran-bus, even the dash looked foreign to her.

"This shouldn't be hard for you to drive." The cynical tone Tor used proved he'd seen the obvious as well. "Go back to the pond. We're grabbing the transmitter."

"We aren't going home?" Peg shifted the thing into gear and it lurched forward.

Tor ignored her question and looked over his shoulder at Syndi. "Find that water the driver mentioned."

A large black box was full of bottles of water. At least she recognized them, having seen the coveted bottles when they'd made trips to the commissary. Anyone in the village would have thought they'd died and gone to heaven to see a case this full with bottles.

Pulling two bottles from the box, she twisted the lids and then handed one to Tor and the other to Peg. Both gulped at the water greedily. Tor stopped before half finishing it and looked again at her.

"What did you agree to do?" he asked and at the same time handed her the bottle.

She shook her head. "There's plenty of water back here. You need it on your skin."

Grabbing another bottle, she dipped her fingers in it, and then rubbed them down her skin. Tor watched the action.

"Tell me what you were sent here to do." His gaze dropped down her body slowly.

Even with burns on his body, the way he looked at her made her heart pound furiously in her chest. He was fucking gorgeous no matter what condition he was in. Ignoring the sudden desire that rushed through her, she took a small sip, moistening her mouth so she could talk.

"Fern called Peg and me to your control center and asked that I come here to find you. She told me that my status up here wouldn't help you, and that they'd created an account so that I would have money, and appear to be one of the city people. There was more. I could tell she held back information. She did tell me that there was a conspiracy going on up here. But she said Peg would explain the rest."

Tor nodded and turned to Peg. Apparently it was debriefing time. She ignored the wave of disappointment when he no longer gave her any attention and started questioning Peg.

Using her bottle of water, Syndi revived Roln, who came to, coughing and sputtering. The driver next to him groaned, but remained unconscious. Nonetheless, when Syndi returned to her side of the back of the vehicle, she sat behind Tor.

"You want to explain to me why you were leaving in this vehicle." Tor's tone was so cold both women looked at him.

Peg sighed. "We should go back home."

"No. Damn it." Tor hit the dash so hard that Syndi jumped. "I want to know right this fucking minute what the plan was."

Peg managed to find her way back to the pond and slowed the vehicle alongside the water, the transmitter visible through the windshield.

"Syndi. Get the transmitter."

"Aren't you afraid she might run?" Suddenly Peg sounded hurt. An expression crossed her face that Syndi hadn't seen before. Her voice softened. "I've known you most of my life. We've fought alongside each other. I helped you gain control of the West Passage."

"Which is why you are going to tell me right now why you were ready to leave in this vehicle. And if you tell me you were coming to look for me, I swear I'll take you home and drag you ashore by your hair."

Peg gave him a condemning look. Syndi glanced from one of them to the other. There was a bond between these two, one that at the moment she felt she intruded upon. Her hand on the door handle, she hesitated, curious to hear what Peg knew.

Peg spoke so quietly it was hard to hear her. "Fern is second-in-command. She made a decision that she thought was in the best interest of all our people."

"And what was that decision?"

"Ran Mose would destroy the surface and Undrworld. He's insane. And all he wanted was the death of his bastard."

Tor's hand fisted as it rested on the dash. He seemed to grow in the seat next to Peg. "And so suddenly we know who this bastard is? We're in a situation to appease the East Passage leader?"

Peg nodded, staring Tor in the face. Wrinkling her brow, she dared to brush her fingertips over Tor's arm.

"Fern intercepted more transmissions. She found the name of his bastard."

Tor grabbed Peg's wrist. He squeezed hard enough that it had to be painful yet Peg's expression didn't change, and she didn't look away from him.

"What is his bastard's name?" he asked through gritted teeth.

"Syndi Stone."

Syndi's heart stopped beating. Suddenly there wasn't enough air in the vehicle. A cry escaped her lips. There had been so many unanswered questions throughout her life. But she'd never dreamed, never thought for a moment...

Holy fucking shit. She was the illegitimate child of one of Undrworld's leaders. And he wanted her dead.

Tor shoved Peg's wrist toward her body, looking for a moment like he would hit her. "And so you were simply going to deliver Syndi over to Ran?"

Peg bit her lip but then straightened. "I had hoped that we'd find you first."

Chapter Eleven

∞

Syndi's golden tan complexion had turned pale gray. She sat there, frozen, her hand on the handle to the door. But those small green eyes looked almost golden against her skin as she stared wide-eyed at Peg.

"You were taking me to a man who would kill me?" she asked, her voice barely a whisper.

Roln straightened, his attention on Syndi. Tor half expected her to pounce at any moment, and guessed the same thoughts ran through his guard's head too.

Peg twisted her body so she could see Syndi. "I'm a soldier. I follow orders. Just because I don't like them doesn't mean I'm going to question my commanding officer."

"Then your training is questionable," Syndi hissed, opening the car door so that burning heat flooded the car. "You were given a bad order, and if you aren't intelligent enough to see that then I'd question your ability to know right from wrong. Your land has been attacked, and already water seeps to the surface because of it. None of that can be reversed. What happens now will determine how our lives on the surface, and your lives underground will be. And you were just about to give the person who started all of that more power."

She jumped out of the vehicle, marching around it toward the transmitter, leaving the door open and the intense heat almost choking them.

"Fern believed your feelings for her might affect your judgment toward Undrworld." Peg spoke quickly, obviously trying to get back on his good side. "If I questioned her, she wouldn't allow us to come to the surface. I didn't know where or when we'd find you. But I damn well knew we wouldn't find you by waiting for you in your home."

"Are you supposed to report in?" He didn't like that Ran Mose might be infiltrating the West Passage.

Fern would be no match for Mose. Tor believed she mastered penetrating through his transmissions. She'd felt that she had leverage over Mose with Syndi. But her decision to hand Syndi over to Mose had just cost her rank.

"Yes. Once we met our contact," Peg said.

"Make that call. Don't mention that you've found me." He ignored Peg's frown.

Syndi had the transmitter in her arms as she walked toward the vehicle. Her brown hair floated around her narrow hips. She held her head high, her expression determined as she moved with ease. It was as if she didn't notice the overwhelming heat. She didn't squint. Her dark skin glistened under the sun.

Yet she was one of his kind. At least half of her was. And not only that, but she was the daughter of the greatest leader Undrworld had ever known. At least, once he'd been a great leader.

No woman he'd ever known compared with Syndi's style and grace. Her actions were simple yet dignified. She fought like a warrior, determined, ready to demand that everyone around her see what was right, and that they act to their fullest potential. Tor never imagined what the perfect woman to swim by his side would be like. His heart swelled, pain tightening through him when he realized Syndi was that woman. She stirred more than need in him, she touched his soul. Whatever it took, he would make her his—permanently. There was no other woman for him.

Remembering what he'd heard Ran Mose say about threats from the surface, there were others who knew who Syndi was, knew of her heritage. She dropped the transmitter on the floor of the back of the vehicle, the thud stirring the driver to consciousness. Immediately Roln pointed a gun to the driver's head. Syndi stepped on the driver's foot when she climbed in. He moved toward her, and Roln shoved the gun into his temple.

She adjusted herself on the bench seat behind him. "I need to make contact with my village," she told him.

If Ran Mose were this close to her village, more than likely he knew where she lived. Contacting them might not be in her best interest. Syndi was pissed though. He would share his decisions on that matter with her later.

"Make the call," he told Peg.

She adjusted the band on her wrist and then spoke quietly into it, verifying that they were on their way to Detroit.

"Now then." Tor stared into the blank expression of the driver, more than likely one of Ran Mose's men. "You'll give her directions to your destination."

"What?" Syndi cried out, grabbing the back of his seat and looking like she wanted to wring his neck.

He put his hand over hers, and clamped down when she tried to pull away. "Trust me," he said quietly. "We're going to have a little discussion with Ran Mose."

"He won't be there," the driver told him.

Which was damned good news. That bought them planning time.

"Oh yes. He will be," Tor told him.

Roln kept his gun aimed at the driver as they entered into the city. Peg wiped moisture from her forehead while navigating through cars that drove over paved surfaces in between tall buildings. In spite of the overwhelming heat, people walked up and down the sides of the street. They were all dark-skinned like Syndi, yet most of them seemed to have very light-colored hair.

"Pull in here and then stop at the gate," the driver told Peg. "There's a card in the storage box on the dash. You slide it into the box that's on that post. Roll down the window by pushing the button next to your arm."

"If this is a trick," Tor told him, "I promise you won't live through the day."

"All the people here live behind locked gates. It gives them protection."

"He's right," Syndi said, brushing her hair over her shoulder. "Theft is a common crime in the city."

Moisture glistened over her skin. Tor noticed it on all of them. Their skin seemed to be creating its own water, although once when he tapped his finger to his lips, he realized it was salty. And even though he was damp with this moisture, his skin still stretched like it was too dry. Heat glared through the windows, burning his skin, which itched miserably from the sand and dirt still covering him. More than likely they were all as miserable.

Peg found the card and rolled her window down, which slid silently into the door. The terrible heat outside immediately suffocated him and he wondered why the cars were even designed so the windows would go down. Maybe humans on the surface didn't have the laser technology his people had which would have allowed the box to simply read it was them and open the gate.

Peg slid the card into the box, and the gate opened.

"Drive to the second building, and the door with the number two on it is the home that we want," the driver instructed.

"Who will be there?" Tor asked.

"No one. Once we arrive there I notify my commanding officer."

No one stood outside around the tall gray buildings. Peg stopped the vehicle, parking it in between two other similar-looking vehicles and then pocketing the keys. Tor held his hand out to her.

"I'll take those," he told her quietly.

She didn't say anything but handed the keys to him. She bit her lower lip though, looking down. They got out, heading toward the door with the number two on it. Peg and Roln walked on either side of the driver. Tor remained behind, his attention turning to Syndi.

The sun glared so hard his eyes burned. His flesh burned, feeling like it would ignite into flame if he stood under the sun another minute. Syndi's world was void of color, nothing but the deadly sun and a planet of gray ground, hard and cracked where exposed, showing its years of abuse and old age. Even the buildings were gray. The lack of color, of life, of any sign of happiness, would make this a tough place to live.

Yet Syndi had run from him, returned to this place. She was at home here, walking tall by his side, her strong personality and natural beauty the only thing appealing around him.

He wanted to assure her that she was safe, that absolutely no one would harm her. Syndi held her head high, not looking up at him, but watching while the driver slid the card into a slot on the door and it slid open.

"We'll make sure no one's here," Roln said quietly.

"That's okay. I'm anxious to meet my father." Her words stunned everyone.

They were inside, and the door closed behind them when all of them looked at her. Roln and Peg moved quickly through the home, Roln taking the driver by the arm while inspecting every room.

Syndi seemed oblivious to their search but instead walked into the large room, running her hand over furniture, her gaze darting from object to object. She had the same look of awe on her expression that she'd had when she'd first entered his home.

"Have you ever been in a city home before?" he whispered, coming up behind her and brushing his fingers down her neck, stroking her gill.

Her shoulders lifted slightly, an obvious chill rushing through her. Instead of leaning back into him though, she moved forward, walking away from his touch.

"No." Her clothes clung to her damp body, offering an incredible view of her narrow waist, and that tight perfect ass as it swayed when she walked.

He stayed within hand reach, following her into another room, the kitchen. She walked up to a hole in the counter and turned a knob. Water flowed from a silver tube and she laughed, although there was little humor in it.

"Come here," she instructed, cupping her hands and then turning.

She seemed surprised that he was right behind her. Looking up at him, her dark eyes sparked for a moment. The interest was there. Lust swarmed inside her. Alive and vibrant, there wasn't another woman like her. She looked down quickly. Her expression turned serious and she let the water drip from her fingers, soaking his arms and chest as she continually cupped her hands and poured the water over him.

"So many of us die without water while it runs this freely in the city," she murmured, her bitterness over the discrimination obvious.

She ran her hands down his arms, around his neck, over his face, letting the water soak through him. He never looked away from her, allowing her to soak his flesh, rinse the dried sand and dirt from him. Her touch was gentle, moist, and the water cold. She created a fever inside him though. With every stroke, every caress, her expression focused on her task, his muscles hardened with a desire more carnal than he'd ever experienced before.

Standing just a few inches shorter than he, her long lashes fanned over her eyes while she cupped her hands, filled them with water, and then let it flow down his chest, soaking his shirt. She rejuvenated him. She cared for him like a mother would a child. Yet there was nothing motherly about her touch. Her long narrow fingers spread over his chest, pressing against his heart, bringing the fever inside him to a boiling point.

She cupped her hands with more water. If she touched him again he would take her right here in this odd kitchen. Grabbing her wrists, he forced the water in her hands to drip down her front. Her shirt clung with moisture to her full ripe breasts. The view drained all blood from his brain.

"We're the only ones here," Peg announced, walking in on them.

She walked right up to them, leaning against the counter next to Syndi and staring him in the face.

"Did you expect there to be others?" Syndi didn't blush.

She met Peg's hard stare with an equally defiant one.

"Allow me to bring in the transmitter and make sure this place is secure," Roln suggested, following Peg into the room.

Syndi turned and filled her hands with more water, then poured it over his chest, running her hands down his shirt.

Tor looked at Roln, nodding.

"You should soak yourself down with water," Syndi said, finally giving Peg her attention.

"I'm fine," Peg said quickly, ignoring Syndi and looking at him. "What do we do with the driver?"

"Find something to tie him up with," Tor ordered.

He doubted the driver would give them any trouble. But Ran Mose knew he was here. And the man would bring trouble. Not knowing when it would arrive, they didn't have time to waste.

Syndi stopped Peg from leaving, grabbing her arm. "You're not fine. You'll dry out if you don't soak yourself down."

"You aren't in charge here," Peg said, and pulled her arm free from Syndi.

"Nor are you." Syndi stood as tall as Peg. Even though he doubted she had any warrior training, she moved to stand directly in front of Peg. "But I've lived on the surface all of my life. If I go more than a few hours without rubbing water on my skin, it starts to peel. Go a day, and it begins to shed right off me. It will make you stand out. We can't afford that right now. So put whatever animosity you have toward me to the side. We work together, or I'm out of here."

He'd be damned if she was going anywhere.

Peg looked up at him, that look he knew so well. She was about to explode. And her temper wasn't pretty.

"Go tie him up," he told her quietly.

Peg ignored the water and walked out of the room. Roln turned and left also. Tor swore he saw an amused look on the man's face. He couldn't help feeling a bit of pride over the way Syndi stood up to Peg. She had no idea how strong a warrior Peg was. He wasn't pleased with the way she'd followed Fern's orders, but that could be discussed later.

"She's jealous of me," Syndi said quietly when they were alone.

If that were true, Peg had a hell of a lot to be jealous about. He had no intentions of letting Syndi get away. He reached around her, pressing her against the counter.

"She's not jealous. Protective maybe, but not jealous." Now wasn't the time to explain his almost lifelong friendship with Peg. He cupped his hands under the running water behind her, and then let the water drip over her hair. "And you have no reason to be jealous of her."

Her eyes had fluttered shut when the water dripped down her. She didn't open them, but a chuckle escaped her.

"You have your world to protect. And I will never turn my back on my home. Don't get any expectations." She spoke so calmly, as if her words wouldn't affect him.

Pressing into her, allowing her to feel his cock stir to life, he whispered, "Expectations allow us to move forward. Without them, we die."

He poured more water over her head, watching the streams flow over her lashes, down her cheeks. More than anything he wanted to lick the water droplets from her face, devour her, make her weak with need for him.

"Do you want to fulfill my expectations?" she asked, lazily raising her lashes and looking up at him.

"I'm sure I can," he said, pouring more water over her head, and then letting his fingers stroll down to her neck, caressing her gills.

She sucked in a breath, her cheeks blushing a warm shade of pink. Her breasts swelled against his chest, her nipples puckering like hard pebbles. He fought the urge to cup them in his hand. Lust swarmed in her expression. An ache hardened every muscle inside him. She craved him, her arousal adding to her wild spirit.

"Bring my father to me," she said.

It was the last thing he expected her to say. But it shouldn't surprise him that discovering who'd sired her had her curiosity piqued.

"I promise you'll meet him." And he'd make damn sure the man wouldn't hurt her either.

"Tor," Roln called from the other room.

He backed away from Syndi, reaching to brush his finger over her lips, a silent promise that he'd take care of the other needs she had that she was too stubborn to voice.

Roln had the phone that attached to the transmitter to his ear when Tor joined them in the living area. Peg stood next to the driver, who was bound to a chair. They all looked at him when they entered the room.

Roln cupped his hand over the voice piece of the phone. "Fern has broken in to more transmissions from Ran Mose."

Tor watched the driver fidget in his chair.

"What has she learned?"

"He knows we're here. Apparently he has several of his people on their way over. The plan is to bring Syndi to him. Sounds like he has no intention of coming to the surface." Roln watched him, waiting to hear what he should tell Fern.

"How soon will his people be here?" Tor asked.

"All she heard was that they were on their way," Roln told him and then looked at the driver. "Are they already on the surface?"

The driver straightened, glaring at Tor, but remained silent.

"How many are coming?" There were just the three of them. He wouldn't rely on Syndi's abilities to fight, even though she'd already bested Peg once.

"But Ran Mose isn't one of them." Syndi crossed her arms over her chest, pacing to the other side of the room, her damp hair clinging to her back.

She turned and looked at all of them. "I'm returning to my village."

"Like hell you are," Tor said.

"Ran wants me. But he's assuming his people will bring me to him." Syndi shook her head, that determined look he was coming to know crossing her face. "Here he can take me without anyone noticing. But in my village, it would cause quite a scene if his people strolled in and tried to walk away with me."

Peg looked at him. She wanted to say something. In fact, it ate at her to remain silent.

Tor let out a sigh, meeting Peg's gaze, seeing that she understood. He didn't want to lose Syndi, but this was a matter of protecting their nation. Peg worried he'd put his growing attraction for Syndi over the wellbeing of the West Passage. She should know him better than that.

"Take Peg with you. I can stay here with him," Roln said, pointing to the driver. "If there are too many of them, I just won't let them in."

Tor stared at Syndi.

"We don't have much time," she urged.

"Peg stays here." Tor pointed a finger at her when she would have objected. "Unless you are grossly outnumbered, capture the men who come to take Syndi."

He then walked over to Syndi, brainstorming as he took her by the back of the neck and guided her out the door. The sun instantly burnt his skin, which was already too tender from being out in that sand and dirt for a few hours. Moisture unlike anything he'd ever experienced clung to his skin, making him feel sticky and itchy. Looking down to avoid the glare, he hurried her to the car, pushing her in the driver's side and then climbing in when she scooted to the other seat.

"Wait a minute," she said, climbing into the back and then scurrying around while he turned in time to see her sweet ass facing him.

"What are you doing?"

She straightened, her hands full of empty water bottles. "I'll be right back," she told him, leaving the vehicle through the back door before he could stop her.

She ran back to the door, banging on it with her elbow, until it opened slightly and she was let in. Within minutes she was back out again, the bottles full with water. Hurrying into the backseat, she arranged the bottles in the box where the remaining water bottles still were.

"A box like this would be a gift none of us would expect in our lifetime," she told him.

Tor nodded, taking a minute to familiarize himself with the console of the vehicle.

"Can you drive it?" she asked, climbing up to sit next to him.

"Yes." It was rather interesting that the vehicle had a similar layout to tran-buses. "Obviously our technology originated from the surface."

"That would make sense," she said quietly. "What doesn't make sense is why some of us stayed on the surface while others of us moved underground."

"We don't have much reliable history prior to World War Three," he said, igniting the engines, and then pulling the gearshift until he found the right gear to make the vehicle move. "Of course we know prior to the war we lived on the surface, but our history states the surface became uninhabitable."

"The war was over a hundred and fifty years ago. The planet was destroyed. The atmosphere torn apart. And I know it was impossible to go outside. Back then we lived in shelters connected to each other by tunnels." She nibbled at her lip, looking outside as they moved on to the paved area where lines of vehicles moved slowly between the tall buildings. "I've seen pictures in history books. Maybe I can get my hands on one to show to you sometime."

Driving the vehicle didn't take much effort. Even through the tinted windows, the glare hurt his eyes. There wasn't much out there worth looking at anyway, a gray world filled with people who didn't seem to give each other the time of day. It wouldn't surprise him at all if he could walk down their street and no one noticed the difference in their physical appearance. Most everyone wore the dark sunglasses and seemed intent on getting where they were going. Ran Mose could have hundreds of his warriors up here, and none of these people would even know.

Reaching out, he brushed her hair behind her shoulder so that he could see her face. Syndi turned and looked at him.

"This visit of yours to your village will be short-lived," he told her. "I'll come for you tonight."

She shook her head. "Already you have burns on your skin from the sun."

"This isn't up for debate." She wasn't safe unless she was with him. He wouldn't have any arguments. "Offer whatever explanation that you wish to your people, but I won't have you up here where I can't ensure your safety."

She pointed toward the front window. "You need to get off this street. Turn right up here and that will take you out of town. We'll find a side road and head out into the dead lands."

Making note of the landmarks around him—he would need to return for Roln and Peg, and hopefully a few prisoners—he followed her instructions. They drove in silence until the city was behind them, and a dead world of sand and dirt surrounded them as far as he could see. She guided him over the baked ground, somehow able to tell when everything around them looked the same, which way to go until the small pond glistened under the sun in front of them.

"I'll get out here," she said, climbing into the back to get the box of water.

There wasn't much time. Leaving Roln and Peg in the home in Detroit alone for very long wouldn't be safe. There were matters to discuss with Fern once he returned home. The sooner he was brought up to date with everything concerning Ran Mose, the better he'd be at making a call as to what to do next. Finding Ran Mose, questioning him, would have to be top priority.

Grabbing Syndi's wrist, he pulled her to him. She didn't put up much of a fight. No matter that she felt the need to help her people, she wanted him. And he knew she needed him.

"Use this communicator," he told her, rubbing the band that was on her wrist with his thumb. He could feel the rapid beat of her pulse when he touched her skin. "If anything goes wrong, contact me."

She nodded. "I'll be fine."

"You'll be better once I have you with me again." Pulling her into his arms, he cradled her into his lap and then crushed his mouth over hers.

Syndi let out a small cry, opening to him, her arms wrapping around his neck as she returned the kiss.

Running his fingers through her hair, he tangled them in the thick strands and pulled. Her head fell back and he traced kisses down her cheek, to her chin, and then tasted her flesh as he stroked her neck with his tongue.

God. He didn't want to let her go. Everything inside him screamed to turn this vehicle around and force her to go back with him.

Tangling his fingers in her hair, he pulled her face inches from his, watching as she panted for air. Her lashes fluttered over her eyes as she took a moment to focus up at him.

"You have four hours." Giving her that much time was dangerous.

She tried to shake her head but he gripped her hair and she couldn't move.

"Too much is at risk." Her lips were wet and swollen from his kiss. "I won't have you coming back up here when the city is already looking for people from Undrworld."

He frowned, remembering that she'd mentioned that before. Again, confirmation that Ran Mose had his soldiers scouring the surface for her.

"You will give no indication of knowing about Undrworld." Letting go of her hair, he ran his hand down her shirt, cupping her breast, watching as the nipple puckered against the fabric.

"I've already decided how to handle matters," she said on a breath. "After dark, I'll return to the pond. Meet me there, or I'll come to you."

Syndi was young. But she would be the perfect lady to swim by his side. Yet she was willful, determined. More than likely, years of hard living had made her ruthless, convinced she could handle life on her own.

That and the simple fact that she came from the bloodline of his history's greatest leader excited him.

"If I don't hear from you, I will come after you." And he better hear from her soon.

Chapter Twelve

ॐ

Sweat soaked her clothes, and every muscle ached when Syndi reached the edge of her village carrying the box of water. A handful of children noticed her first.

"What is it?"

"What do you have?"

They circled around her, drawing attention, as she forced every step until she made it to her tent. Putting the box down, she struggled to remove the transmitter from her wrist. Her heart exploded in her chest when her tent flap opened behind her. Quickly she shoved the transmitter under her mat.

"Where have you been?" Aunt Mary wiped her hands on her dress as she hurried to Syndi.

Syndi almost collapsed on to her mat, exhausted from the heat and anxiety over whether her half-plotted plan would work or not.

"You wouldn't believe me if I told you," she answered, keeping her voice at a whisper.

Children huddled around the tent, more than likely assuming that whatever was in the box wasn't for them, but still bested by curiosity.

The flap pulled back fully, her uncle filling the opening, blocking the glare of light behind him with his husky presence.

"Tell me it's not starting again," he said, his attention focused on his wife.

"I don't know anything yet." Aunt Mary shook her head then looked at Syndi. "The entire village has been looking for you."

"I guessed as much," she said, fingering the box still on her lap. "And I'm sorry. I didn't realize I'd been gone so long." She squinted at Uncle Paul. "And what is happening again?"

Her uncle waved a chubby finger at her. "I won't have you sending your aunt into a fit of worry like your mother did."

"My mother," Syndi whispered. "She would disappear for lengths at time?"

"Never mind that," her uncle said, suddenly cross. "You better have a believable explanation as to where you've been."

"I found water," she told them, smiling and patting the box in her lap.

Her aunt and uncle stared as she opened the box and showed them all the bottles of water.

"What have you done?" her aunt whispered.

"Nothing wrong. Nothing illegal," she assured both of them.

Pulling two bottles from the box, she handed one to each of them. Her aunt pulled the lid, taking a quick drink. Her uncle hesitated for a moment, as if the bottle might transform into something hideous, before taking it.

"How could you have all this water and then tell us you've done nothing wrong?" Her uncle held the water, but didn't open the bottle. Instead, he turned it in his hand, looking at the label. "This came from a store. Who gave it to you?"

Syndi sighed quietly, knowing no matter what form of the truth she offered, they wouldn't believe her.

"How many know I've been gone all day?" she asked.

"Perry told me this morning that you weren't in your tent last night," Uncle Paul said, lowering his voice to a grumbly whisper. "Bertha sent the kids over for you around noon. When they came up empty-handed old Ralph was sent over to see if we knew where you were. You know how loud he speaks. Damn fool can't hear a thing anyone says."

"Yeah. I know." And she imagined that by her uncle's brief soliloquy, practically the entire village of Camden knew she'd been gone since sometime during the night.

"Tell us you've found a nice man from the city, that he can't live without you, and wants to bless you with all of his riches," her aunt suggested.

Syndi had always enjoyed the way her aunt's eyes sparkled when she said something amusing. If only her aunt knew how close to the truth she was. Although nice wasn't the word she would use to describe Tor. Stunning maybe, demanding definitely, aggressive…controlling.

She reached for one of the bottles and opened it, drinking freely. The water did nothing to cool down the heat that swarmed through her, heat that wasn't from the intensity of the sun against her tent walls.

"Perry was right. I did leave during the night. One of the men resembling the man in the pictures the council members posted entered the village last night. I followed him."

Her aunt gasped and her uncle crossed his arms against his thick chest. Someone nudged her uncle, and he jumped then turned quickly. Both women squinted against the sudden light, which Perry blocked when he filled the opening of the tent.

"Where the hell have you been?" he barked, as if he had a right to know. "We about had all the men scouring the dead lands for you."

Her uncle stepped inside her tent, with Perry now filling the opening, his hand gripping the tent flap so that enough light filled the small area. With three adults in her tent, there was little room to move. Claustrophobia made her heart race, along with Perry's words. The last thing she needed was half the village burning to death in the dead lands looking for her.

Of course, if they found the pond, they would be better off than they'd been all their lives.

She ignored Perry's demanding question. "I followed him into the dead lands. They had so much water. I just happened to get a hold of this box and carried it back with me. They had it in their car."

"Look at all that water," Perry said, but then his eyebrows almost touched each other when he frowned, squinting at her with a scrutinizing stare. "Where have you been? I never noticed a car."

"I carried the box back here." She needed to get them off the questions and get them to focus on something else. "But I learned some things. Things that can help us. I need your help though, and your trust that I'm not crazy."

Her aunt had been looking at her uncle. Syndi had been staring at the box, talking to them. But her aunt and uncle had worried expressions on their faces. Her aunt worried her lower lip with her teeth, while she rolled the bottle of water in her hands and focused on her husband.

"What do you need help with?" Perry asked.

"To dig," Syndi told him. "I want us to dig for water."

"Oh God. No," her aunt suddenly wailed.

Uncle Paul reached down for her, lifting Aunt Mary into his arms.

"I won't be able to handle it if she disappears too," her aunt said, suddenly sobbing. "They'll kill you, Syndi. They will come and take you away and I won't ever see you again."

Syndi shoved the box of water off her lap, standing quickly and squeezing her aunt's arm.

"I'm not going to die," she told her aunt. "I don't know what my mother knew," she said quietly. "But she had some information. And she wasn't crazy. Please trust me."

"What are you all babbling about?" Perry was suddenly annoyed. "Why do you want us to dig?"

"I want to find out if what I heard the…umm…mutant saying was true." Tor didn't want her mentioning anything about Undrworld to them. But if they learned on their own, discovered the water, and then possibly with time, found out about the people beneath them, she wouldn't be going against Tor's wishes.

He looked out for the best interests of his people. She had to keep that in mind. And her focus had to be on what was best for her family, her friends, her village.

They needed water.

"We're going back to our tent," Uncle Paul announced.

"Uncle Paul," Syndi began.

"No," he said harshly, raising his hand while keeping a firm hold on his wife, who'd buried her face in his chest. "It was this kind of nonsense that got your mother killed. Now you go find out if Bertha still needs your help. Get your mind off this foolish digging notion of yours."

The two of them moved around Perry, who stepped to the side so they could leave. He watched from right outside of their tent for a moment, before turning his attention back to her.

"Who did you leave with?" he asked, entering the tent and letting the flap fall behind him.

"I didn't leave with anyone. I followed him," she lied, looking Perry straight in the eye.

Fooling him wouldn't be hard. And he would tell the others. Once the villagers believed her, they would band together and do what she asked. Whatever mistakes her mother made, she wouldn't make the same ones. If only she knew exactly what those mistakes had been.

Perry scowled, and then without warning, leapt at her. Grabbing her arms, his fingers pinched her flesh until it hurt.

"You aren't strong enough to overtake a man," he hissed. "Now tell me the fucking truth."

She struggled against his grip. "You're hurting me," she whispered. "Let go of me."

"I could force you to fuck me, make you give me what you willingly gave me years ago," he continued, ignoring her pleas.

More than anything she wanted to spit in his face, knee him in the groin, anything to make him take his sweaty hands off her. A sudden pain twisted through her as Tor appeared in her mind. He'd send Perry flying for grabbing her like that. But then what would he think of her plan on creating awareness among the villagers?

She shoved thoughts of him out of her mind.

"Perry. I didn't fight off any man. They never saw me." His point was clear. And although he was more than annoying with the way he was making it, he'd see that she understood. "Now let go of me."

He let out a heavy sigh and released her, shrugging as he took a step backward.

"And how is it that you were never seen?" He didn't believe her.

She had to make herself more convincing. "They don't do well with the heat. I wanted to know what he was doing here. It wasn't hard to stay in the shadows. He almost staggered out of the heat. More than once I fought the urge to go help him."

They'd played games as children hiding in the shadows, seeing how long they could go unnoticed. He'd been at her side more than once as they spied on the city people, managing not to be seen for long periods of time.

"Where did you go?" He squatted in front of the box, pulling out one of the bottles of water and examining it.

"I followed him into the dead lands, to a car. But like I said, he didn't handle the heat well. He passed out when he reached the car. I decided to explore it, since he was out flat on the ground. There was a radio transmitter in the car. I listened for a while. Then I saw this box of water and brought it back with me."

"What did you hear on the radio?" He opened one of the bottles and sniffed at it before taking a small sip.

He was starting to believe her story. This was going to work.

"I didn't understand most of it." If she came up with too many answers at once, she would be questioned. Best to be vague and let him feel he would figure out the rest. "But wherever they are from, they have a lot of water. They kept commenting on how they couldn't believe how we had no water."

Perry frowned, studying the box, and then straightening, looking down at her. "Do your best to remember every word and tell me."

She nodded, putting on a show of concentrating. "I remember something about keeping an eye out for someone. I don't think they all trust each other. Then there was the comment about the water. And something about the heat killing them if they didn't get back soon."

"Back where?"

"Back home. And wherever their home is, I don't think it's far from here."

"Why do you say that?"

She opened one of the bottles and dipped her finger into the narrow opening, moistening her flesh and then wiping the drops of water over her arm. Already her skin stretched painfully over her body from the heat.

She took her time answering. Frowning as if trying to remember, she spoke slowly. "Something about returning home and bringing back more enforcements in the morning."

"Enforcements for what? And why do you think digging will accomplish something?" he asked.

Syndi shrugged. She had his interest. Perry would help convince the other villagers if he believed her.

"These people don't look like us. But they don't live that far away. And they talk about all this water. Well, if there was somewhere around here where there was a lot of water, we'd know about it, right?"

Perry raised an eyebrow, nodding slightly.

"I think they live underground," she said quietly, conspiratorially. "It would explain their really big eyes. They aren't accustomed to the light."

"Damn, girl." He shook his head.

For a moment he looked at her as if she'd lost all sense in her head.

"We'll discuss this with everyone else, pass out the water."

Not realizing she'd been holding her breath, she exhaled, smiling. "The water is going to be such a treat."

She'd been looking forward to everyone's faces when she passed the water around. "Let's carry it over to the main tent."

"Not so fast." Perry held up his hand.

Syndi frowned. "Now what?"

"There are many who remember your parents. Your aunt and uncle didn't like anything you had to say. I don't know why. But there will be others who might react the same way, thinking a pattern is occurring."

Conspiring with Perry seemed weird. She'd known him all of her life, but trusted him about as far as she could throw him. He would help her with this, as long as he saw gain in it for him. At the moment, hopefully that gain was more respect out of the villagers, especially if they found water. Also bringing news to the main tent always gave the one bringing it prestige.

"You're right," she said, willing to allow him to feel control over how the news of strangers in the village, and possibly water they could dig for. "Maybe we should approach a few at a time."

"That's what I was thinking. Bertha was looking for you. Go see her, talk to her if she's alone. She probably knew your mother pretty well." He grabbed a few bottles of the water and tucked them under his shirt. "I'm going to talk to a few people too. Make sure you're back at your tent by dark."

He pulled the tent flap open. She grabbed a few of the bottles, using her shirt to hold them against her, and ducked out of the tent. Taking off before he could order her around further, she ignored the pain that stretched through her skin as the sun beat down on her. For now, Perry at least backed her story, and hopefully would help convince the villagers to start digging.

They couldn't possibly dig big enough of a hole that it would bring any suffering damage to Undrworld. And making the villagers more aware of people from Undrworld being around them would make it harder for Ran Mose to come in and try and kidnap her.

She had every intention of meeting her father, and soon. But she would do it under her terms, not his.

Thinking of what Tor might think of her half-formed plan didn't make her tummy sit well. His dark eyes glowed in her mind.

Fortunately, Perry had his own agenda. For now, she wouldn't worry about what that might be. As long as he convinced others in the village that these "mutants" were both good and bad, and that a lot of water might exist underground, she would let him be to jaw his head off.

Approaching the main tent, Perry already knelt next to a couple other men, speaking in hushed tones. She ignored the looks they gave her, searching through those lingering before returning to their tents for dark. Bertha wasn't there.

And that was a good thing. Hurrying toward the village doctor's tent, she found Bertha searching through several dilapidated boxes inside her tent.

"Now is a good time for you to show up," the old woman said, scowling at her. "I had more work than a soul should endure during a day. And where were you then? Nowhere. Not around when there is work to do."

Her voice faded as she continued to mumble her discontentment with Syndi.

"I'm sorry, Bertha," Syndi said, meaning it. "I brought you a gift."

She unwrapped the bottles of water that she'd kept concealed in her shirt and handed them to the old woman.

Bertha quit searching for whatever it was she was looking for and took the bottles.

"I'll be damned." She sat on her tent floor, a gaunt and petite woman, looking little more than a bony figure covered by a too loose-fitting dress. "What do we have here?"

"They're for you." Syndi smiled. "May I talk with you for a bit?"

"Problems. You bring me problems." Bertha clucked her tongue and waved at the space in front of her. Not that there was a lot of it. "Sit. Tell me what bothers you. Everyone expects Bertha to fix everything."

Syndi did her best to make herself comfortable opposite Bertha on the uneven tent floor. The old woman brushed gray strands of thinning hair from her face. Her tanned skin was covered with large freckles, and wrinkled. She made a show of hiding two of the bottles of water, and then opened the third, taking a long drink and then pouring water into her palm before patting her face. Pale eyes studied her, while Syndi took a minute to figure out the best way to start the conversation.

"I found an old journal that belonged to my mother," Syndi began, watching Bertha closely to capture her immediate reaction to the subject she broached.

"I never knew Samantha kept a journal. What did it say?" If Bertha had any preconceived opinions of her mother, her expression gave no indication.

"She mentioned adopting me, bringing me home."

Bertha clucked. "Adopted you?" She snorted. "I guess maybe it was better to call it that."

"What do you mean?" No one had ever given any indication that there was anything wrong with the way her parent's had obtained her. "Will you tell me what you remember?"

"I remember all of it." Bertha straightened, frowning, as if her memory had just been questioned.

"I'd love to hear about it."

"And what good will that do you?" Bertha snapped, her usual harsh personality coming through as she pursed her lips.

Knowing Bertha all her life helped in dealing with her. "I bet I was a pain in the ass baby," she said, making a face that she hoped looked apologetic.

"What baby isn't?" Bertha looked at the ceiling of her tent, as if hoping some deity had patience with her for all she'd endured.

"There were some things my mother mentioned in her journal that didn't make a lot of sense to me. I figured you'd be the one to talk to about it."

Bertha took another long drink of her water, the clear fluid dampening her thin lips and dribbling to her chin. She wiped her face with the back of her leathered hand. "You know I see everything. Everyone knows it. A burden, I tell you. Knowing all that happens in the village—although back then I guess we were still on the streets—but it wasn't too much longer after you came along that we got this village—a blessing they tell us."

Again she snorted, looking around her place as if the condition of her existence spoke for itself. Bertha would sway from the subject if Syndi didn't keep her focused.

"So you remember Mom bringing me home?" she prompted.

Bertha looked at her for a long moment until Syndi was convinced the old woman had forgotten what they talked about.

"I remember helping to birth you," she finally said, whispering the words.

Syndi's heart caught in her throat. The words seemed to creep through the air, taking their time reaching her, and then even longer to sink in. It was her turn to take too long to speak. Bertha nodded slowly, as if knowing the moment that understanding crept through Syndi.

"I wasn't adopted?" That didn't make any sense. Bertha's memory must not be as intact as Syndi had hoped.

Bertha made a hushing noise, her finger going to her lips, but then shook her head. "They are both gone now. But their memory is strong among us—may their souls rest in peace," she uttered. "Your mother wanted to avoid scandal. She loved your father. I really think she did. And he'd forgiven her, taken her back. It was best for both of them, so they could move forward. And I never saw him love you any less than if he'd been your real father."

"What are you saying?" Syndi shook her head, Bertha's words coming too fast, and making absolutely no sense. "My mother didn't adopt me? But the journal…"

She'd have to read it again, but she swore her mother had written that she'd brought Syndi home.

The older woman put the bottle of water down and took her time standing, moving to the corner of her tent and then kneeling over one of her boxes. She fiddled through the contents, muttering to herself about her lack of organization. Years of dealing with Bertha was enough to remain still, let her go through her show of searching for something. There was more to this story. Bertha knew the facts. And it would take a lot of patience to sit there and wait for the story to be told. But if she did just that, she would hear all Bertha could remember.

"You're saying that my mom gave birth to me, but that my father wasn't my real father," she said to Bertha's back.

The woman turned around, pulling a small box out from under some other things, and then brushing dirt off the surface of it. She once again situated herself on the floor of her tent, holding the box in her lap.

"You're quick, girl." She pursed her lips and lifted the cover of the box. "Sometimes a person wonders why they save things. I swear, most of it would be better burnt. This old woman would have a lot more room to stretch out her bones at night. That's for sure."

If Samantha Stone was her mother, and Ran Mose claimed to be her father, then her mother had an affair. Now it made sense why her mom had begged the villagers to dig. She understood the pain in her aunt and uncle's face when she'd made the same suggestion, and had been gone for so long. They worried history would repeat itself. And to an extent, it already had. She had found a man from Undrworld.

Her heart swelled painfully in her chest. The air was too tight in the tent. She wasn't married though. Her mother had cheated on her father, had an affair, and come home pregnant. The pain that must have caused all of them. And she was the product of it. Yet everyone had kept that from her, allowing her to believe she had two parents who'd loved her dearly. They'd kept that pain and humiliation from her so that she could have a happy childhood.

Her heart had swelled into her throat, but she had to ask. "Did you ever meet my father? Do you know who he is?"

Bertha gave her an odd look, as if Syndi were out of line for asking. Instead of answering, she returned to the contents of her box, pulling out everything, and then lifting a tattered envelope from the bottom of the box.

She held it out to Syndi, who took it as trepidation seeped through her. The envelope threatened to crumble in her hand, and she opened the slit cautiously, worried whatever was inside would tear before she could discover what Bertha had gone to such efforts to find for her.

"What is this?" she asked, at the same time pulling very old newspaper articles out of the envelope.

They almost tore as she unfolded them.

"That should answer all the questions you seem too nervous to ask me." Bertha adjusted herself on her tent floor, straightening her plain tan smock around her bony legs.

Syndi glanced up at Bertha's knowing expression. Sometimes she swore the woman seemed to know things before you brought them up to her. Now was no different. Bertha nodded at the papers in Syndi's hands, and then reclined against rags that were probably stuffed with newspapers but offered back support for the old woman.

The lump in her throat seemed to grow. And suddenly she wished she'd brought one of those bottles of water with her. Her skin itched, but she wouldn't rub it. Delicately opening the old articles, she stared down at the faded picture and print of the first one in her hands.

Paradise Found Underground. The headline of the first article grabbed her so hard she could only stare at it for a moment before glancing at the picture, which was almost too faded to see. It appeared to be a large hole in the ground, or the entrance to a cave. The article was short, obviously not front page news.

Street people announce the discovery of an underground water world. The article accurately described Undrworld. She looked up at Bertha in disbelief.

"Read the others," the old woman said, pointing her bony finger at the scraps of paper in Syndi's hand.

Orphaned Child Returned To Family. Again the article was short. *City officials show they have a heart, returning young Syndi Stone to her street people family after tragic death of parents.*

The third piece of paper wasn't an article, but some official form. After a moment of staring at it, she recognized a sentencing report. Donald and Samantha Stone convicted of theft of water, sentenced to sixty days in local jail, and ninety days of hard labor.

She read the report and then looked again at the article claiming their tragic death. Basically the papers confirmed the hearsay she'd heard over the years.

She looked at the first article again. "What do you know about this?" she asked.

Bertha shook her head. "Some things are best left alone, my child. Disturbing how it's always been could make life worse."

Bertha knew about Undrworld. Syndi couldn't believe it. She stared at the older woman for a minute, her thoughts coming too quickly to sort them out all at once.

"Bertha, there is so much water," she began.

But Bertha hushed her, waving her hands in the air as if she didn't want to hear about it.

"What might appear to be a paradise to you, child, could actually be all of our death sentences." Her tone was harsh, but then she sighed, and reached out with her leathery hand and patted Syndi's leg. "You let alone whatever you think you've discovered. Do you hear me? It's bad. And it will come back to haunt you. Take the word of an old woman. You stay away from there."

The swelling in her throat sank to her stomach, like a heavy rock that settled with an unpleasant thud. She looked down at the articles in her hands and then folded them as they were before, then slid them into the tattered envelope.

"I'm not sure I can," she said quietly.

Bertha was so adamant about leaving things as they were now that Syndi hesitated in questioning her more, or offering what she already knew. The old woman had always been good to her, although set in her ways, and often acting like she was a crotchety old thing. She had a good heart, and Syndi knew if she took her into her confidence, Bertha wouldn't do anything to cause her pain. But she didn't want to hear that it was best to stay away.

Tor was down there. She wouldn't deny that she wanted to see him again.

"What's his name?" Bertha's question startled her.

She looked up quickly, catching the shrewd glare the old woman gave her.

"Tell me now," Bertha said before Syndi could answer. "I'm not as senile as most think. Don't assume for a minute that I don't know why you came to see me. Now tell me his name."

Syndi would have loved to ask why Bertha thought she'd come. At the moment, she wasn't completely sure herself. Bringing up digging for water seemed ridiculous at this point. But there was no getting out of answering Bertha's question.

"His name is Tor Geinz, and he's one of their leaders," she said quietly, not taking her gaze from Bertha's.

Bertha's pale eyes studied Syndi for a long moment. She fought the urge to squirm, like a child waiting for punishment to be handed down under a parent's intent stare.

"Did you know my father?" she dared to ask when too much silence had passed and still Bertha hadn't said anything.

"Your father was a terrible man. Promise me now you'll never try to find him." Bertha shook so hard as she spoke that Syndi reached out to steady her hand.

But how could she make such a promise?

Chapter Thirteen

80

Tor pulled Fern from the control room. Assigning her to overseeing the rebuilding of the passages would be good for her. She'd spent too much time in that cave.

"Not to mention, I wouldn't be surprised if she had an agenda she doesn't want you to know about." Roln voiced Tor's concerns.

"I thought I had her loyalty." Tor didn't mind sharing his disappointment in her with Roln.

They jumped into the narrow tunnel of water and left the Control Room. None of the people in New Dallas seemed any the wiser about him heading to the surface. For that he was grateful. Any leaks of information getting out to the general masses would cause chaos and panic. News of the damaged passages had hit all the main websites. A simple statement on his part that crews should have them open and safe to the public satisfied the press.

Coming ashore near the edge of the mountain where his tran-bus waited, thoughts of what Syndi was doing right now plagued him. Ensuring all was well with the West Passage came first. But damn it if he didn't want her safe here instead of on the surface where he had no idea what she was doing, or if she were in danger.

His phone buzzed while he walked toward the tran-bus.

"We've received a transmission from Ran Mose," Ben Osk told him when he answered. "He's definitely not happy. When he couldn't reach you personally he contacted the

Control Center. He didn't appreciate having to convey his message to me."

Damn shame phones weren't perfect. Tor didn't like it that signals faded in and out with strength any more than the next person did. At the moment, he was rather glad it caused Ran such an inconvenience. "What does he have to say?"

"He views it as an act of aggression that you've captured three of his men."

He'd been damned proud of Roln and Peg for having Mose's three soldiers under gunpoint when he'd returned to the home after leaving Syndi. Once they'd returned home and confined the soldiers, they'd managed to get a little more out of them. The most important news he'd learned from them being that Ran Mose had quite a few people on the surface.

"He says entering his territory and attacking and capturing his men is an act of war."

"Those are some pretty strong words." Tor met Roln's inquisitive gaze when the two of them climbed into the tran-bus. "I didn't know he ruled over territory on the surface."

"Neither did I," Ben Osk muttered through the phone.

"Don't answer him yet." Tor would let the man stew. He doubted Ran Mose was any more powerful than he was. "We're headed to the four passages now to see how things are going there. If he sends any more messages let me know."

Before hanging up, a thought hit him. "And Ben, increase security throughout the passage. We might need to organize armies. Let's get them ready just in case."

"Understood." Ben Osk terminated the transmission and Tor secured his phone to his belt, lost in thought.

Ran Mose had been plotting something for a while. And he couldn't believe all his soldiers on the surface were simply up there looking for Syndi. She played a part in all of this.

But there was a bigger picture. One he didn't see clearly yet. And that bothered him.

"Ran Mose sent a transmission," Tor told Roln, knowing his soldier waited quietly, yet anxiously, to hear what was up. "Apparently our capturing his soldiers on the surface is an act of war."

"Oh really?" Roln cocked an eyebrow. His jaw twitched, the words upsetting him. "If he attacks the West Passage over that, then there is a lot to this that we don't see."

"Exactly what I was thinking." Tor stared through the front window as they moved through the large ocean, which was relatively calm in the early evening. A calm he'd like to see maintained. "I'm going to have to tighten our military," he added with resignation. "It's going to be hard to keep a lid on this."

"You'll have to make a public statement. Probably better sooner than later."

None of this sat well with him. They reached the four passages, and he waded to shore, his mood souring as he thought of how Ran Mose would disrupt the peace they'd worked so hard to obtain.

He'd grown up in battle, as most of them had. Fighting to secure the West Passage, gaining control over it, they'd worked hard to get what they had now—a peaceful, prosperous society. Damn Mose to hell for stirring up trouble now.

Whatever it took, there would be no more war. If he had to take Ran Mose out himself, he'd see to it peace remained in the West Passage. Imagine, the leader he'd once admired, had studied and strived to follow in his footsteps, convinced there was no one better, was now the same man Tor wanted to wipe off the face of this planet.

The way he felt right now, the only public statement he'd need to make was apologizing to the East Passage for annihilating their demented leader. Syndi would worry now, her life wouldn't be the same. Until something was done about Ran Mose, she would know her life had a mark on it. He fought not to clench his hands into fists at his side, but couldn't keep his muscles from hardening throughout his body as he moved through the forest with Roln toward the four passages. For Syndi's sake, for the sake of peace in the West Passage, for the sake of the world, Ran Mose wouldn't live long.

His phone buzzed as they reached the South Passage. He stared down at the muddy water, which a day ago had been a sparkling blue, and grabbed his phone.

"Tren Fal and Shara Dar have both contacted us," Ben Osk said over the phone.

It didn't surprise him that the leaders of the North and South passage had checked in.

"They've offered assistance in rebuilding the passages. They have work crews on their way to assist."

"Send both of them my heartfelt thanks," Tor said. "And see if you can establish a conference call with the two of them. I think it would be in our best interests to inform the two of them what is going on."

And to ensure their alliance.

"I'll set it up," Ben told him.

"Keep me posted," Tor said, and then hung up the phone.

Fern walked around the edge of the pond toward him. "How are things going?" she asked.

"I was about to ask you that same question."

She wanted to be kept abreast of what went on in the control room. He ignored her frustrated look that he didn't immediately brief her on current events. None of that was her concern any longer.

She straightened, realizing his unspoken message, and clasped her hands behind her back. "We're digging out debris in both passages." Her tone was dry, as if all of this bored her terribly. "I've got crews working in both passages. We should have the passages functioning again in a day or so."

Her blonde hair clung to the curve in her neck, water dripping from strands of her hair down her shoulders. Her dark eyes stared at him defiantly. What bothered him more than anything was her lack of remorse for her poor decision-making.

With a quick, sharp nod, Tor looked past her through the trees where the North Passage was. "You should have help from the North and South Passages within a few hours," he told her.

"You've been in contact with Tren Fal and Shara Dar," she asked, a light sparking in her dark eyes. "What have you discussed with them?"

Something prevented him from sharing the entire truth with her. Her expression filled with interest, and when she sensed his hesitation, her features softened, her small mouth forming a reassuring smile.

"Tren Fal has a thick accent, but I've dealt with him in the past. He comes across as difficult, but he's not." The Fern who was all confident, comfortable with her rank as someone accustomed to being acknowledged, returned before him. The sulkiness at being assigned to such menial labor faded as new spirit resounded through her. "Be careful discussing too much with either one of them, Tor. I'd advise you to not discuss any matter concerning Ran Mose with them."

"Advising is no longer your job," he told her, watching her expression deflate.

Fern wrinkled her brow at him, for a moment her anger over the situation coming through brilliantly as her dark eyes turned almost black with emotion.

"You're a fool, Tor," she snapped, and then turned from him, jumping into the pond before he'd dismissed her.

Tor stared at the rippling water she'd created as her body disappeared into the deep murky water. For some reason, her not wanting him to discuss Ran Mose with the other leaders made him want to talk to them even more about him.

Roln had been talking to his guards that he'd stationed around the passages, and walked over to him when Fern jumped into the water.

"Problems?" he asked.

"Possibly."

Fern's loyalty to him had diminished. That much he realized. What he wanted to know now was where exactly did her loyalties lie. And God help any of his guards who might have sided with her.

"The area is secure," Roln offered.

Tor nodded. "And I've requested a conference call between myself and the other two Passage leaders. We don't have a lot of time."

He didn't have to tell Roln what they needed to do now. It had been over several hours since he'd left Syndi on the surface. By now, it would be dark above, and time for her to come to him. Turning toward the small pond, Roln fell into stride alongside him.

Roln's phone buzzed and he answered it, speaking briefly with one of his men then ending the call.

"Tell me it's not more trouble," Tor said.

"One of our patrol officers noted a higher content of debris just offshore in the ocean. I'm sure it's nothing. But considering the debris content from the ponds, he wanted to let me know. They're investigating now for a source."

Tor nodded. "If it's just offshore, the ground surrounding the ocean would be closest to the surface. Erosion might cause the water to seep to the surface."

"The water would fry and evaporate up there before anyone noticed it," Roln said, making a face.

Tor wasn't enthused about the torturous heat on the surface any more than his guard was. And more than likely, Roln was right.

"Let's hope so," he muttered. The last thing he needed was people on the surface discovering them, especially while a possible upsurge from the East Passage existed.

Reaching the pond that was the passage to Syndi's world, Tor stared down into the water. Obviously Syndi hadn't swum to him yet. There was no sign of her.

"Stay here," he told Roln, and then raised his hand when his guard started to protest. "Keep guard and if anything urgent happens, buzz my phone. I won't be long. If she isn't on the other side, I'll return. Right now, I can't risk entering her village. Maybe later tonight, after the conference call with Shara Dar and Tren Fal."

"All right then. Fifteen minutes, or I'm coming after you," Roln told him.

"I'll be back." Tor doubted he'd need fifteen minutes. "Unless of course, Syndi wants to show me how much she missed me."

Roln snorted, and gave him a smirk. "Then I guess you can buzz me," he said halfheartedly.

Both knew too much was going on right now to allow Tor the privilege of getting some, while down in the pond. Tor's phone buzzed and he grabbed it.

"Yes," he said impatiently, wishing Syndi would just appear in the pond and eliminate one of his worries.

At the same time Roln's phone buzzed.

"I have a conference call lined up for one hour from now with Shara Dar and Tren Fal," Ben told him.

Roln looked up at him while listening to his call. "What is the exact location?" Roln said into his phone.

"I'll be there," Tor said.

Hanging up his phone, he made sure everything he needed was secured to his belt.

Roln hung his phone up as well. "We've got a problem."

The last thing they needed was more problems. "What?"

"About a quarter mile north of here offshore," Roln began, his face lining with worry. "The debris is clogging the water to zero visibility. Now they are reporting chunks of dirt that are slowing traffic in that area. One of the entrances to the rural caves is out that way."

"A quarter mile north of here." Tor looked that direction. "None of the other passages could access our passage from there."

A sinking feeling twisted his gut as he met Roln's gaze.

"So if the debris is caused by someone digging, or an explosion," Roln began.

"It would have to be coming from the surface," Tor finished the thought.

Trying to visualize what would be above ground a quarter mile north of here, he let out a slow breath.

"Syndi's village would be above ground at that location," he said. Standing there thinking about this wasted time. He headed toward the pond, more determined now to get that little vixen back under his wing. "Secure that area," he told Roln. "Detour all traffic. I'll be back shortly."

Syndi wouldn't instigate any digging. That would strongly affect the West Passage. He walked into the pond until he stood waist deep and then dove, kicking fiercely as he hurried toward the underwater tunnels. Water rushed through his hair, soaking through his flesh as his gills opened, clearing his mind. Sucking in the oxygen from the water, he pressed harder, flying through the dark water and then floating into the narrow tunnel.

If there was digging going on in her village that had to mean trouble. Syndi had been so damned determined to return to her people. No reason came to mind though as to why digging would start after she'd returned. Possibly his mental calculations were off, and the digging wasn't instigated in her village. There was also a chance the debris wasn't a result of digging, although he couldn't think of what else might cause it.

He kicked harder, pushing his muscles, feeling the strain as he flew through the darkness toward the warmer water and the pond in her dead world. He'd get her back, and then take on the leaders of the other passages. Once he had Syndi back with him, it would clear a lot of his thoughts, allow him to focus on leading his people, keeping them out of war.

The water warmed around him, although darkness surrounded him. Exiting the tunnel, he kicked toward the surface, the heat of the water making it harder to breathe.

A fire inside him burned as well. Realizing how badly he wanted Syndi back, not just to protect her, but because he missed her, was an emotion that confused him. Always in control, focused on what was best to better his leadership, a woman had never distracted him like Syndi.

Yet he ached to touch her again. Her long dark hair, her tanned skin and lean body, every bit of her called to him. The heat that burned inside him, along with the increasing temperature of the water, made him almost lightheaded.

He came out of the water, sucking in air that was so hot it burnt his lungs. Blackness surrounded him, but as he wiped water from his eyes, a flash of light almost blinded him.

Tor quit moving, bracing himself in the water for possible attack. Instinctively he reached for his gun at his belt. A booming sound shook the ground.

"What the fuck?" he mumbled, turning slowly in the water, fighting to get his eyes to adjust to the darkness.

Another light flashed before his eyes, so bright it blinded him. A streak of white screamed from the sky, attacking the ground at the same time the loud rumbling sounded again. For a split second, everything around him lit as if daytime had broken into the night. For that moment, he had a clear view of everything surrounding the pond. He didn't see a damned soul.

Complete darkness engulfed him as if the light had never shown. Syndi wasn't here. The stillness that surrounded him, blanketed with smothering heat, unnerved him. Treading water, he moved slowly in a circle, struggling to see beyond the shores of the pond. Where in the hell was she?

Another streak of light rushed above him, making the hairs on his body stand on end. Every muscle in his body spasmed, as if he'd just endured a full body hit. He didn't see the light this time, it must have come from behind him. But the jolt to his body made it hard to turn quickly enough before the rumbling once again shook the ground. The water around him rippled.

The light was electricity and he'd guess he just took a pretty good shock. It took a minute for his muscles to quit quivering. Water and electricity didn't mix. This wasn't good.

Before he could recover light struck again, the invisible attacker showing no mercy. This time he saw it streak down from the sky, attacking the ground by the water so that flames jumped up from the dirt. The explosion that accompanied the light splashed the water around him.

Whatever attacked the surface would destroy it and him with it if he didn't move quickly. Maybe the catastrophic event explained the debris in the ocean. Diving down into the water, he swam to the tunnel, returning to his own world. Something was terribly wrong.

Minutes later he swam to the shore of the pond in his own world. Climbing out of the water quickly, his gills still struggled for air while he gulped it in through his mouth. Adrenaline surged through him too quickly, and it took a minute to slow the oxygen to his brain. His phone buzzed while water dripped down him.

"Yes," he said, looking around him and realizing Roln was gone.

"You're back faster than I thought," Roln said into the phone. "There's a problem in the ocean. I'm headed that way now. I'd have waited if I knew you two would have been back so soon."

"I'm here alone." And it pissed him off. "What's the problem?"

"I had the area where the debris was building closed off. But some of the guards I posted there have reported an anomaly."

"What anomaly?" Tor headed through the trees toward the ocean.

"I'm not sure by the description. But I have this sinking feeling that someone from the surface has dug a hole into our world."

It wasn't common knowledge that people lived on the surface. Other than the few in his government who'd been made aware of the situation, the citizens of Undrworld had no clue. For the time being, it had to stay that way.

"The area is sealed off from the public, right?" he asked, trusting Roln to have followed his orders but needing confirmation.

"Yes." Roln didn't hesitate.

"I'm using my phone to track you and I'll meet you at the location." Tor hung up the phone and then adjusted the settings so that he could determine Roln's exact location.

Studying the small screen on his phone, it wasn't the best of maps, but it gave him a good idea where to head. Reaching the ocean, he again walked into water. And again, he wasn't sure what he'd find when he reached his destination.

A sinking feeling settled through him. Something was wrong with Syndi's world. He had no idea what he'd just witnessed on the surface, some kind of natural catastrophic event possibly. It had prevented Syndi from coming to him. All he could do was pray she was safe. Although there was nowhere she'd be safer other than at his side. And until he had her there, he wouldn't be satisfied.

Syndi was strong. Considering how young she was, he gave her credit for having more sense than many women he'd met. She had enough fight in her to make the women who worked around him nervous. The leadership blood that ran through her was the only thing she could thank her sire for. Ran Mose was a fool to wish her destroyed.

Although maybe not, he thought somewhat sardonically. Syndi had what it took to make quick decisions. She would take on the unknown, and battle anyone who stood in her way. Ran Mose wouldn't succeed, but Tor suddenly understood why the man feared his offspring. Syndi had the strength to take him down. All she needed was the education. And Tor was willing to give her that.

Swimming through the open sea, he finally spotted the tran-bus, hovering underwater ahead of him. Within minutes, he swam around it, spotting Roln under the water, investigating the underwater ground along with several guards.

Tor swam closer, noticing what his men looked at. There was a hole in the ocean wall. Dirt muddled the water turning it to mud, and making it hard to see where the hole led. His men turned to acknowledge his presence, and parted to give him a better view. The ocean wall had crumbled, creating a tunnel similar to the one that led to the surface from the pond. Darkness loomed in the hole, making it impossible to see how far it went. His insides hardened, while an ill feeling sunk through him. Pulling his flashlight from his belt, he had a feeling what he would find once he entered the hole.

Chapter Fourteen

෨

The darkness weighed with so much humidity after the storm that Syndi swore she could cut it with a knife. Sweat dripped from her body, adding to her dehydrated feeling. Praying that most everyone had gone to sleep with the storm preventing any evening activity, she sat on her mat, finishing up the last of her tasks.

Her oversensitive senses picked up the noise outside before she heard someone grab her tent flap.

"Syndi? Wake up." Perry whispered as he struggled with the flap.

He didn't use a flashlight, which gave her time to shove the box holding her mother's journal into her large plastic bag. During the storm, she'd tediously wrapped it in old plastic bags, praying she'd waterproofed it. Habits left over from living on the streets, many of them still carried plastic bags with all of their possessions in them. Hardly anyone stole in the village, but as a child if she wanted to hold on to something, she kept it with her at all times.

"What do you want?" she asked, grabbing her flashlight and stuffing it in the bag.

Perry managed to open her tent flap and then stepped inside, kneeling down next to her. He smelled of sweat and dirt. When she squinted at him, he looked even dirtier than usual.

"You need a bath," she told him, curling her lip.

"We started digging," he told her, his eyes wide in the dark and his toothy grin making him look even more stupid than usual. "And you were right. Come on."

He grabbed her hand, almost dragging her to her feet.

"What?" She yanked her hand away from him, forgetting to whisper. "You started without telling me?"

"Shh…" He put his finger to her lips, the salty sweat from his touch making her jerk backward. "You were busy with Bertha."

And she'd hurried to her tent when the first signs of the storm appeared. There was no way she could venture into the dead land until it stopped. But sitting here had given her time to organize some things. There was little doubt that her mother was dead. But learning that Ran Mose claimed to be her father had made her think more about her parents than she had in years. Talking with Bertha, with her aunt, and reading the journal had brought her closer to the woman who'd birthed her, and shown her that she was a lot like Syndi. If even the slightest chance existed that her mother still lived, maybe the computers in Undrworld would help her find her.

She hadn't moved fast enough though. Perry showing up meant she couldn't take off for the pond. Yet if she had escaped before he'd arrived, once again he'd be reporting she wasn't in her tent at night. Frustration over how closely he watched her added to her uneasiness.

"You should have told me," she snapped.

"But you were right," he said, her mood not fazing him. "Come on. You've got to see."

All she wanted to see right now was Tor. He would have shown up at the pond. She had no doubts about that. And more than likely right now he was pissed. But if he'd surfaced, witnessed the storm, then he would understand their meeting was simply delayed. Relying on his intelligence, his understanding that weather couldn't be controlled, she'd managed to sit in her tent and take her time preparing what she wanted to take with her on her next visit to his world.

It had also given her time to miss him, want to be in his arms again, to feel his hard body pressed against hers. As the storm had coursed through the village, need had pulsed through her. With every clap of lightning, she'd ached for him. With every roar of thunder that made her jump, she'd thought about him. Tor had worked his way into her system and she didn't have a damned clue what to do about it. Neither of them could just walk away from their world. Somehow, there had to be a way to keep seeing him. The more she saw him though, the more she'd want him.

Perry opened her tent flap and waited for her. Rolling her bag to protect its contents as best that she could, she stuffed it under her arm and stood.

"What do you have there?" he asked, still whispering.

"Things I had prepared to help you dig," she said, thinking of the first thing that came to mind.

Giving him her usual disgusted look, she pressed past him, brushing against his body, which irritated her even more. Touching him just made her want to touch Tor even more.

It wasn't as hot outside as it had been in her tent. The fresh air felt good, the winds from the storm making the air seem a bit cleaner, fresher. One thing she'd always enjoyed about nighttime, when the temperatures dropped under a hundred degrees, was that it was so much easier to breathe.

"You know I would have come for you," Perry said, sounding apologetic, and running his hand down her hair, which made it stick to her back. "When the guys agreed to give it a try, and it was getting dark, we decided now was as good as any. I couldn't wait to show you when water bubbled over the ground. We had to stop because of the storm. Come on, it's over this way."

His continual whispered jabber in her ear while he stroked her back and guided her through the quiet tents distracted her. Her mother had begged everyone to dig, and they hadn't. Already she'd accomplished what her mother hadn't. That had to be a good thing.

On the outer edge of the village, far enough away that most wouldn't notice, Syndi spotted the uprooted ground. Hurrying from Perry's side, she reached the overturned earth.

"Water," she breathed, going down on her knees and running her fingers through the trickles of water that had flowed long enough now that a miniature stream crept over the dead land.

"You were right, sweetheart." Perry gripped the back of her neck, giving it an affectionate squeeze.

"I'm not your sweetheart." She shrugged him away, resituating herself on the ground so she wouldn't fall over. "How deep did you dig?"

"Quite a ways actually." Perry moved around the hole in the ground and pulled out his flashlight, beaming it over the ground so she could see what they'd done.

Footsteps behind them had both of them jumping to their feet. Syndi's heartbeat thudded in her chest as Perry beamed his light on Shef Winfrey.

"Storm didn't appear to do that much damage," he said in a hushed tone. "Do we still have water?"

He joined the two of them, staring down at the tiny crooked path of water that had streamed away from the hole.

"Fucking unbelievable," he muttered. "I tell you Syndi. When Perry told me your idea, I thought you'd plumb lost it just like your mother. But you were right. You were fucking right."

"Who else helped you?" she asked, moving dirt from the source of the water.

"Jeff Marley helped," Perry said. "Doubt he'll be back out though. He's got a family."

Shef produced a broken tent pole and started jabbing at the earth, tearing at the entrance where the water came from. Within minutes more water bubbled free.

The fresh water was cold, clear, and ran easily over Syndi's hands. "You realize how this could change our lives," she whispered, as too many thoughts ran through her mind at once. She'd keep Tor's order not to tell them about Undrworld, but this water was a significant discovery for her people. And it was one that wouldn't remain a secret for that long.

"Once we tell everyone, they'll be out here like wild dogs, hurrying to fill their bottles and cups." Perry told the truth.

"I wonder how much of it there is," Shef said. "Do we want everyone to know?"

"We can't keep something like this to ourselves." She wouldn't suggest there was an unlimited supply. They would learn that on their own soon enough.

Perry dug at the hard ground with his hands, scooping away the dirt that Shef broke loose. Syndi grabbed the flashlight, offering light while the two men created a bigger hole. Within minutes water flooded over their shoes, soaking all of them. She couldn't help joining the two men in laughter as the water continued to flow freely from the ground.

"It goes down pretty deep," Shef told her, and then showed her by pushing his broken tent pole into the ground.

It disappeared along with most of his arm before he pulled it back out. "The tent pole is a good three feet. I'd say we got a hole almost the length of a man here."

And they'd now made it almost a foot wide. She couldn't picture where it might show up on the other side, but prayed it was somewhere that wouldn't be noticed. A hole that small wouldn't possibly draw attention. With all the water underneath them, they'd barely made a dent.

"Let's fill our water bottles for now," she told them. "In the morning we'll decide what to do. I'm exhausted."

And she wanted to have some of the night so she could slip over to the pond, see if she could find Tor. He wouldn't be there still. But with any luck, she'd be able to find him once she reached the other side.

"That sounds good," Perry said.

She gave silent thanks when he didn't follow her back to her tent. It wouldn't surprise her if he had his own agenda with the water. Not knowing how much of it there was, he'd probably try to get a monopoly on it. She could only hope it would keep him occupied through the night, and he wouldn't come to her tent and realize she wasn't there.

Nonetheless, she waited in her tent for a while before daring to sneak back out. The village was silent as she crept toward the dead lands.

Even after enjoying the fresh water that had bubbled from the ground over her skin, and the cooling winds from the storm bringing down the temperature, she still craved the pond. To feel the water soak through her body, fill her pores, had her picking up her pace. A tightening in her belly couldn't be ignored either. She wanted to see Tor. He'd brought adventure to her life, excitement, the risk of being caught, and sexual pleasure. She needed all of that to live. Without a focus, a reason to get up every morning, she'd wither and die. And Tor had brought all of that into her life.

The dead ground cracked underneath her feet. The simple dress she'd put on while in her tent clung to her, rubbing against her legs right above her knees where the material ended. Sleeveless and simple in design, the material that rubbed against her shoulders made her itch. Not too long ago, she would have stripped from the dress and swam through the water naked. It was better than paradise to experience the water against her bare flesh, feel it rush past her as she kicked into the pond's depths. The sensation almost matched the pleasure of Tor's hands stroking her flesh.

Tingles rushed over her in spite of the heat. Quickening her pace, she hurried through the black night, anxious to reach the pond.

A sound grabbed her attention, the soft patting against the ground, the sound of someone running. Or in this case, something—animals, the wild dogs, and lots of them. Their paws hit the ground, a repetitive beat alerting her long before she saw the shadows of the creatures through the night.

The tingles that had prickled over her skin changed to chills. Her heart stopped painfully in her chest. They were gaining on her. Whether she walked or ran, they would show no mercy. The winds from the storm had stirred up the smells of the night, and they were hungry, on the prowl, and she was as good a catch as any.

Suddenly her heart raced too fast. The silhouettes of the dogs, running in a pack, were visible through the darkness. Across the dead lands, pounding the earth as they raced toward her, the sight of them made her want to freeze in fear.

That would cost her life!

Outrunning them would be impossible too. They ran faster than she did.

She was too far from the village. But was she close enough to the pond?

There were no other options.

"God. Oh God." She broke into a sprint.

Sweat rolled down her forehead, her hair sticking to her face as she ran as fast as she could. Their barking filled the night. Growling, yelping, as if they laughed at her, mocked her efforts at escape.

"Please," she cried out, seeing the pond ahead of her.

The dogs were close enough now she could hear them panting. Their paws pounded the ground, a repetitive vibration that beat through her. Her heart raced in an uneven pattern, her breathing so loud it was deafening.

"No!" she screamed when she saw the first beast leap through the air, diving toward her, ready to take her down and then fight the others for the right to tear at her alone.

The water was so close. She leapt toward it, landing on her hands and knees while she got splashed in the face. Crawling forward, skinning her knees, she screamed again when the dogs lunged into the water behind her.

"Help me! No!" Her screams were futile, no one hearing her but the dogs.

They barked and splashed, eager to capture her, make her their dinner.

Lunging forward, she dove underwater, kicking furiously. A pain so sharp it froze her ability to move, surged through her with lightning speed. She tried to kick, a weight hampering her movements. Twisting in the water, she stared into pale eyes that reeked of hatred and determination. The dog's mouth clamped down on her leg, tearing into her flesh.

"No!" She screamed underwater, causing bubbles to blind her vision and choking on the water that hurried to fill her lungs.

Kicking furiously with her unhindered leg, she felt her foot hit the hard skull of the dog. Pain tore at her, the water around her turning red. She kicked and kicked, losing her sense of direction, flailing her arms around her with a fury that matched the dog's attack.

Blinded and not sure where she was in the pond, the weight lifted from her leg. She'd freed herself from the dog, but couldn't tell if the surface of the pond was above or below her. Pain surged through her with more fierceness than anything she'd ever experienced before.

And her gills wouldn't open. Her lungs burned. Her leg was on fire. The water around her was red. Her brain raced for the right thing to do.

Kick.

The tunnel.

Find the tunnel.

Her fingers hurt, clamped down, holding on to something too hard.

It took a minute to realize she grasped her plastic bag and she brought it to her chest, holding on to it with everything she had, as if it would stop the pain, while kicking with her uninjured leg. Trying her best to think, focus, pay attention to her gills so they would open, everything around her seemed a blur.

Tor. God. Help her. Know that she was hurt and rescue her.

But that wasn't going to happen. No one would rescue her. Survive on her own or die. As it had always been.

Holding her bag to her chest, she did her best to block out the throbbing pain that rushed up her leg. Not looking down, not wanting to see how bad her injury was, she took her free hand and massaged her left gill, just as Tor had. Closing her eyes, thinking only of her hand touching her neck, of her fingers as they caressed her skin, her world around her seemed to be nothing but a floating blackness.

Oxygen suddenly rushed to her brain so quickly she swore she floated upward. Opening her eyes quickly, she scrambled to straighten herself. *Don't go to the top.* The dogs — the dogs were at the top.

Pain throbbed through her. Her gills opened. She quit moving for a moment, not sure if she sank or floated upward.

There was no turning back. The only thing that kept the dogs from her was their inability to hold their breath long enough to get to her. But her blood would keep them at the pond, howling and fighting among each other waiting for her to surface. She had to move forward.

Struggling with her bag, she fought to free her flashlight. It wouldn't surprise her if she'd destroyed her mother's journal the way she'd flung the bag around in the water while desperately trying to escape the dog. That thought was too depressing to focus on.

But the only thing else that she could focus on was the pain. Her entire leg seemed to weigh a ton, throbbing as if her heart had grown five sizes larger and now existed below her right thigh. With every pulse, waves of anguish racked her body.

Think about something else.

With some effort she turned on her flashlight and then had to use the same hand, and her one good leg, to push herself through the water. It would take forever to get to the other side at this rate. In fact, she was sure hours had passed before she even found the tunnel. And then it seemed to go on forever, the walls narrowing around her. The painted pictures on either side of her seemed to glow, contort as the beam of her light brushed over them. The water had to be washing out her wound, minimizing infection, so it had to be the level of pain that distorted her vision.

She'd left the tunnel and started rising before she gave it thought. The cool water helped her focus a bit. The surface of the pond was visible, the large trees above her slowly coming into focus.

"I can do it," she cried, sounding too pathetic, as she lifted her head out of the water.

The shore seemed too far away. Shallow water surrounded her. If she could stand, she would have. But it was all she could do to crawl to the edge of the pond, dumping her soaked bag on to the ground, and simply staring at it.

"I can do it," she said again.

No way would she let the tear in her leg take her down. Damn the dogs. Damn the pain.

"Shit. Hey. Over here." A man's voice boomed above her.

It was almost too much effort to pull herself out of the water. Large hands grabbed her under her arms, lifting her up and then holding on to her.

"Tor." She looked into a man's face that she didn't recognize.

Were her eyes playing games with her? Being unable to determine her surroundings meant not being in control. She squinted, sucking a breath of air through her mouth into her lungs. The man wasn't Tor.

"I need Tor," she said, doing her best to sound more coherent.

"It's okay. We'll get him." He turned his head, reaching for something on his belt.

Leaning against a complete stranger didn't sit well with her.

"I've pulled someone out of the pond over here off the edge of the passages. She's hurt." The man spoke into his phone, eyeing her with those large dark eyes that were similar to Tor's but not Tor.

"I'm fine." Instinct kicked in.

No one would take care of her but her.

Syndi pushed away from him, but then promptly fell on her rear. Pain jerked through her with enough ferocity that for a moment she couldn't see. Ringing in her ears disoriented her. One of her hands landed on her bag and she clutched it to her side.

Her vision cleared and she stared down at her legs, her dress bunched up around her thighs. One of her legs had a nasty gash, the flesh hanging open, the water having cleaned it enough that she swore she saw bone. Just the sight of it made her stomach turn and her vision blur again. Closing her eyes, she took long slow breaths.

The man above her was talking. There were other voices. Focus on them. Block out the pain.

"What do we have here?" It was a woman.

The man who'd pulled her out of the water spoke. "She asked for Tor. That leg looks pretty bad."

"Help me get her to the tran-bus," the woman said.

Syndi looked up, recognizing the woman. "I need Tor," she said.

"It's okay, Syndi. Put your arm around my shoulder. Can you walk?" Fern looked down at her leg. "Maybe you should carry her, Rev."

She didn't have time to answer before the man scooped her into his arms. Holding on to her bag, her injured leg stuck up in the air, in full view. Her dress was wrinkled around her thighs. She couldn't pull it down. It left her feeling exposed and vulnerable—two feelings she hated. She held her bag to her waist, doing her best to look anywhere but at the blood that had begun trickling down toward her dress.

For a moment everything around her seemed a world of color. She didn't seem able to focus and the words she fought to speak didn't want to come out. The next thing she knew she was being placed in a seat in the back of a tran-bus.

"Get the medic kit," Fern said, kneeling in front of her. "That must really hurt."

A scream ripped from her throat when it seemed Fern clamped her hand over the gash. Her stomach churned and she pushed her bag off her lap, freeing her hand. Reaching out, all she could think about was stop the pain.

"Don't strike out at the person who is trying to help you." Fern sounded angry.

"I wasn't...I'm sorry." She hadn't thought of hitting the woman.

Taking slow, long breaths, she stared at Fern, at her large eyes, her dark blonde hair that was wet and pressed back against her head. The woman's lips pressed into a thin line. This was the woman who'd try to send her to Ran Mose, who believed Tor's involvement with her might jeopardize their people. She couldn't trust her.

But how was she supposed to get away from her when she could barely move?

The guard, Rev, handed a small white box to Fern, who opened it up and searched through its contents.

"I can take care of her," Fern said, glancing quickly at Rev. "Return to your post."

He hesitated for only a moment, glancing at Syndi before nodding.

"Contact Tor and tell him I'm here. Tell him Syndi is here." She spoke quickly.

The guard, who blinked, heavy lids falling over those large eyes, and then looked at her, was obviously surprised at her sudden initiative and strength to give him an order.

"I'll take care of her," Fern said again.

"You're not going to tell him I'm here, are you?" Syndi asked after the guard had left.

"Now why would you think that?" Fern didn't sound offended.

Fern pulled out a clear bottle and sprayed something on Syndi's leg that burned so badly she did lash out this time. Grabbing Fern by the shoulders, she leaned forward, holding on while she rode out the intense sting.

"It will keep down infection," Fern said quietly, her own hands gripping Syndi's wrist.

Either Fern wasn't using all of her strength, or Syndi was the stronger. She held the woman's gaze. For a moment, she stared into Fern's large eyes, watching her pupil's dilate. The color drained from the woman's cheeks. Fern feared Syndi. Her mouth moved before she spoke.

"I can wrap that wound, and probably ensure a minimal scar. But I can't do anything if you don't let go." Her voice was quiet, unemotional.

Slowly Syndi loosened her grip on the woman's shoulders. Fern gave a quick nod, again pressing her mouth into a thin line, her gaze lowering to the box. Syndi watched her pull out another bottle, similar to the first one.

"How did you get this nasty tear in your leg?" If she was trying to make conversation, Syndi wouldn't play along.

"Is it going to hurt?" She didn't mind sounding like the pain was too much.

First of all, it was. But more importantly, for some reason, all of her defensive instincts had kicked in. *Don't let the opponent know your strengths, and misguide them about your weaknesses.*

"This will numb your leg," Fern said without looking up. "Did someone attack you?"

Syndi nodded although Fern didn't see her. The woman moved quickly, applying the medicine that indeed numbed her leg, clearing her head but making her leg feel like it weighed ten times as much as it should. Fern applied a white bandage that covered the wound, and stuck to her skin around the gash.

Just as quickly as she'd tended the wound, she put the items back in the little white box and then moved away from Syndi. Stepping out of the van, Syndi watched her reach for her phone, turning her back to Syndi while she spoke. Something told her Fern wasn't contacting Tor. Reaching for her bag, she searched quickly until she found the wristband Tor had left with her. Pushing the button on it, she signaled for help. Another button on the band began blinking, but she didn't know what to do. Staring at the small button as it flashed, she decided to push it.

"This is the control room," a man's voice said, sounding tinny and hollow coming out of the wristband.

Fern turned around quickly.

Syndi met her gaze, immediately seeing annoyance on the woman's face.

"I need to speak to Tor," she said, holding the wristband below her mouth and watching Fern the entire time.

"Who is this?" the man's voice said.

Fern reached for the wristband, moving quickly. Syndi was ready for her, and put the medicine on her leg to the test when she jerked backward, keeping the wristband out of Fern's reach.

"This is Syndi," she said quickly. "I'm at the pond."

"What's wrong with you?" Fern sounded astonished, but her expression showed her outrage.

Jumping into the tran-bus, she didn't care that she almost tripped over Syndi's injured leg. Fern grabbed the wristband in Syndi's hand. But Syndi had guessed right. She was stronger. And more determined. Pushing with all her strength, she shoved Fern backward. The two of them fell out of the tran-bus, Syndi landing on top of Fern since she couldn't balance her weight.

The wristband flew from Syndi's hand, rolling over the ground until it lodged against a nearby tree.

"You're not going to take down Tor," Fern hissed, managing to kick Syndi hard enough in the leg that even through the effects of the medication, she felt the sting of the blow.

"Don't judge me when you don't even know me." Syndi endured the pain, biting her lip until it stung and she tasted blood.

Fern almost had Syndi rolled over, and worked to grab her arms. Too many years on the streets, fighting just for the right to live, aided Syndi. Her leg was useless, dead weight under her, but she pushed herself up with her good leg, and then used every bit of strength she could muster to pull Fern's arms down. Clasping the woman's wrists together, she pushed with her body. If only she could stand, use her body to apply more force, but her handicap made it impossible to do so.

"I know enough about you," Fern spoke through gritted teeth. "Your father would have you creep your way into Tor's bed."

Fury added to her strength. She knocked Fern backward, toppling on top of her. Holding on to the woman's hands, she twisted Fern around so that she was trapped facedown between the ground and Syndi's body.

"I don't even know my father," Syndi hissed, although she doubted the woman cared, or believed her.

Fern fought underneath her, swearing under her breath. Syndi held her there, not sure what to do with her, while searching the area for some means to confine her while she tried again to reach Tor.

Footsteps sounded behind her, and Syndi turned, so sure she'd see Tor that she smiled. Several men, and another woman, hurried toward them. Before Syndi could speak she was yanked off Fern.

"Let's get her out of here," Fern said, jumping up as if she hadn't been the one just overcome in the skirmish.

Gesturing to the two men who half held, half dragged Syndi after the quickly moving Fern, they moved quickly away from the tran-bus.

"What are you doing?" Syndi struggled fruitlessly. "She attacked me, not the other way around. Where is Tor?"

They neared a pond, although it wasn't the one that Syndi had just come out of.

"Listen to you." Fern turned around, staring at Syndi triumphantly. "You wish to kill Tor just as you tried to kill me. Do you think Tor's guards stupid that they would pay attention to a word out of your mouth?"

Syndi stilled at Fern's words, catching that she'd just implied Syndi had tried to kill her. The woman painted a picture of lies for the other guards to hear. Syndi straightened, doing her best to balance herself with her one dead leg. She quit struggling and the guards on either side of her held her by her arms. Ignoring them she stared at Fern.

"Whatever plot you've devised, it won't work," she said in a low whisper, wishing for only Fern to hear.

Fern's triumphant smile didn't fade. She continued staring Syndi in the eye. "How long until they get here?" she asked.

"Should be any minute," the woman who stood alongside the guards answered.

"Good." Fern's gaze darkened, something cold and terrifying making her dark eyes almost turn black. "My dear, today is your lucky day. We're reuniting you with your family."

Her chuckle almost curdled Syndi's blood.

Behind her, limbs crackled and the sound of approaching footsteps made Syndi's heart lurch in her chest. She couldn't turn around to see who approached.

But she didn't have to.

"What the hell is going on?" Tor barked from directly behind her.

Chapter Fifteen

ഌ

Tor didn't know what to expect when he got to the four passages. But he sure as hell hadn't expected to see this.

He and Roln had just returned to the tran-bus, in need of better equipment in order to determine how close to the surface the hole in the ocean went. Immediately his phone had gone off.

The young guard who'd contacted him had sounded nervous, but determined. "I know I'm skipping rank by speaking with you directly, Sir," the young man had said as an introduction. "I'll take the punishment but something isn't right, and you need to be here."

That had alerted Tor more than control center contacting him with the message from Syndi—a message that had been terminated before she'd finished speaking with them.

Arriving at the four passages, Tor and Roln had barely made it out of the tran-bus when a young man, wearing the uniform of a junior soldier, just out of the academy, hurried to them.

"Like I said, Sir," the young man immediately stammered, forgetting all about protocol and rank, "something isn't right. She was hurt. And she didn't come out of any of the four passages."

That had Tor's attention.

"Slow down, lad." He gripped the young man's shoulder, sensing how the excitement of something other than his usual drills had the man overdosed on adrenaline. "Who did you find? And you said she's hurt?"

"Yes. But Fern took care of her." The guard seemed to sense he wasn't in immediate fear of a reprimand and gained some of his confidence. "I'll take you to her. She asked for you specifically. And, Sir, she doesn't look like anyone I've ever seen before."

The young guard had hurried off through the trees, leaving Roln and Tor to follow him. They reached the tran-bus but no one was there. Tor looked inside the tran-bus, its door open, and pulled out the worn-looking bag on the seat. It was soaking wet, as were its contents, but something caught his eye.

A small box, wrapped carefully in plastic, with faded colored carvings on it, dripped with water as he lifted it from the bag.

"What is it?" Roln asked.

"Not sure. But those are the same carvings that are on the tunnel walls," he said quietly.

"I'm pretty sure that woman had that bag with her. She had one of the nastiest gashes on her leg that I'd seen in a long time. She couldn't walk. I'm not sure where Fern would have taken her." The young guard scratched his head, looking around at the trees. "Sir, if I may speak openly."

"Speak your mind," Tor said, also searching the area with his gaze.

"The woman seemed determined that you be told she was here, as if you expected her. But Fern," he hesitated, and it was obvious he respected Fern's rank.

"Go ahead," Tor prompted.

The young guard nodded and straightened, locking his feet together and staring Tor in the eye, his expression relaxing as he took on full military stance.

"Sir. I got the impression that Fern didn't want you told that the young woman was here. I wish it noted that she never ordered me not to contact you, Sir."

"It's noted," Tor said, believing every word of the young soldier. "Let's find them."

Roln had walked around the tran-bus, searching through the trees, and looking on the ground.

"Look here," he said, reaching down and picking up a transmitting wristband. "Might be the wristband Syndi used to contact control center."

Interesting that it was lodged up next to a tree. Tor didn't like this. On a hunch that didn't sit well with him at all, he gestured for the two men to follow him. He headed straight to the East Passage.

And that was when he saw exactly what he didn't want to see.

"What the hell is going on?" he barked at Fern and the guards who held Syndi between them.

She struggled to turn around but couldn't, and there was something very obviously wrong with her leg.

"Tor," Fern said, nodding and looking quite relaxed as she moved around the men who held Syndi. She patted the young soldier on the shoulder, smiling. "Good job for contacting Tor, soldier," she said.

Then turning her attention to him, she spoke quietly. "I'm sorry you have to see this, Tor."

"What is it exactly that I'm seeing?" Tor asked.

"She attacked me," Fern explained. "I tended to her wound and then she attacked me."

"You lying little bitch." Syndi struggled against the guards holding her. "She just told me that she's bringing me…"

"Didn't you two just pull her off me?" Fern interrupted, turning quickly and pointing to the two guards who held Syndi.

"Yes," both of them said, nodding.

Tor noticed immediately the confused yet outraged expression on Syndi's face. Her wet dress clung to every curve on her body, her long hair unbrushed, tangled, and falling in thick strands over her shoulders and down her arms. Those small dark eyes glowed with a passion that alerted him to her level of outrage. Other emotions surged through her as well. The way one of her legs, a leg with a clean bandage covering her shin bone, seemed limp and unusable, he guessed what he saw on her face was pain.

Two guards held her arms, refusing to let go of her when she struggled. She then staggered, and used the guards as crutches when they prevented her from falling. Every muscle in his body hardened as he watched her struggle, and then almost fall.

"Why are you here at the East Passage?" That bothered him more than how they were treating her.

He sensed the worst and waved his hand at the two guards. "She can barely stand, let's get her back to the tran-bus," he added quickly.

The guards glanced at Fern, confusion quickly showing in their expressions, but at the same time moved forward to carry out their leader's orders.

At that moment a group of men rose out of the East Passage. His view of them was partially blocked by Syndi and the guards, who had their backs to the passage.

"What is this?" Roln immediately jumped in front of him.

Tor managed to move around Roln and grab Syndi just as the men behind her reached for her. For a moment it was a struggling match. They seemed intent on taking her and focused on no one else.

Within mere feet of each other, opening fire would be ridiculous. Tor aimed a hard punch at the face of the closest man who'd emerged out of the East Passage.

"Get your hands off her," he hissed, knocking the man back into the water.

"Tor," Syndi cried out, falling into him when the men behind her let go.

There were more of them. Reaching for her, grabbing her shoulders, wrapping their arms around her waist. Determination made their expressions hard. They were on a mission, here for one reason. And he wondered how they knew to show up at this exact minute.

With all the scuffle going on, it was hard to determine who fought whom. People were all around him. He held Syndi, and she latched on to him with incredible strength.

"Go. Get her out of here," Roln hissed next to him.

"She's coming with us." One of the East Passage guards was close enough to hear Roln. "You have no right to prevent us."

"Well, I do." Syndi twisted in his arms, kicking out with her uninjured leg. "You have no right over me."

Her quick attack surprised the guard, and he fell backward. But Tor wasn't ready for her to move so quickly either, almost dropping her. She staggered to the side, her injured leg unable to hold her. A woman, one of the East Passage guards, made a dive for her, and the young soldier pulled a gun, firing. The woman screamed, and fell on top of Syndi. She went down hard and he saw the pain contort her face when her back hit the ground.

Outrage filled him with an intensity so severe, he lifted the dead soldier off Syndi and hurled her toward the other guards. Immediately Syndi sat up, scurrying backward with her one leg dragging.

"Get her," one of the East Passage guards yelled.

But Tor was faster.

Wrapping his arm around her waist, he lifted her off the ground, running toward the tran-bus while he carried her pinned to his side.

"What the fuck?" she yelled when he pushed her against the side of the vehicle, pressing his body against her.

Looking over her shoulder, his gaze pierced into the trees toward the East Passage, there was no time to waste in getting back up over there. God only knew how many more soldiers Ran Mose would send through that passage.

Her dry hand gripped his biceps, clinging to him. He couldn't afford to linger on her worried expression. Right now wasn't the time to determine the reason the fire burned in her eyes as she pinned her gaze on his face.

The control room answered on the first buzz. "We have unannounced troops coming through the East Passage," he told Ben Osk. "Send me backup and quickly."

"How many men do you need?"

"Get a unit over here right now." Twenty guards should stabilize the situation. "Better put several more units on alert. I'm not sure what is happening here yet."

A scream came from the East Passage. Someone came running through the trees, a figure too fast to distinguish if it was one of his men or not. Syndi jumped against him, her fingers digging in to his flesh.

"They're on their way," Ben Osk said. "What's going on there?"

"I'm not sure. Search for any transmissions that might help give me a clue."

"On it now."

Tor pulled Syndi toward the side door of the tran-bus. "Get in there," he told her.

"I can help fight. I don't want to hide." She surprised him by fighting him.

Damn fool woman. She could barely walk.

"I don't have time for heroics," he hissed. "Do as you're told."

"They are attacking because of me," she shot back at him. "And I'm not going to hide while your people die. There's got to be something I can do."

Gunfire screamed through the air, attacking leaves and branches on the trees as it flew toward its destination. The tran-bus shook, the front end of it receiving a direct attack.

"Damn it," he moaned, pulling Syndi in against him. He'd almost sent her into the damn thing.

Tor dared to step around it, aiming at the woods until he found his mark. Firing at the guard who'd attacked him, he sent him sprawling back into the trees.

"Over there," Syndi said, pointing.

He aimed, taking out another guard. Where the hell were his men?

Fury burned through him while his muscles hardened, his gun aimed at the trees while he searched for any more of them. Syndi pulled his phone from his other hand before he realized her intent.

"This is Syndi Stone," she said into the still open line. "They've attacked the tran-bus. Yes. We need another one."

Quickly she started answering questions, filling Ben Osk, and him at the same time, in on what had happened directly before he arrived.

"Your men should be here now," she said, looking up at him.

She leaned heavily against him. As much as she tried to show him that she could stand up and fight, he saw her stressed expression. She took long breaths in between her comments, and her heart raced against his chest. Her long brown hair, unbrushed and waving around her face and over her shoulders, contrasted against her flushed face.

Staring down at her, the drive that kept her going fueled his need for her as much as her raw beauty. Carrying her out of there, taking care of her, sounded like the ideal thing to do at the moment. Those dark green eyes, hints of brown swarming in them, were warm with passion, understanding what he craved. She ached to be with him too. The look on her face told him as much. Ached to be in his arms, away from this spot, in a much more intimate setting.

"You'll be better soon," he whispered in a husky tone.

Her dry lips parted and then closed. Defiance making her nose look a bit perkier, her chin stick out slightly. One eyebrow raised just a bit. "I'm fine," she lied, looking sexier at that moment in her defiant state than she had a few minutes ago.

The rustle of trees behind him was his only warning.

Syndi tensed in his arms, her eyes widening as she looked past him.

"The woman is coming with us," a man's voice said from directly behind him.

At the same time, something sharp pressed between Tor's shoulder blades. Another person moved around him, one of the East Passage guards, water dripping from their hair and clothes.

"We don't wish to harm anyone," the female guard said quietly, her gun pulled but held firmly in her hand at her side. Her dark eyes didn't blink as she held his gaze. "If you'll kindly let her go, we have orders to bring her back with us."

Syndi stiffened in his arms. She didn't move when the sound of twenty of his men grabbed the group's attention. His guards appeared through the trees, looking surprised and then quickly pulling their weapons.

"She's not going anywhere," he told the woman. "You can start a war today, or you can go back to Ran Mose and tell him if he wants to speak with Syndi, he may come here and do so."

It was too quiet as the growing amount of men and women, all with weapons pulled, stood watching — waiting. The hard metal pressed into his back irritated him. Syndi's hands curled into fists against his chest, her long hair stroking his arms as it fell down her back. But he wouldn't break the awkward silence. Let his enemy ponder. They could kill him, but he doubted those were their orders. And they had a dilemma, one he would let occupy their minds. They knew getting Syndi out of there right now would be damn near impossible. Raising the death count would be likely. Walking away in defeat was their best option.

Syndi's fists pressed against his chest. "No," she whispered, pushing away from him.

Everyone around him moved slightly, on edge, the tension growing thick in the air. One overanxious shot, and they would have a bloodbath on their hands.

"You won't have war because of me." She looked up at him, her small eyes tormented. "I'll go with them."

He shifted, the point of the gun aimed at his back rubbing against him, irritating him further. Grabbing her, forcing her to remain in his arms, or better yet, holding her firmly with one hand while he turned around and belted the coward who dared hold him at gunpoint, rushed through his mind.

"Like hell," he began.

She puckered her lips, shaking her head slightly while her hand stroked his arm. "It's okay. I'll be okay," she told him, taking an awkward step to the side.

The woman who held her gun at her side, watched him carefully, her gaze drifting to Syndi when she moved. Tor shifted enough to catch a mere glimpse of the soldier behind him, and that there were others behind them. The fact that he didn't see Roln, or Fern, or any of the other guards bothered him. But right now, all he could focus on was Syndi. If she'd kept her mouth shut, possibly he could have convinced them to leave. But her interruption of the silence threw a new angle on the situation.

She took another step, and the woman to the side of him reached for her. Every muscle in his body tightened while he fought the urge to punch the woman in the face.

Just then, Syndi stumbled, going down behind him. He turned just as she grabbed the gun from the hesitating soldier who'd held the blasted thing at his back. Twisting it from his grip, she aimed, firing at close range. The soldier flew backward, surprising the other men who'd stood waiting for orders.

Apparently their leader was the woman who stood next to him. As Syndi fell, the woman raised her arm, as if ready to issue an order. He wouldn't allow that command to be directed though. Punching her square in the face, he felt her nose crush against the impact. Falling backward, Tor ducked at the same time, grabbing Syndi as she fell to all fours.

"Fire!" he screamed, diving with Syndi into the opened door of the tran-bus.

His men were more than ready. Bursting into action, they took out the East Passage guards, who hesitated that one moment too long when they didn't know whether to attack or run. It seemed apparent they were to bring Syndi back alive. He guessed he should give thanks for small favors. But at the moment, all he wanted to do was get his hands around Ran Mose's neck.

A couple of hours later he wanted to do a hell of a lot more than strangle the man.

"Ten of our soldiers are dead, and you imply we've attacked you?" The smug look on Ran Mose's face urged Tor to send his fist through the monitor. "We were invited through the passage, told that Syndi was waiting for us. Pray tell, dear boy, who opened fire on whom?"

He wanted to *dear boy* him right up the ass.

"Your people tried to take her against her will. And as for who opened fire first, I have ample testimony here that your men attacked first." This was worse than beating a dead fish. "What has my curiosity piqued at this point is why you are going to such measures to capture this homeless woman from the surface?"

"If she means so little to you, send her to me." Ran Mose smiled with calm confidence.

Tor wouldn't be bullied, even by this smooth pro. "I don't believe I've discussed my feelings toward her with you," he said in a low voice. "If you wish to see her, we'll have escorts at the East Passage to bring you here to her."

Ran Mose laughed. "You'd like that, wouldn't you, boy?"

Ignoring the man's insulting tone took so much strength his jaw hurt from clenching it.

"What is your interest in her?"

Ran Mose leaned forward, raising his eyebrows, which caused his forehead to wrinkle. Large eyes pierced him victoriously.

"You'll be receiving a file soon verifying the blood type and pupil scan of my daughter, who was stolen from me when she was a child. Running a test on Syndi Stone would be appreciated. Needless to say, if the tests match, holding her will be viewed as a kidnapping of a citizen of East Passage." Ran Mose crossed his arms over his chest, leaning back as he stared at his screen.

Tor wouldn't let the man get to him. Keeping his expression relaxed, he leaned back in his chair, relaxing behind his desk in the quiet office. Outside in the control room, he knew they were incredibly busy preparing for battle, searching for transmissions, running scans throughout the West Passage, and trying to gain as much information as they could to prepare themselves for whatever attack this leader might have lined up.

As attracted as he was to Syndi, he couldn't accept that all of this was because of her. Ran Mose had started the motions of turning their world upside down. He'd sent men to the surface, sabotaged the passages—the man had a mission. And the picture was a hell of a lot larger than just obtaining a lost daughter.

Not to mention, they'd tapped into transmissions verifying he wanted her dead. This wasn't a father blinded with love and searching desperately for a lost child. Ran Mose probably had little concern for Syndi, other than the simple fact that she stood in the way of his legitimate son ruling after Ran. Even then, if he'd kept quiet about Syndi, no one, including Syndi, would have known she was his daughter. There were missing pieces here.

Letting out a breath, he stared at the man who'd so quickly become his nemesis. Mourning Fern's death for a moment, one of a handful of his soldiers who'd been found dead after the skirmish ended, he feared she'd probably been an informant to Ran, and more than likely the one who'd contacted him telling him to come get Syndi at the East Passage. Five of his soldiers were dead. And the rest were in the infirmary right now. That would be his next stop, after this private conference call ended. He needed to see Syndi, confirm that Roln was okay. But with the amount of deaths, he'd have a harder time knowing exactly what happened at the passages.

"You know as well as I do that Syndi isn't a citizen of the East Passage, regardless of who may or may not have birthed her." The way Ran raised an eyebrow, Tor didn't doubt the older leader seldom had his words questioned. Tor ignored the slight gesture, deciding that broadening the picture might be to his advantage. "Turning her over to you won't stop the knowledge that the surface is populated, that it's a matter of time before they learn of us. She's found us, and so will others. Admitting you're her father tells me that you've known for quite a long time about the cities above ground. What has me curious is what you're doing with that knowledge."

Ran's grin made Tor bristle. An uneasy feeling sank through him.

"I always knew you showed potential. I doubt it takes you long to gather your answers." Ran looked down, arranging something in front of him on his desk. "The identification information on the infant stolen from me is being loaded to you now. I expect a day is ample time to run your verification tests."

With that the transmission terminated. Tor stared at the blank screen for a moment, digesting everything just said. He had no intention of running any test on Syndi. That barely concerned him. She was safe with him, and that was where she was going to stay. What did concern him was the realization that Ran Mose had men on the surface. His agenda had to have something to do with the people up there.

A strange thought formed somewhere in the back of his mind, something that didn't sit well, leaving a foul taste in his mouth. Pushing away from his desk, he stood, running his hand through his almost dry hair as he stared at his quiet office. Not focusing on any one thing, he allowed the thought to take life, develop in his mind.

Images popped into his mind. Bottles of water that Syndi had been so excited over, the intense heat and dead ground that he'd seen while up there, the pathetic living conditions that Syndi called home. The surface was dead. People existed up there, fighting for water.

But, where was that water coming from?

Hitting his fist against the top of his desk, Tor hurried out of his office. He needed to see Syndi.

Chapter Sixteen

ଛ

Without the sun, it was damned hard to know how much time had passed without a clock to go by.

Syndi sat on the edge of the bed, looking around the large cave that was brighter than most of the other caves she'd been in since she'd been in Tor's world. It seemed an unbearable amount of time had passed since the nice young man, who barely seemed grown, had looked at her leg, applied a new dressing and some medicine that he told her should help eliminate any scarring.

Ever since then, she'd sat there, growing more and more restless, while watching Roln and another young guard sleep in nearby beds. More than anything she wanted to get out of there.

A lot of people had died shortly after she'd arrived. There was no denying it had all been because of her. Ran Mose wanted her bad enough to kill for her. Not the first time, she hopped off the bed, amazed at how little her leg hurt now, and walked over to the natural waterfall that bubbled down about five feet of rocks in the middle of the room. Sitting on the manmade ledge surrounding the water, she ran her hands through the cool water, watching it flow over her palm.

She hadn't seen Tor since they'd left the passages. More than likely he was working, trying to figure out the mess she'd caused. He hadn't questioned her but had simply instructed his men to take her and the other injured to the infirmary. Sitting there and waiting for him to come to her, or for anyone to come for her, was making her nuts.

Water trickled over her wrist, soaking into her skin. Bringing her hand to her face, she rubbed the water over her, relishing its coolness. This world was more than a paradise, yet complicated with so many problems. The biggest one being her entering into it. It was as if she weren't supposed to be here, and now that she was, she'd set off balance the natural course of everyone's lives.

For some reason, she couldn't get her mind to accept that knowing Tor was all that wrong though. Granted they were from different worlds. But it was the same damned planet. There had to be a way she could keep seeing him without destroying the lives both of them had always known.

Accept that her world, her life, was dying—and his world could save hers.

Already she'd tapped into his world, shown a few of the villagers how to gain access to the water. She'd have to tell Tor, make him aware that water now bubbled in more than one place on the surface.

That is, if he would ever come for her. Running her wet hand over her arm, she soaked both hands, moistened her skin and then stood, straightening the dress she'd had on since she'd changed during the storm in her tent. Her damp hand made the material cling to her, and she looked down at herself. Her nipples hardened while she watched.

In the matter of one night, she'd been attacked by dogs, captured by guards, shot at and almost abducted—not to mention almost killed. She let out a breath, shaking her head that in spite of all of that, what she wanted more than anything at the moment was Tor.

There was no other man like him. Ever since she'd left him, returned home, all of her attention had been focused on hurrying through what she had to do so she could be with him again. It wasn't right. Their being together, experiencing some kind of normal relationship, could never happen.

Walking into her village with him at her side could never happen. And the leader of this world, this passage, would be gawked at with her by his side. Everyone down here stared at her, her physical differences. And that wouldn't change.

But her heart wouldn't accept that she couldn't be with him. Just trying on the thought for size brought excruciating pain that made it hard to breathe. Images of him floated through her mind, smothering the unbearable thoughts. So tall and well built. Dark hair, darker than a sky at midnight, that fell around a rugged face, a sexy face, made him a man who would stand out in a crowd. But it was more than his good looks, that muscular body. Tor had a way of seeing into her soul.

Standing there, imagining him entering the room, coming to her, she returned to the water, suddenly feeling way too warm. Tor was a born leader, with an aggressive nature, and ways of making everyone around him turn to him for guidance. That was exactly the kind of man she wanted at her side. Someone strong, not afraid to take chances, willing to always fight for what was right. Someone she could trust. Trust with her life.

A lump formed in her throat while her heart started beating too fast. Tingles rushed over her. Damn it. Just sitting there, waiting, and thinking about him, need poured through her. A pulse in her pussy began throbbing harder, her breasts felt swollen. She watched droplets of water fall from her fingers over her legs, then create small paths between her thighs. Moisture mixed with heat inside her, soaking her.

Dear Lord. She needed to fuck him soon.

It was that strong side to Tor that turned her on so much. She had to have someone stronger than her. No man in Camden had even come close. They all balked when authority entered the town. None of them would stand up and fight, try to improve their life. They were content to dry out and die without trying.

"But not you, Tor Geinz," she whispered, playing with the water.

Now to figure out how to keep seeing him without destroying both of their worlds.

Soaking her arms one last time, she headed toward the door, her pace slowed only slightly by the dull throb in her leg.

"I'm going nuts sitting in there," she said, immediately holding her hands out in a sign of nonaggression when two people in white shorts and shirts approached her.

"We have orders to keep you here," a young man said, the one closer to her, as he gestured for her to return to the room.

"I'm sure you do," she said with a sigh. "Isn't there something I can do though? I'm going nuts."

Escaping wasn't on her mind this time. It was still the middle of the night at home, not to mention she really had no clue where she was, or what direction to head to get back to the passages.

The cave she'd entered wasn't much bigger than the one she'd been in. This room had its walls painted white and had computers and other equipment lining the walls. There were several people in the room other than the two who approached her, their looks wary as if they expected trouble from her. A woman who'd been working at one of the computers turned, frowning as she wiped her hands on her hips. She looked at Syndi as if she'd never seen anyone like her in her life. Which, in fact, was probably true.

"What's the problem here?" she asked, sounding annoyed.

"No problem." Syndi shook her head. "I'm restless. Bored. My leg feels better."

"I'm sorry we aren't entertaining you." The woman scowled.

Syndi nibbled at her lip. They didn't want anything to do with her. Well, she didn't want to be there either. "Would it be okay if I contacted Tor?"

"Of course not." The woman shook her head, looking at her coworkers as if they'd just learned they were dealing with a nut.

"Then how about Ben Osk?" There had to be something she could be doing other than sitting and twiddling her thumbs, going nuts thinking about Tor, who obviously was busy enough that he wasn't seeking her out. "You can monitor the conversation."

The woman waved her hand in the air. "Fine," she said, sounding exasperated. "Open a transmission for her. But watch her."

"I'm not going to do anything," Syndi mumbled, wondering what they'd heard about her.

After a minute of watching the man press several buttons on a keyboard, she stared at the screen until images of the control room and Ben Osk frowning appeared before her.

"Ben, I…" she started.

"What is this?" Ben's large eyes opened wide, his expression one of complete astonishment. "Cut this transmission immediately."

The screen went blank with no further explanation. Immediately a phone began buzzing on a counter alongside the wall. The woman who appeared to be in charge answered it, mumbled a few short words then hung up. Turning around, she pointed a finger at Syndi.

"Get back in that room," she barked, as if Syndi had done something wrong.

She started to turn, more than put out with how they were treating her, when the phone buzzed again. The woman grabbed it.

This time she almost slammed it down after agreeing to whoever was on the other end.

"Take her down to the main entrance. Several guards are coming to pick her up."

Syndi hid her smile, more than pleased to be getting out of there.

Only the man led her out of the room, leading the way down the narrow hallway that Syndi had grown accustomed to seeing outside all of the caves. Wondering how much effort must have gone into carving out their homes and businesses in these underwater mountains, she imagined how this civilization had come to be. Once their ancestors had lived on the surface. Tor had told her how scientists had managed to mutate humans. For whatever reasons, her ancestors had been left out of that mutation.

Those who had moved underground to live had to have worked hard to create these cities, carve tunnels and build rooms inside of rock.

The opening in the ground full of water was wider and longer than the openings at Tor's home and control central. Dark water barely rippled as she looked down at what reminded her of a watery grave. The man in front of her jumped into the water, splashing it around the rocky ground. Syndi licked her lips, jumping in after him, hating this part. There was no way of knowing how deep the water was, or which way it led once she was in it.

Her eyes didn't adjust immediately and she found herself in black water, with no light around her. It seemed odd for a medical facility to have such a dark entrance. If this was where they brought their injured, they must use some kind of light. She couldn't see a damned thing.

A hand wrapped around her arm and she jumped, coughing water. It took a minute to focus on the man's face underwater, the white of his eyes standing out against his black pupils. He began pulling her through the water and she focused on her heart beating, and the throbbing in her leg that matched the beat. If she didn't relax her gills wouldn't open. And the last thing she wanted was this man to see her panic underwater.

They moved quickly through the underwater cavern. It seemed there was too much water around her for this to be a tunnel and she had no idea where he was taking her. This didn't seem a typical way out of a cave-room like the other tunnels.

Water rushed past her while she held her breath, tolerating him holding her arm while leading her through the dark cold water. Her lungs burned. Her eyes were wide open, although they might as well have been closed because she couldn't see a damned thing. Her lips pressed together, holding the air in her lungs, the pressure building as she ached to breathe.

She could really only kick one leg, although that was barely necessary the way he propelled the two of them through the inky blackness. Her brain began pulsing, matching the throbbing that now seemed to beat from her head to her toes.

Air. She needed air. The urge to yank her arm free, fight to reach the surface, became a thought that she couldn't make go away. More than likely there was no surface though. They swam underground, through a tunnel so large and so dark she couldn't see the walls, had no idea where the ceiling or floor were. The blackness closed in around her.

And still she couldn't breathe.

Her heart thudded harder, beating against her ribs, struggling for freedom just as she ached to do. The man kept pulling her, cold water moving over her body, her hair flowing behind her. It seemed it would never end. On and on, through the darkness, wet blackness blanketing her, suffocating her, drowning her.

Pop!

Her gills opened so quickly she swore she floated over the man who held on to her arm. His grip didn't change. It had to be her imagination. The quick gush of oxygen to her lungs made her lightheaded.

At first she thought her eyes played tricks on her when she saw the white dot. Ahead of them, growing, getting brighter, until she could see the man's legs and body who led her. He swam with a solid rhythm, his legs kicking, barely moving, yet creating enough power that it thrust them forward. He guided her toward the light.

It was a beam. No. A headlight. They were approaching a tran-bus. The light grew, enabling her to see through the murky water, see that they were in fact in a large underwater tunnel. The tran-bus fit easily within the walls, hovering underwater, waiting for them.

When they floated up to the tran-bus, the side door opened, giving way to a small closet-like entrance. The man pushed Syndi forward, placing her inside the tran-bus and then let go of her arm. Instantly the door to the tran-bus closed. She was inside a closet filled with water—and it was starting to drain.

First her head was out of water, then her shoulders, then she stood with water only to her waist. Within a minute all water had drained out of the confined area and a door slid open behind her. She turned, swallowing thickly, and stepped into the tran-bus.

"You are such a little troublemaker." Tor grabbed her and pulled her into his arms with enough fierceness that she almost stumbled forward.

Before she could react, or respond, he'd gripped her hair, angling her head and devouring her mouth. His lips were hot, his actions so aggressive she forgot to breathe.

Strong arms wrapped around her, crushing against his powerful torso. Her nipples hardened so quickly they ached. She couldn't breathe. At that moment she didn't give a damn. Leaning into him, collapsing against him, she opened up, tasting him, drinking in his passion.

He'd called her a troublemaker. But why, she had no clue. And if this were her punishment for her unknown crime, she'd do it again in a second.

His hands pressed against her back, his long fingers stretching over her skin, sliding down her until he gripped her ass. Squeezing, he groaned into her mouth and impaled her with his tongue. Their tongues moved around each other, quickly at first, and then slowing, while he stretched her mouth open, taking all she could give and demanding more.

Water dripped down her body. Her heart pounded against his chest. Barely able to move, she did her best to cling to him. Holding his shoulders, feeling his muscles twitch against her fingers, she arched into him further, wanting more.

Her pussy throbbed. Heat swarmed through her. Humidity rose between her legs.

He broke off the kiss as aggressively as he'd started it, ripping his mouth from hers. Staring down at her with lust-filled large black eyes, his panting matched hers.

"I'm not a troublemaker," she whispered, barely able to catch her breath.

He moved his hands under her dress, gripping her panties and pulling them up the crack of her ass. The material pressed against her pussy, against her clit, rubbing the sensitive flesh while he pushed his fist against the top of her rear.

"Anyone tracking our transmissions now knows where you are." His voice was barely a whisper.

"What do you mean?" Her panties were soaked, and the sensation he gave her as he tugged on the material made her want to buck into him. She couldn't think.

"What I mean is that I think a war is about to break out. That's why I had the medical technician bring you to me." Tor's other hand cupped her breast. His finger and thumb found her nipple and twisted it.

Her mouth fell open. His words were too serious yet he was sending her into a pool of desire. Thinking became a chore she didn't want to mess with.

Letting out a gasp, she fought not to start panting. Her voice was no more than a husky whisper.

"Don't go to war over me."

The corner of his mouth twitched, possibly the beginning of a smile. "You are more than worth going to war over," he said, squeezing her breast. "But I have a feeling the picture is a lot bigger than that."

God. She wanted to yank her dress down and demand he suck on her nipples right now. She blinked a few times, barely able to see past his broad shoulders into the small space of the tran-bus. The dark water outside made the windows look black. Glancing up at his brooding expression, she tried thinking about anything but his hands slowly torturing her.

"Why are they trying to take me then?" Even thinking about Ran Mose couldn't take away the sensations rushing through her as his fingers let go of her panties and started a wicked trip down the crack of her ass.

"Because, my dear, under his own laws, if you are his daughter, you could claim your right to rule the East Passage after his death."

His words made her heart stop beating. Everything around her seemed to stop. All she could do was stare at him, struggling with the meaning of what he just said.

"I don't want to rule his Passage."

"By law that rulership might fall in your hands." His words were sobering.

Pushing against that hard chest, she stepped around him, his hands slowly gliding off her body. Her limp was slight as she took a step or two into the small area of the tran-bus. Pressing her fingers into the back of the passenger seat, she stared into the dark abyss outside the windows.

"I wonder at the thinking of a man who would turn the entire world upside down because of his own wishes." No matter what she did, lives on the surface and below were going to change.

Something on the panel buzzed and Tor moved around her, sliding into the driver's chair. Pushing several buttons on the dash, he then reached for her, trying to pull her into his lap.

Although her leg didn't hurt like it had before, she still wasn't as stable as usual. She collapsed on his lap, instantly feeling the steel rod of his cock press against her ass.

"This is Tor," he said into a mouthpiece that attached to the dash by a wire.

Syndi moved quickly to the other seat. Sitting on his lap was a hell of a lot more than just a distraction. Pressing her legs together, she fought to keep the throbbing ache for him down to a dull roar. His eyes focused in on her, boring through her, knowing that she wanted him. It was obvious by his expression.

"There are explosions reported at the passages," the piped voice said through the small speaker on the dash. "I'm sending five more units over there."

"Good. I'll be there in less than ten minutes." Tor immediately brought the tran-bus to life, turning it around so quickly that Syndi held on to her chair.

"I'm afraid the explosions have done some serious damage this time." It was Ben Osk's voice.

"What damage?" Tor asked.

"I'd hate to speculate, but I swear they were intent on bombing the small pond that isn't one of the passages." Ben cleared his throat. "They did a damned good job. The pond is nothing but mud now."

Tor met her gaze. The tunnel to the surface had been destroyed. Her heart beat in an uneven rapid patter. Suddenly she couldn't breathe. Being trapped down there would mean her people would fight to learn what had happened to her. And right after showing Perry that there was water. This wouldn't look good at all.

"Do we have casualties?" Tor's expression looked strained. His jaw clenched and a small muscle at the edge of his mouth twitched.

He no longer focused on her as he pushed the tran-bus through the water. Light added shadows to his face when they entered into brighter water, and left the large cavern. The blackness outside the windows slowly changed to a milky blue-green, lights off other tran-buses slowly flooding the water around them.

"None reported yet," Ben said. "I have a request from the infirmary. Roln is asking to return to his post."

"If he's okay to release," Tor told him.

Ben acknowledged and the conversation ended.

Her heart continued racing as they moved into the open sea. Schools of fish swam around them while other tran-buses flooded the area. It baffled her brain that for over a hundred years such a sophisticated society lived underneath them and they never knew. In fact, the more she thought about it, the harder it was to believe. But if her government had known of all of this, surely they would have gained access to the water.

As it was, water purification plants in the city were heavily guarded. Breaking into the heavily secure areas was a death sentence. Not once had she questioned where the water came from. Had her government known about this world all along?

But Tor hadn't known about her world. She believed his sincerity and had seen his reaction when he'd first surfaced. He hadn't been prepared for the intensity of the heat and the brightness of the sun. He believed all humans had been mutated, and lived underground.

If Ran Mose really was her father, he'd known about the surface at least twenty years ago. Maybe the picture of war was a lot bigger than simply trying to steal her back. Ran Mose very well could be planning war with her world. An unpleasant taste rose from her throat. And somehow, she fell into play with all of this.

Icy chills rushed down her spine. She had no army. And she sure as hell had no clout. Her world would turn her over to Ran Mose in a second to keep peace. The villagers were loyal to each other—to an extent. But intentionally she'd always kept her distance, knowing she was different.

It dawned on her at that moment that she'd lost the bag she'd brought with her. "Tor," she said, breaking the unpleasant train of her thoughts. "I brought some things with me. They were in that tran-bus before we left the passages."

"Tell me what they were. I'll have them sent to my home." He looked over at her, his expression firm but those dark eyes penetrating through her.

She twisted the bottom of her hair, wringing the water out on her already soaked dress. The material clung to her and she guessed probably gave him a damned good view. Looking down she saw how her nipples peaked into hard nubs, the swell of her breasts stretching her dress as she breathed.

There had to be something wrong with her. In the middle of a deadly situation, she wanted him. And she knew when a man wanted her. That kiss he'd given her when he pulled her into the tran-bus wasn't a friendly greeting. They had a physical need for each other. Allowing emotions she seldom paid attention to surface for a moment, it had been all she could do to get back here to him. Granted, taking care of the villagers, learning more about her mother, all of that mattered. But she wanted Tor too.

Looking into those large dark eyes, the same compassion ran as deep through him. He'd hurried over to get her, using a back tunnel to help keep her hidden, but then they rushed off to protect his people. He wanted her, but just as badly, wanted to ensure the safety of his world.

"Everything was in a dark plastic bag. It was on the seat next to me when I was in the tran-bus." The small box that held her mother's journal could be damaging if it got into the wrong hands. "I'd brought something to show you that I found out in the dead lands before I met you."

"What was that?" He watched her when she glanced his way.

"My mom's journal. It was in a box that had similar designs on it that were painted on the tunnel walls that led from my world to yours."

"I have men working on learning what those designs are." He picked up the small speakerphone, giving the order that the bag in the tran-bus be taken to his house. "Or I did until Fern died," he added, staring at her.

"Will you miss her?" She couldn't read his dark stare.

"She betrayed me." Obviously he wouldn't share his feelings.

All she could go by was the darkening of his eyes at her question. The hard edge of his jawline, the intent dark gaze in his eyes, made him so powerful looking. Warmth spread through her, something that felt as dangerous as he looked.

The dash buzzed and he reached for the small speakerphone, corded muscles flexing in his arm. His mouth barely moved as he spoke.

"Roln here, checking in." The voice sounded raspy through the small speaker. "I've been in touch with all the unit commanders. The situation at the passages appears to be stable, although interesting."

"How so?" Tor asked.

"Our readings show they've collapsed the pond that leads to Syndi's world, but they've extended the East Passage. My guess is they've made their own exit to her world."

Syndi sucked in a breath. Things were about to get ugly for both worlds. Would it be better to be stuck down here, or on the surface when it all went to hell? The pain in her heart made that answer too clear. She wanted to be by Tor's side.

"Have the men reopen that passage. We might have to prepare some of them to head to the surface." Still he showed no emotion, other than that one muscle that twitched next to his mouth.

"We might not have to do that." Roln's words had her pulling her gaze from Tor and staring at the small speaker.

"That small hole we discovered in the ocean leading to the surface has just gotten larger."

"Small hole?" she whispered.

Tor looked at her. "I was investigating a hole that had developed in the ocean wall when word reached me that you had been attacked."

She nodded. The timing was right.

"Do you know about it?"

"I couldn't say until we reach the location." Her insides tightened. There was no way to guess what his reaction would be when she told him they had dug for water. But, damn it. Her people had a right to survive. "Before I left to come here, I convinced a few of the villagers to dig for water."

She straightened in her seat, sliding slightly in the puddle created from her wet clothes. No way she'd back down from that penetrating gaze of his. He needed to see that her people meant as much to her as his did to him.

He took his time looking at her, as if forming some conclusion. Her tummy twisted in knots. That power that had turned her on filled the small confinement of the tran-bus. And those sensual large eyes, with that almost black hair bordering the hard features of his face, made it seem suddenly very warm.

He slowly raised his hand, putting the small speakerphone to his mouth. "We're headed over to the hole in the ocean wall. Meet us there."

Putting the handheld device back on its hook on the dash, he finally pulled his gaze from hers, adjusting their course. For a long moment he said nothing. She didn't look away but studied his profile. There was no longer a twitch by his jaw. He focused on the view in front of them. All of that water.

"I had to do it. We're dying without water." She bit her lip. There was no reason why she had to explain her actions. She didn't need to prove herself to him.

"Any good leader would have done the same thing." He didn't look at her.

"I'm not a leader."

"It's in your blood." Obviously he accepted her bloodline without any questions.

The tran-bus slowed, and silver cylindrical objects appeared floating in the water, the bright yellow tape stretching between them catching her attention. Tor glided around them, moving through the water and in between several other tran-buses. He brought them to a stop then moved out of his seat.

"I'll be back," he said, moving toward the door.

Syndi jumped up, her leg throbbing slightly. "No. I'm going with you. If this is from the hole we dug in the village, I need to know."

Tor looked down at her, their bodies inches from each other. She ached to run her hands up his chest, get that hard as a rock body to twitch under her touch. It took more than just a little bit of effort to keep her hands at her side. He made no effort to touch her, and she wouldn't touch him. He gave no indication of how upset he was about her telling him she'd helped dig for water. And he had no right to be upset at all.

"And what if it is?" he asked her.

"Then I'd rather have the villagers see me appear in the water than one of you."

Chapter Seventeen

ജ

The irony of it was unbelievable. In her world Syndi was a nobody, a cast-out among her people. Yet the woman standing before him would take care of those people who deemed her unfit to live in their cities. She would protect them, see that they survived. Not many would do that.

Syndi would die trying to take care of her people, and few would remember her efforts after she was gone. He wouldn't let that happen. Never had a woman worked her way under his skin like she had. With all the chaos surrounding them, handling matters was a lot easier with her at his side. For one thing, he didn't have to worry if she were safe. Syndi had no training, reacted from pure, untamed emotion. There was no way he wanted that raw energy that he saw glowing in her small dark green eyes to crumble. No one would take that from her.

Stroking a wet strand of hair that stuck to the side of her face out of the way, he loved how she turned her head into his touch.

"What would you tell your people if they were at that hole when you surfaced?"

"Simply that I'd been swimming in the water." She didn't hesitate. She'd already thought through her answer. "You asked me not to tell anyone of your existence, and I won't. Although I think the time is coming when all will be made aware that there are two worlds on this planet."

She was right. More than likely, since Syndi existed, Ran Mose had been dealing with people on the surface for a number of years. Whatever those dealings were, Tor would find out soon. The people didn't know. He was pretty sure of that. But her government probably already knew his world existed.

Nothing bugged him worse than being in the dark about something. He'd be damned if he approached her people before knowing what Ran Mose knew. Unfortunately, he'd be willing to bet Fern had a hand in keeping him in the dark. The fucking bitch. Good riddance. Ben Osk was a good man though. If he could be in several places at once, he'd do his own snooping and learn what Ran Mose knew. And he had every intention of doing that once he could get home. Until then, he had to rely on his government to back him and support him.

"And then you would stay on the surface." He didn't want her leaving him.

Her breath tickled his palm as she spoke. "It can't be morning yet. I brought a small clock with me, but it's in that bag. I'm not sure of the exact time. I doubt there would be anyone at the hole at this time."

Her concept of morning and night was new to him. But he understood that she based time on the rotation of the Earth.

Running his hand down her face, and then over her soft full round breast, he tortured himself momentarily. Damn. What he wouldn't do to fuck the shit out of her right now. Every muscle in his body hardened just watching her, touching her, seeing her passionate gaze as she stared up at him.

"You may come with me, but you are not returning to the surface." He wouldn't let her argue that fact. It wasn't open for discussion.

Sensing his finality with his words, she shut her mouth, and nodded silently. The way she pressed her lips together, he didn't doubt she wanted to say something. That was too damned bad. There would be time for discussion later. Right now, he still needed more answers. He wouldn't lose her before he had all those answers.

"Good," he said, giving her nipple a slight tug. Then reaching for her hair, he pulled her closer, leaning down to nibble on her lip. "Later, my dear, when we get back to my house…"

"I can't wait," she whispered against his mouth.

The blood rushing through his veins began to boil, and drained quickly to his cock. Her passion for lovemaking matched her passion for everything else in life. He straightened as another tran-bus glided into view through the front windows. At the same time, his phone buzzed. Clearing his thoughts, he grabbed his phone, but didn't let go of her wet hair that wrapped around his fingers at the back of her head.

The small screen on the phone told him it was Roln. Staring at his guard's tran-bus that floated alongside them, he answered the phone.

"I've ordered the guards here to remain in their tran-buses and just keep an eye on the hole," Roln told him. "Reports are that it's now a good five feet in diameter."

"I'll meet you out there." Tor hung up the phone and placed it back on his belt. "Let's go. We're a half mile or so from the passages right now. I thought your village was closer than that."

"We dug outside the village," she told him, running her fingers through her hair when he let go.

He pressed the button to open the inner door of the tran-bus and then put in a quick call to Ben Osk.

"Once I've determined the safety of this hole, I'll head over to the passages," he told Ben.

As long as none of the villagers entered the ocean and drowned, he'd be satisfied. What he really wanted to know was if they had access to her world from here. If they did, he'd let Ran Mose think he'd sealed them off from the surface.

"I'll buzz you if anything changes, but right now we appear to have a respite over there."

"Keep searching their transmissions," Tor told him. "I want to know everything there is to know about Ran Mose."

Ben told him he was on it, and that would have to be good enough for now. The great leader of the East Passage wouldn't have an easy trail to follow. If there were a trail at all, Tor would find it.

They entered into the small compartment between doors, the door behind them closing securely before the other door opened. He heard Syndi gasp when the water quickly filled the small area, pulling them out into the ocean.

Habit had him leaping forward, quickly falling into line with Roln, when he realized Syndi hadn't kept up. Roln noticed at the same time. She was just outside the tran-bus, struggling to move through the deep water. Her small eyes were wide, and a beautiful shade of green next to the deep blue water that surrounded her. Long brown hair floated around her, and her thin dark limbs kicked furiously and waved in the water, showing her lack of swimming skills. Her cheeks puffed out. Her lips puckered into a small circle. The more she gyrated around, the less she moved.

Roln was probably his only officer who wouldn't laugh at the sight. Hurrying back to get her, he wrapped his arm around her waist, pulling her up against him. Her face was inches from his and she blew a stream of bubbles into his face. Pinning her to him, he rubbed one of her gills, brushing the sensitive skin with the edge of his finger. She didn't know this was how they treated their children. Her facial expression relaxed as her gills opened, and she smiled warmly at him.

His heart swelled at her innocence. Trust and gratitude warmed her cheeks, making her eyes even greener. Letting go of her, he took her hand, and swam back to Roln.

The hole he'd seen earlier that day didn't look a thing like the gaping dark abyss they swam up to now. Looking into the dark tunnel, he realized the water had a fair amount to do with how large it had become. Dirt from the ocean wall had quickly eroded, creating a natural tunnel.

Syndi kicked forward, ready to enter the tunnel, and he pulled her back. There was no light in the tunnel, although there wouldn't be if it were still dark on the surface. He also had no clue how far the tunnel went. Letting her lead the way didn't sit well with him.

She turned on him, glancing quickly at Roln who floated next to them, but then returning her gaze to him. She pointed to the tunnel and tried to pull her hand away. The woman was determined. And there was only one way to get answers.

He kept a firm grip on her hand, but moved into the tunnel with her. The three of them floated into the dark murky water. And surprisingly, they weren't in it long before he could see the other end.

The surface was a hell of a lot closer than he'd imagined.

Syndi stopped them and put her palm up toward their faces, gesturing for them to stay put while she swam to the surface. Frustration hardened Tor. He didn't like giving her the lead but understood she had to be the one to surface. Letting go of her hand, he and Roln treaded underneath the water while she moved above them.

Her legs kicked in an untrained fashion, more like a scissor kick. Her dress floated around her offering a wonderful view of her crotch, and the panties that barely covered her ass.

Glancing at Roln, his officer met his gaze, raising one eyebrow. Amusement almost flickered in Roln's eyes. But he had the good sense to keep his expression blank. The man would have to be blind not to be enjoying the view. Tor looked above him to see that Syndi had surfaced and now all they could see were her legs kicking and her sweet pussy and ass barely covered by her underwear.

Then she pulled herself out of the water, and he had a brief glimpse of her before she disappeared. This wasn't the plan. Floating there for only a minute, his mind raced as he needed to make a quick decision. Going to the surface could reveal his existence to anyone who might also be up there. Syndi didn't reappear, which told him nothing. Either she was ensuring no one was around, or she was talking to someone. There was no way to know without waiting.

Having spent a lifetime learning patience, Tor remained below the surface a bit longer, knowing they were underwater far enough that no one would see them. But Syndi didn't reappear. She'd agreed to come back to him. And he trusted her. If she didn't return, something wasn't right. They hadn't discussed how much time she should stay above ground.

If something were wrong, he would have to help her. Tor's thoughts raced. Giving away his presence would make her people aware of him. The ramifications of that act weren't clear to him. But leaving Syndi, not going after her if she were in trouble, would mean she could get hurt. That wasn't an option.

A few more minutes passed, and he met Roln's gaze. The worry in his friend's expression matched how Tor felt. Whatever act he made at this moment could change their lives forever.

Syndi was worth making that move for.

Pointing toward the surface, Tor kicked ahead. They were going after her. In the next second he lifted his head out of the water. Dim light and heat greeted him. There was enough room for the two of them to surface. Tor saw Syndi immediately, with another man holding her arm. There was no need to contemplate his next move. The man's angered expression was all Tor needed to see to know she needed protection.

"Don't try and make me think you just walked over here," the man hissed at her, shaking her as he held her arm. "Tell me the fucking truth, I've been at this hole all evening."

"What have you been doing? Why didn't you let me know you were over here?" Her familiar manner of speaking with the puny ass who held onto her only fed Tor's fire.

Ignoring the intense heat that instantly burned his skin, in spite of the fact that there was no visible sun, Tor pushed himself out of the water. The ground seared his hands. Moving quickly toward Syndi, his growing anger helped him ignore how the hot dirt tortured his bare feet.

"Get your fucking hands off her," he told the man.

The scrawny excuse for a man looked at him with pale blue eyes, his blond hair streaked with water and dirt around his face. His surprised expression turned quickly to shock as he let go of Syndi and took a step backward.

A quick glance showed him the man wasn't armed. His clothes hung on his thin body. Little muscle tone and hesitation were enough for Tor to know he could take him out without even using his weapon. He glowered down at the man, grabbing Syndi at the same time.

She surprised him by putting her hand on his chest, her tone calm and quiet.

"It's okay, Tor. He won't hurt me." She gave him a placid smile that he didn't like, and then turned to look at the man. Her other hand went out to him. "Perry. Calm down. Listen to me."

"They're fucking mutants." Perry took another step backward, almost stumbling over himself. He pointed a shaking finger at Tor and Roln. "That's what the council members told us to watch out for. If they've infected this water…"

He tried to turn, as if to run. Syndi jumped after him. She moved so quickly that Tor was surprised. Tackling Perry, she tried to pin him down. He was bigger than she was, and stronger.

"You aren't going anywhere until you hear the truth," she spat.

"We'll get money if we turn them in. Then we'll have money and water." Perry wrestled with Syndi, quickly gaining the advantage.

Tor gave Roln a quick look, which was all his officer needed. He interfered with the struggle, and quickly pinned Perry down.

"Don't hurt him," Syndi said, rubbing her arms as she took a step backward and stared at Roln, who'd pinned Perry to the ground. "Let him up. Perry if you run, so help me, I'll kick your ass."

"Who is this man?" Tor asked, pulling Syndi out of Perry's reach.

The tents of the village weren't too far away. He saw no movement among them and could only hope for the moment that the four of them were alone. There was a wet path, looking well trodden, leading from the hole of water in the ground back to the village. If Syndi had helped create this hole before she'd left, this Perry had been working at hauling water ever since then. His marks in the ground were proof of that.

Perry struggled against Roln, but was no match. His officer had Perry's arms pinned behind his back and held Perry so that he stood facing Tor and Syndi.

"How do you know them?" Perry asked, frowning when he saw Tor hold on to Syndi. "Syndi, what have you done?"

She ignored his questions and glanced at her village, then up at Tor.

"Perry is a friend, I guess," she said, hesitating on the word friend. "I've known him all my life."

"Friend?" Perry hissed. "Just a friend?"

Tor didn't like the man's tone.

"Yes, Perry. Just a friend," she said with conviction. "And at the moment, you're pushing it."

There wasn't time at the moment to question why Perry would think himself more than a friend. He would get answers to that later. There were two buckets near the water, more than likely what Perry had used to haul water back to the village. One of them lay on its side, its contents having soaked the parched ground, filling the cracks at Tor's feet. More than likely, Syndi had startled Perry when she came out of the water.

This water meant everything to these people. He'd establish authority first then get his answers.

"What have you been doing with my water?" he asked Perry.

"This is my water." Perry struggled again against Roln's grasp. "Find your own water."

"Your water?" Syndi sounded surprised.

Perry gave her a quick look, but dismissed her with a mere glance. He narrowed his gaze on Tor.

"Why are you here?" he asked, trying to look stern but failing miserably.

It wasn't hard to tell that Roln used little effort in restraining the puny runt.

Tor looked at Roln. "Let him go."

Perry shrugged out of Roln's grip when his guard released him, as if he'd had some effort in freeing himself. His personality was obvious. Tor knew the kind. They'd play nice to whoever they thought could get them the farthest, and stab them in the back just as quickly. There was no question in how best to handle him.

Tor pointed at the hole in the ground behind him. "You're using my water, from my land. With little to no effort I can block it at my end and you won't get a drop. Tell me what your motives are right now, or I block the water."

Perry's back straightened. The man had no muscle tone at all. His small beady eyes shifted from him to Syndi.

"Who the hell is this man?" he whispered to Syndi. "What have you done?"

"I showed you where to dig for the water," she reminded him.

Tor wondered if this was how it happened twenty some years ago. Had Ran Mose followed his woman to the surface, only to find a people who needed his water so desperately they would do anything for it?

The man would have cut a deal, made a prosperous contract for himself. His greed was about to destroy both of their worlds. Tor had worried about their government, about being able to contact and talk to them, but it was the people who would respond to him. These cast-outs would protect him to keep their water. The desperate look in Perry's eyes told him as much.

"I'm Tor Geinz," he said, grabbing Perry's attention. "I rule the West Passage, which exists underneath you, and is where this water is coming from."

"Then why do you look like the picture of the men wanted for destroying the water?" Perry challenged.

"Does this water look destroyed to you?" Tor gestured to the water bubbling to the surface. Just looking at it reminded him how quickly his skin was drying out. If they stayed up there much longer they would weaken. But he had to make a decision. Perry had seen them. Now he needed to decide whether to leave him above ground, or haul him down to the tran-bus. "Sounds to me like you've been fed a bunch of lies."

Perry shook his head. He gave Syndi an imploring look. "You need to explain all of this to me."

"Why? Does it surprise you that our government has again lied to us?" she asked.

She looked up at Tor, her gaze lingering on his chest before rising to meet his gaze. He didn't miss the hunger that still lingered in her eyes.

"What are you going to do?" she asked quietly.

Glancing at Roln, he then looked past him at the quiet village that would be waking up soon. They now had water, a simple necessity to life that they'd been denied all their lives.

"We could make him come with us, that would keep him quiet," he mused, not giving his attention but taking in the desolate surroundings of the dying surface of his planet.

"He can't swim. What would he do down there?" Syndi asked, her tone rising as if she didn't like the idea at all of making him come with them.

"At least then I would have assurance that he wouldn't tell everyone he saw us rise from the water."

"You let that water be, let me keep it, and I swear no one will know I saw you here." Perry held up a dirty hand, as if showing allegiance. "We won't say a word, will we, Syndi?"

Tor was about to say Syndi was coming with him. He looked down at her, watching as she studied Perry.

"You realize if word gets out about this the government will take this water," she said to Perry.

"Do you think I'm stupid?" he snapped at her. "I've been hoarding as much as I can, filling all the barrels. I've been working all night to ensure there would be water."

"What are you going to tell everyone when they wake up?" Syndi shook her head at him.

"That I cut a deal and got us all water." Perry sounded very proud of himself. "No one will even know this is here."

Syndi continued shaking her head, but didn't say anything. She thought Perry no more than a fool, and Tor would have to agree with her. But he wasn't sure he'd write the man off as innocent as he tried to sound.

"We'll be back. If word has spread about us, there will be no more water." Tor pointed a finger at Perry, doubting seriously the man's sincerity as he nodded vigorously and agreed it would be their secret. Time would tell though. He reached for Syndi. "Let's go."

"Wait a minute." Perry took a step forward but then hesitated. "Syndi, what are you doing?" he whispered.

"I'm going back underground. It's okay, Perry. I'll be back in a little bit. And God, please, if you've ever kept a secret in your life, keep this one. There will be water for everyone if you do."

Perry didn't say anything but watched as Syndi jumped in the water. Tor jumped in after her, positive the man would turn tail and run to the village as soon as they'd all disappeared. Most cowards hurried to spread their news, finding safety in the more who knew what they did. From what he'd seen, the villagers didn't have great communication access with the rest of the world, and they had no rank on the planet. For the time being, he wouldn't worry.

Chapter Eighteen

ಬಿ

Tor led the way inside when they reached his home several hours later. His phone buzzed, and he headed into the other room that housed his computer without a word.

Syndi spotted her bag that she'd brought sitting on his couch and hurried to it. Everything she'd brought with her was still inside. Thank God!

For the first time, she wasn't in any hurry to return home. Knowing there would be questions, and possibly heated arguments, was damn good reason to take her time and plot out her defense. Not to mention, this was the first time she'd been alone with Tor. Every inch of her ached to have him inside her again.

Lifting the box she'd found in the dead lands, she slowly unwrapped the plastic that encased it, and then ran her hands over the strange symbols painted on it. Everything inside was intact. The journal was still worn, hard to read, but no worse for wear than before. Taking it and the old newspaper articles, she entered Tor's office.

"Nothing surprises me anymore," he said into his phone, while studying his monitor in front of him.

She moved around the desk, holding the items. Tor stared at a group of pictures on the screen of his monitor, each with a date and time underneath. His calendar was different from hers, and she didn't understand the numbers, but the pictures spoke for themselves.

"That's the governor," she said, pointing at one of the men in the pictures.

He actually appeared in several shots. Shown getting out of a dark car with another man, who was balding with thick, dark sunglasses. Another shot showed the same two men, except this time the bald man didn't have on sunglasses. His too large dark eyes gave away his nationality. The governor was shaking hands with the man. The next shot showed the same two men walking through a secured gate. Syndi studied it for a moment.

"That's one of the water purification centers." The governor was working with men from Undrworld, and the business obviously involved water. She shook her head. "You've been supplying us with water all along."

Tor looked up at her. "Do you know who that man is?" He pointed to the man with the governor.

She shook her head.

"That is Ran Mose."

He might as well have hit her in the gut because all wind flew out of her. For the first time she stared at an image of her father. No immediate reaction flowed through her, she just felt numb.

He said something quickly into his phone and then hung it up. With a quick movement, his strong arms pulled her onto his lap. Powerful and confident, his strength flooded through her, allowing her to take in the obvious.

Her father worked with her government in controlling the water. Hundreds of thousands of gallons of water so readily at his disposal, and he rationed it out at a devastating five dollars a gallon. Emotions broke through the numbness. She despised the man that she stared at in front of her. People died daily without water while he floated in it at his leisure.

She choked down the lump in her throat, her heart hardening with hatred toward the man who'd helped conceive her. Realizing her hands shook, she steadied the box in her lap, and then placed it in front of the monitor.

"What's this?" Tor asked, shifting her so that she sat on one leg.

His hard muscular leg, with its corded steel muscles, pressed hard against her soft rear end. She turned, brushing her hair over her shoulders, catching the attention of his soft dark eyes. A fire smoldered deep in his gaze, matching the burning need that pumped through her. It would be so much easier to seduce him, fuck him hard. She'd be comfortable with little conversation right now, allowing more primal emotions to surface.

"I...uh..." She cleared her throat. Closing her eyes didn't work. She could still see that brooding stare, feel his hard body touching her everywhere. She gripped the box in her hands. "I brought something to show you."

It sucked how her fingers shook when she held the box out in front of him. More than anything she wanted him to see her as strong, possessing every quality her father obviously lacked.

"What's this?" Tor moved underneath her again, forcing her to shift on his lap.

Her legs brushed together, her panties stretching against the sensitive moist flesh between her legs. Need surged through her with so much force it stole her breath. She sucked in a long slow breath.

"I found it in the dead lands the day I found the pool that led to you." Her fingers trembled as she brushed them over the odd symbols. "They match the pictures that were in the tunnel."

"And so far, those symbols match nothing in our history." Tor lifted the box and she pulled her hand back.

"It had that journal inside. These articles came from one of the old women in the village." She picked up the torn pieces of paper and opened them slowly.

Placing them on his desk in front of them, she pressed her hands over each one, flattening them. The headlines of each article were bold, glaring up at them.

Paradise Found Underground.

Street people announce the discovery of an underground water world.

"Explain these dates to me," Tor said, pointing to the dates at the top corner of each page.

"Both articles came out right before I was born." She read through them again, wondering how such news could have hit the papers and then been brushed aside without the entire world turning upside down.

"And this," she said, holding her mother's journal for him to read.

For a moment she thought his large fingers would crush the paper inside the journal. Tor showed surprising gentleness as he read the entries, turning the pages slowly, until he'd reached the end of the book. Without saying anything, he again looked at the box they had come in.

"These are exactly what are on the tunnel walls," he said, almost to himself, and then leaned forward, holding her to him with one arm as he gripped his pointer with his free hand and changed the images on the screen. The pictures he'd taken of the paintings on the tunnel wall appeared.

"These four paintings look like a hand, with the fingers in strange positions." Syndi compared the images on the monitor to those on the box. "That last image, of the two people dancing…"

"I should have realized this before," Tor said, interrupting her. "They aren't dancing. They're swimming. It's a celebration swim."

"A celebration swim?" Looking from the screen, she saw the excitement that made his dark eyes glow.

"Yes. It's a wedding celebration swim."

Her gaze dropped to his mouth. "A wedding swim? They're naked."

"When we get married," he said, his lips barely moved as his tone became quiet, growing huskier. "The couple performs the wedding swim. It's very erotic."

She ran her tongue over her lips, thoughts of moving against his body, naked in the water, making her insides throb. "Sounds kinky," she whispered.

"Depending on the couple, it can be."

Her heart skipped a beat, and then started racing too quickly. Marriage was something she'd never given any thought to. And she sure hadn't known Tor long enough to even entertain the thought. Something about how he said, *when we get married*, sent a fiery tingle rushing through her.

Her mouth went dry, and then too wet. "I can imagine," she managed to say.

"I'd like hearing what you imagine," he whispered, cupping her cheek and pulling her mouth to his.

His mouth was moist, hot and demanding. Parting her lips with his tongue, he moved slowly, with a determination that had her melting into him. Wrapping her arms around his neck, she pulled him closer, demanding more—needing more.

Everything inside her exploded. God. She couldn't get enough of him. Tangling her fingers through his thick hair, turning her head to deepen the kiss, she dove into his mouth, drinking from him as if he were her source for survival.

Twisting in his arms, she moved her legs so that she straddled him, forcing him to lean back. Every nerve ending that he ran his hands over sprang to life, tingling and charging her with energy that needed release.

His touch made her wild, his fingers gliding under her arms, down her sides, until he reached her hips. Grabbing the hem of her dress, he hiked it up her thighs, exposing her ass. She cried into his mouth, needing every bit of him.

Tor moved forward, taking her with him. Lifting her, he pulled his mouth from hers, leaving her gasping for breath. Brushing her hair from her face, for a moment she suffered from a fog of lust, unable to focus.

Her ass plopped down on the side of his desk, the hard surface cool against her exposed flesh. She had to smile when she focused on his messed-up hair, aching to run her fingers through it again. Tor straightened though, looking down at her with those large dark eyes, his focus intent, watching her while he reached for his shirt.

Feeling so alive with the energy that pulsed through her, she leaned back on his desk, pushing papers to the side, while she spread her legs, pulling one up and resting her heel on the edge of the desk.

Pulling his shirt off, his gaze riveted to her exposed crotch, the thin fabric of her panties stretching over her soaked pussy. Power fueled her cravings. Controlling him like this, watching lust fog his expression, she rested one arm on her knee casually, and then ran her fingers delicately over her underwear.

"What are you doing?" His voice was so damned husky.

She was driving herself nuts. That's what she was doing.

"Making you watch," she said, keeping her expression serious when he raised an eyebrow.

"You're in charge, huh?" His shorts went next, falling down his muscular legs when he pushed them past his hips.

His cock was hard as steel, jutting forward, eager and swollen. Her mouth went dry, while her breath caught in her throat. A throbbing started pulsing against her fingers as she stroked herself.

"You'll do what I want." She grinned into those large dark eyes, and then squealed when he lunged at her.

Tor lifted her rear end off the table as if she were no more than a child. He showed no strain, no effort, but simply picked her up. And with a fluid movement, had her panties sliding down her legs. He didn't let her down as easily, but allowed her rear end to slap against the hard surface.

"And you'll do what I want," he told her, not letting go of her legs but spreading them.

Syndi went back on her elbows as she fought for balance. Landing on a pile of papers, she tried not to mess up whatever she lay on. Tor took advantage of her hesitation in lying back and slid her forward. His hands moved down her legs until he gripped her ankles. Spreading her, opening her legs like scissors, he held her legs so she couldn't move them and pressed his cock against her throbbing pussy.

There was nothing to grab on to, nothing to brace herself. Clawing at air, she looked up at him when he thrust inside her. Her pussy stretched, his cock moving deep inside her, stroking the inner walls of her cunt. God. Her head fell back, her mouth opening in a silent scream when she couldn't catch her breath.

"Tor," she finally managed to say, barely managing to brace herself against her elbows while he pushed her ankles so that they were on either side of her head.

He would twist her into a fucking knot. And the spot he hit!

"Damn it!" She found her voice.

"Oh, hell yeah. I love how you control me," he said through clenched teeth as he began a faster pace.

Brushing in and out of her, stroking her pussy with his thick shaft, he hit her hard and fast. She scooted back against the desk, unable to hold on. Tor's hands wrapped around her ankles, holding on to her, while he leaned into her and filled her. Never had anything felt so damned good. Again and again he hit the spot that had craved his attention since she'd last been with him.

"Syndi," he growled, while she watched his entire body harden.

Chest muscles bulged. His eyes closed. His mouth formed a thin line.

"Come for me," she demanded, and at the same time felt him explode, his cock convulsing deep inside her.

Tor fell forward, making her think for a moment that he would collapse on top of her. Quickly she fell backward, raising her hands to catch him before he hit her. At the last moment his hands slapped the desk on either side of her and he stopped his body, just a few inches above her.

She smiled. "Told you I was in charge."

Tor growled, wrapping her into his arms and lifting her off his desk. Papers fluttered to the ground around them.

She wrapped her legs around him, feeling his wet cock slide out of her as he carried her from his office. When they reached the kitchen he stepped into his shallow pool, then dropped her.

The water felt so good splashing against her legs. She laughed, kneeling and lapping at his still semihard cock with her tongue as she ran her hands through the water.

"Syndi," he said, kneeling in front of her and then cupping her face with his hands.

She stilled, staring into those incredible eyes of his. His expression sobered, his gaze searching her face. Not daring to move, her heart started a hard, slow pounding in her chest.

He leaned forward, brushing his lips over hers and then rested his forehead against hers.

"You're starting to mean a lot to me," he whispered, as if the confession were hard for him to admit.

Oh God. They were from different worlds, meeting at the moment everything both of them took for granted was about to crash. She was at the lowest of ranks in her world. And he ruled his. His people didn't trust her. There were mysteries about her that could cause him problems. Hell, there were facts about her that already caused him problems.

She didn't move, made no effort to look at him, or pull away. "You mean a lot to me too," she finally said.

He ran his hand over her hair, a soothing gesture. A confession of feelings like what they'd just shared shouldn't result in a gesture to relax her. Unless he felt just as she did. And that was simply that a relationship between them would be close to impossible in pulling off.

Leaning back in the water, she pulled away from him, crossing her legs and sitting. "Are you going to take me home?"

"No." He sounded so stern she looked up at him.

His phone buzzed in the other room and he stood, leaving her. She followed his wet footprints into the other room. He paced naked in his office, listening to someone. Reaching for her dress, she pulled it over her wet body. Suddenly her heart was so heavy it hurt. When he should take her home, the determination in his voice had to mean that in spite of the dangers in them pursuing a relationship, he wanted it.

And damn it, so did she.

But she didn't want him brought down because of his attraction to her. If he wasn't thinking clearly, then she had to. God, that sucked.

"Show me when you get here," he said, moving to his desk.

She picked up the papers they'd scattered on the floor, and put them on his desk, curious about his call.

"I'm not sure what it means. That's fine." He ended the call.

Large muscles bulged against perfectly hairy skin when he bent and picked up his shorts. She swallowed a heavy lump, enjoying the view. Hell, she more than enjoyed the view. Her body tingled from damned good sex. Yet watching him dress, his hair falling around his face, long corded muscles stretching in his arms, in his legs, she ached to touch him, to walk into his arms, to know his thoughts. Already she wanted him again.

"Peg is on her way. She's discovered something about the images on the tunnel."

"What?" She took her underwear when he handed them to her.

"We'll find out when she gets here. She sounded pretty excited." Suddenly he was all business.

Switching gears wasn't quite as easy for her.

"Tor," she said quietly, watching as she traced an invisible line with her finger along the edge of her desk.

He didn't say anything and she really didn't want to see his hard all-business expression right now. She didn't look up.

"I'd like to hear about the images," she began, moistening her lips. Her stomach twisted and her heart felt like a heavy rock in her chest. She didn't want to leave him. "But then you should take me home. I have matters to deal with. And you'll think better without me around."

She choked on her last words but forced them out. Turning quickly and looking blindly at the doorway to his office, she didn't want him to see the moisture burning in her eyes.

Something pounded behind her. Her heart exploded, forcing a gasp out of her as she spun around. Tor looked ready to pounce, his fist resting on the top of his desk where he'd just hit it.

"If you ever tell me again what you don't mean..." he said slowly, standing and moving around his desk.

She automatically took a step backward. His fists clenched at his side. Muscles bulged through his arms and chest. And those eyes—they blazed with anger as he glared at her.

Moving in on her, he gripped her chin, lifting her head so she was forced to stare at him. "I swear I'll bend you over my knee and spank that sweet ass of yours."

She slapped his hand away from her. "I'm not a child. And this—" She waved her hand in the air between them. "War could destroy both of our lives. Your being with me could make it worse."

"No." He grabbed her wrist, pulling her to him. "I'm not letting you go, Syndi. You know as well as I do that we're stronger together. Deny it and I'll bend you over right now."

She stared at him, breathing so hard she worried she'd hyperventilate. There was nothing worse than not being in control. Standing next to him, with him holding her so she couldn't move, made her thoughts race, her mind spin while her body instantly reacted to him.

A tear burned down her cheek and she turned, suddenly very angry that she couldn't control her emotions. A buzz sounded in the living room, and she yanked her hand from his. Her heart fluttered with realization that they'd fight all of this together. But it scared her. And that pissed her off even more.

Tor gripped her shoulders, his hard body pressing against her back. Leaning down, his lips brushed over her cheek.

"Everything will be fine. We'll make it through this—together."

She wiped at her tears, hating herself for suddenly having so many damned emotions. She straightened, walking away from him. Leading the way into the living room, she held herself tall, quickly wiping away the blasted tears that had insisted on falling.

Control. She needed control. All her life she'd been in charge of herself. That wouldn't stop now. Something about having Tor to lean against sent a warmth through her too strong to subside. Fearing she was too damned close to losing her heart, losing that control she'd always had, she forced her emotions under check.

Staring hard at the door as Tor went to open it, she told herself that she too would be all business. No more of this thinking she was way too in love with him to back out now.

Peg stepped into the living room, looked past Tor and gave her a disapproving gaze. "I didn't know she was here."

There was nothing worse than being talked about like she wasn't there. "What did you learn about the images?" she asked, before Tor could say anything.

Peg frowned, looking down, as if trying to decide something. Carrying a black case with her which dripped with water, she walked past both of them into Tor's office. Obviously she was quite at home in Tor's house. Her tan shorts and short tan shirt clung to her wet body. She set the case down on the desk where just a short bit ago, Tor had fucked the shit out of her.

"I think I know what those images are," Peg said, her back to both of them.

Tor moved next to her, crossing his arms and watching while she pulled papers out of her case. The papers were encased in a see-through plastic, which had kept them dry. Syndi watched her spread the papers out over the desk. They were pictures of the painted images on the tunnel, and then some other pictures, more faded, in black and white. Syndi moved closer until she stood next to Peg, studying the pictures spread out before them.

"What are these?" Tor asked.

"I've been doing some research," Peg began, "going through many of the transmissions that are from the surface. They have quite a bit of their history on file." She looked up at Tor. "A lot of history from before the war—history we've lost."

A few of the black and white pictures looked a lot like the painted images from the tunnel. "So what are these?" Syndi asked.

Peg grinned, looking rather proud of herself. "You don't know?"

Syndi shook her head.

"They are from your history books. It's called sign language. A long time ago, when people couldn't talk, they held their hands in different positions and it meant things." Peg pointed to one of the pages. "This page shows how you hold your hand and what it means."

Then she pointed to the page next to it. "I printed the hand positions that match what is on the wall. If you put it in this order, and then use this key to determine what each word is, the message is, 'you must marry'."

"You must marry?" Tor frowned. "And the last image is the wedding dance."

"You figured that out too." Peg nodded quickly. "Someone painted a message on that tunnel wall. The question is, who did it?"

The three of them fell into a deep silence. There was only one person who could answer that question.

Chapter Nineteen

ॐ

The phone buzzed and Tor walked around his desk. His control room was calling him.

"What is it?" he asked, noticing Syndi's box she'd brought on the floor by his side of the desk and picking it up. He put it with the pictures so Peg could see it.

"Everything's just gone to hell." Ben sounded exasperated. "Several more explosions just went off around the East Passage. I've had several transmissions come through from Tren Fal with the North Passage. He's offering help. Shara Dar has also contacted us agreeing to send units as well."

The situation hadn't gotten so bad that they need the other passages help. "I'll head to the control room."

"The casualties are lining up, Tor," Ben told him.

Tor pinched his nose at his brow, feeling a dull throb start at his temples. War between the passages would only make matters worse. He feared there would be confrontation with the people on the surface soon, and he wanted to show them a calm strength, not chaos.

His phone buzzed again, showing another call, this one from Roln, coming through.

"I'm on my way," he said and then ended the transmission, taking the other call.

"You're not going to believe this." Roln sounded disgusted.

"Right now I'd believe about anything." He prepared himself for bad news, while watching Peg who'd picked up Syndi's box and was studying the paintings on it.

Glancing at Syndi, her attention was riveted on him. She worried so much for her people, for their safety. Her cheeks warmed a lovely rose hue while he watched. She nibbled at her lower lip, but didn't take her eyes off him. And she thought he'd do better without her. There was no way he wanted to go a day without her by his side.

"The hole leading to the surface has almost doubled in size." Roln paused and Tor had a feeling this wasn't the part he would have a hard time believing. "And damn it, Tor, we just pulled someone from the surface out of the ocean."

"What?" Tor yelled and both women next to him jumped. "Damn it, man. What did you do with him?"

"Right now we have him in a tran-bus. Poor guy is shaking in fear."

Tor cursed. This isn't what he needed right now. The damn fools would drown and their government would blame him.

"What's wrong?" Syndi asked, frowning.

"I think I've got this figured out," Peg said, also frowning. "What is this box?"

"I found it outside the pond in the dead land by my village," Syndi told her, looking now at the box in Peg's hand. "Do those images say something?"

"Okay, hold him there." Tor didn't like this at all.

Listening to the women, and imagining the worst at the passages and from the hole leading to the surface, a definite plan of action was needed.

"He's not going anywhere. But you might want to send Syndi over here."

He would have to send her to the surface. In the heat of their day, he wouldn't last long up there. There was no way she'd go up there alone though. He hung up the phone, heading around the desk and then putting his hands on Syndi's shoulders. He didn't miss the look Peg gave him, one of concern and reservations.

"The images on this box say, 'follow your heart'." Peg put the box down on his desk.

"We're headed out. Peg, you can take us to the control center." He looked down at Syndi. "We'll be there for a few and then we're headed to the hole leading to your village. Seems some of your people have floated into our world."

"What?" Syndi turned on him, her eyes widening. "I need to get over there now, then."

"I can take her to her people if you need to get to the control center. Do we have more problems at the passage?"

"Sounds like war is about to break out." Although he would do everything in his power to stop it. "But Syndi is staying with me. Let's go."

He turned Syndi toward the door but Peg grabbed his arm, pulling him back. "Can I talk to you for a moment? Alone?"

"There's nothing you can say to me that I wouldn't want her to hear." Tor let go of Syndi, crossing his arms.

He didn't think for a minute that Peg would turn traitor like Fern did. He'd known Peg too damned long. If she had a problem with him, she told it to his face—like she was getting ready to do right now.

Peg glared at him, crossing her arms. "Fine. Starting a relationship with her right now is a bad move."

"That's what I told him," Syndi said.

Peg slowly let her arms fall to her side. "It is, huh?"

"Yes." Syndi stepped around Tor, facing Peg. "Tor is the most incredible man I've ever met. I can see that you really care for him so I'll tell you that I might be falling in love with him. But my people can't live down here. And I won't desert them. You can't survive without water. And if left to their own methods, I'm worried my people could drain your world. So yes. You're right. There may never be a right time."

"And you've told Tor this?"

Suddenly he wasn't in the room. Tor crossed his arms, looking over Syndi at Peg. Syndi had just confessed what he knew already. She made love with every emotion involved. And their sex was too damned good for him not to see the truth.

"She told me this." Tor wouldn't have them discussing whether a relationship should exist or not. It wasn't open for debate. "And our worlds will have to learn to accept each other. She stays with me. Now let's go."

Once again he grabbed Syndi and this time left no room for argument. He almost dragged her out of his home.

"You are a stubborn pain in the ass," Peg mumbled.

"I'm noticing that," Syndi muttered.

Peg huffed from behind them but he ignored the two of them. Keeping his hold on Syndi, he jumped into the dark tunnel outside his home, yanking her into the water with him.

"We've got units crawling out of the East Passage worse than minnows," Ben reported in as soon as the three of them were in the tran-bus.

"I'm sick of Ran Mose's shit. Collapse the East Passage tunnel. Keep them over on their own side." Tor would take that man down before it was done. And he'd love to do it personally.

"Yes, Sir." Ben sounded excited with the order.

"Is there any way you can capture Ran Mose?" Syndi sat behind them.

Peg looked over her shoulder at her at the same time that he did.

She glanced at both of them quickly. "I want to talk to him before he dies."

"I'd love to give you that right." He guessed having never known her parents, she'd want to at least see the man who helped conceive her. He stared at her dress, wet and clinging to her firm curves. "Actually, that might be a damned good idea."

"What?" Peg had known him long enough to know that tone. "What are you going to do?"

Tor grabbed the speaker. "Ben," he said into the handheld speaker.

"I'm here."

"Send a message to Ran Mose. Tell him his daughter wants to see him."

He heard Syndi gasp behind him. Peg stared at him in disbelief, and there was silence on the other end of the line for a moment.

"Yes, Sir," Ben said, and then ended the transmission.

"What are you going to do?" Peg asked again.

"I'm going to take the motherfucker down," he whispered, turning toward the windshield.

The large ocean spread out in front of them. Tran-buses cruised around them, a usual busy day for New Dallas. His people were happy, led productive lives. And he'd see to it that they kept that life.

Ran Mose had struck a deal with the people on the surface. But he'd been selfish, greedy. He couldn't imagine the surface had much to offer them. Ran Mose saw it as a way to control more people, and the asshole got off on power.

If it were in his power, he'd do what he could to help those on the surface. But even if they turned all the water they had loose, and let it flow on the ground above, the sun would dry it out. They would still all die.

The speaker on the dash buzzed, and Tor grabbed the handheld. "Go ahead," he said.

"Tor," Roln said through the speaker on the dash. "Three more men came through the hole leading to the surface. We got two of them. One of them is dead."

"Take me over to that hole right now." Syndi leaned forward, grabbing Peg's shoulder.

Peg looked at the hand that gripped her, and then frowned up at him. He saw her hand reach for the controls but knew she wouldn't take the order without his consent.

"Do it," he told her, and the tran-bus swerved hard while Peg accelerated toward the hole in the ocean.

He ended the transmission and then quickly contacted the control room.

"We've got an emergency over at the hole Roln is patrolling."

"So I've heard," Ben told him.

"There are units just inside the South and North passages. No conflict, although a few guards swam ashore asking if assistance is needed. Shara Dar has asked to speak with you."

He would need to speak with all of the passage leaders before this was done. "Let her know at my earliest opportunity," he said. "Is the East Passage collapsed yet?"

"The order just went in," Ben told him. "No reports back yet."

"Keep me posted."

By the time they'd reached the part of the ocean where the hole had formed in the wall, Tor noticed the darkening of the water. Sediment floated heavily in the area. There were several tran-buses holding station just past the secured surroundings. Peg navigated around the other tran-buses and brought them to a stop.

His phone buzzed.

"Can you bring her over here?" Roln asked without greeting. "We've got a handful of upset people."

Tor heard someone say something in the background. Roln didn't respond to whoever it was, obviously waiting his answer.

"On our way." He secured his phone to his belt and moved to the back of the tran-bus with Syndi. "Peg. Wait here."

"Tor," she began.

"I said wait here." He took Syndi's arm and guided her toward the door.

Out in the water, he immediately noticed they'd need a purifier. As dirty as it was, it would be hard to breathe. Holding on to Syndi, who looked at him wide-eyed with her cheeks puffed out—a look he was getting accustomed to—he moved quickly through the water to the other tran-bus. The door slid open and he pulled her up against him into the small chamber. Her arms slid around his waist while bubbles filled the water when she exhaled. She had no idea how damned sexy she looked with her hair floating around her like that. Never would he have imagined such long hair looking so good on a woman. It wasn't practical, would always make it harder for her in the water. But damn if he ever wanted her to cut it.

The water lowered around them and he brushed a soaked strand away from her face. Coaching her right now probably wouldn't do him a damn bit of good. These were her people. He'd let her talk to them. She licked her lips, glancing past him when the door to the tran-bus opened.

"Syndi!" A child bolted from the seat and jumped into her arms.

"It's okay, Joey." She held on to the child and looked around at the crowded tran-bus.

The man he remembered as Perry stood slowly, meeting his gaze. Anger and fear were obvious in his expression. The man's small eyes shifted to where Tor had his hand on her shoulder.

"No one will answer my questions," he demanded of Syndi.

"What were your questions?" Syndi asked.

Roln was the only other guard in there. Obviously these people hadn't been any trouble. There was a man and a woman, the child in Syndi's arms, and Perry. Tor didn't doubt that the villagers were wondering where they were.

"What is this place?" Perry asked, his attention darting from Syndi to him.

"These people live here, just like we live on the surface," Syndi told him as she stroked the boy's hair. "How did you get down here, Joey?"

"I fell," the child said.

"And I went in after him." Perry shifted, a worried look darting around the small confines of the tran-bus. "Now why are we being kept here?"

"Can you swim your way out of here?" Tor asked.

Perry glared at him then ignoring the question, looked at Syndi. "Have they hurt you?"

"No." She turned and looked up at Tor. "We've got to take them back to the surface."

Tor nodded, in full agreement. He wouldn't have word getting out that they were holding hostages. No matter how they treated these people, he wouldn't doubt Perry would make them all out to be inhumane. Obviously he was quite jealous of him. Jealousy was a dangerous emotion, one Tor knew he needed to keep an eye on.

"Move this thing as close to the tunnel as you can get it. We'll haul them up to the surface one by one." He looked at Roln, who nodded and took the driver's seat.

Within minutes they had the door positioned at the entrance to the tunnel. The couple clung to each other and Roln and Tor stood behind them, gripping their arms, and catapulted to the surface when the doors opened. Next were the boy and Perry.

"Like I'm going to let you put your hands on me and drag me through that water." Perry crossed his arms, looking at Tor and Roln as if they were some type of hideous creature.

"I can tie a rope to you and pull you through the water," Tor suggested.

Syndi gave him a frustrated look. "There's no reason for you two not to like each other." She turned to Perry and sighed. "You know you can't swim. You try and get to the surface by yourself and you'll drown."

"Are we going to die?" Joey asked, tugging on Syndi's dress.

"No. We're going to be in the village in just a minute." She ruffled the boy's already tousled hair and he wrapped his arms around her.

"Roln, you haul him up there." Tor looked at Syndi. "I'll hold you while you hold the boy and take both of you up there. It will be the fastest way."

Guiding Syndi toward the door, he held her while she picked up the child and hung on to him, whispering reassuring words and making it all sound like an adventure. Moving quickly, he pulled the two of them through the water, having no doubts that Roln would have little trouble with Perry. The man didn't want to be away from Syndi. He would follow them quickly enough.

They were greeted by a small crowd and glaring sunlight when they surfaced. The heat was so intense, Tor could hardly breathe. His arm wrapped around Syndi's waist, he held her while she lifted the child out of the water. No grateful parent ran to him. The child simply turned and offered his hand to help pull Syndi out.

"What happened?"

"Where did you go?"

"How can there be people down there?"

All the questions buzzed around them. Focusing on the people was difficult with the sun making it so hard to see.

Syndi slipped out of his hands and lifted herself out of the water. Knowing disappearing back in to the water would mean leaving her there, Tor climbed out as well. There were more people hurrying toward them from the tents until he swore everyone who lived in her village had to be standing around them. Roln surfaced with Perry who sputtered and cursed, going into a coughing fit so that Roln had to almost shove him out of the water.

"There's enough water down there to last us the rest of our lives," Perry announced to the growing crowd, causing whoops and cheers.

The asshole made it sound like he'd just discovered it of his own accord.

"You know damned good and well as soon as the government learns this water is here they will mark it and we won't be able to have it," someone yelled.

Immediate arguments broke out. So many people were talking at once, and the glare made it so hard to focus on them, that Tor wondered how to calm the crowd.

"Enough!" Syndi yelled, standing next to him. "Listen to me. The water belongs to these two men. Now you all get to hear what I have to tell you. And the first one of you who tells me I'm crazy like my mom was, I swear, I'll belt you."

Apparently the mention of her mother was enough to hush the crowd. A few mumbled, and Tor cursed the sun silently for making it so hard for him to focus on them. He was seriously handicapped on the surface. Not being able to take control of this matter pissed him off. But there wasn't a damn thing he could do about the fact that his eyes weren't made for the sun.

"First of all, I need someone to bring me two pairs of sunglasses. Hurry now. This is important and you all need to hear it, but these two men can't see that well under our sun. They want to help us. And they've given us this water. Now we need to help them. We need sunglasses."

"Their sun is going to dry up this water sooner than they anticipate." Roln stood next to him and when Tor looked at him he noticed Roln had his head down, not looking at him.

"Not if we cover it," Syndi said, still standing next to him.

"Quick! A tarp for the water, and sunglasses," someone yelled.

The people around them moved quickly, surprisingly fast. Tor was impressed that within a short time a handful of them were hauling supplies from the village toward the water.

The sunglasses were amazing. Everything darkened when he put them on and suddenly he could see the people around him dragging a large plastic blanket and poles. In spite of the heat, he and Roln helped shove the poles into the baked ground and secure the covering over the water. Within a short amount of time they were shaded from the sun.

"Sit down by the water," Syndi suggested to him. "It will keep your skin from drying out if you at least keep your legs wet. We can't leave them now without an explanation."

Staring at the villagers who grouped around the waterhole, which now was almost ten feet in diameter, he saw their excited expressions. Leaving them like this, with them knowing he'd come from the water, would cause news to travel quickly. For the sake of her village and his people, a satisfying explanation needed to be given—or more lives would be lost.

Syndi sat at the edge of the water next to him, and as many who could, crowded in around them. The rest stood behind them, watching and whispering among themselves.

"I should have told all of you this sooner," Syndi began, silencing the crowd, who huddled around them. "There is another pond larger than this one out in the dead lands. I almost drowned in it and these people saved me."

She put her hand on his leg, and he put his hand over hers, keeping it there. Her hand was warm and damp but she didn't pull away when he intertwined their fingers together. Instead she tightened her grip and continued with her speech.

"That pond doesn't lead anywhere now, but this one does. When I found it, there was a tunnel that led to their world. But just like here on the surface, there are bad and good people below us. And it's the bad people who have been selling us our water, probably as long back as the last war."

"How did you find this out?"

"How much are they going to charge us for this water?"

The questions shot out from the villagers.

"We aren't paying a cent for this water," Perry yelled out.

"Quiet!" Syndi grabbed their attention. "We all need this water to survive. But the last thing I'll have is everyone fighting over who is in charge of it. Now I told you to dig this hole. I knew the water was down there. This water is part of their home."

She lifted Tor's hand in hers as she spoke. If anyone doubted that they were a couple, she eliminated it, drawing all eyes to their clasped hands.

"The man who has been selling water to our government collapsed the tunnel in the pond out in the dead land. He's trying to start a war underneath us. And it's going to affect us on the surface too. The only way we can make sure we have this water for our village is if all of us swear right now not to tell anyone that it's here."

An older woman, holding on to a stick that she leaned on when she walked, pushed and cursed her way toward the front of the crowd. "Let an old woman speak," she yelled at those around her, and then used the stick to point at Syndi. "How do you know all of this, Syndi? It seems like yesterday to an old lady when your mother came home with terrific stories. Look what happened to her."

"Bertha." Another woman in the crowd pushed her way toward Syndi, touching Syndi's head and scowling at the old woman. "My sister never produced water. Maybe if we'd listened to her she'd still be alive. Syndi has given us a great gift. I say we pay attention here."

"I've lived my entire life with the whispers from all of you about my mother," Syndi said, silencing everyone around her. "Well, she wasn't crazy. Maybe she made some bad choices, but she discovered something—something that hit the papers." Syndi pointed a finger at Bertha. A few of the others around them shuffled, giving clue that they knew and remembered another time when Syndi's mother had tried to tell them about underground water. "Now all of us have another chance. Here is water. If we're quiet about it, we'll have water to bathe, water for our meals, to cook with."

"No one cares about us." An older man looked at the group surrounding him while he spoke. "We keep this water for us, and we'll have it a lot better."

Quick agreement sounded among the villagers.

"What about these people?" Perry piped up, his disgust not having dwindled. He glared at Tor as he spoke. "What part do you plan on taking in all of this?"

"Don't abuse the water and keep your people from falling into it. I can't save you every day." Tor watched the man fume.

Obviously he had some clout among his people, for they grew quiet, watching him. Perry shifted his gaze to Syndi, his anger not subsiding.

"Do you think this water is going to hide what's really going on here?"

Syndi's fingers twisted under his grasp, but Tor held on to her hand firmly.

"There is another world down there, with cars that move underwater. Who knows what else? I saw it! How long before they try to take over? And look at you...you would turn against your own people." Perry waved his hand in disgust at the way Syndi held Tor's hand.

"If I were turning my back on my own people, I wouldn't have told you to dig," she said, her voice quiet although her anger was mounting.

Perry threw his hands up in the air. "I've heard enough. You don't want us to know what else is down there, what will happen next. You think we'll just sit back and be happy with having a little pool of water."

Perry turned, pushing his way through the group surrounding the water. Something made him stumble backward. It wasn't a normal movement.

Tor jumped to his feet, pulling Syndi up with him. In the intense heat, the quick movement made him dizzy, but he ignored the sensation, struggling to see what made the man act so strangely.

Then he saw them. Slowly surrounding the villagers who'd huddled around the water and underneath the makeshift covering, soldiers moved in on them.

Damn it!

Sitting on the edge of the small pool, the villagers had blocked his view. Soldiers from Undrworld that he didn't recognize, wearing some kind of backpack, and all heavily armed, closed in toward them in a half circle.

"What?" Syndi whispered, seeing what he saw.

"No one move and you won't get hurt." One of the soldiers, his gun aimed at the villagers, gestured with the weapon. "Don't anyone get stupid, and no one try to be a hero. All we want is Syndi Stone."

"Oh God," Syndi whispered, her hand wrapping his arm with more strength than he knew she had.

His gut reaction was to send her into the water, have her swim to the tran-bus. All of the villagers around him blocked his view of the soldiers. They also hindered his ability to get a good shot fired.

"She's not here." It was Bertha, the old woman, who pushed her way forward. "You think an old woman doesn't remember? Who do you think you are coming at a bunch of unarmed villagers with your goons like this?"

"I remember too." The woman standing next to Syndi moved quickly around the water, pushing her way through the crowd. "You took my sister. And if you're going to point those guns at us, why don't you take me too?"

The outburst from the two women seemed to put the guards surrounding them in an awkward position. Tor counted ten men, and realized the one talking was Ran Mose. The packs on their backs leaked water, and he guessed that somehow they'd rigged up a contraption that aided them in staying on the surface longer.

Villagers moved away from the water, creating a more visible line of fire. Tor reached for his gun, but Syndi moved faster, snatching it off his waist and darting around the water before he could grab her.

Holding it behind her back, she stepped forward. Damn woman. He pushed his way after her, knowing he made his presence known. Ran Mose smiled when he saw him. Tor wanted to send his fist right through that smug grin.

"So you are Ran Mose," she said, before he could reach her. "What a joyful reunion you've created for me."

"Syndi." Ran's tone grew softer. "You're even more beautiful than I imagined — prettier than your mother."

"And you're too ugly to live," she hissed, and pulled the gun out from behind her back, firing at close enough range to send the man flying backward across the parched ground.

Tor grabbed her, snatching the gun before she could lower it. Roln was right next to him, his weapon pulled. There was no way two of them could defend the entire village against nine of Ran Mose's men.

"No one fires." Tor held the gun down, staring at the men who seemed shocked that their leader had just been assassinated in cold blood. "I don't think anyone wants to start a war today."

The soldiers shifted, their weapons still aimed at the villagers. Water splashed behind him and several of the villagers cried out in surprise. Tor turned as a handful of his guards hurried out of the water. He glanced at Roln.

His guard gave him a half smile, tapping his phone. "Had a signal," he muttered.

Someone yelled, and Tor shoved Syndi behind him, aiming his gun when a man raced toward one of Ran Mose's guards, tackling him.

"Perry! No!" Syndi screamed.

Gunfire sounded and suddenly everyone was screaming and running. It was complete chaos.

"Hold your fire!" Tor screamed, as several more villagers stormed into the soldiers surrounding them. "Everyone hold your fire! These people aren't armed."

More than a handful of villagers raced past the guards, heading toward the shelter of their tents. Within minutes, a few villagers remained, two of them dead, one of them being Perry. Two of Ran Mose's guards held villagers down, pinning them to the ground. His men lined up next to them, pointing their guns at the East Passage guards.

Syndi started shaking in his arms, the reality of what she'd done obviously sinking in. He doubted she'd ever killed a person before and the trembling increased as she leaned into him.

"Everyone put their guns away," he said quietly, sliding his own gun onto his belt. "Let the villagers go," he told the men in front of him.

No one moved for a moment, but then slowly weapons were lowered, the pinned down villagers allowed to scamper to their feet.

Two dead men lay at the feet between the soldiers.

"Perry," Syndi whimpered, pushing away from him. "God. You stupid idiot."

No one moved as she knelt down next to him, the tears flowing. She stroked hair away from his face, closing his sightless eyes.

"You always had something to prove, and look where it got you," she said through choked sobs. Looking up at the men around her, she turned, staring at each of them. "Help me. We've got to carry him back to the village."

She stared at the East Passage guards, who didn't move. "Help me now, damn it. I'm not your fucking enemy, and I never was. Now I can't lift him by myself. Help me carry him."

One of the guards moved, and then one of Tor's men stepped around Syndi. The two men squatted, and then stared at each other for a moment before lifting the dead man. Syndi stepped back, nodding. She turned to the other guards.

"Take your man through the water. He deserves to be buried in his own world."

The guards obeyed her without questions. Tor nodded to the men, moving so they could carry the dead guard to the water.

She put her hand on his chest, looking up at him with a tear-stained face. "Go," she said quietly.

"I'm not leaving you here." Something hardened inside when she shook her head slowly.

"I need to take care of Perry," she said quietly. "And I need to talk to my people. I need some time, Tor. Go home."

She wiped her eyes then turned from him, leading the way as the guards helped carry the dead man back toward the tents.

Lorie O'Clare

Chapter Twenty

ဢ

Syndi walked through the village toward her aunt's tent. Her uncle spotted her, and pulled back the tent flap, saying something to his aunt who was inside. She stuck her head out as Syndi approached.

"How are you doing?" her aunt asked, stroking a strand of Syndi's hair away from her face.

"A little better, I guess." Two days had passed since they'd buried Perry, and since she'd killed her father. The numbness still hadn't worn off. "I came to tell you that I'm going to go see Tor."

Her aunt nodded. "We figured you'd go to him."

Syndi had known she would too. Every bit of her ached to be with him, to be in his arms again. There had been matters to take care of here though. She wouldn't walk away from her people.

"How long will you be gone?" her uncle asked.

Syndi shook her head. "I don't know. I'll be back. I just know I have to be with him."

She searched their faces, looking for understanding.

Her aunt pulled her into a hug. "We're going to miss you."

Then pushing her back, she turned toward her tent. "Wait. There's something you should have."

The midday sun fried her back as she stood outside the tent waiting for her aunt to reappear. Her uncle turned back to his work, his usual quiet presence not disturbing her.

"I've saved this knowing there would be a time when you should see it," her aunt said, wiping sweat from her brow as she pushed her way out of the tent.

Moving to the side of her tent where two chairs were semi-hidden by an old blanket clipped to a clothesline, Syndi looked at the items her aunt held in her hands.

"These were Samantha's," her aunt began, relaxing in one of the chairs, her fingers delicately going over the items in her lap. "She was a good woman. Don was a good man too. He married my sister when he learned she was pregnant and the man wouldn't marry her."

Syndi let out a choked sigh, the knowledge that her mother hadn't disgraced her marriage like that more reassuring than she'd thought it would be. Accepting that her mother had been less than scrupulous had torn her up. A major weight lifted from her shoulders with that knowledge.

"Why did they say I was adopted?" Syndi asked, dying to see what lay in her aunt's lap, but realizing there was a story to be told and she'd have to be patient to learn about each item.

"Like I said, Samantha was a good person, strong in her beliefs, and always determined to make everyone happy. You were born just a few months after Don married her. She managed to keep the pregnancy a secret, which was easier back then on the streets in the city. They just told everyone that they got a baby—and you were that baby."

Syndi remembered the box with her mom's journal, which was still at Tor's home. "One of Tor's people learned what the images were that were painted on that box I showed you with Mom's journal in it."

Her aunt looked up at her.

"It was some old language where people used their hands to talk if they couldn't speak. The hands painted were in different positions and each position was a word."

"That sounds like Samantha. She always seemed to know about some antiquated thing that didn't matter to anyone else." For the first time her aunt seemed content, relaxed in talking about her sister. She smiled as if remembering something. "What did it say?"

"The message on the box said, 'follow your heart'."

"I'm sure you'll do that," Aunt Mary said, looking down at the items on her lap. "When you were little, barely walking, Samantha came to me one day." Aunt Mary took a slow breath, her head lowered so that Syndi couldn't see her face. She let out a choked sigh, continuing. "Somehow she knew her days were numbered. But she came to me with this letter."

When she looked up the tears streamed down her face. Lifting an envelope off her lap, she handed it to Syndi. "I've never opened it. But she told me to give it to you when you were grown."

Her mother knew she would die. Suddenly trembling, she took the still sealed envelope, staring at the dried-out paper. The glue crumbled easily when she ran her finger against it, revealing the piece of paper sealed inside.

My dear Syndi,

Your father is going to take me. Not the father that you've always known, but the one who gave you life. I won't tell you that he's a good man. But he's a strong man, daring, willing to change life as we know it. Forgive me for falling in love with that adventure.

Sweet child, know that I love you with all of my heart. Already I see that you crave that same adventure, just as you crave the water. You will find what I have. I know you will. And when you do, take it on with full force. I know it will be your calm nature that succeeds in doing what your father can't do.

Make the world without shadows your home.

Goodbye and know that your life is blessed!

Your mother,

Samantha Stone

The tears wouldn't stop. They hit the page too quickly, blurring the ink. Syndi handed it back to her aunt who shook her head.

"Keep it, my dear. I know that's what Samantha wants."

"What she wants?" Syndi looked up, wiping her eyes to clear her vision.

Aunt Mary waved her hand in the air. "What she wanted. I don't know. There are days when I feel she is still alive, then I tell myself that is just me being a foolish old woman."

Her aunt shoved the rest of the items on Syndi's lap. "I saved what I could out of their tent. She carried this bag, and I think it probably came from that world underground. But it's all yours now."

Syndi ran her hand over the black texture, cracked from years of being exposed to the intense heat. Once it was probably waterproof, an easy way to carry things back and forth from underground to the surface.

Standing, she clasped the bag to her chest, aching to feel the water around her again. Her aunt stood as well.

"You're leaving." Her comment grabbed her uncle's attention, who had walked over to stand by them.

"Yes. For now. Thank you. Both of you. Thank you for raising me, and for giving me good memories of Mom." She pulled her aunt into a hug, holding the woman tight to her.

"Follow your heart," Aunt Mary said, which brought forth a round of new tears.

"I am," Syndi managed to choke out. "My heart is already underground. And I'm going there now."

She put her aunt at arm's length, smiling at her, and then reached for her uncle, hugging him as well.

When she left the semiprivate side of her aunt and uncle's tent, a handful of villagers had gathered, slowly walking alongside her while wishing her well, instructing her not to be a stranger. Old Bertha stopped her, and Syndi hugged the woman, laughing.

"You all act like you're never going to see me again."

She laughed through tears. The villagers followed her to the waterhole, and the realization sank through her that for the first time she approached water with no fear. She didn't worry about getting caught. No one would see her who wasn't supposed to. Even under the covering they'd made to keep the water from evaporating as quickly, it glistened like rare jewels against the dead ground.

A fresh start. A new beginning. And hopefully, a peaceful one. That water represented so much, just as her walk with her village alongside her did.

Mom, are you proud of me?

Securing her items under her arm, she sat on the edge of the water, the moisture soaking through every pore in her legs like a sweet lifeline being reconnected, rejuvenating her.

"Take care of all of you," she said, grinning as she slipped into the water.

She heard their goodbyes even after she dipped her head under the water. Grinning while the water filled her mouth, her gills opened on their own, without having to wait until her lungs were about to explode.

It was meant to be. Just as she'd done it. Kicking through the water, heading for the large ocean, butterflies swarmed in her tummy, excitement, nerves, anticipation.

Tor wanted her. And damn, did she want him. Her hair floated around her as she worked her leg muscles, forcing herself down through the water, kicking hard to move through the tunnel that led to the large ocean. It was harder than she thought, and took a lot longer than the few minutes it had taken Tor and Roln to move against the water.

By the time she reached the hole in the wall of the ocean, her heart beat so hard that for a minute she gripped the dirt wall with one hand, and her bag with the other. Simply staring out at the large underwater world in all its beauty, she took a minute.

The place had faults just like her home did. These people weren't perfect — hell, they were human. But she was part of this. And Tor was here. As she stared, a tran-bus, stationed at the side where the ocean had been roped off, protecting the hole, lit up. It began moving closer to her, splitting the water in two as it glided toward her. The door to the tran-bus slid open when it was right in front of her.

Her leg muscles ached when she kicked away from the hole, grabbing the side of the bus and then forcing her way inside. The door slid shut and the water began draining. She spit when her head was no longer underwater and waited for the other door to open.

When it slid open, she stepped inside, almost collapsing onto the chair inside. A driver she didn't recognize looked back at her.

"Take me to Tor, please," she said, feeling giddy like suddenly she was rich enough to call for a cab in the city.

Simply nodding, he turned to face front, and navigated the machine away from the hole, from her village, from her old life.

Her grin didn't fade as she gripped the wet bag on her lap. Everything her mother owned was in that bag. And somehow, that made her feel her mother was a part of her, experiencing this new adventure. She had a feeling her mother would be laughing with excitement just the way Syndi felt like doing.

The large underground mountain actually looked familiar while they cruised around other tran-buses and schools of fish. The guard driving the tran-bus never spoke to her, but she wasn't uncomfortable.

"I know the way from here," she told him when they reached the cave entrance that led to the tunnel which took her to Tor's home.

Again the guard was compliant. It crossed her mind that he'd been told to bring her to Tor when she showed up. Knowing that he had waited for her, given her the time she needed to take care of her village, made her even more anxious to see him.

The tran-bus came to a stop, and the door next to her opened.

"Thank you," she told the guard, and then grabbed her mother's bag, clutching it to her as she entered the small space between the doors.

It was even a longer swim through the dark cavern toward the tunnel that led to Tor's. Dark water surrounded her and her progress was slow with one hand holding the bag. Her leg muscles burned from kicking and more than once she wondered if she went in the right direction.

Remembering the snake they'd encountered in the water when she'd been with Tor, she shivered, forcing herself to kick harder. There seemed no end to the dark water, so cool against her skin, drifting through her hair, pushing against her face as she pressed forward.

When she was convinced that she must have swum in the wrong direction, the tunnel that led to his house finally appeared in the dark water, a black hole staring at her. Never had it seemed so dark before. Yet she'd always had Tor with her, guiding the way, holding on to her as he swam like a fish through the water.

Wondering if she'd ever have his skills, she entered the dark tunnel. The water grew even cooler, making her cramping muscles shiver. At least now she couldn't get lost. The narrow tunnel only went one way, and soon she would be popping her head out of the water. Focusing on seeing Tor, on being in his arms, hear him tell her how much he'd missed her, she continued kicking. Her muscles cramped, burned, stretched and ached but she kept moving them. Determination pushed her through the black tunnel.

When she reached the end and lifted her head out of the water, she dropped her mother's bag on the cold damp stone floor then simply rested her head against it. The coolness felt good on her cheek, her legs limp in the water. She was so tired from swimming she wondered if she had the strength to lift herself out of the water.

If she didn't, she wouldn't see Tor. And he was so close. Sucking in a breath, she pressed her palms on the wet stone ground, and pushed her body out of the water. Her legs were like limp noodles, wobbly and making her footing unstable as she moved along the edge of the stone wall toward the door to Tor's home.

The door opened as she reached it. Stepping inside, she stopped in her tracks when Tor stood before her. Tall and so powerful-looking, he was even more damned sexy than when she'd last seen him. Wearing nothing but his shorts, his muscles rippled under his creamy white flesh while dark hair tumbled in waves around his chiseled face. Eyes so large and dark stared down at her.

There was no doubt in her mind that she would collapse right there at his feet. Smoldering heat gripped her insides, tightening her muscles and making her tummy twist in nervous anticipation.

"I'm back," she whispered, her voice seeming suddenly incapable of uttering anything louder.

"No." He shook his head slowly, moving in on her, taking the bag from her hands.

"No?" The knot in her tummy soared to her throat, lodging there as she stared up at those dark unblinking eyes.

He tossed the bag onto the chair to the side of them. "No," he repeated.

Taking a strand of her wet hair in his hand, he twisted it, tugging slightly as he pulled her closer to him.

"You're home." He cupped her cheek, bringing her mouth to his, and then kissed her with a passion that sealed his words.

She'd followed her heart and it brought her home.

Why an electronic book?

We live in the Information Age—an exciting time in the history of human civilization, in which technology rules supreme and continues to progress in leaps and bounds every minute of every day. For a multitude of reasons, more and more avid literary fans are opting to purchase e-books instead of paper books. The question from those not yet initiated into the world of electronic reading is simply: *Why?*

1. *Price.* An electronic title at Ellora's Cave Publishing and Cerridwen Press runs anywhere from 40% to 75% less than the cover price of the exact same title in paperback format. Why? Basic mathematics and cost. It is less expensive to publish an e-book (no paper and printing, no warehousing and shipping) than it is to publish a paperback, so the savings are passed along to the consumer.

2. *Space.* Running out of room in your house for your books? That is one worry you will never have with electronic books. For a low one-time cost, you can purchase a handheld device specifically designed for e-reading. Many e-readers have large, convenient screens for viewing. Better yet, hundreds of titles can be stored within your new library—on a single microchip. There are a variety of e-readers from different manufacturers. You can also read e-books on your PC or laptop computer. (Please note that Ellora's

Cave does not endorse any specific brands. You can check our websites at www.ellorascave.com or www.cerridwenpress.com for information we make available to new consumers.)

3. *Mobility.* Because your new e-library consists of only a microchip within a small, easily transportable e-reader, your entire cache of books can be taken with you wherever you go.

4. *Personal Viewing Preferences.* Are the words you are currently reading too small? Too large? Too... ANNOYING? Paperback books cannot be modified according to personal preferences, but e-books can.

5. *Instant Gratification.* Is it the middle of the night and all the bookstores near you are closed? Are you tired of waiting days, sometimes weeks, for bookstores to ship the novels you bought? Ellora's Cave Publishing sells instantaneous downloads twenty-four hours a day, seven days a week, every day of the year. Our webstore is never closed. Our e-book delivery system is 100% automated, meaning your order is filled as soon as you pay for it.

Those are a few of the top reasons why electronic books are replacing paperbacks for many avid readers.

As always, Ellora's Cave and Cerridwen Press welcome your questions and comments. We invite you to email us at Comments@ellorascave.com or write to us directly at Ellora's Cave Publishing Inc., 1056 Home Avenue, Akron, OH 44310-3502.

THE
☥ ELLORA'S CAVE ☥
LIBRARY

Stay up to date with Ellora's Cave Titles in
Print with our Quarterly Catalog.

TO RECIEVE A CATALOG,
SEND AN EMAIL WITH YOUR NAME
AND MAILING ADDRESS TO:

CATALOG@ELLORASCAVE.COM

OR SEND A LETTER OR POSTCARD
WITH YOUR MAILING ADDRESS TO:

CATALOG REQUEST
c/o ELLORA'S CAVE PUBLISHING, INC.
1056 HOME AVENUE
AKRON, OHIO 44310-3502

Make each day more *EXCITING* With our

Ellora's Cavemen

Calendar

www.EllorasCave.com

Cerridwen Press
Monthly Newsletter

News
Author Appearances
Book Signings
New Releases
Contests
Author Profiles
Feature Articles

Available online at
www.CerridwenPress.com

Cerridwen, the Celtic Goddess of wisdom, was the muse who brought inspiration to storytellers and those in the creative arts. Cerridwen Press encompasses the best and most innovative stories in all genres of today's fiction. Visit our site and discover the newest titles by talented authors who still get inspired - much like the ancient storytellers did, once upon a time.

Cerridwen Press
www.cerridwenpress.com